the Conqueror's Child

Suzy McKee Charnas

the Conqueror's Child

A Tom Doherty Associates Book
New York

This is a work of fiction. All the characters and events portrayed in this novel are either fictitious or are used fictitiously.

THE CONQUEROR'S CHILD

This book is printed on acid-free paper.

Edited by Debbie Notkin

A Tor Book
Published by Tom Doherty Associates, Inc.
175 Fifth Avenue
New York, NY 10010

Tor Books on the World Wide Web:
http://www.tor.com

Library of Congress Cataloging-in-Publication Data

Charnas, Suzy McKee.
The conqueror's child: book iv of the Holdfast chronicles / Suzy McKee Charnas. —1st ed.
p. cm.
Sequel to: The furies.
ISBN 0-312-85719-5 (acid-free paper)
I. Title.
PS3553.H325C66 1999
813'.54—dc21 99-19544

First Edition: June 1999

Printed in the United States of America

0 9 8 7 6 5 4 3 2 1

This is for the grandkids;
mine, yours, everybody's

Contents

ACKNOWLEDGMENTS 11
MAP 12
PROLOG: HOW I DID SOMETHING FOOLISH 15

BOOK ONE

THE RUNAWAY 31
PAPER 45
DOWNRIVER 51
SLAVES 63
SALALLI'S TEARS 72

BOOK TWO

OATHMOTHER 85
MEMORY MARKS 91
THE READING LESSON 101
CRIME 111
PUNISHMENT 117
A HELPER AT THE CHILDREN'S HOUSE 125
OUTLAWS 136
A FAMILY QUARREL 142
A DARK ROOM 153
SIGHT OF HOME 164

BOOK THREE

Bear Dancers 181
Lovers 191
Monument 195
Bug Bites 205
Sharemother 216
Reading the Signs 225
The Ice Stair 237
Migayl's Raid 243

BOOK FOUR

Envoy 255
The View from the Watchtower 264
Clearfalls 278
A Promise 284
The Demon 291
Stalkers in the Forest 304
Setteo's Fall 314
D Layo's Woman 323

BOOK FIVE

Fever 335
Malice 342
Taken 353
Demands 361
Heroes 370

FATHERS 382
A STORY ENDS 393

EPILOG: THE WIND 411

Acknowledgments

Many thanks are due at the conclusion of what has turned out to be a thirty-year project: to the readers who kept gently prodding me for the rest of the story; to the editors who held the doors open to publication long past any reasonable expectation; to the book dealers who struggled to keep the earlier volumes available; to the family and friends who supported and appreciated the apparently endless effort; to the creators of the many works in all the arts whose achievements spurred me on and nourished my own ideas and ambitions; and to the misogynists whose tireless efforts to keep women down have made it impossible *not* to complete the tale of Alldera and her world.

More specifically, deepest gratitude to editors Debbie Notkin and Patrick Nielsen Hayden for their encouragement and receptivity; and to those who took on the task of giving a critical reading to the 814-page typescript that became this book: Jeanne Gomoll, Susanna Sturgis, Timmi DuChamp, Rich Dutcher, Jae Adams, and Steve Charnas.

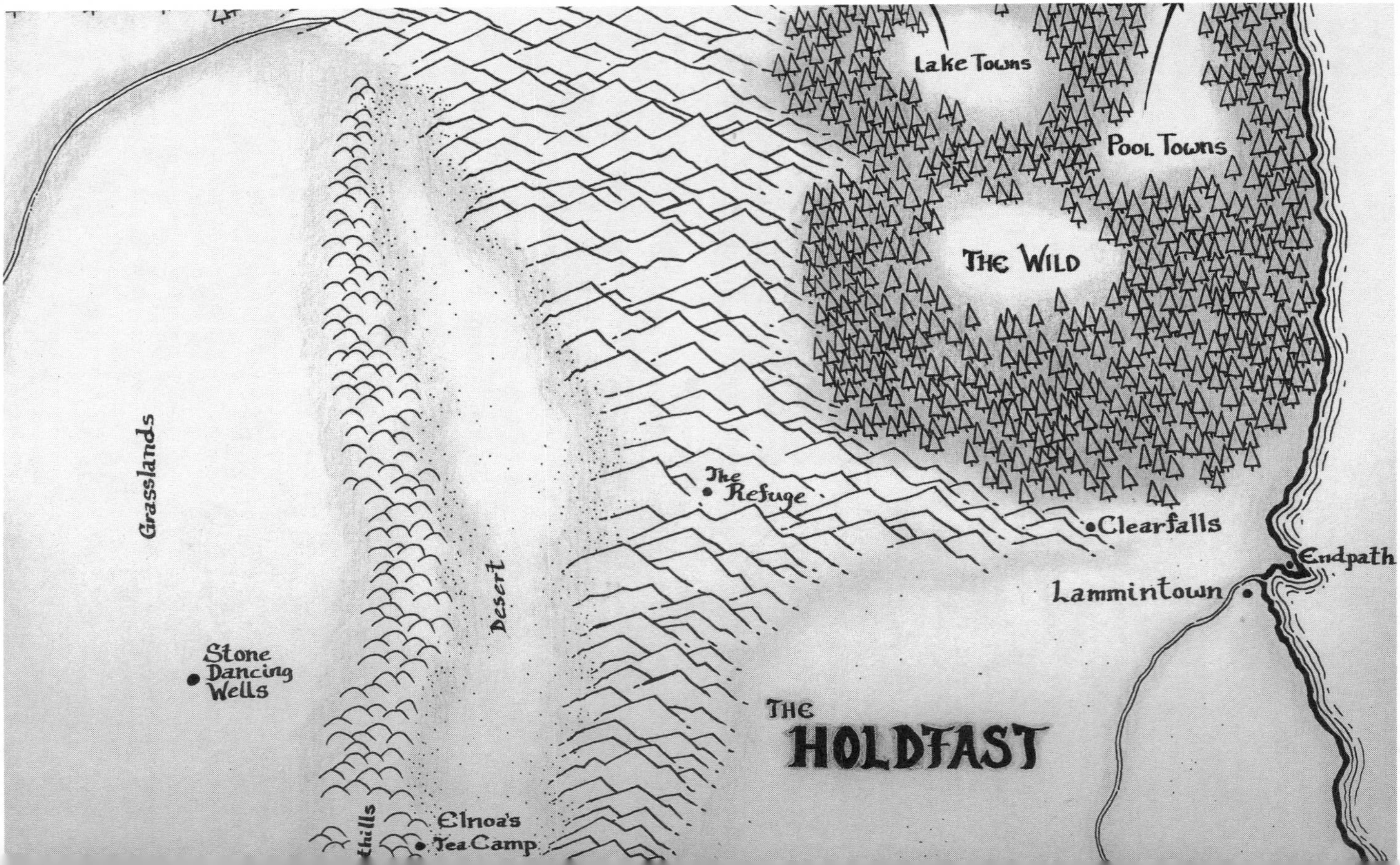

Lake Towns
Pool Towns
The Wild
The Refuge
Clearfalls
Endpath
Lammintown
Grasslands
Desert
Stone Dancing Wells
The Holdfast
hills
Elnoa's Tea Camp

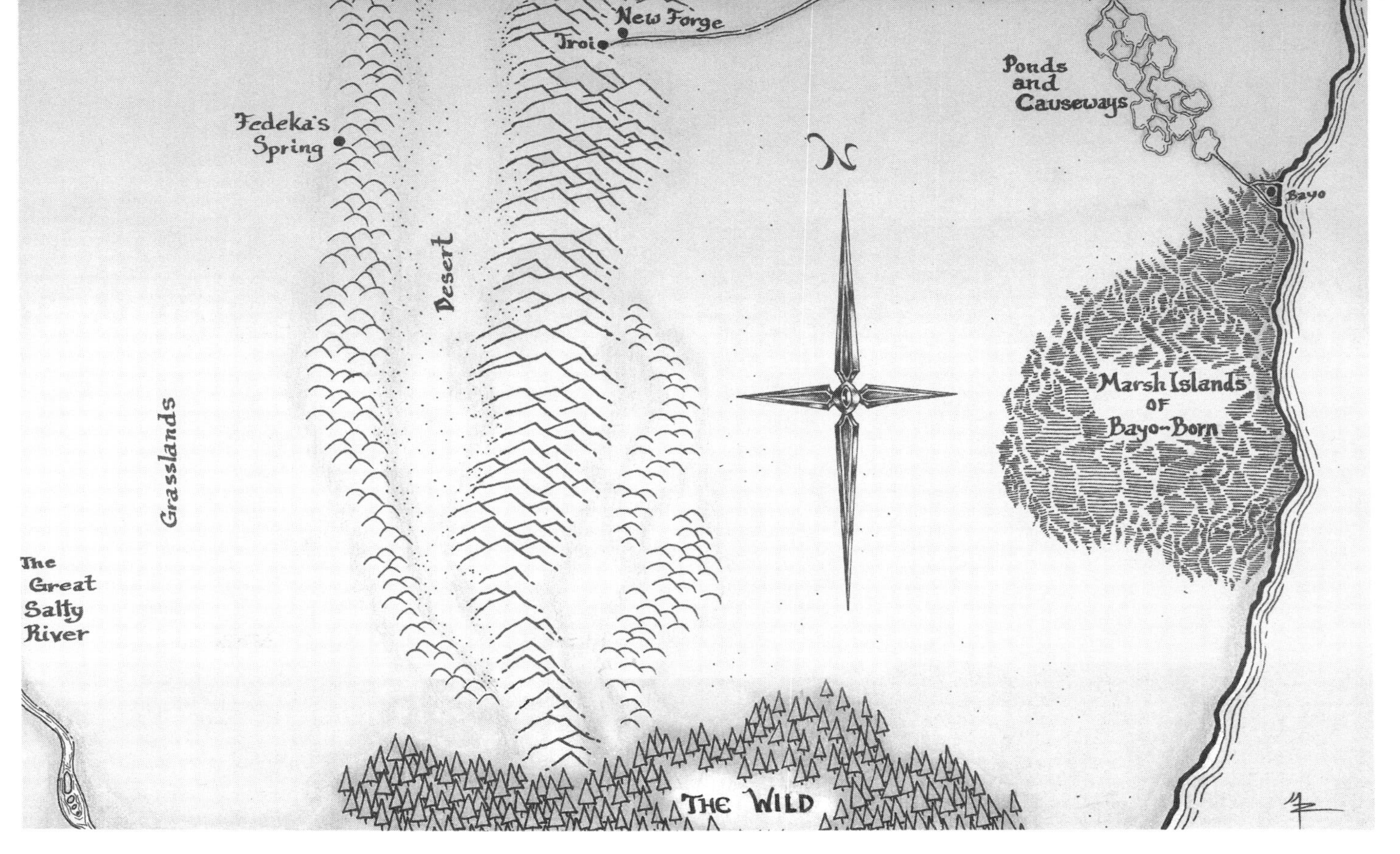
New Forge
Troi
Ponds and Causeways
Fedeka's Spring
N
Bayo
Desert
Marsh Islands OF Bayo-Born
Grasslands
The Great Salty River
THE WILD

Prolog: How I Did Something Foolish

I was angry with my mother, so I did a foolish thing.

Some people say you can't be angry "with" someone you haven't seen for years, you can only be angry "at" them. So: maybe I was angry *at* Alldera the runner, Alldera Messenger, Alldera Conqueror, and all the other titles that my bloodmother went by after the fall of the Holdfast. I wasn't angry because she had ridden off to war without me (well, I wasn't *very* angry about that any more), but because after she and her little army of ex-slaves conquered the homeland in which they had all been slaves of men, they stayed there; and she didn't send for me.

Over months of anguish at her betrayal, I slowly hardened my heart to stone. Stone is heavy and awkward to carry, but it gives you weight and balance so that you don't get blown around by the winds of your feelings.

But you can still do something foolish.

Now, this is all part of a much older story, which began with the crash of the mighty nation of the Ones Before who, led by men, greedily devoured all the bounty of Earth, which then drew into itself to heal. The men fell to fighting each other over the remnants of good food and clean water, and over fertile women; and millions died.

The men, growing impotent in the world they had poisoned and frantic for sons, made a secret camp where they sent women to be changed to conceive children without men's seed. Their science used the blood and sweat of horses, say the stories. When the women of that place rose up and took command of it, they freed captive horses also.

They rode out onto the plains driving their small mother-herd before them into the wakening world, those foremothers of all the great lines of the Riding Women.

But they brought no men, having no need of them.

Their daughters lived without men ever after, following

the grass their horses grazed and raising their families' tents beside springs and wells. Each woman's children were started with the seed of a stud colt and grew up to look just like the mother, creating the Motherlines of the Grassland camps.

Meanwhile another new world was coming into being. In the mountains bounding the Grasslands to the east, others of the Ones Before had built a city below ground to hide in from the ruin they had brought about; for this "Refuge," as they called it, was prepared by men who were Chiefs in those last days.

They took women there with them, and, being maddened by the loss of the fertile world they had once called "Mother Earth," those men reduced those women to mere brood-stock and slaves.

Their descendants emerged in time as men—Seniors commanding their Juniors in strict hierarchy—and fems. They cleared a strip of coast, the Holdfast, out of the surrounding scrub forest (which they named "the Wild" and peopled with imaginary ghosts and demons). They farmed that hardy survivor, the hemp plant, taking food and fiber from it and also the drug "manna," which men used to dream visions from their tales of masculine virtue triumphant. From the sea they harvested long green kelp, and from sewage ponds the red weed laver, for food.

They founded towns for the working of metal in the hills at 'Troi; for retting hemp on the river at Oldtown; for cooking seaweed at the cliffs of Lammintown; and, for trading and dreaming and conducting quarrels among the "companies" of men, the City at the center of the Holdfast, where the river forked.

By the delta of the southern stream they built Bayo, a mud-brick village on the edge of a marsh. There female children were raised by tame old fems, the Matris, who weeded out the more spirited kits (before they could cause trouble) and taught the rest to become good, obedient slaves.

The Riding Women on the far side of the mountains knew of these people from runaways fleeing westward—escaped fems, men run rogue from bad manna, or others escaping sentence of death by poison at Endpath for being ill, or criminal, or for standing in the way of influential Seniors.

No fugitives returned to the Holdfast to speak of the Riding Women, however. Mounted patrols tracked stray men and killed them, and took runaway fems home to the Grasslands.

Now, a time came in the Holdfast when one man, Raff Maggomas "the Engineer," began to reclaim the lost science of the Ones Before, the "Ancients" as men called them. He found out the identity of his son, Eykar Bek (by trickery, since Holdfast rules kept fathers and sons strictly ignorant of each other, as natural rivals and enemies). Seeing that the Holdfast was faltering, Maggomas meant to pass on his mastery of science to this son of his, and make a richer, better life for its men.

The new wealth would be based on Ancient ways—guns, grain, and power sucked up from the river by great wheels—and on reducing fems from slaves to livestock and subsisting on their flesh.

Eykar Bek, marked always from other young men by his forbidden knowledge of his father's identity, had been sent to Endpath to be the poison giver as punishment for his own youthful errors. A questioner and a thinker like his father, it was inevitable that he should run up against the Seniors' laws. In time, Maggomas contrived to bring him out of that black tombhouse again and set him seeking his father up in 'Troi-town, in the hills.

And thus it happened by Maggomas' design, through troubles and adventures; except that Eykar Bek brought with him his longtime lover Servan d Layo, a reckless and violent young man outlawed himself for using manna for unlawful dreams; and Alldera the fem, a speed-trained messenger, who was herself secretly in search of the legendary "Free Fems" surviving in the Wild.

Because of what she told him, Eykar Bek refused his awful inheritance and (bearing out the theory of enmity between father and son) struck his father down. With that evil man fell the Holdfast itself, other Junior men rising against all the old men who oppressed them.

Alldera, with Eykar's aid, escaped into the Wild. She

was carrying, as she discovered with dismay, a child—Eykar's child, or Servan's child, a child of rape like all Holdfast children in those days.

Pregnant, starving, and desperate, Alldera was rescued by a patrol of Riding Women from the plains. She bore her daughter in Stone Dancing Camp, after which she left that child—me—and her own lover among the Women, Nenisi Conor, and went to live with the other runaways, the Free Fems, who did in fact exist—but not as the mighty warriors of femmish legend.

They were a clutch of quarrelsome fugitives who lived by harvesting tea from the foothills, which they traded from their great wooden wagons to the Women of the far-flung camps. Alldera fell afoul of their leader, Elnoa the Green-eyed, and also of a schemer named Daya, a once-pretty pet fem with a scarred face. The runner's life went badly at Elnoa's Tea Camp.

Sick, betrayed, drunk on Grassland beer and disappointment, she went away to heal with the one-armed hermit Fedeka, who gathered plants and medicines on the plains. Daya, betrayed in turn, came there too, and Alldera and the pet fem became lovers.

At age six or so, I joined the childpack (for the camp children ran free from then till the menarche, in order to wash out the unfit and keep the Motherlines strong). When I emerged again for my naming as an adult woman, Alldera returned to Stone Dancing Camp. Unexpectedly, other Free Fems arrived also, and stayed; for on the plains Alldera had found her strength, and they wished to become like her—riders and warriors, instead of ex-slaves dying out in a corner of someone else's country.

And a time came when they took horses and weapons of their own and rode east, under Alldera's leadership, to conquer their own homeland and set free any fems still held bond there. But her daughter, Sorrel Holdfaster, Alldera left behind.

As I discovered when I returned from my maiden raid in my fifteenth year, having lifted a famous horse called the Hayscall Racer from Red Sand Camp.

Alldera and the Free had done what no one had believed they ever really would do—they had gone home. In the light of this, I and my passage into adulthood vanished from view. Everyone was busy arguing: the fems would never make it home; they wouldn't, they couldn't, and if they did the men would wipe them out, and if not—

I went off by myself to cry. Eelayenn Soolay, my first serious lover since my childpack days, came and hugged me and asked me what I would do now.

I couldn't even think that far. "How could she ride away without a word, as if we weren't even related?"

"No one was told," my friend pointed out. "They planned it all in secret, otherwise we wouldn't have let them go."

"This was my first raid!" I stormed. "I could have been caught at Red Sand, I could have been hurt by those angry women! I would have needed my bloodmother to come argue down my fine."

Eelayenn said, "Fems have different wants than ours."

I said, "She can't just leave me here!"

Eelayenn patted my hair and offered me a gourd of cold, sweetened tea. "She loves you too much to risk your life in that horrible place she comes from," she said reasonably. "What if the men caught you?"

"Shut up!" I slapped the gourd out of her hand.

So she got up and went off a little way and waited while I cried and cursed and made plans and unmade them again. When I woke the next morning, Eelayenn was lying snugged against my back with her arms around me, snoring softly into my hair that was still filthy from the hard ride home from Red Sand Camp.

After we'd made some slow, sleepy morning love and eaten the dried meat she had with her, we rode back among the tents of Stone Dancing Camp together—to a fresh uproar!

My sharemother Sheel Torrinor, scarcely pausing to rest after going raiding with me, was gone after the Free Fems—to stop them, of course, though how she meant to do that I couldn't imagine. She had slipped away without waiting for a Gather of the camps and the palaver it would take for that assembly to agree on what to do.

Sheel had collected a few friends and relations ready to hand, called in some debts in order to get horses, weapons, and supplies for a journey, and galloped away in the night.

And she hadn't asked me to ride with her. I was stunned by this second blow right on top of the first. My eyes felt like pools of grief that went all the way down into my heart.

Now everybody began hugging and patting and pulling me into the middle of the Chief Tent. They talked over and around me about how I had lost *three* of my five mothers now (for my heartmother Barvaran had died not long before), and what could my future be?

I could go after the Free Fems and Sheel Torrinor myself. The way they had taken was no mystery. Women from Stone Dancing had already scouted the trail as far as the Tea Camp in the foothills, where the Free Fems used to live. Any Grassland girl could have tracked the expedition from there.

But, realistically speaking, my mother Sheel would send me right back again if she caught me trailing her. She was a proud, impetuous woman (not sad and understanding like Nenisi Conor or stolid and accepting like Shayeen Bawn). I shrank from the idea of being shamed by her.

Sheel, slim and blonde as a wand of wood hardened in fire and sanded smooth, was the one among my mothers whom I most admired and wished to be like. I couldn't bear the thought of her watching me make a fool of myself (which anyone might do in a strange country).

And anyway, why should I go traipsing after my bloodmother Alldera, when she hadn't thought enough of me to tell me that she was departing on the greatest adventure of her already legendary career? Why run after my raidmother Sheel, who had also left me behind?

When someone turned to me and asked me what I meant to do about two of my mothers going off like that, the one chasing the other, I said, "I'm going to start my own family, like the rest of my age-mates."

Oh, they were delighted with that. People I scarcely knew called out names of daughters of their own lines whom they wished me to take as sharemothers in my bloodchild. That child would have been the foundation of the first new Grassland line since the Riding Women's ancestormothers had left the Lab of the Old Ones and ridden out onto the plains.

Shayeen Bawn, another of my mothers, began boasting now in the Chief Tent about how I had lifted the Hayscall Racer from Red Sand Camp on my maiden raid. What fine children a woman like me would bring into the world, children anyone would be proud to be related to!

A little late for praise, I thought angrily. Despite what she tried to do for me, I hated her for what she could not do.

Well, nothing anyone could have said would have changed my mood. Unless Alldera herself had galloped back and reached a hand down to me, crying, "Sorrel, I couldn't leave without you, child. Jump up behind me and ride with me to war!"

Like it or not—and I must admit that sometimes I liked it very much—my bloodmother was a hero. Maybe she was right to leave me behind. What place could there be for me in her gigantic life? And even if there was a place, did I want it? Did I wish to ride always in her shadow, knowing that she didn't like me and didn't care what happened to me?

She was more a mother to the rest of the Free Fems than she had ever been to me, Shayeen had said once. It made sense, when I thought about it. With them Alldera shared memories of bitter slave life in the Holdfast, while my life as an infant in my mothers' tent and then a wildling of the childpack were things she, a foreigner, had never experienced.

I was done with weeping. Abandoned and bereft, insulted in front of everyone by my own mothers, my newly achieved adulthood overshadowed by their deeds, I turned my back in the days following on all argument over what to do about the Free Fems. I practiced hard and long with bow and lance, just in case someone should call for riders to follow Sheel Torrinor's lead.

No one did. Or rather, several people did, but the call always got bogged down in argument from other quarters. Everyone had an opinion.

Nobody asked me for mine. This was also hard for me to bear.

I had been suckled by all my share-mas, like any Grassland girl, and swept up by the childpack to live or die among them, like any Grassland girl. Now I target-shot and wrestled and cooked and rode and hunted sharu and made love with my age-mates, like any Grassland girl.

But I felt people watching, measuring, gauging the distances between myself and my cohort in this regard or that. I was unique in a way that no one else in the camps ever had been, not even Alldera herself. Uniqueness in a person made the people of the Grassland camps nervous.

Oh, I had my remaining mothers, Shayeen and Nenisi, and I loved them. I had friends and lovers and mentors among their friends and relations. I had my age-mates. But Alldera and her Free Fems, the people from whom I had come, were gone. I found, very resentfully, that I missed them. They had taken with them their passionate stories, their scars and intrigues, their colorful oddities of clothing and custom and belief.

Perhaps most of all I missed their sad, wild songs in which I had caught glimpses of exotic possibilities that I sometimes thought by rights belonged to me too, perhaps more so than anything life offered me in the Women's tents.

So I felt a need to be not unique any longer but to be just like my age-mates (if I could). They were all settling down into families, preparing to bear children for their lines.

But could I, conceived by customary Holdfast rape but born and raised in a Grassland camp, do the same? I was not the only one to ask this question.

"Don't worry," Sheel's old heartmother, Jesselee, had told me often enough. "The Women who mothered you fed you the milk of their bodies, the spit of their mouths, and the love of their hearts. They made you one of us with their care and their nurturing. No mere man-seed could outweigh that! You'll start a child to the stud colt the same as any other girl."

But Jesselee also said, in another mood on another day, "Don't worry; even if you have no bloodchildren, nobody will think any the less of you."

Part of what had driven the Free Fems home was desperation over their inability to get pregnant without men. I had dreams about this. They were not good dreams. Unreasonably, I added my many restless and fearful nights to the tally of blame against my bloodmother and her femmish kin.

* * *

Before the next Dry Season, when still nothing had been decided among our tents, two of the women who had ridden east with Sheel Torrinor returned. Both were weary and thin (Margora Garriday was noticeably more quarrelsome than normal even for a Garriday).

Their news, however, was good: the Free Fems had swept over the Holdfast like a Grassland fire, bearing down by armed and mounted assault the remnant of men living there. All the fems still in bonds to those men had been freed.

There had been deaths in the little army, but more deaths among their enemies. Alldera was Alldera Conqueror now. They thought that she might not visit the Grasslands again for some time, as there was a great deal still to do in her homeland. Sheel Torrinor and four other Riding Women had stayed behind with her to observe with Grassland eyes, that might see Holdfast matters more clearly than femmish eyes could.

The two who brought this news also brought a stranger-fem with them. She was one of the "NewFree," Holdfast slaves liberated by Alldera's army of "First Free." She was pregnant.

"I was Juya," this person said when she first spoke in the Chief Tent. "Sheel Torrinor gave me a free name, 'Veree,' in exchange for my coming to bear my child in this camp. The child will be Sheel's gift and mine to her Motherline, the Torrinors."

The Torrinors present said nothing. They left soon after to ride to other camps and talk with other Women of their line. Nobody was comfortable with what Juya-Veree had said.

People of the camps didn't "give" children to other people. And hadn't it brought enough trouble to take in Alldera Holdfaster herself, so many years ago? What did it mean now to take in another such person, her belly swelling with the get of a Holdfast man?

I swallowed my tears, seeing how I was part of this "trouble" that had vexed the people around me for so long.

Later I went and sat by Juya-Veree's bedding under the

fly of Holdfaster Tent. She was already heavy in front. I said, "Did Sheel give you special messages for anyone?"

"Oh!" she said, turning a startled shade of pink that showed up some dusky designs marked into the skin of her face. "You must be the Conqueror's child! I've looked forward to meeting you, but there's been so much confusion—I've heard people talk about you. Free Fems, I mean. They all wondered when Alldera would send for you. Some said she already had, but that these people wouldn't let you come. But some said that she would never uproot you from among the Riding Women, where you have all of your close ties."

I didn't really care what the fems said. "Did you ever hear Alldera herself say anything about me?"

"No." I could see that she was embarrassed that my own bloodmother didn't talk about me. "We were in a war. People didn't talk much about other things."

"It's nothing to me," I said. People were always making excuses for Alldera the Hero. "We were never close."

She babbled on about battles, sieges, killings, and pursuits until Shayeen came and told me to leave her alone. Didn't I understand that Juya was pregnant and that she needed rest after a hard journey?

When I went to the stud colt that first time (sooner than was wise, wiser people told me), I meant to prove something. And when no conception followed, that time or the next, I saw that I had proven the opposite: that I was not really a Riding Woman at all, just the daughter of an escaped Holdfast slave, as Juya's child would be.

Meanwhile word came with a trading party that Daya the pet fem—she who had been Alldera's lover and my own best auntie among the Free in Stone Dancing Camp—had led an assassination attempt against my bloodmother.

The attack had been foiled; Alldera was recovering. I would have gone to her, but how could I face her, a childless child? And still she did not send for me.

Juya-Veree got a fever and died after birthing her baby despite everything anyone could do. The infant was male.

Nenisi said in the Chief Tent, "All Women know that it is wrong to destroy a child, any child, at its birth."

People came from all over to look at him. Nobody volunteered to be the one to take him back over the mountains to Sheel Torrinor, who had thought she was sending us a daughter.

I lingered by Strangerchild Tent one hot morning when three visitors from Steep Cloud Camp—two Tuluns and a pie-skinned Kang—squatted around the coltskin sling studying the infant. Sannader Borrin, sharemothering the boy to pay off a debt she owed to Sheel's line, had drawn his wrappings aside to give the visitors a better look.

The Kang prodded him, not ungently, with her finger. "A tiddly, tiny baby," she said, "and look at the bag-and-hanger on him! It's like a challenge, isn't it?"

Sannader, who treated the little creature better than its other shares did, reminded them that infant girls had to grow into their cunnies too, babies being naturally big between the legs. The little boy kicked in that jerk-limbed way of infants and grinned his gummy grin. I had to turn away from his cheerful trust in those about him.

He became a quiet child who could play contentedly with a lump of sandblasted glass for an hour; a good thing, as his unhappy sharemothers spent as little time with him as they could and clearly all longed for his departure into the childpack.

At first I avoided him, except when curiosity got the better of me; I didn't want to think about what was similar in our circumstances, his and mine. The differences were greater; my mothers had loved me. Most of them.

But I didn't like to see him left out in the sun too long because someone had forgotten about him, or playing with a slice of hoof-paring in the absence of real toys. I made him a grass horse and when that fell apart one of leather, which he slept with and would not be parted from without a tempest.

He would have to be sent back to the Holdfast, people said; but no one could imagine how, or when. Meantime, I began to tell him stories of that place which the Free had once told me, as his own sharemothers should have done. Any child must learn to speak, to remember, and to think.

As a toddler, he sought me out. Even when other little ones played with him, as they did when nobody called them away, he would leave their games and run to where I sat knotting menstrual plugs or cutting leather laces, and he would beg a story or show me a stone or find out what I was doing and why.

One day he asked me if his name was "Boy," since that was what his shares called him. He was becoming a pretty creature in his own way, slim and brown, though small in stature for his age (he had never thriven in infancy, and no wonder). He had developed alert and winning ways, for those who bothered to notice.

I had seen little girls tease him till he ran away wailing, which did not augur well for his future in the rough and tumble of the childpack itself.

I told him his tent-name was "Veree," since Sheel had given that name to his bloodmother; and he ran about announcing it to everyone, which made people laugh. That night, Sannader asked if I would take her place in Strangerchild Tent. As if a child's mothers could be switched about like that!

"You worry about him anyway," she said, "and he speaks of you as his 'story-ma.' "

"When?" I said uncomfortably, but I was pleased, too. "I never heard it."

"All the time," she said.

But I turned away from her, and from him too, which was very hard since he now came to me whether I wanted him or not.

He was almost six years old then, and a few weeks later the childpack of Stone Dancing swept him away with them. (His reluctant sharemothers hurriedly dispersed as soon as he was gone.) I knew that I had dropped from his thoughts, along with his mothers and everyone else he had known till then, which was a relief but an emptiness to me also.

Grays Omelly said she had seen him dancing the horses, as the pack children did on bright nights; but the Omellys are crazy, and no one believed her.

I went out to see for myself. I was at that time not lovers with anyone except in a casual way, so there was no one to mark my comings and goings at night. I did see him, leaping over the backs of the restless herd with the pack of girls. On another night, I saw them chase him over tent ropes and meat-smoking fires, and whoever managed to dart a hand between his legs—which made him squeal—apparently won the game, which immediately began again. When they were too exhausted to run any more and collapsed to sleep, Veree piled in among them as if they had never singled him out.

I saw him staring at me with a terrible, craving look when I came upon him devouring some ground-egg strips that had been left out for the pack. I saw how violently he turned away and ran with the others, forcing his way right into their midst as they veered off in a screeching throng, grabbing food from each others' dirty hands.

It was sad but not surprising when the pack dropped him, bruised and nearly unconscious, at the squats by High Wells. They had expelled him, a thing that never happened. A sickly or crippled child simply vanished in the course of the pack's wide-ranging rampages of games and thievery. That was terrible enough, and the Riding Women seldom spoke of the grief such losses cost them. But this was different and terrible in its own way.

I watched from horseback as he stumbled, blubbering, into the shade of a sharu skin stretched to dry, drank the water from the pot that was used to moisten the skin, and fell asleep with a bit of the skin, that he had ravenously tried to eat, hanging out of his mouth.

Grays Omelly, surfacing from some private ritual of her own involving bones and torn-up grass, saw too, and went off toward the Chief Tent, to make some Omelly-style trouble, no doubt.

I dismounted and knelt by Veree's ribby little body, looking at the filthy, matted hair and the scabs and scrapes on his sunburned skin. The smell of him was familiar: sweet, rank, and utterly blameless.

So I woke him, kissed him quiet, and told him that we were going away to the place of all the strange, exciting tales I used to tell him. Then I gathered some horses of my own and in the full brightness of afternoon I rode for the mountains, and the Holdfast beyond, with Veree slung sleeping on my back.

No one followed us or tried to call us home.

That was the beginning of the foolish thing I did.

I

The Runaway

Like many things that are done without planning and alone, it went badly from the start. Veree got tired of riding clinging to my back, was heavy to carry in a leather sling, and cried a lot. The childpack had left him bruised and sore with their rough handling, and I had not brought enough warm clothes for the higher elevations of the mountains. And he was at this time inclined to be weepy and whiny anyway.

But we got through the poisoned barrens and across the lower pass over the mountains, although this took us farther north than I would have liked and more slowly.

Still, one warm and cloudy morning I found myself looking down on a sight I had been told about often enough: the foothills on the eastern side of the mountains. The timbered land fell away toward a broad plateau of scrub woodland out of which the Holdfast had been cleared generations ago by the people from the Refuge.

I sat by my fire on a rocky outcrop in the upland forest, drinking a very thin brew of tea and thinking about what I meant to do down there. I had it in mind to deliver Veree to a place where there were others like him, so that he would not live as a freak all his life in the Grasslands.

But when I looked around for him, Veree was gone. I saw nothing but looming trees, and the upcountry sky which mounted very high and shone intensely blue but which didn't feel big as Grassland skies did.

Over the panic in my heart I began to call, "Veree!"

The Free Fems had always laughed at the men of the Holdfast for believing that the forested mountains were full of evil spirits. Such beliefs seemed less strange now. I had done two turns as a border scout watching for men from the Holdfast, and I had heard tales from other scouts of the deaths of such strays. The Riding Women had ghosts of their own to deal with in the land between the nations.

I scrabbled a hole in the ground for the ashes of my fire and covered them over with dirt. Then I stood turning in a circle, craning my neck and stretching my eyes wide to see into the shadows of the trees. Such shadows! So different from in the Grasslands, which lay everywhere open to the sky.

"Veree!" I screamed. "Where are you? Answer me!"

My voice was swallowed by the trees. Patch, the mare I had saddled for the day's ride, barely turned an ear. All my horses went on quietly grazing among the roots and rocks. They were used to the note of alarm in my voice, having heard it often enough lately. A child is not an easy traveling companion, and I had no shares to help.

I squeezed my eyes shut and tried to use my breathing to calm my panic, a technique of relaxation I had learned before going to my first stud colt. Having had the training, I might as well get some use out of it.

I couldn't bear to think about what Sheel would say when I told her that the child she had sent us was lost or dead. In truth, I cared very much myself that he was lost: Holdfast-bred but Grassland-born, he was more like me than any other living person. I had become his only mother.

Should I mount up and go looking for him, or would it be better to search more slowly and thoroughly on foot? What if meantime he came back and found me gone?

While I stood dithering, the lead pack mare nickered and was answered with a snort from beyond the clearing. I crouched with my knife clutched in my hand. Two riders burst from among the trees, ready-armed with drawn bows.

They were not Grasslanders, I saw that at once; fems, of course, what else would they be on this side of the mountains? I was so relieved to see them that I simply discounted their arrows that were trained on me and dashed toward them.

"Free people!" I cried, agitated enough by Veree's disappearance that it never occurred to me to present myself properly with my self-song. "Have you seen my companion? A little child has wandered away from me."

The riders looked at each other and lowered their weapons. Their clothes were more fabric than leather and both wore their hair braided. One, a short-waisted brunette with a squinting glance, looked familiar.

"Who are you, and what are you doing here?" the taller one asked sternly. "With a child, too, wandering on our border?"

She sounded so hostile that I hesitated to answer. The dark one stood in her stirrups, looking anxiously around as if fearing an ambush. Now I recognized her; she had always been a timid soul.

I held out my hands to her: "Don't you know me, Lora?"

Lora-Lan—it was she, though her high forehead was now stamped with lines of time and weather—stared at me, her lips parted in amazement. Then she put her head back and laughed the staccato laugh that I remembered so well.

"I'd say you were Sorrel Holdfaster," she said, "but when I was at that person's naming in Holdfaster Tent, she swore to ride only red horses. I don't see a red horse among your stock."

"It's me, it's me," I said, squeezing her hand in my two. She leaned down and kissed me.

The other one said brusquely, "I'm Ebba-Basarr, and I don't know you. There's a runaway stick on the loose. How old is your little girl? How could you let her ride off on her own?"

"Stick," "stickie," and "muck" were all, in the conversation of Free Fems who came over the mountains to trade, terms for men. Hearing now how she said "stick," the depth of her loathing and contempt, I made a decision without even thinking about it.

"I didn't 'let' her do anything," I said. "I just turned around for a second to put out the campfire and she was gone."

"On foot? She can't have gone far then," Lora said.

I said, "If your stick gets to that child before we do, I'll never forgive myself."

"Nobody else will either," the other fem said and reined her horse around.

I mounted Patch and we rode together, leaning from our saddles and searching for sign. After an hour or so we heard crying, and in short order we came upon Veree sitting on the ground among some stunted junipers, wailing.

Could they tell he was a boy by the way he sounded? I rode ahead and scooped him up, rejoicing to feel his thin little arms around my neck.

"You should smack her for wandering off alone," Lora said severely, but she reached out to pat Veree's springy curls.

I hugged him close, put my lips against his wet cheek, and whispered, "Don't ever do that again! This isn't the Grasslands. It's full of—full of dangers here, worse than swarming sharu. Do you hear me, Veree?"

He snuggled deeper against my neck. "I couldn't find you, ma," he mourned, hiccuping.

"It's all right," I said. "Now I've found you." I smoothed his sweaty hair and listened to the calming of both our heartbeats.

"Not yours, is she?" said Ebba-Basarr. "We'd have heard of it if Alldera's daughter had had a child."

It amazed me, how much I could dislike somebody I'd never even met before. She was homely, too, with a blunt-featured, concave face. If she'd been a Riding Woman, I would naturally have had to dislike all of her blood kin as well; a big job. Maybe there was something to be said for Holdfast singularity.

But Ebba-Basarr was neither Riding Woman nor one of the Free Fems I had known as a child in Holdfaster Tent. She must be NewFree, as Juya had been—a slave freed only a half-dozen years ago by Alldera's army. They could be touchy people.

Since the Conquest, some NewFree had come bartering for Grassland horses to improve their Holdfast herds. I had kept my distance. Sometimes Sheel Torrinor came with them for long talks with influential people about events over the mountains. I had not wanted Sheel to meet me and then ride back and tell my bloodmother all about it.

If Alldera Conqueror wanted firsthand news of her daughter, she could come see for herself.

Gossip was always exchanged, of course. No doubt questions were asked and stories carried back to the Holdfast, so my name and life couldn't be completely unknown here. I thanked the luck of my home tent that I had not sung my self-song, which would have revealed my childlessness. It occurred to me that it might be harder to be Alldera's daughter on this side of the mountains than it had been on the farther side.

However, having told one great roaring great lie I had no choice but to build upon it.

"She's my daughter, yes," I said. Veree wouldn't object. He was used to being called "her" and "she" in a casual way. He even insisted on it if you didn't, as he wanted so badly to be like the other Grassland children (a feeling I knew well).

"The Riding Women asked me to keep her birth a secret," I explained, improvising wildly, "for fear my femmish kin would come and to take her away. Now the childpack has rejected her. I've come to see if Alldera's people will bring her up here."

"What a pity you chose just now," Lora exclaimed. "Alldera's gone to talk with the Bayo-born about pasturage."

Well, that was a shock. I had heard of the people living in the swamps south of Bayo, but had never imagined that Alldera would travel there. I also hadn't realized till that moment how tense I was about seeing my bloodmother after so long. Why else would I feel so relieved to hear that she was away?

Who said I had come all this distance to see her anyway?

"Fedeka hasn't gone, too?" I asked casually, as if the old dye-maker was just as important to me as my bloodmother. Well, in some ways she had been.

"Fedeka's in Midfast," Lora said enthusiastically, "at the Moon's House. She'll be so happy to see you!"

I silently blessed my luck again. Fedeka had once sworn to give me any help I asked if I called on her, making herself oathmother to me even though I was already grown by then. She certainly had more plain sense and sympathy (as I remembered her) than Mighty Alldera anyway, at least when not obsessed by the fems' god, the Lady in the Moon.

I asked about Sheel Torrinor and the Rois cousins who were still living on this side of the mountains. Lora-Lan said they were somewhere north of us in the Wild, investigating the Refuge, an underground fortress from which all present-day Holdfasters' ancestors had emerged after the Wasting.

More good news. Better to deal with Fedeka than with Sheel.

Veree whispered, "We have to go back now, ma."

"Back where, sweetcakes?"

He pointed vaguely, but I knew what he meant: back over the mountains, back home.

"No, not yet."

He rubbed his moist, round cheek against mine. "But we have to. We left Notch-ear; he has nobody to play with him except Nip, and she kicks him too much. We left—"

"Yes, we did," I said firmly, trying to forestall sulks or tears. He was already badly rattled by having gotten himself lost. "We're not going back yet so just rest quietly, Vee, while I talk with these friends."

He sighed mightily but subsided. He had become a very grave, self-possessed, and generally obedient child. Too much so, I had sometimes thought, but that can be the effect of a life filled with rejection. Now I was grateful for his meekness.

"What's her name?" Lora asked warmly. "She has your eyes."

"I call her Veree after your Juya, that died." Juya's child didn't have my eyes at all, and I didn't want to encourage closer scrutiny.

Ebba-Basarr said, "I don't think she looks much like you." She might have been one of those abrasive Managena Women, except that they at least had the virtue of beautiful, tawny skin that never seemed to age.

"Look," I said, "we still have your runaway stick to find. I don't feel easy being out here with a child while a man is running loose."

"It's not far to New Forge," Ebba-Basarr said, glancing up at the sun. "We'll set you back on the trail—"

"No, no," Lora protested. "She can't travel alone with this pretty kit. She's not used to finding her way in our country." She shook her finger at me, scolding. "Nobody crosses the mountains alone! You're as rash as your blood-mother."

I frowned—I always frowned when someone compared

me to Alldera—and to hide my ill temper I turned to nuzzle the child's hair again. Well, some good came at last out of being bloodchild to Alldera the Great. Lora and Ebba-Basarr wouldn't like having to explain how they had let Alldera's daughter and granddaughter wander off alone into danger.

Ebba said, "All right, then, help us search."

Lora nodded. "I'll haze your horses along with ours. Three of us will find that stickie faster than two anyway, unless another patrol picks him up first."

"But you must keep the little one quiet," Ebba-Basarr warned.

I said, "Oh, she's exhausted, aren't you, little pony? She'll sleep." I gave Veree a sweetgrass twist from my pocket. "Quiet time now, Veree. Remember what I've taught you."

He leaned back in my arms to look at me, nodded solemnly, and began sucking loudly on the sweet. I mounted Patch and pulled Veree up behind me. Using a leather snugger strap, I buckled him tightly to my back for safety.

We didn't talk much, searching that rough upland country. I rode in overlapping arcs with Ebba-Basarr, while Lora trailed us driving the spare mounts. It was much like scouting on the other side of the mountains with a Grassland patrol.

But I had never gone into danger with a child. My nerves were strung tighter than the bow in my hand.

At midmorning, Ebba-Basarr drew rein suddenly. "I smell him!" She got off her horse to search closer to the ground. I stayed in my saddle, casting my gaze more widely about in case our quarry lurked nearby.

We found a flattened swathe of grass where someone had slept by a stream. At that instant we heard a choking yell of alarm behind us. We both rode hard back toward Lora and the spare horses.

Two grappling figures rolled, thrashing and grunting, on the ground. Lora was struggling with a near-naked stranger while our frightened horses jostled away down a brushy defile.

We galloped up, arrows nocked but unable to shoot for fear of hitting Lora. She heaved her torso clear enough to use the strength of her legs, which were locked around the stranger's body. Twisting, she just managed to avoid a vicious blow from a rock clutched in her opponent's fist.

I kept an arrow trained on the enemy as best I could. Ebba-Basarr rode in close, her lance hiked up to stab him to the earth.

The stranger stared wildly up at her, dropped the rock, and clapped his hands to his head.

"Heras," he cried, "spare me, I beg! I am hungry, I am mad, I thought myself attacked by a demon of the Wild!"

Lora, red in the face and panting, scrambled up, angrily slapping dust from her tunic. "Oh, be quiet, Galligan, save it for the Steps. You ran, you're caught, that's all."

Ebba shook her lance menacingly. "Why bother with the Steps?"

What "steps"? But it seemed a poor time to ask.

"Oh, leave it, Ebba," Lora said. "There's no great harm done." Her bruised lips were already beginning to swell.

Ebba-Basarr swore and slipped the lance back into its straps.

My fingers were frozen to the grip of my bow. I rode nearer—but not much nearer—and kept my arrowpoint centered on this Galligan while the other two bound him with thongs. Of course they knew him—there were not so many men left alive in the Holdfast now, and the Free had good reason to keep close track of each and every one of their former masters.

At my back, Veree breathed soft, frightened breaths. I had forgotten him. I whispered over my shoulder that there was nothing to fear now, but I knew he could feel the pounding of my heart.

"Was she very bad, that big ma?" he asked me tremulously.

"Very bad," I said. "Like that dun horse that bit my leg, remember? So they have to tie this ma up, to keep her from hurting people."

"Would she hurt me?" he said.

"No," I said. "I won't let her." I sighted down the shaft of my arrow at the fellow, who gaped at me. If the Free knew every one of them, wouldn't he know every one of the Free? He must think I was a Riding Woman, with my daughter.

"I won't let her hurt anybody," Veree echoed. He began to whisper, squirming as he acted out his words, "I can hit her and smack her, I can push her in the squats so she gets all stinky."

And the like, a list of vengeful fancies. I let him talk his fear out to himself.

I had seen one dead man in the mountains, never a live one close up. That corpse (long dead when my patrol found him) had looked like the oddly shrunken carcass of a horse, all disordered bones and rags of skin and small things scuttling about.

This fellow quivered and sweated with life and the desire to keep hold of it. He wore a long, coarse-woven shirt (torn now at the collar), and slung round his neck was a shapeless mess of what looked like hair—a wig! He must have been passing himself off (or trying to) as one of the Free in his escape.

He said hoarsely, "It's not my fault. I was fed bad manna by a man who hates me—"

Ebba-Basarr jammed her headcloth into his open mouth and tied it tightly in place. "None of your lies, muckie."

"Don't look any more at that bad ma," I murmured to Veree, putting up my bow. His dark eyes missed little. I hoped that he couldn't guess that the captive man and he were of the same kind (how *could* they be?).

But Veree must know it someday.

The spare horses, being unpursued, had gone no great distance. Only two of the packs they carried had to be remade. Then we paused for a bite to eat before descending to New Forge.

Galligan, who had had to trot along at a rope's end behind us, was unceremoniously tied to a tree. I sat with my back against a juniper trunk and held Veree on my lap so that he faced away from the others and from Galligan.

By now all the strains of the morning had put Veree into a drowsy mood. He lay loose and heavy against me, whispering to himself a story that Nenisi had made up for him about a little white horse made of cloud.

I said over the child's head, trying not to sound too critical, "What if your stickie gets loose again? We kill them outright if we find them in the borderlands."

Ebba-Basarr raised her eyebrows. "You do?" She dipped her fingers into a small crockery pot she had taken from her saddlebags. Lora sat shirtless so that Ebba-Basarr could anoint her scrapes, cuts, and at least one bitemark. "You're supposed to send runaways back to us alive."

"That's your rule, not ours," I said. I didn't mean to sound rude. The look Ebba gave me was one of outrage. In fact, it was two years since any of the Riding Women had had occasion to hunt down a male fugitive on the border.

"Oh, Ebba, it's one of those rules that everybody ignores," Lora chided, trying to keep the peace. "The plains people have always considered the mucks dangerous vermin, to be got rid of when the chance offers. They don't mate with men, so why risk living with them? It's different for us, more's the pity."

She caught Veree's eye and waved. He said, "Why is that ma all shiny?"

"That's medicine, Veree," I said, "for her scratches, see?"

"I have scratches," he said, beginning to squirm around to find some, chattering away about the history of each one.

"Did the little white cloud horse have scratches?" I asked. He considered aloud whether it was possible for anything to scratch a cloud. When I said not so far as I knew, he seemed satisfied and returned to the cloud-horse story.

Ebba-Basarr said to me, "As we ride down into New Forge, watch for stacks of stones by the roadside and in the fields. I know of three at least that you'll see on the way."

"Oh, leave it, Ebba," Lora said, making an unhappy face. "What can our cairns mean to someone raised in the Grasslands?"

"Each cairn," Ebba-Basarr pressed on, "shows where someone saw a bond fem they knew, maybe one of their work gang or part of their own master's femhold, killed in slavery or in the war.

"The cairn closest to New Forge, right by the river, is where two teams of Rovers cut a runaway fem to pieces in sight of a labor crew out mending 'Troi dam. That was many years ago, but we don't forget." She raised her voice, for Galligan's benefit no doubt: "We don't forget anything."

I recollected the Free Fems at Stone Dancing Camp telling just such grim tales, and myself as a girl listening avidly. In those days I drank in their stories with a jealous yearning, sad that I myself would never be tested as strongly as they had been.

Now I wondered how hard the Free worked at keeping such memories fresh, and whether it could be a good thing to dwell on so much suffering and rage. My self-song had changed as I'd grown older—each significant event took less space as new ones were added, although the depth of original feelings stayed the same. Didn't harking back always to ancient wrongs distort perspective, distracting from more recent happenings?

What was memory anyway, in a country where each person must remember for herself alone because she doesn't even know her own mother or her own children, or if she has any kin living?

"Did you ever see such terrible things yourself?" I asked politely.

"More than once," Ebba began, "in the old, bad days—"

"But that's over and done," Lora said, probably saving me from hours of gruesome reminiscences by her dour companion. "Your little kit will only know such things from the stories that go with the cairns." She reached over and stroked Veree's bare arm. He shrank against me, turning his face into my shoulder.

Lora sat back again. "Shy little creature. May I hold her?" she asked wistfully. "Just for a minute."

"Maybe later," I said uneasily. He was too old to be dandled by strangers, but then these people naturally regarded children a little differently than we did in the Grasslands. More importantly, a knowing hand might discover Veree's sex through a chance caress. (Did Galligan know just by looking? A terrifying thought that I quickly dismissed for my sanity's sake.)

"So you named your daughter after Juya-Veree," Ebba-Basarr remarked, putting the final touches on Lora's injuries with shiny fingers. "If that fem had stayed here where she belonged, she might still be alive to carry her own name."

Lora said, "We heard that Juya's cub was male. What

would the Riding Women have done with it if it had lived?"

I shrugged, keeping my face as blank as I could. This was not a conversation for Veree to hear, but he was now dozing against me and I doubted that our talk was anything but a background droning to his fleeting dreams.

"Poor Juya," Lora said. "We worked together in the old days. She was always impulsive."

"Impulsive?" Ebba-Basarr said, tying the lid back on her ointment pot. "Stupid, to leave her own people at such a time."

Veree squirmed, mumbling, "You're squeezing me, ma!"

"Sshh, now," I murmured to him. "Do you have to pee? We'll be riding for a while. Let's go empty out over by those bushes."

"Don't have to."

"You're sure? We don't want to have to stop once we're up and riding. You're really sure?"

A nod.

"Then settle down and go back to sleep."

"I'm not tired," he whispered, but he drooped against me.

"Sleep anyway."

Veree gave a few tentative moans and then fell quiet; good. I didn't want any more attention drawn to him than was absolutely necessary.

Galligan coughed and spat dust he had inhaled from the bark of the tree he was tied to. He was young, with a sharp profile and very short, dirty hair of indeterminate color. He looked harmless now.

I said, "What happens when you get him back to where he came from?"

Lora said, "He'll have to be punished. They may give him a public death, as a warning to the others." She shook her head. "I won't watch. I hate those things."

"That's why you say 'they' will punish him, instead of 'we' will punish him," Ebba-Basarr said darkly. "What do you think he would have done to you if we hadn't arrived in time to save your neck?"

"Oh, what can you expect?" Lora said. "He's a man, Ebba!"

I said, "Has he hurt anybody else?"

"He did a little damage," Lora said cheerfully. I think she

was still lightheaded with the energy charge of the fight. "At least he had the sense not to try to escape on horseback."

Ebba-Basarr spat. "The first rule is, no man rides a horse."

Having seen this Galligan in action, I heartily agreed. The idea of such savagery backed up by the speed, strength, and mobility of horses sent a shiver down my spine.

Or maybe my shiver was for the knowledge that at some point these people must discover that Veree had already lived most of his life on horseback, like any Grassland child his age.

Ebba-Basarr said, turning her head to keep her words from the tender ears of my "daughter," "We should burn him alive, the way they used to burn us for witchery every time something went wrong in *their* Holdfast. You wouldn't be able to keep me away from that spectacle!"

She wiped her fingers on the grass and tucked the ointment pot into a saddlebag. "Let's go. I don't want to be responsible for him any longer than I have to."

Towing our captive at a rope's end again, we descended toward the smokes and sounds of New Forge, a town rising on a site above the black ruins of old 'Troi which Lora pointed out to me. She rode close to me and reached out now and then to touch Veree's arm or his cheek. He snoozed, unaware.

He was a dead weight at my back. I felt saddle-sore, tired, and filled with trepidation.

"Lovely skin she has," Lora murmured. "She didn't take your color hair, though. I thought, among the Mares—"

I had had some time to come up with an answer to the inevitable questions about this. "Nobody knows why she doesn't look just like me," I said, as casually as I could. "Something about the stud milk meeting Holdfast seed instead of Grassland seed, they think. They say she'll grow into a closer resemblance, with time."

Lora looked dubious, but at that moment Ebba-Basarr interjected, "That's the cairn I meant."

Inwardly, I blessed her stubborn nature. She indicated a pile of stones rising alongside the trail some distance away. Four big Holdfast horses grazing near it moved off as we approached.

Ebba-Basarr exclaimed angrily. "Those are Partan Hearth horses running loose again! There'll be hell to pay if they've been through anyone's fields."

"Loose from what?" I asked, puzzled.

"Oh, we keep our horses in fenced pastures here," Lora-Lan said, "so they don't damage the crops."

This was such an odd idea that I couldn't imagine what to reply. Horses wander; horse people follow them. But of course there had been neither horses nor herders in the Holdfast before Alldera's return. I could see that they hadn't the space for great, free-ranging herds, their country being a patchwork of fenced fields and clusters of buildings.

The two fems each added a stone to the lopsided cone of rocks. Lora scooped up a stone for me, saving me having to dismount with the burden of the child on my back. I rode close and tucked the pebble into a gap near the top of the pile.

"What do you do if there are no stones handy?" I asked.

"In any of the Lady's sanctuaries," Lora said, "you'll find a bucket of chips from the quarries. Travelers take some with them to add to the cairns they pass. You won't be expected to do that, being Grassland-raised."

"The cairns at 'Troi," Ebba-Basarr said, giving Galligan's rope a jerk so that he stumbled wide of the cairn as he passed it, "are a hundred strong. When the mucks have finished leveling that place, nothing will be left except our monuments."

I had made a terrible mistake, I told myself as we came out of the trees and descended the trail toward New Forge. I should never have brought Juya's little boy into the Holdfast of the Free Fems.

Paper

Beyarra-Bey ran her palm over the pale green page.

"Closer," she said, "much closer to what we're looking for. See, here's a sheet we use as a standard—" She reached for a stack of papers on her work table. Several loose sheets glided onto the floor.

Roona bent with a grunt, retrieved the pages, and handed them to her. "Well, I'm not doing it any more. I don't like anything about this reading and writing—it's men's things. Look at that!"

The top page was covered with printed text and an image of a stilt-legged, fantastical-looking beast with a large patchwork design on its body. It had two tiny, knob-ended horns on its triangular head, giving it an insectlike aspect.

Roona regarded the image malevolently. "Not everything that was lost in the Wasting was worth keeping."

" 'Gee-ra-fee,' " Beyarra read. "I think that's a creature that died out before the Wasting really took hold."

"You're saying the name wrong. *He* says he thinks the a was short because of the two f's, you see, so it's 'geer-*aff*,' *he* says. Damned know-it-all. We should lock up his Book Room and throw away the key."

What hope for change was there, given this attitude about a man who had helped to save Alldera's life? Sometimes Beyarra despaired.

With Alldera gone, she felt her own unease more sharply. She was as discontented as Roona was, but she could not say, *This life is so much better, but it's not yet good enough. It's not what I joined you for, what I fought alongside you for—a state of permanent enmity between us and the men, between us and our own sons. I have a daughter. She deserves peace, not war; brothers, not slaves.*

Indeed, there were few she could say this to; only other mothers of freeborn children, and not to all of them. They had seen the bond fems' situation slowly improving after the old men had been overthrown. Some said that they would have eventually come to their own workable accommodation with the younger men even without Alldera's army, maybe even a better arrangement; but they only said it among themselves.

Beyarra took the old woman's knuckly hand in a soothing grip. "Roona, nobody's forcing you. Only people who are interested study reading."

Roona frowned but consented to let her hand be held. She had declined noticeably of late. One sign of this change was an increased hunger for the touch of younger people. Involving her in the paper-making project was in part meant to root her deeper in life.

"It makes me sick," the old woman grumbled. "That damned muck can tell me what marks on a page mean and how to say them, and all I get to say back is yes. You'd think he was one of the winners, and me one of the losers of our war. Anyway, we got along fine before without men's book knowledge."

Beyarra sighed. She herself had sparked the literacy effort. When Eykar Bek had shown her Maggomas' notes on paper making, she had approached the Council about writing down a record of the Conquest. Despite the difficulty finding time for such "frills" with a whole country to be rebuilt, Alldera had agreed (she had been a messenger once and knew the value of preserving the truth). Others had followed her lead.

So the skills and materials needed to write history had begun to come into being, but not without criticism and dire warnings which Roona had never been reluctant to articulate.

"You know what this is for," Beyarra coaxed. "Anybody can lie about the past to make herself seem more important or to injure someone else. Without records of others' experiences, who could correct the lies?"

"Writing doesn't prevent lying!" the old fem hooted. "The men still tell plenty of lies among themselves about how wonderful life was before we defeated them."

"Exactly. You don't want anyone taking those lies for truth, do you?" *My daughter. Other children.*

Roona gave her an outraged look. "Well, what fool would ever believe what a *man* says?"

Beyarra got up and brought a small stack of pages to

the table. "Kenanna-Kai wrote this part in her writing class: see?"

Roona snorted. "How do you know any of it's true? Men wrote down plenty of shit in Ancient times!"

Beyarra said patiently, "That's why we're so careful. We check everything with other people to weed out mistakes at the start." A name on the top page caught her eye. "This is about Alldera's life in the Grasslands, at Stone Dancing Camp. You remember, I read it to you last week."

She peered more closely at the blotted writing. "What's this underneath? A list? 'Mares who were sharemothers of Sorrel in Holdfaster Tent'—I wish she hadn't written 'Mares.' "

"It's what we called them," Roona said obstinately. "Some still do." She came around to look over Beyarra's shoulder. Her breathing sounded laborious but her sight was keen; she still called the scores in archery contests. "Anyway, everybody knows all that stuff. The First Free have it in their self-songs, even."

"People are letting their self-songs go," Beyarra said. "When's the last time you sang yours?"

"Well, if we can't remember our own past with songs or without them, we're worse off than I thought!"

Why do I bother? We're just going in circles, Beyarra fretted. But this old fem could be her grand-dam; she could not help but try to induce her to understand, and approve. "We're writing things to make sure we do remember, and for our children. We can't trust Daya to keep our stories any more—"

"Daya!" Roona growled. "That sly, selfish, coward! But her damned lies are scribbled down someplace in here too, aren't they? Because she taught them to you, and you wrote them down."

Beyarra's eyes stung briefly and she didn't answer at once. Daya had once trained Beyarra to remember femmish stories and histories. Beyarra had idolized the exotic liberator whose tales wove such magic, and had loved her desperately.

She'd had good reason to hate Daya since. Now she hated being reminded of that earlier, hot-burning affair.

"Roona, I was a slave until you and the rest of Alldera's

army freed me," she said. Her voice trembled, something she couldn't help when she was upset. "I never lived free in the Tea Camp with Elnoa the Green-eyed. But Daya was there. I put down her version of events as I did other people's. Yours too."

Roona clapped her lumpy old hands together. "When Daya and Alldera went to live with the Mares, my wagon crew was first to join them there. Did Daya tell you that? Ha! 'Course not! And why not? Jealousy, the vice of pet fems!"

"Well," Beyarra said, "we all have failings. When there are questions, we need evidence, the accounts of eyewitnesses—"

"Evidence, witnesses—it's plain as daylight. Daya's a murderer, her and her cronies too. They shamed us all."

Her faded eyes glared accusingly at Beyarra-Bey, as if the young unslave had been one of the traitors instead of one of Alldera's rescuers. Then Roona turned away, dabbing at her cheek with her sleeve.

"It was a very close thing," Beyarra agreed faintly. She still dreamed sometimes about the blood showing black on Alldera's bleached face in the firelight, and Eykar Bek's skin smeared with that same liquid black as he held her against him and waited to die with her.

In these dreams she would scream at the shadowy figures with the bloody knives, and they would laugh. But as long as they laughed, they did not strike the final blows.

Roona, seeing something troubled in her face, said more gently, "You should have gone south with Alldera. This world is a heartless place. It's too easy to lose people you love."

"I'm not her shadow," Beyarra said. "I have work to do. Geeda was dying. I needed to write her story down."

"And you don't like to ride horseback," Roona said shrewdly, "so you preferred to stay behind. You *could* have gone instead of sending Chisti, that prissy little snot. Eykar's writing students here could have recorded Geeda's story."

Beyarra shifted in her seat. "No one else writes fast enough to keep up with Geeda once she got talking—"

"Oh, nobody else can do this, nobody else can do that," Roona said in irritation. "A few years of freedom and people become very elevated in their own eyes! That's what comes of taking on Marish ways."

"If we were Mares we'd just kill all the men and forget about them," Beyarra retorted, "as some people still want us to do."

She fell silent, shamed by her own outburst.

Temper was not something she had been able to indulge as a bond fem. She hadn't known she'd had a temper. It was not a revelation of her own character that she liked. Of course partly it was due to being tired all the time. She hadn't expected to work harder for her own people than she had worked for her masters.

"I don't want to argue with you, Roona—"

"Too high and mighty to wrangle with me, just because Alldera favors you?" the old woman sneered.

That stung. "I hope people don't see me as haughty on that account."

Roona groaned and pressed her hands to her mottled scalp. "Oh, forget I said that, child! I'm truly sorry. It's just all these men's ways, all this paper and ink! People will lose the knack of remembering if they can always go look at a piece of writing instead."

"Daya says the same thing."

"Oh, Daya, Daya," Roona replied, waving her crooked old hands in the air in frustration. "A man's plaything, that one, all her life. Don't put her stamp on my words!"

They probably say that about me, Beyarra thought, *some of them anyway: that I'm soft on the men. Because I work with Eykar. Because I want something better than rage and hatred and contempt between women and men. In that one thing, Daya and I do see eye to eye.*

"Did you know the pet," she ventured, "in the Old Holdfast, before she ran away west?"

"I didn't write that down," Roona said slyly, "so I don't remember."

Beyarra almost told her, then, about the Bibles: it was true that not all the old books were worth keeping. Eykar had brought her several copies of the book of the Ancient religion. The Ancients must have taken numbers of these books with them into the Refuge, for so many copies to have survived.

She had read one (it was in plainer speech than the other two, but told the same tale), forcing her way through. Then she had told Eykar that she was going to destroy these Bibles. If he had objected she might have changed her mind, for she understood his love of books to be deeper rooted than her own, and wiser out of greater familiarity if nothing else.

But he had said, "Good," and he helped her burn them, watching with her in grim satisfaction as it all went up in smoke—the boasts, the grandiloquent promises and raging threats of the great father called "God" and his prophets; the crowing tales of self-righteous slaughter; and the women who, in the background or (briefly) the foreground, never belonged to themselves. Up in smoke, and good riddance.

Sometimes now she wondered if the destruction had been right. So many books were lost already, so many clues to the past obliterated. But the best thing about the past was that it was over, and it lifted her heart to think of the stories being written now, new stories, stories of the Free.

That was why writing was so important.

Roona said, "Elnoa wrote too. She used to write things down in big leather books that nobody else ever got to read. Secrets. She held them over our heads—secrets that could never be forgotten because she'd written them down."

"This is different," Beyarra protested. "We write to spread knowledge around, not to hide it away. This isn't a Tea Camp full of intriguers."

"Oh, you know everything," Roona said spitefully. "You're NewFree, you were never even there, but you know everything better than I do, and I lived in the Mares' country!"

In a sober tone the old fem added, "I'm just an old fool with big patches of forgetting in her head, but I can tell you this, my girl: any skill can be put to good use or evil, depending on the hand that wields it."

Downriver

I left New Forge early in the morning on a barge loaded with metal goods, and sacks of grain harvested from upland fields that had once served 'Troi. The idea of traveling in a huge, wheelless wagon on the top of the water was terrifying; but Ebba-Basarr was riding down to Midfast, and she set about including me in her expedition with such grim efficiency that I consented, on Lora's suggestion, to take the boat instead.

Veree sat on my lap questioning and pointing and grabbing at anything within reach. He was too shy of all these new people in a new place to go far from me, which suited me very well.

The fems who crewed the barge came by often to smile at "her" and pat her on the head as they pointed out the sights for her delectation. We passed two villages, which I was told were hearths for people tending the crops along the banks. Fields of tall green hemp rose beyond these riverside hay meadows.

The Riding Women gathered a scrawny plains version of this same hemp for medicine, as I'd learned while recovering from a separated shoulder. The stuff had made my legs go numb as well as my injury, and I hadn't much liked it.

Veree kept piping up, "Look, ma! What's that?" and whoever was nearby would kindly take pains to answer. Some looked perplexed when they heard he was mine. If they found our lack of perfect resemblance suspicious or disappointing, they were too polite to say so to me.

I felt very strange; I had never expected to enter the Holdfast as a trickster, hiding a secret that could get me—and my little companion—into deep trouble.

Well, what *had* I expected? That Alldera would rush to meet me, I suppose, and take Veree under her protection for my sake. Certainly she owed me that much, and, I was sure, it was within her power to do for Veree as she had done for Eykar Bek and for a madman called Setteo.

I had never thought of *not* meeting her. All the Free lived in fixed houses of stone and wood on this narrow coastal strip. How could I miss her?

Lora had told me that if I had come last spring, I would have found Alldera weeding fields like everyone else. The remnant men had let much of the land grow rank with neglect. Bosses like Erl the Scrapper had been more inclined to scavenge than to create.

After the Conquest, providing food for a population swollen by the addition of Alldera's army had not been easy. The lammin harvest had been dwindling for years anyway. (I remembered the Free Fems' tales of starving inside their own country almost as much as they did when they wandered in the Wild.)

Information about raising field crops had been found in Maggomas' Ancient books. (He had over time gathered—or stolen—almost all the surviving practical volumes.) But the first harvests had been lean.

This year, with yields higher and storehouses full, a bit of leisure was possible. Friends had urged Alldera to make use of it, Lora said. About a month before my arrival, Alldera left for the land of the Bayo-born, albeit with serious matters to discuss as well as hope for a rest.

I took this to mean that she was unable to settle in one place even now that it was her own hard-won territory. Off she must go to visit these interesting and reclusive strangers. Fine; I had plenty to keep me occupied in her absence.

Galligan, naked except for his bruises and his chains, rode with us, locked by a metal collar to a great wooden goods chest in the middle of the deck. His ankles were encircled by metal cuffs, linked together by short lengths of chain fastened in turn to the two ends of a wooden bar as long as my forearm.

This "stick" chained between his feet kept them spread apart and limited his stride. He could barely walk, let alone run or get a leg over a horse's back. This was what they meant when they said a man was punished by being put "on the stick."

He had, I was told, run away from Oldtown, but it was to Midfast, the Holdfast's central city, that he must go for judgment "on the steps," whatever that meant. Nothing good for him, I thought. He sat motionless and silent with his head bowed over his manacled hands.

The crew never spoke to him or touched him, but I saw how closely they watched him. I watched, too.

I thought he had the visual appeal of a wiry, well-made plains horse, although his wide shoulders made him look top-heavy and small-headed. I had heard femmish talk, in my childhood, of masculine beauty. Such ideas, laughable then, were important to me now. Veree would grow up to be a man.

I regarded with apprehension this savage image of his future, searching for any signs of grace or goodness. How unjust, that my tender boy must in time turn into a creature like this!

I missed having someone familiar to talk all this over with. My own fault: it had simply never occurred to me to drag anybody away from her own business (and good reputation) to cross the mountains with me and Veree, the two outsiders.

Veree came running back from a short excursion down the deck bawling over a splinter in his thumb. I drew it out and started a word game to distract him from the sting of the tiny wound: "A white horse grazing on new grass," I said, pulling him onto my lap.

He said, "A black horse rolling on her back."

I said, "A dappled horse rubbing his face on his foreleg."

He thought. "A dun horse nursing from his ma."

When he ran out of possibilities he would say one about a sorrel horse, for my hair color. That ended the game, unless we started all over again.

I was saved from a fourth round of "Colored Horses" when the person on the stern-sweep began to sing. Veree, caught by the unfamiliar tune, consented to be still and listen:

Hey! You, with the small, sweet hands
And hair like my black mare's mane,
I think I love you.
Hey! You, with that battle scar on your temple

Like a little, shiny star,
I think I love you.
But I see that you have two shadows
When you come riding this way,
One that follows you over the ground
And one that darkens your eyes from within.
One you were born with,
But the other joined you in hard times past.
Oh, the kisses of shadows are sweeter
Than the kisses of living lips,
And the embraces of shadows are warmer
Than those of living arms.
I should know. Look into my eyes,
My second shadow is watching you with longing.
Hey! You, with the small, sweet hands,
I think I love you.
Come look into my eyes.
I think I love you,
And my shadow and its shadow
Reach shadow hands toward yours.

I turned to one of Galligan's guards who stood near me. "What kind of song is that?"

She cocked an ironic brow at me. "Don't they have love songs on the other side of the mountains?"

She was a spare, elegant-looking person with sun-bleached hair and fine, weathered creases in her face. She never took her eyes off Galligan for more than a few seconds while she spoke to me. A good person to have with you on a raid.

I said, "It must be a new song. There were no horses in the Old Holdfast."

"Old tune, new song," the guard replied. "Korija, there, says she got it from someone in New Forge and it's called 'Sweet Hands,' but a horse tamer I know over at Lammintown says one of her hearthmates, a musician who makes very fine clay flutes, composed it. On the other hand, the horse tamer and Korija-Kon hate each other, so maybe that's not true."

"Why do they hate each other?" I asked.

"Oh, it's a long story," she answered with a shrug. "I

don't much like the second part of the song, about the singer's own two shadows; too complicated for such a simple melody."

People in the Grasslands didn't criticize each other's self-songs, and other songs were traditional and so beyond criticism. But they didn't sing self-songs here, I'd noticed; everyone knew everyone else without them.

Diffidently I asked, "Will she sing it again if I ask her to?"

The guard leaned closer to me. "Korija had a lover like that, a person with 'two shadows'. Old griefs and angers drove that woman to get into fights. A NewFree from Midfast had to kill her in self-defense. It's not just a song to Korija-Kon."

An older NewFree sitting across from me on a crate reached over and tapped my knee. "Some people find the only way to get rid of their troubles is to get rid of themselves. Isn't it like that over the mountains where you come from?"

I admitted that sometimes it was.

The guard remarked, "Me, I just bite my nails."

I said, "I used to suck my hair when I was little. My mothers had to dip the end of my braid in horse piss to make me stop."

They both laughed. The older one introduced herself as Tikkin-Tuva. I barely noticed. I was wishing that the guard, who said her name was Raysa, would laugh again. Her laughter stirred my blood up.

The two of them fell to talking over the noon meal, arguing about friends of Raysa's who wanted to take some horses off south to pasture them west of Bayo and live like Riding Women, in camps that followed the grazing. Tikkin-Tuva said they were just too lazy for real work. Raysa said they wanted to be away from men altogether and to live truly free.

Korija-Kon began a new song, which Raysa joined in. I knew it from Holdfaster Tent, the sad ballad of "Shy Ann." For the first time since I had entered the Holdfast, I felt happy and at peace.

That evening, the barge put in at a loading dock by a village called Reed Hearths. Three passengers settled themselves on a bench in back. It was a while before I noticed, in that late summer light, that one was a man, a grizzled, unsticked slave accompanying two weavers transporting bales of cloth.

A slump-shouldered figure in a plain smock with close-cut, graying hair, this man ignored our prisoner, looking instead at the water gliding by. He spoke only to the weavers. His feet were bare, and he wore a metal circlet around one ankle.

I had only to look at him to despise him. That was when I realized uncomfortably that in comparison to him, I had some respect for the runaway. After all, Galligan had tried to do what my bloodmother had done: escape.

I nudged Raysa. "What about that one, what's he?"

"Relki? Nothing. A sponsored man."

I stared at that stooped, gray figure. Veree could never look like that, not ever!

"I heard he bred a sickly child," Tikkin-Tuva said (she had been drinking with Korija-Kon and smelled of liquor now). She didn't bother to lower her voice, but if Relki heard, he gave no sign. "I knew men who should have survived instead of him."

I said, "Were many killed? I thought you meant to catch them alive, for breeding." Yet the thought of either of these Free folk mating with Relki, or Galligan either, made me nauseous.

"Lots died," Raysa said judiciously. "We put them all on the stick at first, to keep better track of them. They kept dying of accidents, sickness, fights. People said the stick was too harsh, that it was killing even the younger ones who had been much softer masters after the Fall of the Seniors.

"We argued for half a year over it. Then we told them all, 'You go freefoot from now on, unless you give us reason to put you on the stick.' Relki, there, has two sponsors in charge of him; two, to prevent some silly NewFree from being made a fool of by some pretty, cunning fellow with no other woman there to prevent it."

She spoke dryly, plainly not believing that such a thing could happen to *her*, at any rate.

"We told them," she went on, " 'Do as you're told and you'll die in peace like civilized people. But if you lay a willful hand on any of us, or mount a horse or draw a bow, we'll kill you out of hand.' That weeded out the ones who couldn't accept the new way of things. Resistance and sabotage got them put back on the stick, if they survived."

I looked over at Galligan. "Maybe that one wanted to be killed too, so he made a doomed bid for freedom."

Raysa shook her head. "Don't make a romance of it; he snapped, that's all. There aren't enough grown men left to overturn things again, and we have enough sons off them now to replace the men if needs be; we don't really need them at all. When they think about that, sometimes they snap."

Tikkin-Tuva chuckled. "Not that all of them want to change things back, coddled as they are these days. We feed them better than their Seniors did and they get to fuck as much as they're able. Cleverer people than me say most sticks have learned to like it."

I was conceiving a dislike of Tikkin-Tuva, imagining her busy gaze picking out Veree as one of the people she thought were being "coddled." I turned toward Raysa.

"Wouldn't it be an awful risk, to kill the men and have only your young sons to depend on for the next generation?"

She trailed her fingers over the side, watching the ripples they made. "I'd rather the world be empty of any people at all than chance our daughters' freedom."

"She speaks it," Tikkin-Tuva said fervently, "the Lady's truth."

Silenced by this glimpse of the vast distances between my history and theirs, I retreated into a daydream of going gambling at Midfast with Raysa, who in my mind became a famous hero of the Femmish Conquest (well, for all I knew, she was). In my dream she taught me more of Korija's song, rare and intimate verses, and we ended in each other's arms. Old hurts were soothed, old hungers fed, and for my sake she even came to love Veree.

We tied up at Oldtown a day later. The docks looked new-built, raw, and unhandsome in the way of many practical femmish things. Raysa (who had to stay on board to watch

Galligan) directed me to a friend's house and offered to lend me tea brick or some of the small metal links they called "trade chain" to pay my way. I declined but thanked her with a full heart.

Lora-Lan had assured me at New Forge that finding remounts would be easy. In exchange for my spare horses, she and her hearthmates had filled my saddlebags with provisions and my belt pouch with chain. I felt poor with only two horses and wished I hadn't let my pack string go, but I was glad not to have to make my way trading on my connection with Alldera.

Oldtown itself was built of red sandstone and baked red brick. The air stank of rotting hemp plants. There were few people about when we docked. A half-dozen raggedy figures passed heavy sacks down a line from a warehouse to the end of the pier. By their wide-legged, clumsy steps, they were stickmen. I was curious, but went no nearer.

The free people I had seen so far were dressed for riding, Grassland-style, in long, loose shirts, trousers, and soft boots tied under the knee. Most wore a headcloth draped over the hair or slung loosely around the neck. I was glad to see that my own hard-worn clothing was not out of place.

Some Oldtown fems wore instead of a shirt a sleeveless, woven garment that closed with toggles or belt and sported capacious pockets on the front of the long skirts. I wondered how I could obtain one of these for myself, for they looked handsome and useful.

At a cross-street I halted Patch, on whose back Veree sat staring about. I glanced uncertainly around. A small crowd, following at a distance, had stopped when I stopped.

There came a sudden commotion of music: drums, chimes, and a piercing rill of pipes. I had to steady Patch, who threw her head up and danced backward. Veree squealed with excitement.

A procession came into view bearing down upon us, riders on white horses, each carrying a banner tied to an upright lance. In the lead walked a slender figure in pale, fluttering robes, flanked by musicians also on foot. They halted before us at a signal—the dramatically upflung arm of their leader.

She said in a high, carrying voice, "Greetings from the servants of the Lady, Alldera's child!"

She smiled—a freakish, scar-rucked smile that made Veree stare. Me, too: I knew that nightmare face, but I scarcely recognized the frail-looking figure, slightly bowed at the shoulders now.

"Daya?" I faltered, backing a step. The hard-riding Free Fem of the plains and the devilish traitor in the Watchtower—my imagination's masks, in recent years, for Alldera's lover and betrayer—dissolved in the face of reality: she was just an aging pet with a scarred face. To my horror, I felt a stab of pity for her.

She modestly inclined her head, looking at me from under her long, curved eyelashes. "Did you think that Alldera's own bloodchild could enter Alldera's country and no one would know? We've been quarreling over who to send to New Forge to escort you here."

A rebellious thought whispered in my mind: who said I had to be bound by my mother's feuds? I was my own person, born and raised in another country, and Daya had always been good to me, encouraging me, enthralling me with slave tales of Holdfast life.

Her gaze shifted past me, to Veree. "And here's the child people have been talking about!" My blood jolted with alarm. *She* would see that he was no Grasslands double of his "blood-ma."

But "Pretty!" was all she said, and then, "Now come, we have a quiet place for you to stay tonight."

I shook my head, fearful that to her keen eyes Veree's secret must be revealed if she had more time with us. But she leaned forward and gripped my arms as I tried to retreat, adding in that public voice, "Come with me, child. I did wrong to Alldera, but I am in Moonwoman's service now. That Lady keeps me on the pathways of her light."

As I tried to frame a refusal, she added in a whisper, "Sorrel, don't force me to explain to everyone how this child can't possibly be your own."

And so I closed my mouth, took a deep breath, and went with my bloodmother's enemy, my heart pounding with apprehension.

She led me to the central hall of the Moon's House, a sparely furnished, domed space, its tiled floor dotted with circular rugs knotted of pale cloth rope. As soon as she shut the door to the outside court, I turned on her in fearful anger.

"Why are you doing this? What do you want?"

"I sleep in the adjoining room," she said, ignoring my question. "It's small, but adequate. You can sleep here, with the child."

I looked up from settling Veree, who was nodding off, on a couch by the window. Through the window I saw two fems walk past, talking together in low voices and looking in my direction. "Who are those people in the courtyard?"

Daya said with amusement, "My followers, or rather the Lady's own; and my guards. I'm in exile here, child, kept out of the center of things. But my wits are still sharp. I know that child wasn't sired on you by a stud colt in the Grassland manner.

"And no one here has challenged you about the lack of resemblance between you two, have they? Alldera's daughter is an honored guest, not to be questioned. You abuse our hospitality, Sorrel. I'm surprised at you."

I burst out, "I don't know why they let you live at all, after what you tried to do to Alldera!"

She answered calmly, "In the midst of the blood and flying blades that night at the tower, I knew that we had made a terrible mistake. I mended what I could. Fedeka offered me the shelter of Moonwoman because she, and the Lady, understood that however badly I had acted I was still a First Free, and not an evil person."

She poured me a bowl of beer, but I refused it. I wasn't sure what drinking with someone signified in the New Holdfast. For all I knew, this could be part of some trap.

On the couch Veree sighed and squirmed restlessly. The excitement of the barge journey and our arrival had not quite worn him out. I went to him, bending to brush kisses onto his face.

"Can I have a story, ma?" he murmured.

"I can't tell you one right now, precious," I said. "You tell yourself a story until you fall asleep."

"I don't know any stories," he whined.

" 'Sabadi and the Whispering Water.' I'll start it for you." I got two sentences along and he let out a couple of bugging little snores. I tucked my headcloth around his body.

"A quiet child," Daya observed, when I returned to her. She was pouring a drink for herself.

Anxious to deflect her attention from Veree, I returned to the attack. "I've never understood what you did. Alldera was your friend, your lover."

"We didn't start as friends," Daya corrected quietly. "When she came to live at the Tea Camp, it was perfectly clear that she despised me as a conniving little pet fem, which I suppose I was. I thought her a callow, arrogant lout." She smiled and sipped her drink. "Which in many ways she was."

That smile enraged me. "And that's why you tried to kill her in the Watchtower?"

"I stopped the attack. I sent for help."

"The NewFree Beyarra-Bey stopped it, that's what I heard."

"Without my help she would have been killed too." She set down her bowl on the matting beside her knee.

"You call that help!" I jeered.

She lifted her slender hand, palm outward. "Hush, child; I am thinking of how I can tell you this." Eyelids lowered and face pensive, she could almost be mistaken for beautiful.

How I longed to be outside and away from her. I had occasionally pictured a conversation with my bloodma's chief attacker—myself the righteous accuser, the generous pardoner, the indifferent adult above it all—nothing like this actuality, now. And I had never imagined finding Daya so composed, so elegant in the moon's colors of white and gray, with white rings gleaming on her agile fingers.

She said at last, "I thought Alldera despised me. She had taken other lovers, drawn others close in counsel, people whose warlike virtues were beyond the reach of a mere pet." She looked at me with a soft, meditative gaze. "Being in the Holdfast again sapped my courage. I thought we were reckless with victory, inviting a men's uprising that could destroy us all. So I let myself become the thing I most feared. I behaved like a frightened slave, turning against her own.

"Well, I was never very good at being free."

She blotted tears or the suggestion of tears with her sleeve. I was moved in spite of myself but I resented having been maneuvered into sympathy for her, for I was sure that she played on my feelings for purposes of her own.

Expect treachery, I reminded myself. This isn't really your attentive auntie any more—the glamorous, tragedy-marked foreigner who had always treated me, flatteringly, like an adult. This is the criminal that person later became.

Daya suddenly rose, crossed the room, and bent to stroke Veree's sleeping head. If I had been closer by, I would have been unable to stop myself striking her hand aside.

She said, "What will you do with this little one, since Alldera is away? It's Juya's child, isn't it? And the Mares don't want it. Will Alldera want it?"

I stood up, taut with nerves. "Fedeka is my oathmother; I'll ask her help."

"But she isn't your only friend in the New Holdfast," Daya said. The insinuation in her tone made me feel ill.

I began pacing the room again. "What do you want with me? I haven't come here to mix into your affairs. I just want to settle Veree in friendly hands and then go home."

With breathtaking lightness she said, "Leave Veree with me."

I gaped at her. I said, "You tried to kill my bloodmother. Don't ask me to trust you with a child!"

"Ah," Daya said. She made the strings of white pebbles tied at her belt ripple over her fingers like magic. "But I should trust *you*."

She straightened and shot me a piercing glare. "How can you, Alldera's daughter, lie yourself silly pretending you've had a baby when everyone in the world would know about it if you had?" She stabbed her finger at Veree. "Worse yet, pretending that this is a girl, when in fact it is a male child?"

I felt as if a horse had kicked me.

She smiled faintly, a truly horrible smile. "I can smell

them, young or old, alive or dead; I know when there's a male in a room with me. Now, tell me again about how *I* am not *trustworthy.*"

I could not speak. She nodded gravely. "Good, silence is best, and silence I will keep about this boy, if you do as I ask. Don't worry, my request is simple. I must travel on with you to Midfast. If you take me with you, no one here will venture to object."

"Midfast," I said stupidly, my brain ringing with shock. "What's in Midfast?"

"I have business there," she said, "of the Lady's. Is it agreed? I will keep my word. I'm your auntie, Sorrel, and I'm on your side. Even in the tents of your precious Grassland relations, kindred keep the secrets of their kin."

Slaves

Eykar was puzzling over the shelving of a water-stained volume with its front cover and first few pages missing—"sheriff grabbed for his six-gun, Rankin brought up his Winchester one-handed and pumped three shots"—when the crooked door to the anteroom was kicked back against the wall with a thump.

He turned, clutching the book to his chest. Two figures came staggering out of the dark: Setteo, limp as a rag, supported by a muscular young man who called, "Help me! He's heavy."

Eykar hurried forward to seize the sagging form round the waist, stumbling under the sudden weight. "What happened?"

"Don't blame me," Payder panted. "Arjvall said to bring him to you."

"Those Bear-cult idiots!" Eykar said bitterly. "They didn't feed him manna, did they?"

"Wouldn't waste it on him," the other said.

"I hope you're not one of Arjvall's band of plotters," Eykar said, peering at him. "They'll all go back on the stick or worse if they don't come to their senses! No? So why are you running their errands for them?"

"Because I'm freefoot," Payder said smugly, "and the Heras like me." He had in fact acquired a reputation as a dancer who entertained sometimes for his hearth-heras.

"Not for much longer, if Kobba's patrols catch you out after curfew!"

With Payder's help Eykar brought Setteo to the sleeping alcove, where a small lamp burned over a nest of tangled bedding. The cutboy coughed as they eased him down onto the pallet of blankets and sacking, but did not wake.

Payder said, "There's no blood. It's just a fit."

Eykar's swift examination—he was used to doing this—confirmed that Setteo bore only his usual complement of casual scrapes and scabs. "Help me roll him over; he sleeps on his stomach. Now come help me close the front door again."

The younger man courteously fitted his lithe stride to Eykar's halting one, which made Eykar feel old. Of course by the standards of the men's Holdfast, he *was* old, a Senior himself and the "natural" enemy of a young man like Payder.

"Arjvall's talking against you," Payder said in a confidential tone.

Eykar laughed. "No news there."

"He says you're not going to help Galligan."

"You can't help an idiot."

The door had jumped its top hinge again. They jockeyed the heavy panel between them, trying to get the pin back into the slightly twisted socket. Payder grunted, "Galligan snapped, that's all. Could be worse; I know cockies who'd have slit a few throats on their way out. Let go, I'll do it."

Eykar stepped back gladly. He couldn't see into the gloom up there anyway. " 'Snapping' is a luxury we never could afford, not under the Seniors and not under Erl the Scrapper's rule either."

Payder grinned over his shoulder. "Erl could be got round."

"Well, the Free folk can't," Eykar said. "I hope Galligan isn't special to you, because his chances—"

"Nobody's special to me," Payder grunted. "Which is how I like it." The hinge came together, and the door swung, creaking, into place. "I'm not a romantic, like some people."

"Good," Eykar said brusquely. "So; what are you waiting for? Your sponsors will be wondering where you are, surely? There's no wiser master than an upstart slave."

Payder brushed his hands clean. "I need your advice, sir."

Eykar longed to get away before some tale of trouble could be unfolded, but where to? "Find someone your own age to talk to. You're not thinking of bolting like Galligan?"

"Why? There's no place to go. They've even looted the Refuge now. Vargindo says you told them where to find it."

"I might have," Eykar said dryly, "except that it turns out not to be where I thought it was."

The young man squared his broad shoulders, looked Eykar in the eye, and said, "It's one of the Heras. We had a fine time in breed-bed. I think she's interested in me."

Eykar groaned inwardly.

"Trouble is," the young man continued, sinking gracefully down to sit on his heels, "it's not all from her side." He cracked his knuckles, one by one, with a disgusting sound. "She's killer-beautiful. We laugh together."

Eykar rubbed his hands over his face. He felt very tired. "Don't tell me her name. You think she returns your feelings?"

Payder nodded. "Now, I'm no pervert, I love my own kind as any real man does." A modest cough. "A little too freely, if you ask some people."

"Spare me your protestations," Eykar said coldly. "Cross-sexing was the way of the world before the Wasting; it took the strictest application of Old Holdfast doctrine to suppress it. With that pressure removed, things are changing. Don't let anyone—not the Free, and not Arjvall and his lads either—tell you who you do or don't love. You are the only authority on that."

"Then do *you*—I mean, are you attracted by—" The young man faltered, grinning nervously, clearly aware that he had stepped over the line.

Eykar liked him for it and chose to answer. "No. I'm one of those who is same-sex as a natural inclination. But that doesn't mean that you, or anybody else, must be so too. And," he added, warming to the point of his theme, "none of this means that you can afford to ignore the actual rules in place, regardless of who's enforcing them."

"Oh, rules," Payder said. "A smart fellow can learn to play that game to his own advantage."

There was something of Servan in his manner, some flavor of careless rebellion, that impelled Eykar to press the point. It would be so easy for this lad to destroy himself on a reckless whim.

Eykar said, "The Seniors punished love between men and women for religious reasons, while mandating cross-sexing for reproduction; and a fine, twisted mess that made for everybody, too. The Free, although their reasons are rooted in their own experience rather than in imagined evils, have come up with a very similar arrangement. Already some of them see the likeness to what the old men did, and they don't like it; but change won't come quickly, and it won't be smooth.

"Which means that as things stand now, my advice to you is to fuck this woman all you like, but keep your feelings out of it."

"Well, you can say that," Payder answered warmly, "but if she were here, even you would see, there's something about her—"

"Nothing worth risking your neck for," Eykar barked. "Work it off in breed-bed. No secret meetings, no private conversations, no wiggling around trying to get yourself sent to her hearth. Pray she gets pregnant; then she'll have something on her mind besides you."

"But if we like each other—"

"All the worse! You asked my advice. That's it. Say 'thank you' and go home to your sponsors."

Payder rose to his feet. "I thought *you'd* have something else to say."

Because of Eykar's special relationship with Alldera and Beyarra, of course. Foolish boy. Eykar said, "No. Men did the same as this Hera of yours when we sat in the master's chair. Dallying across the rule for the thrill of the forbidden always ended badly then. You're not too young to remember, and it's perilous to forget."

"But you and Alldera—"

Eykar rapped the young man's chest with his forefinger. "You aren't me and your Hera isn't Alldera. And that's not what people think it is anyway."

"Who's to say what's right, though?" Payder said earnestly. "Nobody knows any more how things 'have' to be."

"So why are you wasting your time asking me?"

"Well, what about something else, then?" Payder said, stepping close and reaching for Eykar's hand, the hand that had tapped him in the sternum a moment ago. "Maybe I have something for you. Setteo won't mind, he's light with people."

An acquisitive light gleamed in his eyes: *He thinks it will be a thrill,* Eykar thought, *to sleep with the Man Who Knew His Father, to fuck the Oracle. Maybe he thinks he'll catch a glimpse of his future. He wouldn't be the first, Christ knows.*

He turned his hand, slipping the younger man's grip. "You want too much from me. I would disappoint you."

The tension went out of Payder's frame. He lifted one shoulder in feigned indifference. "You're the Senior." He gulped. "God-son, I'm sorry! That was really stupid—"

"Oh, get out, go back to your hearth," Eykar said, "before you're missed. And don't talk about this again. You understand? Guard your words or change your friends. If your pal Arjvall finds out about this Hera of yours, he'll do something to make an example of you to the others. Do you hear me?"

Eykar pushed the door shut after Payder and went back to sit with the cutboy, who snored gently. Eykar shut his aching eyes. Inside his head, Payder walked into a femmish patrol and gave as his excuse, "I was consulting the Oracle."

Cascades of pictures poured through Eykar's mind, images of death and ruin. He slipped helplessly back to find himself on a bluff at dawn looking down at the fems that men had left impaled there, contorted on blackened stakes fixed upright in the riverside mud; and feeling the blood of the man standing next to him pooling under his bare feet in the shrieking furnace of femmish retaliation on Judgment Day; and even looking into the face of his father that shone exultantly as the man went on talking, talking, talking unendurable horrors, while fiery rage and despair coiled tighter and tighter in Eykar's body, and he couldn't stop what was coming, didn't want to stop the overpowering need to obliterate that face . . .

"Don't," Setteo said in a thready whisper. Eykar looked down to find his hands gripped in the cutboy's sinewy fingers. "If you make sounds like small things calling, you know, like child sounds, it draws their attention."

The attention, he meant, of his blasted Bears.

"You'll be fine," Setteo said, letting go his hands with a prim, reassuring pat to each one. He leaned back on his elbows. "You have to be. I can't help if they come now."

He was melancholy since his hallucinations had stopped, pining for his lost madness.

"It's all right," Eykar said. "Nobody's coming."

"Well, I wouldn't know. Nobody tells me anything anymore."

"I'm telling you something right now," Eykar said sharply. "Don't go wandering around at night again. There are people out there who would kill you without a thought."

The cutboy shivered hard. "Kobba of the Red Hand."

"Not just her. Men too, Setti."

"No man would dare. Not while I'm yours."

"That's a stupid thing to say," Eykar muttered angrily. "You never used to be stupid, and you can't afford to be now."

Setteo sighed. He would say something about being abandoned by the Bears next, as if that were the cause of any stupidity on his part as it was the cause of everything else in his life.

Eykar wished the damned Bears would come back. Maybe those dream creatures had been good for Setteo, preventing his worst excesses here in the "warm world." Eykar hated the tightness he felt in his chest when Setteo did reckless things and then escaped the consequences by no more than a hair's width of circumstance.

If I die, he thought, *—when I die—who will look after him?*

"There are men," he explained for the hundredth time, "who hate me. They hated me before for their friends and lovers who died at Endpath. Then they hated me for wrecking my father's plans and the Old Holdfast with them; and they hated me because they abused me when I was Servan's tame prophet, and people hate no one so much as someone they've wronged.

"Now they hate me for living among the books that I love with a person I love, under the protection of Alldera Conqueror."

"They envy you," Setteo said.

"It's the same thing. They hate me for teaching the fems to read our books, and probably for many other things that I don't even know about. It's a lot of hatred, Setti, enough to get me killed ten times over. They don't dare touch me, but they might go after you, because they know I love you."

Setteo was quiet for a moment. Then he said, "But you don't love me as much as you love your books."

Eykar put his hands to his head. "Don't start that again."

"And you love your students, the ones who read even outside lesson hours, the ones who draw letters in the dirt to teach others. I see how you look at them: so proud, so loving."

"I've told you," Eykar said, "I'll teach you, too. No one would care if you knew how to read."

But Setteo was shaking his head, shaking so hard that his whole body shook.

"No, no, I told you! That's why the Bears left me. You can't have *all* the kinds of knowing in the world. It was when I looked at books that they began to close the Cold Country to me. It was only right."

Eykar rubbed at his eyes. "Setteo, you're giving me a headache."

"I'm sorry," Setteo said contritely.

Eykar looked into his open, defenseless face. "Where was it so important for you to go tonight? Tell me, I won't be angry."

"You will."

"No, I promise."

"You won't yell or hit, but you'll be angry."

"Here, hold my hand. You'll feel it if I get angry. Then you can stop telling me. Just let go of my hand and I'll go read and leave you alone to sleep."

Setteo blinked anxiously. "Don't read. You'll wear out

your good eye and you won't be able to read at all."

"Setti," Eykar said, winding his fingers between the cut-boy's trembling ones, "tell me where you went."

Setteo turned his face into the bedding so that his voice was blurred. "Chokky Vargindo held a Bear dance."

Eykar wanted to stroke the thin back of Setteo's neck. Or wring it. "You risked getting killed just to hear a lot of crap about a past that never was and a future that never will be? They get drunk on mannabeer and spew their lies, their boasts, their threats—it's all fake, just fuel to feed their hatred."

"The dancing is powerful," Setteo murmured. "The Heras would stop them, if they knew."

"They do know!" Eykar said, exasperated. "They have spies, you know that. I forbid you to risk your neck to be part of those pathetic, drunken hate sessions, do you hear me?"

Setteo coughed.

"Setteo, Kobba walks around at night looking for stray men to punish. Don't give her a chance to break you in those big, angry hands of hers."

"In the Cold Country there are birds that sing with their fingers," Setteo said with a brilliant smile. "They used to say, 'The ice looks like a plain with black holes of water lying about on it, and so you walk on the white parts, carefully, and think about other things. But we who fly, we see that the white ice is an illusion made of the black water that underlies everything everywhere, and no one can go forever without that black water opening at last and gulping them down. That is why we fly and fly and never set foot on the false white ice made of black, black water.' "

Eykar put his hand over Setteo's mouth. "We're not in the country of the Bears. This is the country of Free Fems and slave-men. We can only survive here if you pay attention and obey the rules!"

The mouth under his fingers moved, the tongue licked his skin. Setteo's eyelids drooped, his eyes dreamed.

"Is it salty, like this," he whispered, his breath buzzing between Eykar's fingers, "the black water? It would taste like your hands that once served the death drink, the blackest water there is." He pulled back his head, smiling. "You see? I can learn things about the Cold Country even after I've been shut out of it. I can learn things from you."

"Why did you go tonight?"

Setteo leaned close and breathed in his ear, "They say they see the Bears, those men. The Bears give them their songs."

"Is this real, or is it dreams you're telling me?"

Setteo let out a low giggle. "Men steal manna and use it to go to the Cold Country, and the Bears stand up and promise them the Sunbear will come destroy their enemies."

Eykar's temples throbbed faintly. "You mustn't legitimize some silly, invented ritual by involving yourself—"

"They know a way in," the cutboy interrupted. "I found the Sunbear for them, but I'm shut out now. Those men go, but if they're bringing back lies about the Bears, we'll all have to pay!"

His nose ran, his eyes reddened, his thin hands waggled in front of his face as if in spastic prayer.

Eykar reached out and folded Setteo close in his arms, canted awkwardly toward him because his lame leg, bent as tight as it would go, was wedged between them. Setteo's fingers pressed into Eykar's back.

"How could they put their shackled feet to that pure white ice?" the cutboy wept. "But they say that in the Cold Country their chains fall away, they dance for the Bears. The Bears eat with them and fuck them, fuck their own power into them, and give them drinks of black water to make them strong and fearless.

"None of that ever happened to me. In all the time I went to and fro in the Cold Country, with all that it cost me, why didn't that ever happen to me?"

"They're lying," Eykar whispered, rocking him. "It's a pack of lies, Setti. The Bears are yours."

"They want whole men now, not a cutboy made for the use of greater men. They only fooled me, the Bears. They were mocking me all that time."

"Stop talking." Eykar held the boy's face in both hands and kissed him hard, tasting the salt of tears. "Stop talking, Setteo."

He enclosed both of the mad boy's trembling hands in his own and browsed Setteo's bitten fingertips with his lips as he whispered, "Forget about the Bears and the lies and tighten your mind around us two together, here."

"But you are my mind," Setteo said. He freed one hand and slipped his thin fingers under Eykar's tunic, bars of coolness on hot skin.

Salalli's Tears

She ground the knife blade with slow, circular movements which had become almost sensuous. The dimpled metal, iridescent with wear, hissed softly against the watery surface of the stone. The slow grinding let Salalli lose herself; the work created a self for her that lived only here, and only now.

She had—although it was distant now, receding more every day—a lost self in a lost past. This blade was part of that past. It had plunged through the smooth brown skin of Gayberl's belly, loosing his guts in a slither of scarlet.

D Layo, the killer, liked to watch her sharpen his knife for him. He watched her now, from the fallen tree that he loafed on over there in the shade. She was to grind an edge that would easily shave his whiskers (none of the southmen let their hair grow, preferring an imitation of beardless youthfulness).

He watched for signs of rebellion in her face. She knew better than to show such things. She knew better, most of the time, than to feel them.

On this bitter trek south from home, a ghost-Gaybrel sometimes came to her in her dreams. She knew him by the sense of his spirit, eager and impatient. A tall, strong man, confident of the future, he had always wanted to try new things.

This had made everybody else nervous. It had also made them rich, all the people of Rock Pool, rich and nervous; because deep in their hearts they had known that their riches must cost them dear some day (had not the wealthy people of olden times paid at last with everything they had?).

She remembered festivals marking the first capture of

wild goats from the barren uplands, and Leshee's discovery that certain trees could be tapped for a sweet sap more delicious than love (almost). And then Beejo and Shoady's boat that could sail offshore and not wallow down in the surf. And the pitch-sealed wooden troughs that brought clean water from inland springs.

Too much, too grand; and all gone now, having first been paid for in Gaybrel's blood and Beejo's blood and the blood of all the men of Rock Pool. What remained were women, children, and a handful of goats moving southward in captivity.

The precious remnant of the goat herd was in the care of the Townswomen because these men were still a little afraid of the goats.

Such stupid men, inventors of nothing. Scrawny, ugly men, every one pale as raw clay under his clothes, and hairy in a patchy, mangy way.

"Don't worry," Gaybrel had told the people. "Things are different now. We are the rich ones, the strong ones. Why be afraid of a pack of ragged, starving wanderers?"

He would never have said that, he would never have been so foolish, except that Beejo, with his gimlet eyes and hands big as milk buckets, had begun to challenge Gaybrel's authority. Beejo had said the strangers were dangerous, for hadn't the slavers of Way Before been white?

So Gaybrel said, "That's how things *were*. This is how things *are*, and it's different now. We're not a bunch of savages, to attack strangers just because their skin is pale."

This knife had butchered Tufty, the best of the milkers. It had gutted Gaybrel while he sat with his interesting guests, and then the knifepoint jabbed Salalli just under the right ear, freezing her where she sat.

The knifepoint had stayed there as the chief of the new men jerked her britches down and fucked her on the ground amid the chaos of the other Rock Pool men slaughtered, other women raped, children running and screaming. Her outflung left hand had stained itself in the blood spreading silently from Gaybrel's curled body.

Now she glanced over at Shareem, her son. He had been overlooked by the strangers in that first whirlwind of destruction. Then his knowledge of goats had saved him. He squatted now by their fire, using a stick dipped in ash to draw on the skin of his shoulder, aping the New Men.

Good, she thought. Let him become one of them, and live. Let him become one of those who came smiling out of the wilderness like long-lost brothers, begging a meal and shelter, who then killed men and took women and children and tools and livestock as loot. Let him become one of the winners, even if—she swallowed bile—even if it meant accepting the filthy ways of these pale southern men with each other.

She had seen them eyeing Shar. It had taken time to understand that look, for in the Pool Towns such behavior was rare. Men had been expected to save sex for the making of children so that the Towns could grow and flourish instead of dying out like ill-fated Marsh Pool, where children had died faster than babies were born.

Well, whatever the price, maybe Shar could pay it, join the victors, and flourish. Already this possibility had set a gulf between his sisters and him. He ignored them now, and her too. He wouldn't even look at them.

The men did. They looked often at Shar's sisters, for their appetites were boundless. Lissie had begun to flinch from them, staying dirty, silent, and furtive in an effort to avoid their greedy stares. And what happened to Lissie, when it happened, would tie her forever to these foreign masters. They would use the leverage of her own babies to control her, just as d Layo now controlled Salalli by means of her children as they traveled ever southward, away from home, toward the country of these southmen—the "Holdfast," they called it. She traveled with them, further and further from Rock Pool's silent walls, as d Layo's woman.

She had at first felt only burning, helpless hatred. Now her feelings were slowly scabbing over. Otherwise she would die of rage. While her children lived, she was not ready to die.

Luma scampered about, seemingly oblivious. Salalli's helpless spasms of ineradicable tenderness for the child were futile. The little girl's sexuality would bloom eventually, like Lissie's before her; and Salalli had no protection to offer.

With Gaybrel as their father, no one had dared touch

the girls. Marriages had been arranged with boys from Sand Pool, farther north along the coast. Now Sand Pool was gone the same way as Rock Pool. Salalli had known this from the faces of the two surviving Sand Pool women, now prisoners of the new men, long before she heard their story. Those Sand Pool boys were dead, them and their fathers and their brothers.

Lissie and Luma must toughen up and fend for themselves, just like Shar. These moon-skinned men tolerated no weaknesses. They had left one of their own wounded to die because he could not keep up. D Layo himself had taken his weapons and his tools and shared them out among the others.

They were a scrawny, dangerous breed, with none of the grace of even the paler men of the Pool Towns, like Layser, and the smith, Yellow Dex. These southern men were short, raw-looking, and mean, and they watched each other constantly. They would have killed each other if not for D Layo.

They must know better than anyone how ruthless and unpredictable he could be—a man who could talk peace and then as quick as fire slice open the man he spoke with. Gaybrel hadn't even had time to pull the Rock Pool gun from his belt. (She thought of him with hatred sometimes, furious at his failure to have learned from the old stories of evil whites; but he had chosen the ideal of a new, fair world, and they had all paid for that choice.)

Now D Layo wore the gun as he sunned himself on the trunk of a fallen pine, picking his teeth with a stalk of weed. The bullet belt Gaybrel had made for himself was slung across D Layo's chest. He rarely took it off, not even when he drove himself between Salalli's legs.

The hard truth was, with Gaybrel dead, you could do much worse than be this stranger's bedmate. He was tolerable-looking for a white, cunning, and strong. His men amused each other with boastful stories about him. He was even clever enough to content himself with Salalli, thus standing above the rest of them when they squabbled over the other women from the Pool Towns. He stood above and judged, chiding, joking them out of murdering each other or their prizes.

He carried himself like a leader, a literally pale imitation of Gaybrel. She saved and burnished images of what was admirable in d Layo, storing up glimpses of him at his best, for her sanity's sake.

Nevertheless, a song of hopeless hatred sang silently in her throat for most of her waking hours. He had killed her world.

The children were already forgetting. And would it be right to burden them with their elders' hatreds, compromising their own chances of survival?

Tears wet the blade as she ground it (d Layo punished anger, but ignored grief).

You could do worse; many had (Gaybrel had). N'deen, for instance, was paired up with Dojan, a jealous southman who hit her, often and hard, pretending he had seen her lustfully invite another man's attention. D Layo permitted this, probably as a lesson to the other captives: most of us are not so bad, see how much worse it could be for you!

No women dared to speak to N'deen, for fear of bringing worse treatment upon her or themselves. She was isolated in her bruises and her tears.

Salalli blotted the blade with a rag. The pinkish tinge of the steel was only imagined, of course.

D Layo was the kind of man who acquired a gun but did not let his knife grow dull. He was selfish, but he could be kind when it cost him nothing. If she did exactly as he told her, in time perhaps he would come to lean on her a little (as he already did in matters pertaining to the goats).

Maybe by the time they saw his homeland he would have the beginnings of some feeling for her, providing her a fragile leverage. Something. Anything.

If she just behaved well, if she just didn't think about her sister Wiletta bleeding to death after the southern men had taken turns with her all that first terrible night. Wiletta had been too beautiful, too delicate, to survive such usage. Her corpse lay unburied at Rock Pool with the others.

Think about the girls, about making some leeway for them, some protection, even if it meant turning a blind eye when d Layo began fucking them, too.

She swallowed queasiness. The elders of Rock Pool had

been strict about marrying out of your Town to avoid bearing damaged babies. But would it be so bad to have a brood of children, Lissie and Luma mothering some too, of this one powerful man: sons he would be proud of, daughters he could award as favors to his best, his highest men?

Maybe, working together, she and her daughters could teach him (very carefully) some of the gentler ways of Rock Pool and Sand Pool. Maybe he could be led to see the wisdom of the rules of the Pool Towns elders, so that her grandchildren would not be born poor half-forms, or sickly, or witless.

My mouth will be full of bitterness for the rest of my life, she thought. She wished she had died at Rock Pool. But her hands went on patiently doing the work her captor had set her.

If not for her children, she would use the knife on him and then herself; no, that was a lie. *Coward,* she berated herself silently. With her back to her lost home, she sharpened the knife that had killed the father of her three children.

Two of the men came down with fever. Then one of the women grew sick, too. They crossed a small river near sunset and made camp as rain began to fall. In the morning they found that the river had flooded, splitting into two streams, one behind them and one, deep-cut and rushing, ahead.

"We could wait till the water drops," she said when she came back from helping to milk the goats and found him studying the sliding, muddy waters.

"The clouds are piling up," d Layo said. "From what I remember of traveling in this country, it'll rain inland for days, feeding this flood. Did your men ever come this far south?"

His casual reference to her dead blocked her voice. She shook her head.

"The storms have started early. We could be looking at a week's wait."

She lowered her gaze and said she thought that was

long, given their limited food supplies, but that it would be difficult to ford either stream with sick people. Perhaps wait a day, to see if the rain let up?

He gave her a mocking glance. "A woman's answer. If we stay and more people get sick, we'll be worse off. And my men smell their homeland on the wind."

The unspoken message was that delay meant a risk of losing control; and his control was better than no control. She turned back silently to portioning out the goats' milk.

They began fording the stream across their southward path at midday. All went well until the last of the goats, its feet bound together and its squalling weight hiked across the wide shoulders of a man called Kedge, was carried over. Kedge staggered thigh-deep in the water, slipped, and lost his grip on the squirming animal.

The goat was snatched away by a burst of muddy spume. There was no chance of pursuit; the volume of water doubled in an instant. Only the quick action of the one-eyed man called Hak, on the southern bank, kept Kedge himself from being swept after the goat.

The renewed flood made further passage impossible. The separated parties stood across from each other, peering upstream in the rain, or, more miserably, down, after the vanished goat. It had been Kicker, the only breeding buck.

Salalli crouched in the shelter of the brushwood goat pen where the women waited for the men's decisions. They busied themselves anxiously inspecting greased leather packs that had once bulged with flour and with dried fruits and vegetables harvested that spring and early summer at Rock Pool.

Salalli had never been a gardener. The goats had been her special charge. She counted those that were left—four ewes, one wether, and two kids, only one of them a male—and wept for all the lost work of building the herd.

Lissie petted and crooned to the goats, calming them. She asked no questions. The children had been the first to learn that lesson.

There was a plan now; under d Layo's direction, the men stepped out into the rushing water and made a chain, arms linked at the elbows and hands clasped at the waist.

It was dangerous, but no floodborne trees had swirled past for some few minutes; and two goat carts packed with stores stood on the far side, with the sick. Shareem was with them.

The foremost man, struggling against the current one foot after the other, was d Layo himself. Dripping, muscular, determined, he led the skein of men across to the farther bank. Her traitor heart lifted to see him throw his courage against the spinning waters, pulling the others along after him by sheer strength of will. Not that this would bring Kicker back, or stop d Layo from taking that loss out on her later if he wished.

On the far bank Shar gripped d Layo's hand, bracing himself against a crooked tree. Then Melnie began to drag herself and a bundle of supplies from the larger goat cart across. She used the men like posts in a fence, clawing her way from one to the next. Her mouth showed pale teeth in a grin of terror.

So each one crossed, carrying bits of the dismantled carts, until only the sick remained: three drooping figures shivering in sodden blankets. They should have begun with these. The human chain was wearied, the men lurching and scrambling to hold their places. The line sagged downstream at the center.

Sturdy Hak crossed with Blix clinging to his back like a boy on his father's shoulders, all atremble and eyes squeezed shut. But when it was the turn of Engo, Jendery—who was too slightly built to carry him—stumbled and just managed to thrash his way back to safety, still on the wrong side.

Salalli got up, patted Lissie on the arm, and went to help. She waded out to Migayl near the center, locked her arms around his wet, ribby chest, and threw her strength with his against the pulsing current while Engo was carried across.

It was a clumsy, heart-clenched business. The cold spray blinded her and the water's roar overwhelmed her hearing. She wedged her numb feet among slippery stones. Another woman came to stand with Dojan, who wavered also: N'deen, of all people, backing her brutal keeper.

The men not occupied as links in the chain struggled back and forth to bring the last remnant across. There seemed no end to it.

Salalli felt herself becoming not a prop for Migayl but an additional burden, a weight dragging at his neck. She closed her eyes for a moment, searching within for some reserve of strength. She opened her eyes and saw a tree bearing down on them, the root mass looming wide like a gaping mouth.

"Give way!" she screamed. She dragged Migayl aside by main strength, so that he stumbled upstream with one hand flailing free. The tree yawed wildly through the gap in the line, one jagged branch slashing hard past Laxen's legs. She heard him yelp, but he held his place.

She and Migayl closed the gap again. The last of the fever-stricken, a woman from Sand Pool called Willo, was hauled along the chain clinging to Kedge. Then the whole line of them reeled itself in, soaked, exhausted, and staggering, just as a new flock of torn-away trees came whirling down on the water.

"You've a brain in your head," d Layo said to her that night, hunched with her over a skimpy fire. "Your friends seemed ready to just stand there and see us all swept away, until you made a move."

"Pool Towns people survived by helping each other."

He stretched his legs sideways to the warmth of the flame. "Don't sound so superior. We've been trudging around in these damned forests for five years, my lads and me, keeping each other alive."

After a moment she dared to say, "You left a wounded man of yours to die at Rock Pool."

He handed her a stick to spike a baked root out of the fire for him. "He wouldn't have survived. Our fellows here who are sick may recover. I'll need them when we get to the Holdfast. Who knows what welcome we'll find there, after all this time?"

She considered in bleak silence this new vista of uncertainty opening before them. The men always talked of a hero's homecoming. *Oh, Sallah, where is your help?*

"Watch out for Migayl. He may make too much of all that hugging today." He looked at her consideringly.

"Would you have run into the forest instead of helping, if you had been with those on the other side of the river?"

"No," she said.

"No," he echoed, reaching over to cup her chin in his rough fingers. "Our Seniors used to say that the nigs couldn't reason, but you're a sensible creature, aren't you? In a world roamed by bandits, you need bandits of your own to keep you safe."

Salalli waited in silence until he released her. She had no answer. If that wasn't the meaning of the fate of the Pool Towns, what was?

Oathmother

Daya stayed near, enjoying the power over me that knowing about Veree gave her. She took me with her to the Oldtown docks early in the morning to talk to the dock boss about boat schedules. I sat watching a gang of stickmen unloading a barge.

They were brutish figures, those ragged men with their odd, side-swinging gait. I could no more let Veree be made into one of them than I could breathe riverwater and live. But if he stayed here, how was he to avoid some form of slavery? Was that his future now?

All these men were clean-shaven and stubble-scalped, for shaggy-headed men are more like-looking than the horses of a wild band one to another. The Free knew how easily secret schemes could be masked among people looking all the same.

These men wore loose shirts and twists of cloth around the hips. A few had sandals fashioned from string and straw. All were chained to sticks that jigged and sawed between their feet.

Daya, coming back from her negotiations with an expression of satisfaction, saw me staring.

"What do you think of them?" she asked. "Sheel always says they stink worse than sharu."

"How can you stand to be near them?"

"We get used to it. They did, when it was us scuffling along in our own dirt to do their bidding."

I looked at her sharply. She herself had suffered little that way. A pet prized for her beauty, she had been treated—in slave terms—daintily, until her disfigurement. She shrugged daintily now.

"We let the well-behaved ones live decently enough. Believe me, child, they get a better bargain than we got from them. Your father, of course, lives much better than these because he's Alldera's."

I turned away, not to let her see my confusion. The idea of a man who was supposed to be my sire held as the slave of another person—in particular of my bloodmother, whom he had once raped—was full of shocking contradiction for me.

I said, "What kind of man is he?"

"You'll see," she said. "He's in Midfast, with his wretched books."

So, full of trepidation, I prepared to travel on with my traitorous aunt Daya to see this "father" of mine.

She went off to give final instructions to her acolytes about running the Oldtown Moon's House in her absence. None of them found reason or excuse to detain her; because of me, of course. She counted on the fact that they would not be so discourteous as to interfere with the travel arrangements of Alldera's daughter.

I caught the muted responses and sidelong glances of people on the boat when we boarded. I wondered what reasons they imagined for our companionship. One or two faces seemed familiar, but apparently no one would approach me while I was with Daya. Given my embarrassment at how she had used me, this was just as well. I would not have been gracious company.

How could I have fallen into the power of a pariah?

This was a different boat than before, larger, slower, and loaded with stacks of taydo under canvas covers. A rich, damp odor came off these fat, sweet roots which I only identified later as the smell of deep, fertile soil rather than the sandy, clay-streaked earth of the Grasslands.

Daya unbound her hair to the breeze and chattered like a girl about the beauties of Midfast's festivals, the foremost of which we had just missed. I watched Veree running tirelessly up and down, slaying imaginary sharu with imaginary lance and bow and uttering yells of triumph.

"What would they do if you told them?" I finally said, keeping my voice low. "Kill him?"

"Don't exaggerate, dear child, we're not slaughterers of babies," Daya said. She patted my knee reassuringly. "I'm sure Fedeka will take him in just to please you."

I dug an Ancient nail out of the railing with my knife, just to have something to look at besides water sliding by.

I still hated traveling by boat. "Why should Fedeka care? He's only another little muck to her."

"Not if she believes he's your own bloodchild, Sorrel. Hush, now, people are watching us."

Her silence about Veree would not come for free, that was clear. Seeing again what a fool I had been and who my foolishness had bound me to, I felt despondent and full of self-blame.

"Tell the truth, child," she went on confidentially, "won't it be a relief to give him into the care of others, after being on your own with him so long with no sharemothers to help you?"

With bitter clarity I saw that I had come to the Holdfast without thought, driven by discontent and disappointment with myself, not a fem and not a Woman but a misfit embarked on an ill-conceived gesture of rebellion. And I had carried a helpless child with me into danger. Maybe they should put *me* on the damned stick!

At the Midfast docks I tried to pay for our passage. Daya pushed my hand back and appealed directly to the crew captain. "Surely the Conqueror's daughter rides free."

The captain looked through her and said to me, "I'm pleased to have helped, Sorrel Alldersdaughter. Don't eat at the Moon's House here, the food's not very good. Sioo at the brewery will feed you better. Tell her I sent you."

"Bad food?" Daya looked shocked. "I'm surprised to hear this about the Lady's own hall. But then Fedeka was never very interested in mundane matters."

Which was nonsense, unless Fedeka was very much changed. It was to her that the Free Fems had always gone for herbs and medicines to heal their bodily ills. But I didn't bother arguing. I was beginning to feel more comfortable with Daya again, for her talk and her manner reminded me over and over of the free person I had known in Holdfaster Tent, years ago.

She was not free now. I saw how others turned away from her wherever she went.

Midfast itself, still the center of the Holdfast, was something of a disappointment. The City towers and walls I'd heard of as a girl were nowhere to be seen.

Trailed by a growing crowd of fems (and their murmured criticism of my arrival in such company), we made our way uphill from the water between clumps of squat, plain buildings, newly built or patched up out of older ones. A few walls gleamed with facings of glazed tile; some were even made of cut stone blocks fitted together, but most were bare ochre brick. The ways between them were all wide, bare, beaten earth, streets rather than lanes or alleys.

For horses to pass, of course. I had heard how, in the battle for this place, the Free had had to leave their mounts outside the walls and fight on foot in the narrow City passageways. Now most of the older structures had been razed to the ground and the rubble used to build broad ramps up to the higher street levels of Midfast; entries for riders from the surrounding plain.

Veree must think badly of me, after my stories about our grand destination. For entertainment on the mountain crossing I had dredged up all that I remembered from the Free Fems' talk in Stone Dancing Camp, tales of the great Company Halls full of work-worn young men and the private villas of their privileged Seniors; the busy Market Arc bustling with trade; the secret maze of alleys sectioned without warning by the red ropes, between which passing men were trapped by custom into fighting deadly duels; the heavy barges hauled to and from the docks by femmish labor gangs trudging along the riverside towpaths.

All that was replaced by this straggle of small, homely buildings up a gentle slope. The one barge moving on the river was drawn by horses.

Daya saw my disappointment. "Shelter and utility first," she said. "Someday we'll think again of beauty and grandeur."

She led now, showing me the way to the Midfast Moon's House. Her slim back was the only familiar thing in sight. I felt hemmed in by the buildings and the people, and increasingly eager to get this over with.

Arrived at last, I itched to be home again.

The street we followed opened into a sunny space in front of a squat, whitewashed building. Daya waved to me to stop, drew her wrap over her head, and slipped ahead into the shadows of a deep porch.

I waited. Patch dropped her head and snuffled at my

feet while Veree lay back along the mare's well-padded spine, playing with a cut end of rope he had found somewhere, making it run and jump in his hand.

The spectators kept a polite distance. No one addressed me directly, although I overheard observations about my clothes, my companions, and my horse from time to time. My stomach began to grumble; where was the brewery from here?

I was about to ask when Fedeka came out of the building, her craggy old face changing a scowl for beaming delight.

"Child!" she cried, clapping her broad hand down on my shoulder, "so it's true, you've come to us at last! And look how beautiful you've grown!"

I blushed and embraced her, hiding my face so that no one would see my tears. I was ashamed of how relieved I felt to be snugged against that knotty frame, as if I were still a girl.

Fedeka drew me against her side now so that we both faced the murmuring crowd, and Daya, who stood demurely before us. "I'm surprised by your companions, though," Fedeka went on, looking her coldly up and down. "One of your fellow travelers I ought to have heard about before—a daughter of your own! Good for you, child!

"As for the other—Daya, has the Oldtown Moon's House fallen in, that you venture here?"

People were jostling and craning to see over each other's shoulders.

Daya kept her gaze meek but pitched her voice to be heard by the crowd. "It isn't right for Sorrel Alldersdaughter to travel in our country with no escort."

"Fede," I said hesitantly, using my childhood name for her, "my auntie has been no trouble to me. I hope I haven't done wrong to bring her here."

Fedeka's arm tightened protectively around my shoulders. She answered Daya directly. "Well, this child is with me now, kin as close to me as any except her true sharemothers. I'll escort her from here on. So you can return to the place the Lady made for you out of the kindness of her heart. A boat goes back to Oldtown this afternoon, I believe."

Daya said sweetly, "First let me bring you this child, Fedeka, for you to hug and kiss and welcome, too."

Before I could think to stop her, she whisked Veree down from Patch's back and stepped close with him. Fedeka let me go and caught the child up, straddling him on her hip.

"What are you called, little one?" she said.

"Veree," he said. "Where's your other arm?"

She jogged him a little against her. "The machines at Oldtown ate it, sweetling, but that was years ago. The one that I still have is as strong as anyone else's two."

He looked at me, twisting his fingers in the curls by his ear.

"It's all right, Veree," I said, trying to turn us all back toward the entrance to the Moon's House. I wanted desperately to get out of the open to some privacy, where I could explain.

But Daya said in a carrying voice, "Does the child know that you are not its mother, Sorrel?"

I froze, appalled: how could she do this?

Fedeka turned to look at me. I felt her whole attention pressed against me like the point of a lance.

Daya's face shone with triumph, not over me but over Fedeka, I realized. I was just a weapon in a struggle between them. "Does the child know that it was born of Juya-Veree, a NewFree who was called Juya under the men's rule? And does it know that it is not that NewFree's daughter but her son?"

Shocked exclamations shivered the air. Fedeka went rigid as stone. My hand fell from her waist.

Veree leaned toward me, but Fedeka held him tightly and stepped back, eyes narrowed.

"Is this true?" she said.

I could only nod in tongue-tied misery.

Daya gave a scathing laugh. "Fedeka has to ask! The Lady's Hand on Earth has to ask! I knew it was a boy-child when I looked at it—isn't that so, Sorrel?"

I burned to rush at her and annihilate her on the spot, but shame fixed me where I was.

"I am my own hand and no one else's," Fedeka responded. "The Lady has chosen to see through your eyes and speak through your mouth, Daya, a truth that Sorrel has hidden from us. I don't dispute it."

Then she turned and thrust Veree into the arms of someone behind her. "Take this boy-kit and put him with the other younglings."

"No, Fedeka, wait—Veree!" I shouted. But hands held me back, bodies barred my way. The people closed around us, so that Patch snorted in alarm.

My oathmother turned back the way she had come, saying grimly over her shoulder, "I must sit quiet and think about this, Sorrel. Then we can talk about it."

And the door to the Moon's House closed in my face.

Memory Marks

Six of the Bayo-born sat around a seventh who lay naked on her stomach. The soft grass mats under her darkened with water as the attendants soaped her skin, rinsed it, and patted it dry with wads of soft swamp cotton.

Alldera sat cross-legged and watched. It would be pleasant to be handled like this by friends—for any other purpose.

Chisti, who had come south with her to make notes for Beyarra on what they found in the marshland, had declined this particular experience. Alldera had seen Chisti sew up a gash in her own thigh with a leatherwork needle. People chose odd moments to be squeamish.

She remembered a young Junior, a suitor of her first master, who had come to dinner feverish from the fresh rank tattoo that marked his shoulder. He had later died of blood poisoning. Why did these southerners imitate a loathsome custom of the masters whom their forebears had escaped?

Choggeh mixed seed oil with burnt lamp wick, pounded fine. The sun burned down on the beaten earth of the yard: no shadows must confuse the eyes of the marker.

Alldera got up, easing a cramped ankle, and paced along the enclosing fence of reeds. Blotting sweat from her face with her forearm, she heard giggling whispers from the other watchers, a little clutch of ten-year-old boys and girls under the supervision of a tiny, wizened geld.

It gave her vertigo to see how freely the young of both sexes mixed here. Maybe the Bayo-born were right in declining to share their males with the Free; how would such boys fare in the New Holdfast even just on a visit?

The male yunkers in this gang, bored with waiting, were furtively shoving and pinching each other. Boys were allowed a degree of rambunctiousness so that when they completed their adolescent years of breeding, they would know exactly what parts of their natures they were expected to relinquish along with their testicles.

Meanwhile the gelds gave them instruction in how all humans were conceived female, but some were necessarily cursed with carrying the poison of male seed. Their procreative duty discharged, the boys would be surgically returned to full humanity, their minds unclouded and their hearts calm. They would be respected for the burden they had born.

Male horses were gelded in the Holdfast for much the same reasons with no ill effects. Judging by the durability and even tenor of the Swamp Island society as Alldera had seen it so far, gelding worked well among Bayo-born men, too.

The Free, having suffered at the hands of masters who could cut the tongue from a talkative femmish mouth at a whim, leaned toward defending the integrity of the human body, any human body. The Bayo way was generally dismissed at home as a barbarically simple solution to a complicated problem.

It was not this that Alldera had come south to discuss, but the possibility of obtaining agreement to the pasturing of a small herd of Holdfast horses on the grassy hills west of Bayo Marshes; so far, with no luck. She wasn't sure that it was a good idea, but she felt Raysa and her eager friends deserved at least to have the possibility explored.

"Was it bad news you had this morning, Hera Alldera?" Choggeh asked.

"No," Alldera said, startled out of her thoughts. "I heard that my daughter has come over the mountains to see me."

"I am glad for you," said Choggeh. "She was visiting friends on another island?"

Pointing out that the Holdfast had no island communities, like those of the Bayo-born, would be rude. Alldera said, "She stayed on the plains when we fems rode home."

"Naturally," assented the Bayo-born politely. "She was too young for your war, then?"

Alldera nodded, wondering how young was "too young" for what Sinduann was preparing to undergo here in Choggeh's yard. "I couldn't have felt free to do what was needed and to make the decisions I had to make if I'd had my daughter with me. Even now, the idea of my child falling into the hands of men—"

She stood silent, sweat gliding down her cheek. Damn Sorrel for rousing memories of the brutal past to life again simply by arriving on this side of the mountains! Why couldn't the foolish child have stayed where she'd been put for her safety's sake?

Alldera always asked about her when people returned from the Grasslands. She knew that Sorrel had had plenty of doting family, friends, lovers, horses, songs, and raids to test her mettle. She'd had Nenisi to watch over her and show her the right way to do things, Shayeen to teach her gravity and calm.

And now she comes to me.

Choggeh touched Alldera's arm lightly. "Pardon, Hera, but your face tells that you are imagining bad things. That can bring bad luck." She turned Alldera's back to the inquisitive eyes of the watching children. "Please sit here. You are invited to watch Sinduann take memory marks. Unless you want to start for your home? Anyone might do the same."

"There's no need," Alldera said. "Sorrel is with friends. She'll want to hear everything I can tell her about the Islands of the Bayo-born when I get back."

She leaned closer to observe, thinking that she would have sooner bared her own skin to the serrated points of Choggeh's tools than go to meet her own daughter.

She asked questions—You don't use any mind-clouding dose to ease the pain? Are there traditional patterns, or is each one original? Did your mother also "hammer memory'' for the women of the Islands?—while in her own mind doubts and fears chased each other one after the other:

She'll be nearing twenty, she's gone to stud horses twice, they say. I left her to that. She must hate me for it. But no, mating means to her what it means to the Riding Women, she's one of them. I didn't want her. Maybe her coming here has nothing to do with me.

''Painkiller would turn marks into mere decoration,'' the tattooer said, wiping her fingers on a clean cloth knotted loosely around her neck. ''Only the brave lie under the hammer, to show themselves willing to bear the pain it may take in future to keep our freedom.''

Alldera glanced over her shoulder at the yunkers, who were being lectured in an emphatic whisper by their geld. ''Does everyone agree that this a good thing for children to see?''

The tattooer calmly answered one of her other questions. ''I create the design for Sinduann as I go, but all designs begin on the shoulder where the masters carried their rank marks. I move out from there, inflicting pain that is still only a shadow of what our foremothers suffered in bondage.''

The attendants took hold of Sinduann's arms, stretching the skin tight across her upper back.

What will I see in Sorrel's face? Reproach? Indifference? Mere curiosity?

Choggeh selected a hammer of stone fixed into a wooden handle with intricate braiding. She set a wooden bowl upside down on Sinduann's back. ''I dream designs when I drink. That's what makes me a hammerer. I began these dreams at twelve and was apprenticed in a marker's yard like this one.''

I saw Eykar Bek kill his father. Maybe the Old Holdfast belief is true, that the child is the natural enemy to its parent; daughters as well as sons, why not? No, it's absurd! Must we take on our enemies' burden of madness as we assume their power and authority?

Choggeh took one of the spiked wands from the inkpot and leaned forward, resting her forearm on the fulcrum of the upturned bowl. She positioned the spikes and struck at the head of the wand with the hammer in her other hand, driving the blackened points deep into Sinduann's skin.

Sinduann gasped and quivered. Choggeh's forearm rode up again on the curve of the bowl, plucking the teeth of the tool free. Down came the hammer, quick as thought, punching in the points: another gasp, another row of black punctures. And again. Again, as the wand rode rapidly up and down.

From the clutch of watching children there came no sound now. The old geld sat hugging his knees, watching with a grave expression.

She was so small when I bore her, from starving in my skinny belly while I wandered the Wild. But even that little pain of bearing and the hardship before that she had brought me I couldn't forgive. Everyone else nursed her for me. I was afraid to be bound to her again. She has other mothers, I saw to that.

The Riding Women saw to that, liar; you didn't care one way or the other, you tried to abort her in the Wild (it made perfect sense at the time). Does she know that? Who would tell her? How could she ever understand, with her protected life?

Blood and ink slid down Sinduann's side. One of the attendants mopped the mess away. The hammer chattered, the spikes bit, creating a curving line of minute black punctures from shoulder to spine.

It felt like a choice between her life and mine. I could have survived without her, but not she without me. She was a tough little creature to have hung on. A grown woman now; my blood-child. When I left, six years ago, she looked a bit like me, but handsomer.

"No man of the Holdfast ever carried even this much marking on his shoulder," Choggeh said with satisfaction. She drew away to dip the tool again. Sinduann sighed softly.

If she's changed, if she looks like d Layo now, I'll hate her. I won't be able to help it.

"I dreamed of a fem burning for witchery in the City square," the tattooer said, poised again to strike. *Snap, snap, snap* went the hammer. Sinduann's gasps came in perfect rhythm.

If she's grown to look like Eykar instead, what then? That too was rape, and he didn't carry her in his body, he didn't expel her into the world. What does it mean to either of them, or to me, if she is his child as well as mine?

More mopping, soft talk, and a general shifting as the attendants prepared the other shoulder blade.

She's come with demands, or why come at all? She could have come years ago, right after Daya and her friends nearly killed me. Poor Sinduann, she is suffering even more than I suffered that night, maybe. And Sinduann has paid for the privilege!

Stylized flames began to appear, licking up at the hairline on the back of Sinduann's neck. Her gasps hissed like fire.

She could have come then, when I lay licking my wounds in Endpath. She could have said anything to me, made any demand, cursed me, anything. Helped, even, if she'd chosen to. But she didn't come then. So why now?

Behind her, Alldera heard the geld begin a singsong account of the creation of the Island culture. It was like a dream out of Daya's stories: runaways from the fem-training town of Bayo had hidden in the swamps, constructing rafts of reeds and clay (the original "Islands") on which to live with the mobility necessary to fugitives, eating swampwater creatures like the beardfish and the small, armored gayders that preyed upon them.

Men who had ventured there in search of escaped fems were shot with darts steeped in a sleeping drug, milked of their sperm, and fed to the gayders. So the swamp folk had borne and raised up daughters and sons to suit their own needs.

By stealth, ruthlessness, and secrecy, they had won and kept their watery world with its fecund beauty, its humidity and bugs and diseases, and its protective maze of waterways. Melting into the shadows at the first hint of danger remained their preferred tactic. They regarded with gentle superiority and bemused caution everything and everyone outside their own sodden borders. And they endured.

An attendant turned aside to sneeze. Another commented, and all laughed (except Sinduann). A little girl began to cry and was hugged and comforted by the geld until she was persuaded to continue watching.

There are women in the Grasslands who don't love their children, and people shrug and say some people aren't meant to be bloodmothers, that's why a child has other mothers to turn to. You don't have to love someone just because they've come out of your body. There is no obligation either way.

"Sinduann wants to commemorate your visit," Choggeh said in a diffident tone. The hammer chattered. "She asked me to do the whole design today, while you are here to witness. I must apologize to you, for I refused. People have died from taking a whole skin design at one time. Deciding on the timing of the work is part of my job, so I said no."

They aren't so picky about beauty in the Grasslands, that's a male thing. She could look just like me and not have been made to feel that she was plain.

Choggeh was saying, ". . . a rhythm to hammering, once you get started. The stopping place has to be chosen carefully, to keep the design flowing."

What would Nenisi say? I wish she had come over the mountains instead of this stranger-child of mine. But Nenisi's eyes are bad, and she has another family now. Still, I wish. Mother Moon, where are all the people I've loved in my life?

Perhaps I am bad luck to them.

"Are you well, Hera Alldera?" Choggeh inquired. "Some people feel it more when they watch another marked than when it is done to themselves."

"I'm fine," Alldera said, glancing at the shiny scars on Choggeh's thin, bare legs, marks of swamp parasites. People lived free here, but they aged fast and died young. She wondered if Choggeh was her own age, as she appeared, or a decade or more younger.

"But you think this is heartless?" the Bayo-born pursued, turning her various tools in the ink bowl. "I know what the Free say of our ways."

"I've seen worse," Alldera said. And she could not help but think briefly of Tyn Chowmer and Aksana-Danah, warriors who had destroyed themselves after the peace was won, the former with drink and the latter by leaping from the cliff at Lammintown. And Merima, who had goaded someone into beating her to death.

Maybe they would all be alive now if they had had a better way to express pain, like this pain under the tools in Choggeh's clever hands. *Ugh, what a repellent thought!*

When do we become truly free? What do we have to do? Haven't we earned our peace?

The yunkers got up and quietly left with the geld.

Pehhaps he thought they had seen enough. No males wore tattoos here.

How did he explain that to them?

She forced herself to pay close attention to the marvelous evenness of the lines and double-lines that Choggeh pounded into Sinduann's flesh, using a bright red ink that Alldera had first thought was freer-flowing blood. Did the attendants also find their thoughts wandering in paths of gloom and anguish? Was that an intended part of the process?

Why has she come? She was safe there. No one is safe here, nothing is safe. Where safety may seem to be, we create pain and fear to keep our defenses sharp, our suspicions high, to make sure we aren't taken by surprise by enemies, not ever.

She should pack her things and go home, and not just to meet Sorrel; there were other matters to attend to. She had left unsettled a claim against Smoothwood Hearth for trading green building pegs for a well-broken colt. The pegs had shrunk and dropped out, nearly bringing a 'Troi town threshing floor down during a dance last winter.

But people had moved around a lot since, and also the horse had been found to have a permanent shoulder injury from heavy-handed breaking. Several First Free, Alldera's original warriors, were involved on both sides, so nothing would be settled until Alldera got back to deal with it herself.

She was getting hungry. She wondered how Beyarra was entertaining Sorrel in Midfast, and whether Daya was hiding in shame. Daya could never be trusted so long as she lived, but Alldera acknowledged herself closer to the traitor than she was to Sorrel. Some things could not be explained.

Beyarra might try, though. She felt a stab of longing for Beyarra's sweet, anxious, and unfailingly admiring presence. Poor little NewFree, with her pretty looks sharpened by time and worry, left to cope with this unexpected visitor! She hoped Beyarra would forgive her.

"Before I finish," Choggeh said, sitting back on her heels, "would you wish to take a mark yourself, Hera Alldera, and become a sister in memory to Sinduann? She asked me to propose this when she heard that you would be honoring her marking by your presence."

Sinduann made no move, except for the continual small quiverings of her stained skin. Alldera was glad she did not have to meet the young Islander's eyes.

"Choggeh," she began, "it is I who am honored." She rolled up her sleeve and turned her arm and hand for Choggeh to see. "But I have marks already, scars of bondage, scars of war, to keep the history of my people sharp and lamentable in my heart. If Sinduann can forgive me, I respectfully decline."

"Sinduann was forward to ask it," Choggeh said, with a respectful nod at the slicks of scarring that ran up Alldera's forarm from her palm. "I apologize for her request. Some would disapprove of sharing this way with an outlander, no matter how exalted. You have saved me from their wrath, Hera Alldera. I am in your debt."

There was a knowing and sympathetic (Alldera hoped) glint in her eye. No one would wish to see the Conqueror of the Holdfast faint dead away under the black spikes. Indelible embarrassment was not a courteous gift to an honored visitor.

No wonder the geld had whisked his charges off.

Sinduann was helped up, looking dazed. She stumbled toward a trough full of rainwater to soak her wounds.

"Shouldn't someone go with her?" Alldera said, alarmed by the woman's debilitation. And she had as yet only her upper back designed! Alldera had seen swamp women whose entire torsos were marked by the tattooer's spikes.

"No," Choggeh said, rinsing and wiping her tools. "She goes alone to reflect on the meaning of the marks and of the pain. Unless she comes with a sister, a lover, or a friend who takes marks with her by choice; then they are bonded forever, as you quite rightly declined to be with Sinduann. She only sought to make herself more important by taking pain with you this way."

"How long till she heals?"

"Her skin will burn for days like the fire I picture on it. Now she'll use painkillers, so she can get some sleep."

"It seems a hard custom," Alldera said.

"For a hard world," the tattooer replied tranquilly. "Do your Holdfast people say that too—that this world is perhaps not the real world but a place where we are only tested? No? We have a story I sometimes use in marking—there are symbols for it—that people entered this world drifting in boats from the waters of another world and spread from here north into the Holdfast, not the other way around. Some say that one day we'll find our way back south again, paddling our boats into a world where abundance keeps folk easy with each other, and women and men ride the backs of gayders together in gaiety and rejoicing."

"It's a good-hearted tale," Alldera said. "The Free of the Holdfast are not so generous in their stories, I'm afraid."

She picked up one of the marking wands; the spikes were dull. No wonder the hammer was driven down so hard. These blunt teeth, wide enough to leave a clear mark, had to go deep enough to set the ink bright and strong.

She resisted an impulse to throw the thing down in revulsion. "Are you marked, Choggeh?"

"Marks are for ambitious people," the tattooer said. "People who wish to become Mother to a whole Island, people who want to call out a hunt for a spoiled man or a giant gayder. Others will follow someone so brave. I am not ambitious. To give marks with meaning and beauty satisfies me."

And what am I? Alldera thought. Leaving, she passed two more of the Bayo-born in the shaded entryway, both of them well endowed with Choggeh's inscriptions. They held hands as they sat waiting to be summoned to today's session, and they nodded somberly at Alldera as she passed.

What am I, if I can't risk the pain of rejection or rage from my own daughter? It is time to go home and submit to whatever memory marks she cares to hammer into my soul.

The Reading Lesson

I was lonely in Midfast, at loose ends and bored. I looked for Raysa, the guard, but she had left after delivering Galligan.

The Free were busy folk. I saw none of the loitering and chat that occupied most Grassland Women on summer days. "In the late fall," Lora had told me, "when the harvests are in and the fields prepared for spring, that's when we do our loafing and visiting."

Fedeka would not see me; old Kastia-Kai had told me that at the door to the Moon's House. She said Fedeka had withdrawn to pray and meditate awhile. Meantime, she suggested, I should go see for myself how happy Veree was in the Children's House.

"We raise the boys and girls together," she had said. "The oldest are only six or so. We pray for dreams from the Lady to show us how to bring them up. Perhaps they will say later that they were happiest now." With unexpected sweetness she added, "I go sometimes just to see them being treated as we were never treated. I bring them gifts, so they like me."

I was afraid of seeing fear, misery, maybe even accusation in Veree's face, so I went instead to the western heights of Midfast. Where the great stone causeways strode south on their long stilt legs toward Bayo, I brooded on my own foolishness and the perfidy of the world.

Along the elevated paths of the causeways people moved with trays and baskets, picking some fruit crop from the vines that clung to the stonework. Down below, the ponds bled off the City's wastes to feed waterweeds the Free used as food. This stinking stew was slowly turned, using great wooden churns worked by teams of horses or stickmen.

I walked out to a shelter on the upper walkway. Being up so high off the earth made me nervous, so I sat down on a bench to look out over the patchwork plain west of the City. Shouts and scraps of song drifted on the sultry breeze.

Some way off, a horse-drawn wagon moved slowly along a wide track while people raked a dark substance down from its tailgate to spread on the roadway.

Only I sat idle, missing Veree, his child-smell and his serious gaze that observed without judging. I missed him and I feared for him.

Someone sat down near me; I felt the bench slats shift under me. "You might go to the Children's House and see for yourself how well the little ones are treated, boys and girls both."

Just what Kastia-Kai had said. Not turning my head, I answered coldly: "So what? The girls will grow up to be free people and the boys to be their slaves."

The person let a little time go past. Then she said, "I am Beyarra-Bey."

Alldera's bedmate; I had to look. She had a sharp face like a sharu: clever-looking, serious, with a pointed chin. I said, "Why didn't you go with Alldera to Bayo?"

"I enjoy being by myself sometimes," she said, "like most people."

"Juya said you were the first bond fem to join the Army of the Free when they got here."

She smiled, which made the end of her nose dip down a fraction. "Sometimes I can hardly believe what I did."

I liked her for saying that, although I didn't want to. I didn't want to like any of these people who had taken Veree from me.

I said, "I guess you'd had enough of Alldera for a while." I was immediately ashamed of my nastiness which, to my relief, Beyarra ignored.

"We were sorry to hear about Juya's death," she said. "Did you know her well in the Grasslands?"

"No," I said. "Hardly at all."

A silence fell between us. I got up and walked from one side of the paving to the other and back again.

"What are you going to do until Alldera gets back?" she asked.

"Why should I wait around for Alldera?" And why did I have to keep saying this to people?

"If she'd known you were coming, she'd have rushed home to meet you," Beyarra said. She was hardly older than

I was, by the look of her; why did she think she knew anything?

"Horseshit," I said. "She never did anything on my account before. Why start now?"

Beyarra kept silent, which was a mercy. What I had said was not true. Alldera had come to Holdfaster Tent for my naming and had danced me the plains along with all my sharemothers, in the Grassland ceremony of adulthood.

"I didn't know I was coming myself until I got on my horse and came," I mumbled.

"Will you go back, then," she asked, "now that Veree is in safe hands?"

"Safe hands!" I stopped pacing and glared at her. "I've given him to his worst enemies!"

"Oh, it's not as bad as that," she said, looking down at her small hands, folded neatly in her lap. I could have punched her for her gently chiding tone, as if I'd lost a haircomb, not a child. "And Alldera may come up with a different solution."

"I'm through waiting," I said.

Why didn't it have any shape, this life of mine, nothing but thrashings and boilings that led nowhere, frustrations, meanderings into all the wrong places? Alldera's life was, by comparison, like an arrow shot high to turn and drop neatly into its target. The aim looked wild, but the shot was a true heart shot.

Beyarra stood, brushing at the seat of her tunic. "Before you leave, there is one other person you might like to meet," she said tentatively.

"Who? Sheel? Even she's away, gone to the mountains to dig up some old ruin." I kicked at the base of the wall where a stone leaned inward, loosened from its crumbling mortar bed.

"Considering how Sheel regards males of any age," Beyarra murmured, "I think you're lucky she's not around."

I had had the same thought myself.

"Who do you mean, then?"

"Eykar Bek."

I laughed. "People don't go visit the stud that sired them, not where I come from. Besides, he's only one of two men who could have done it."

"Still, you might like to meet him before you leave."

"What difference could that make to anybody?"

Beyarra's eyes grew wide. "It might make a difference to you and to us! The men of the Old Holdfast were scared of their sons and made sure that no child knew its parents, sire or dam. The boys were sent to the Boyhouse, the girls to the kit pits at Bayo. Even after the Seniors' defeat the younger men didn't change things back."

"Back? To what?"

"In the Ancients' times," she said, "kits lived with their blood parents until they were grown."

I had always imagined Holdfast life as static, its customs fixed in opposition to the perennial patterns of the Grasslands. The idea of making or remaking the shape of how you lived using notions from another time took me aback.

Of course I had been looking at such shapings all through this country. What happened on the causeways, or to the old buildings of the City that was now Midfast, was not due to men's law and custom now. The reasoned decisions of people like Beyarra determined everything.

"But how can you know," I asked, "how things were before the Wasting, I mean? It was so long ago. And maybe those earlier ways were bad for the little ones, too. Are you going to have blood parents living together here?"

"We're still learning," she said patiently, "the things we might try to do, and things to avoid. That's why we read Ancient books; but you and Eykar can teach us, too." She touched my arm. "Come with me."

"Where?"

"To the Book Room."

I pulled free. "That's where *he* is, isn't it? Daya told me he lives with the books."

"Yes." She folded her hands, waiting. I felt like a fractious filly being handled by a seasoned trainer.

"I don't see the point," I grumbled. "I'm not the only person with a father, you know. You're Holdfast-bred; you had a man-sire, too."

She nodded. "But I have no idea who, or if he's still alive or not."

I wanted badly to get away, but I said, "Oh, all right,

then, why not?" She shouldn't imagine that I was afraid of meeting this "father" of mine.

She led me to a fire-marked building, its walls patched up with fresh brickwork. Inside the main room, which was to my eyes of amazing expanse and height, three walls were sheathed in what Beyarra said were shelves of books. The north-facing wall contained a tall, partially completed band of small glass panes that admitted softened daylight. Above that was some canvas fastened to the roof above, to keep the weather out.

In the anteroom, illuminated by a smaller but completed glass panel, a handful of people sat together on the floor: a man and three fems. A stout, bowlegged fem stood with a book open in her hands. She spoke hesitantly in an odd, false tone as she drew one fingertip along the page in front of her.

"—had also fawg-hot in the war," she said.

"Not 'foghot,' the man said, in a flat, expressionless voice. "The gh is silent, as in 'ought' or 'thought.' "

He marked the stone floor in front of him with a lump of white chalk. They all bent to look and then copied the marks on the stone flagging. They moved their lips or whispered aloud as they did this, like people performing a ritual.

I noticed his hands because I had to notice something: wiry hands, agile but not delicate, with black hairs on the backs. His wrist bones stuck out like an adolescent's.

He looked up and froze. The fems turned to stare too, with open curiosity, from my face to his.

Beyarra said, "This is Sorrel, a guest. Will anyone mind if she observes a little?"

A gray-haired fem said, "Sit down, then, join us." I saw one of the others frown and poke her in the ribs.

Bowlegs said, "Nobody likes to be watched making mistakes, Beyarra-Bey. I'm sure your guest wouldn't want to make people feel uncomfortable."

I waited to see what the man would say. He said nothing, of course. He might be their teacher but he was also their slave.

And then I thought, *But I am not; why should I be shunted off for their convenience?* This was the man who had—

perhaps—sired me through a long-ago act of barely imaginable, deeply personal violence. I had come here to see him, and I was seeing him, but slowly, a little at a time. He was hard to take in, somehow, but it was easier this way than if he had been alone and unoccupied.

"I'd like to stay, if I can just listen," I said, and I hunkered down.

Bowlegs continued to read a story about men stealing something valuable from a strong building guarded by enemy men. I thought no raiding party would get far with its members quarreling together as the men in this story did.

I watched Eykar Bek, who kept his gaze bent on a great, fat volume with very thin pages that lay open by his knee, or on the figures he had chalked on the floor.

He didn't look dangerous; maybe it was his not being on the stick, and the fact that his head was not shaven; his dark hair was grizzled white over the ears. He was a lean man, not tall, with stooped shoulders and a sharp face. His bare arms and legs were sinewy and pale, and he had no cuff on either ankle. He wore a frayed slave smock with two patch pockets in the front, for carrying books, I supposed. One of his slippers was worn through at the big toe.

Visually at least, he was—disappointing.

I remembered my bloodmother as having a braid of glossy brown hair, her face well colored by weather but round and glowing with health and energy. He was nearly of an age with her, according to stories; but he looked old, like an elder of the Soolay line, face gaunt and deeply lined. One cheek was sunken in a way suggesting teeth lost. The eye on that side had the milky cast of cataract.

He moved with the nervous tension of those people who never stop being active or sticking their noses into everybody else's business. In this he reminded me of the Torrinors (which Sheel would not, I knew, be pleased to hear). I thought he probably had to remind himself to keep his eyes averted in the presence of his Heras—a person absorbed in what he did and thought rather than mindful of those around him.

No wonder they let him stay in this house of books: he wouldn't survive long out of it, with an attitude like that.

But he wasn't my sire, or if he was, it didn't mean anything. I began to feel bored and restless.

The lesson ended. He said, "Heras, tomorrow who will read?"

One of them sighed loudly and held out her hand with a suffering expression. Bowlegs handed over the storybook with a grin of relief. They put their chalks into a basket on the window seat and left, talking among themselves and glancing back over their shoulders—at me, of course.

"I think Shibann is doing very well," Beyarra said, watching Eykar Bek wrap up his big word book in a blue cloth.

He nodded. "She'll make a teacher herself before long. I can't say as much for Edeez-Ea, unfortunately."

"Edeez is clever. It may come to her later."

"She doesn't study," he said. "I've heard that she has a lover who derides the whole enterprise. Edeez is young and easily distracted, which doesn't help either."

"Don't let people hear you talking like that," she said softly.

He knotted the corners of the cloth, saying nothing.

"We have more teachers now," she added, "thanks to you. You're not needed here as much as you once were."

"The Hera is too kind," he said.

"Can anyone learn to read?" I asked.

"Not anyone," he said, when Beyarra gave no reply. He did glance up at me now, a squinting pale stare, quickly averted again. "For some adults the connection between marks on paper and the sound of a word just never sticks."

"And some don't choose to learn," Beyarra added.

He made an abrupt movement of his narrow shoulders, like someone who knows he ought not to speak but can't hold back. "The Council wouldn't have to worry about literacy being divisive if you would all at least study the alphabet. Certainly the little ones, who are too young to decide for themselves, ought to be required to study. The older children should have started learning already."

"Not now, Eykar."

I said, "Why does reading matter? The person who wrote those old book-words is long since dead. It was a man, anyway. Why would any Free person want to read it?"

He frowned but kept his head turned toward Beyarra, so that he wasn't frowning at me, exactly. If I'd been a Free Fem, I suppose I could have hit him for that frown, or at least demanded an explanation. But I was not offended; to me he was only a curiosity, like a horse speaking up in human language.

"It isn't just stories," he began, then stopped himself and added rather waspishly, "*Hera.* If I may call you that? Sheel Torrinor won't accept that form of address, and since you come from over the mountains—"

"My name is Sorrel," I said, but Beyarra said firmly, " 'Hera' will do very well."

"People who don't know the past, Hera," he said to me, "inevitably keep making the same mistakes their forebears made."

"What have past mistakes got to do with it?" I said, surprised. "All Ohayars gamble their goods away. They always have and they always will, as everybody knows. The strengths and weaknesses bred in our blood are balanced by decisions made in the Chief Tents, not by trying to be different from the ancestors of our lines."

He blinked and changed tack. "I've heard that Grassland people revere the past. They keep it in songs that go far back, which they sing on important occasions."

"The songs are truths about their foremothers' lives," I said. "Your books are full of men's lies."

He thought. Then he said, "No man of the Old Holdfast would admit it, but we have books here written by women as well."

"Women?" Intrigued, I settled more comfortably facing him, my forearms crossed on my upraised knees. I glanced at Beyarra-Bey. "Does he mean the foremothers of the Free?"

She nodded. "I've seen some of their works myself."

He said, "Not many are left, although we find mention of many more in surviving works. Unfortunately there have been purges, over the years, to destroy anything identified as not created by men. Much appears to have been lost."

"But I see so much saved," Beyarra said, taking in the big room beyond us with a gesture.

He said, "Your eyes are better than mine, Hera."

She shook her head slightly and clicked her tongue, chiding. There was something easy between the two of them that annoyed me. She wasn't the one supposed to be related to him.

I said, "Show me one of these books."

He called over his shoulder, "Setteo, fetch *West with the Night,* will you? Striped cover, with a picture of a silver flying machine."

A skinny young man in a ragged kilt popped out from behind a case of shelves just inside the big room. He had such a startled, guilty expression that I laughed. He laughed too, unnaturally loudly and long, and ducked back out of sight.

Eykar said coldly, "His mind's turned. Do you laugh at such people in your homeland—Hera?"

His challenge angered me. "They say that you were my bloodmother's master, muckie, and you raped her, and I am the result."

I heard Beyarra catch her breath.

Eykar answered steadily, "That is a rough description of a complex event, but yes, you may be my child as well as hers."

Surely no man in the Holdfast was allowed to look so directly at a woman—a fem or a Woman—and for so long, and to speak so insolently. Was this some special privilege of "fathers"? The man was insulting, he was unbearable.

"I doubt it's the truth," I retorted. "My bloodmother is strong, not some weakling to be bullied by a creature like you."

He looked away now; I had him on the run. It felt good.

"It must have been the other one," I added, deliberately prodding, wanting to see—something: fear, anger, sorrow? Some sign that that ancient rape meant something to him.

A scar gleamed pale on his forehead above the milky eye. He shook out the damp rag he used to wipe up chalk marks. "I suppose you could be Servan's child."

At that moment the mad boy—Setteo, of course, it had

to be him—reappeared: "Here is the book." He held out a thin set of stained boards with ripply-edged papers pressed between them, the whole thing tied up with a twist of twine.

Setteo's eyes were fixed on me and he said softly, "She looks like her mother. What if *they* made her, not you at all?"

"Go away, mad boy!" I exclaimed. I didn't like being around the Omellys at home, either. Crazy people scared me.

"Go," the older man said gruffly, and took the book. Setteo, still looking at me, backed away among the bookshelves.

"You asked to see this, Hera."

"Ugh. It smells."

"Water damage," Bek said shortly. "Smoke; mold."

"How can you be sure that a woman wrote this?" I held the book away from me. It made me shiver, thinking of someone's voice trapped in the markings inside, like the voice of some long-dead soul that must still speak when commanded. I handed it back to him.

"This is a woman writing about riding a flying machine through the air, as you would ride a horse over the ground." He untied the string and opened the book with a delicate, respectful touch, this man who had violently forced himself upon a helpless slave.

He read out something that I couldn't follow. I felt stupid hearing words I didn't know, and it was boring that he kept stopping to find words in the big, fat book (for he didn't know them all either), which he had unwrapped again for this purpose.

The bits that I could understand affected me strangely; some long-dead woman's thoughts being spoken from a book in a living man's voice made my head spin.

I got up, feeling a little sick to my stomach. "That's enough. I have better things to do."

Beyarra-Bey followed me outside. I whirled upon her and demanded angrily, "Why did you bring me here?"

"He was less afraid of you than I thought he might be," she murmured, her mind clearly much more on him than on me.

"Him, afraid? Rather too bold, if you ask me."

"Oh, he's afraid," she answered with a sad smile, "all

the time. You were never a slave, you wouldn't know."

"Oh, to hell with this!" I was tired of being told how much I didn't know. "I'm heading home tomorrow. When Alldera comes, you can tell her she got back too late."

And if that beat-up slave devoted to his smelly old books was my "father," why, let sharu gnaw his bones, for all I cared. Beyarra and Alldera could keep him; it was nothing to me.

Crime

On the steps of a disused dock at dawn Daya washed her hair. It was holding the dark dye very well. But her reflection showed a slackening of the skin around her eyes; soft pockets of flesh were forming from the corners of her mouth. Time was the cruelest master!

Still, when she washed and dressed and scented herself skillfully, she was beautiful. The inner conviction of that fact, which she had long ago learned to nurture with care for her body, was strong enough to influence the way others saw her.

Now, with Fedeka gone off brooding as she sometimes did, it must fall to Daya to speak for the White Lady. Daya was prepared; she had not approached the Moon's House here in Midfast (from which she might have been turned away by that old bitch Kastia) but had spent the night by the river, praying.

She felt refreshed and eager for Galligan's trial. Fedeka had no stomach for such doings, never had. This was why Daya knew she could outwait the older woman and—despite everything—someday even succeed her as Speaker for the Moon.

Perhaps today, if nothing upset the unrolling of events.

No one challenged her when she went to the common, the open plaza now dotted with slender young shade trees where the Seniors had once burned errant or unlucky fems for "witchery." The common still led toward the Dreaming Hall, but of that great edifice itself nothing remained but the flight of broad, shallow steps up to where the doors had stood. Galligan's trial would take place on the raised platform of the top step and the section of flooring that still extended behind it. People were already assembling on the paving below the Steps in the warm morning sun.

In the first days after the Conquest they had stood or even sat on the Steps on these occasions, claiming ownership of the ceremonial center of the men's world. Now the structure was simply a convenience to be used, without fuss.

Some turned to watch as Daya moved imperturbably by. She was propelled by the power of purpose. The Lady had sent Sorrel to carry Daya out of exile in Oldtown, bringing besides a welcome target for public anger and alarm—the boy Veree. No one would dare to actually harm Sorrel, of course, or the boy.

Someday Sorrel would understand the part she had played in Daya's plans and forgive everything.

Daya did not climb the stairs, not yet. She stood by one of the saplings and cast around her for familiar faces—friends, enemies, pawns. There was Sorrel, arms truculently crossed. Beyarra was at her side, of course, staking her claim.

No, that was the old way of thinking: jealous, competitive, angry. Daya shook herself mentally, struggling to keep aligned to the Lady's will. *Let Alldera's daughter see my beneficent resolve,* she thought, holding tight to her prayer stones. *Let her see beyond my errors in the past. Let them all see!*

Sorrel's resemblance to Alldera came and went with her expressions, gestures, and the fall of the light. She had Alldera's build and features, refined and brightened by youth. Her appearance stirred currents of nostalgia in Daya, but no matter.

I am different than I used to be. Moonwoman has changed me, or else it's all for nothing.

The eight-hour gong rang from the tower of the old Trukker Hall, and the business began. Galligan was brought from the rock-walled cell where he had spent the night. He shuffled, wide-legged, around the stick chained between his ankles. His wrists were locked into the ends of a wide wooden yoke that rode low on his shoulders, bracing his extended arms out and up.

Pellopay and Forrenz walked behind him, each with a short lance in hand. The two guards held ropes, the ends noosed around Galligan's throat above the yoke.

He looks truly terrible, Daya thought with a sigh. Mounting the Steps, he wobbled alarmingly. She was afraid he might stumble and strangle himself right there. But then he stood swaying on the top step, and the guards drew the rope ends through rings set high in the two posts of the old, wide doorway. Daya wondered if Forrenz, who had too soft a heart for this work, had given him any manna to ease his ordeal.

Marajee-Mai, current chief of the Whole Land Council, stumped up the stairs and sat heavily in the wicker chair set out for her. She had arthritic knees and could not comfortably stand for long periods. She reached down under the chair for the speaking horn lying there, ready to hand. A tense silence fell.

"People," she began, speaking through the horn to amplify her voice, "this man fled from his hearth, injuring one of his sponsors in his escape. He was retaken after four days' hunt, with further violence. Who has something to say about him?"

Tila (that showoff!) ran up the Steps and took the horn. "Galligan is a good worker. He didn't take other men on the run with him or attack anyone just to hurt her. Leesann-Leesett thinks he's sired two healthy girls."

Others spoke in turn, addressing the crowd.

"Spies say he's involved in the Bear cult."

"He lived with Zagmendo's crew when I was a slave before Alldera's Return. Zagmendo was a hard master like all those Tekkan men, but Galligan was decent when he could be."

"I heard he had something to do with the death of Kitanna, a slave of Erl the Scrapper's men, two years after the Old Holdfast fell. Who knows about that?"

Someone nearby said, "Why don't they just kill him? I saw what he tried to do to Lora!"

Daya recognized Sorrel's Grassland accent. She tried to catch the girl's eye, but Sorrel gave her a stony stare and turned her back. Beyarra, ever the little diplomat, signaled Daya with a tiny shake of the head: Stay clear.

Plainly it was not yet time to try mending relations with Alldera's child. Not that she mattered much, really. Ignoring the curious glances of those who had witnessed this little byplay, Daya concentrated on what she had come to see.

A NewFree called Muvai was showing the scar on her arm where a rogue stickman had bitten her last year and telling how Galligan had dragged the mucker off her. But wasn't that actually an old scar from the battle for Oldtown? It would be just like Muvai to show the scar anyway and lie about it. Always drawing attention to herself.

Sorrel asked something. Beyarra answered, "He has the right, but most men keep quiet on the Steps."

Another NewFree (Daya refrained from turning to see who it was) interjected, "They know they're bound to say something that will make things worse."

Sorrel said, "What would Alldera do if she were here?"

"Alldera tries to stay out of Step matters," Beyarra said, the mealy-mouthed bitch. "People say she's biased on account of her sponsorship of Eykar Bek and Setteo."

Sorrel said, "Maybe she stays clear because of what Daya did. Who could blame Alldera for stepping back after that? Nobody wants to be a chief among people who hate her."

Despite herself, Daya turned and answered. "I told you! I told you how that was!"

Sorrel glared at her. People around them whispered.

Sometimes Daya thought that her real punishment for the attack at the Watchtower was that nobody heard her words any more. All her stories were suspect now. That was why she no longer told them. Moonwoman had been required to take the place of so much in her life. Sometimes she grieved over her losses, but they were the price she paid for the Lady's protection.

Now Kastia-Kai chose to show herself, drawing all eyes back to the Steps (thank you, Lady!). Her withered arm was hidden by the long, embroidered sleeve of her white gown. She raised the speaking horn with her sound hand.

"Can you all hear me?" she quavered. "Fedeka has gone to think with the Lady. It might be good to put off a decision about this man until she returns."

When in doubt, delay. Or perhaps Eykar had pled for Galligan, to good effect. Daya bit her lip. She hated to leave the last word with Kastia-Kai; was it time to put forward her own ideas yet?

Someone she couldn't see called out, "Swift judgment is sweet judgment!"

She dared not delay. She put one foot on the bottom step and breathed deeply, taking in air to carry her voice without aid. "The Lady dreamed with me last night as I prayed by the river. May I speak?"

Kastia-Kai hesitated, then stepped humbly aside; sweet as cream-cake she looked, as if she had not stabbed Alldera that terrible night herself! Sometimes Daya felt like the only honest fem among the lot of them.

Before she could go up and take the horn, someone pushed rudely past and ran up the steps. Kobba planted herself, her arms crossed, her big hands gripping her biceps, on the top step. "I have a word to speak," she said, staring down at Daya, daring her to object.

Daya heard Sorrel murmur in a surprised tone, "Is that Kobba? She looks younger than I remembered."

Someone answered, "Men say that she drinks men's blood at night as they sleep, and that keeps her young."

The tall fem spoke in a loud, scathing tone: hatred kept her young, couldn't they see that? "This man Galligan hurt Fandua in his escape. He tried to kill Lora-Lan to keep from being caught—a regular macho hero! If he goes back among the others, he'll only do mischief and spread rebellion."

Galligan's throat bobbed in a nervous swallow, but he had the sense to say nothing.

"He should die," Kobba said harshly. "He's broken our rules and done us violence. The sticks will say we're afraid to punish him, and count his return a victory for themselves."

No, she was not going to have Galligan for her meat. Daya had other plans for him.

Daya ran up the stairs to the platform and stood opposite Kobba, the breeze fluttering her robe. Let them all see that she had not left Oldtown to creep about in silent humility. A ward of the Lady could come to Midfast and speak on the Steps if she wished to.

Kobba looked her up and down with a cold gaze out of that long-jawed face of hers with its war scars on cheek and brow. "Well, what have you to say, Moonbeam?"

Daya spoke not to her but to the crowd below. "I say that the Lady speaks in me. She says it is time for a man to be sent to serve her."

How they stared—except for the ones asking others, incredulously, to repeat what she had said.

She clutched her Ladystones. From them flowed the conviction to continue. "Let this stiff-necked man submit to the Lady, let him feel her cold mercy. Then he will teach other men to respect Her and us, Her daughters."

Sorrel's face, upturned with the others, wore a startled look. Now she would see what true leadership was, true courage! Daya flung her arms up to quell the surging voices below the Steps.

"I tell you, the Lady wills it! How else are we to make our lives whole and joyful again? How else are we to sleep sound in our own land, and raise our children free? Moonwoman sustained us through our generations of slavery. Can't she take these men, one by one, and make human beings of them? Give this one to me and to the Lady, and with her help our healing will begin!"

Kobba's hand closed like a vise on her bicep, Kobba's sharp breath stung her nostrils.

"You mad bitch!" the tall fem hissed, shaking her. "Shut up and get back up the river where you belong or you'll regret it!"

Daya cried, "Do you think the Lady wants us with our hearts all soured and shriveled from fearing and punishing the men, as they feared and punished us? If our hearts become the dry, cruel hearts of masters, what welcome will we have from our Lady when we go to her at last? Why should she favor us then?"

"How dare you speak of men?" Kobba said between her teeth. She thumped Daya in the chest, painfully, with the back of her hand. "You never struck a blow against one of them, not even on the Day of Our Judgment! Your heart is still a slave's heart. You can't tell what's real from your stupid, lying stories, you scrawny, treacherous little cock-kisser!"

She turned to the crowd, still holding Daya's arm in a bruising grip. "She'd help them chain us up again, so they'll set her above us like a Matri of the old days! So she speaks up for this worthless heap of shit—"

Then Lora-Lan was between them, dithering. Too bad, really; Daya knew how it looked, with herself pinioned, a poor, marked wisp of a creature, by the hands of tall Kobba who, working the mines of smashed machines, had acquired the hardness and mindless strength of a machine herself.

"No, look," shrilled Lora, "how can we hurt each other over a man? He's only a stickie, two spraddled legs and a hanger between. Just look at him!"

Kobba said, "He tried to brain you with a rock, Lora, by your own account." She turned back to Daya, hissing, "You can't sponsor this man. He'll shove his face between your legs and suck till you screech with pleasure. Out of dizzy-minded lust you'd run behind him on a rope, pet fem to your pet."

"Every word," Daya said steadily, "every word that you say, Kobba Cold-Heart, rises even in daylight to night's mother, who knows the truth behind all words."

"Words is all you know," Kobba spat, "lies and stories!"

Daya moved to the edge of the step. "What better thing to do with this disobedient man than to bend him to the service of our Lady?" As the first murmurs of response began to rise, she added, "That is the tale the Lady tells to me, for I too have had to bend my upstart nature to Her wishes. I leave it in your hands, free people."

As she turned toward the Moon's House, old Roona called, "You just want a stickie of your own, like Alldera's Eykar. Won't she be tickled when she hears!"

Punishment

I should never have gone to Galligan's trial, but how could I stay away? It could be Veree up there on the Steps someday.

I hadn't known Kobba well in Stone Dancing Camp. She

had been too angry to approach, casting nothing but grim glances in my direction. They said at that time that she remembered every terrible story told in the Tea Camp, and that these memories fed her rage.

Now, with Daya withdrawn after making her shocking demand, Kobba turned to Kastia-Kai.

"What does a man need to be able to do, Kastia-Kai," she asked with heavy mock courtesy, "to serve your Lady?"

"Your" Lady, not "the" Lady or "our" Lady. Looking at her, I could well credit that she trusted in no one and nothing but her massive, angry self.

Kastia-Kai said spitefully, "How should I know? The Lady doesn't speak to *me*."

"What if he pisses in the corners of Her house, or sings Bear songs in there?"

Against my better judgment, Galligan's silence had begun to trouble me. He had no one of his line to step forward on his behalf, as any Grassland Woman would have had. His silence demeaned the people who judged him, raising him up at their expense.

I was afraid of Kobba's fury, which all but crisped my eyebrows even at a distance. Still, I found myself advancing, full of misgivings, to the Steps. I had no love for Galligan and supposed myself vulnerable because of Veree, but after Daya's dramatics someone must speak sanely on behalf of Veree's sex. No one else was doing so.

"If I may ask," I said, cleared my throat, and went on, "can this man Galligan speak for himself?"

He stared down at me with what looked like panic.

Kobba jerked on one of the ropes tied to his neck. "Say something, muck," she said.

He coughed.

Someone called, "Oh, let be, Kobba. We're not here to torment the creature."

"Why not?" Kobba snapped. "His kind tormented us casually enough when they were our masters."

A stocky fem with blue love knots tied into her hair called, "The rottenest ones are dead now. You know that, Kobba, you killed some yourself. This one's no worse than the rest of the survivors, and a good deal better than some."

"That's bad enough," Kobba said. She walked closer to Galligan, whose chest was heaving with quick breaths. No wonder. All she had to do was knock him off his feet and put a knee into his back, and he would strangle in the ropes between the pillars unless his neck broke first.

I felt a shift in the feelings of the crowd around me, a stirring from righteous judgment to discomfort. They may have been present to judge Galligan, but Kobba's bare-faced bloodthirst was plainly too much for many of them.

Kastia-Kai, who had been conferring softly with Marajee, said with some spirit, "Fedeka is the Lady's speaker, not Daya, and not me either. But what's the rush? Do we doubt that we can hang on to this fellow till Fedeka gets back?"

Marajee leaned forward in her chair and said through the speaking horn, "I agree with Kastia. Objections could go to the full Council next time they meet."

A long-faced fem near me muttered, "We should chain up Daya too, and send her back upriver where she belongs."

Others glanced in my direction and shushed her; to spare me embarrassment I suppose, over my unwitting part in Daya's escape from exile in the Oldtown Moon's House.

From where I stood, I could see Kobba's jaw set as she caught the drift of opinion toward delay. Quick as summer thunder she kicked out, sweeping Galligan's legs from under him. He toppled with a cry that turned into a gagging rasp as he hit the ropes. He thrashed and struggled, eyes popping and mouth agape, weighed down by the heavy yoke across his shoulders.

Kobba strode contemptuously away, ignoring the people who ran to cut Galligan loose before he could suffocate. She had made her statement, without canceling the councillor's decision.

Beyarra and others bent over Galligan. He had fallen hard to the ground and lay moaning, his arms still held wide by the yoke. Drops of blood spattered from one of his hands as the guards lifted him and hustled him away.

I was appalled by Kobba's swift violence against that trussed, terrified stick. The Riding Women sang praise and prayer even to a worn-out old horse before stunning it with a hammer for slaughter. And these people called *them* savages!

I shouldered my way away through the crowd until I collided with a doorway. There I stopped, waiting for my knees to stop shaking and hoping no one would notice me. How ridiculous, to be upset over the treatment of a convicted man!

Someone touched my arm and asked, "Are you all right?"

Lora-Lan peered into my face with concern.

I smiled some kind of death grin and nodded my head. She urged me inside. The building, a high-roofed, airy space, was a workfloor for curing hides. We sat down at a stained table.

"That was ugly," she sighed. "I wish you hadn't seen it."

I said, "Kobba has gone sharu-bit-crazy."

Lora shook her head. "She's not mad, though you might think so to hear her."

"I don't understand," I said.

"Well, how could you?" she said kindly. "Here's poor Galligan—he's not so bad, I knew him when he and I were both much younger—he lands himself right between Daya and Kobba! He's lucky to have come out alive."

She hesitated, then added, "You didn't help, though I know you meant to. Kobba's not the only one to feel affronted by what you said—as if we were keeping Galligan from speaking!"

"Well, weren't you?" I said.

"He could have spoken at any time," she said earnestly. "For you to stand up for him—a girl of the Grasslands, of all people—and you were there when he fought me!"

"He just seemed so—outnumbered," I said. "And Kobba's a serious enemy, even for a person not bound hand and foot. It was all just so—degrading, for everyone."

She sighed. "Try not to think badly of Kobba. Being a strong hater is good for war, not so good when the fighting's over. I think sometimes she feels left behind these days. You sit there, I'm going to get something to brew up for you."

Soon we sat sipping hot, grassy-tasting tea in that cavernous space. Lora talked seriously to me about Kobba's faction of relentless man-haters, who would as soon see them all dead as not. Recently they had allied themselves with Sheel and the Rois cousins, who felt the same unalterable distrust of males.

These same people had wanted Daya killed, too, after the attack on Alldera, but Fedeka had prevailed. By now most people had grown used to the idea of having the pet fem confined to Oldtown under the protection of Moonwoman—a situation that I had inadvertently altered.

Alldera herself favored a less stringent treatment of the men, Lora said, as a way of moving toward some kind of partial freedom for the little boys when they grew up (and here Lora gave me a very wry look, but forbore to scold me for passing Veree off as a girl).

"It's a lost cause, though," she said. "Galligan's all right—as long as he's bridled and tethered and watched all the time. We all remember how the men treated us when they were masters. The little boys will have to pay too, I'm afraid, when they're grown."

I said nothing but thought about getting back across the mountains as fast as I could ride, taking Veree with me.

Beyarra-Bey joined us, looking flustered and unhappy. "What an uproar. Daya is very inventive in her way, but such a difficult person! I wish she had stayed in Oldtown. Oh, I didn't mean to blame you, Sorrel—"

Lora shook her head in disbelief. "A man in the moon's service! Where did Daya get such an idea?"

I turned to Beyarra. "Will they send Galligan to her?"

"Not exactly," she said with a rueful look. "But a couple of his fingers got mashed by the end of that yoke when it hit the floor. Daya has some healing skill, and who else will want to tend to a man? After what he tried to do to Lora—"

Lora shrugged, putting on a show of nonchalance. "Oh, he was just scared out of his wits."

Beyarra said, "No. He's one of the ones who *uses* his wits, or he wouldn't have gotten away in the first place. We've locked him up behind the quernhouse, but Daya will end up seeing to him. That should keep her busy till Alldera gets back, anyway."

"So in the short run," I said, "Daya wins?"

Lora threw her hands wide in a gesture of surrender. "I can't imagine what she thinks she's doing!"

Beyarra narrowed her eyes, thinking. "It's not a *completely* crazy idea—"

"Sure it is," Lora said, but Beyarra gently persisted: "Fedeka does cleansing ceremonies, using the waning moon. Some people say men could be included—"

"Daya says it, nobody else!" To me, Lora said, "Fedeka invites First Free and NewFree to tell their hardest truths and pains on certain nights, for the Lady to take away into darkness. Some say it helps. But talk of offering cleansing to men is disrespectful of our own dead, and of the Lady Herself."

Beyarra sat silent, looking troubled.

I voiced my own misgivings. "But there has to be some way, for your sons at least. Do you mean for half of your own children to be slaves forever?"

Lora said quietly, "If that's the only way to assure our daughters' safety, yes."

Beyarra murmured, "All our children are very young. People's thinking may change—"

"Not mine," Lora said.

"What?" I said. "When they get a little older, will you bring them to see men mutilated or killed on those Steps for this crime or that? Will you bring your daughters?"

"Of course," Lora answered briskly; Lora, who had once been afraid of her own horses!

"Look," she added earnestly, "I like men, one by one and separated from the Old days of their mastership, and I'm not the only one who does. Maybe you noticed that lovely line of silky, dark hair that Galligan has running down his belly from his navel? It's charming, leading your mind right where many fems' minds are quick to go, especially among the NewFree. And not just minds, either. Being Grassland-raised, Sorrel, you wouldn't know about that kind of attraction, but believe me, it's there, regardless of what people know they ought to feel. And it's very strong.

"But none of that cancels out what men have done to us and would do again if they could—they'll say so, too, when they think themselves safe from being overheard. You know it's true, Beyarra. That's why we have to keep them down. And who's to say for sure that the little boys will turn out differently?"

I had no response, seeing clearly the root of my distress: the children, the future of the children. No, Veree. Just Veree, sucked into the life of a land full of old terrors and hatreds that some people would never let go.

Beyarra turned to me, very solemn-looking for somebody only a few years older than I was myself. "Sorrel, I'd like to be able to put your fears for Veree to rest, but I can't. We're still floundering around with all this, trying to find better ways than the ones we were all taught. We make mistakes. But we'll do our best to keep the little ones safe from our grown-up troubles and confusions as long as we can."

Lora nodded. "The Council discusses the children all the time. People ask questions, suggest things—Kobba thinks we should be telling them horror stories of the Old Holdfast as bedtime tales. It's history, she says, and it's true; but I don't like the idea of pouring such acid in those tender little ears: not yet awhile." She sighed. "But the kits will have to be told something, sometime."

I felt suffocated with apprehension. "Kobba shouldn't be involved with the children at all. She could kill a boy-child to prevent some evil she thinks he might do twenty years from now. Or get him killed, with some lie or other.

"Suppose some fem was angry with Galligan so she made up a story that he attacked her? You could accuse him to distract people so they wouldn't find out something you did yourself. If people found out later he was innocent, it would still be too late for Galligan, wouldn't it?"

Lora raised her eyebrows. "That's how it was for us when we were slaves."

I could find no answer to that.

Beyarra said gently, "You don't mean Galligan. You're talking about what might happen sometime to Veree. Why is he so important to you? He's someone else's son, child of a NewFree and one of her masters."

I stood up, unable to keep still. "He would have died if not for me. You think I don't know what neglect is? That's how it was for me, too. If not for Sheel and her patrol,

Alldera would have dumped me somewhere, if she even let me live to be born!"

Lora held up her hand to stop Beyarra from answering. She leaned toward me and answered, "We explained all that to you years ago, don't you remember? You asked why Alldera was so—distant, and we told you."

"You never told me!" But I wasn't sure, now.

"She had no way to feed herself in the Wild, let alone nourish an infant," Lora said, with that awful, insistent kindness. "In the Old Holdfast there was no *caring* for a child. The masters didn't allow it. We've had to learn to do it ourselves, here in our own country."

I said, "You blame the men for every wicked thing any of you does. Well, my bloodmother left me in Holdfaster Tent as a thanks gift, a breeding mare for the Riding Women to repay them for their hospitality, and no man made her do that!"

Lora sat back staring at me, aghast. "That's not how it was! How could you think such a thing?"

"How could I think such a thing?" I mimicked. "I'm not an idiot. What else could I think?"

But my anger was already draining away. I felt stupid and mean. Although I'd often had such thoughts I hadn't sat around brooding on them, which was the way it sounded now. My sharemothers had loved me; my childhood had been happy.

"So I thought I'd bring Veree across the mountains," I finished surlily, "and consult with my blood-ma, the great expert on what to do with an unwanted child."

Beyarra said in a sympathetic tone that grated on my heart, "Let's not talk any more about this now, Sorrel. I think you're saying things you want to say to Alldera, not to us."

Lora-Lan said, "If only you hadn't brought him here—"

"There was no other place for him!" I cried. "But what's it worth, to have brought him here? He'll grow up to be a man, and a man in your country is just a stick of wood to be snapped in half at Kobba's whim!"

"That's more than he'd grow up to be in the Grasslands," Lora-Lan countered. "They'd kill him there, sooner or later, and you know it."

"Beyarra's right, there's no use talking about this," I said, and I got up and left them.

I had made up my mind to get Veree back, and I didn't want them to read that intention in my eyes or my voice. Where I would take him I could not imagine, but I was not going to leave him here.

A Helper at the Children's House

On the days that Eykar didn't need him at the Library Setteo served the children, played their games, caught their colds and wiped their bottoms. He sang under his breath to protect them from the Bears, with whom he could no longer personally intercede.

No one told him where the new boy, Veree, came from, but he knew. People can have slaves or secrets, but not both.

He was only allowed to help because many of the Free quickly outgrew their initial infatuation with the babies. Restless conquerors, many Heras soon left the Children's House, first to travel the Holdfast as its masters and then to settle into this hearth or that one to tend the herds or the workfloors or the fields and gardens with their hearthmates.

The care of the children required natural slaves, Setteo thought, with an inclination to serve those smaller and weaker than themselves. This came easily to him, now that those great ones he had once served no longer sent for him.

Leesann, chief of the full-time baby crew, had at first jealously watched him, looking, he was sure, for an excuse to exclude him.

Now he thought her reconciled to his presence in the Children's House. There was more and more to be done as new infants were born (though the number of live births dwindled as the bodies of the Free aged). Leesann was so exacting that she narrowed the pool of volunteers.

Right now she was quarreling loudly with Janna over

the freshly washed diapers, complaining that they had been set out to dry too late in the day.

"The sunlight kills molds," she said, shaking out a cloth and eyeing it narrowly. "You're not in that damned foreign desert now. These were in shadow half the day; they're still damp. They'll have to be washed again."

"I came to spend time with the little ones, not with load after load of washing," Janna protested. She was very pretty, with great shining eyes.

"Work first, play after," Leesann said sententiously. "Unless you want to dig a kit pit and toss the children in, to fend for themselves as we had to."

"I know, I know, I grew up there too," Janna said, sniffing dubiously at one of the clean diapers.

"You'd do a better job," Leesann accused, "if you weren't so busy mooning over Belett."

"You're crazy, I don't do anything of the kind!"

"And to think I used to get all teary-eyed," Leesann muttered resentfully, "watching you and Shanuay drinking from one cup, as if you were lovers for life! The war is over. It's time for people to be steady-hearted with each other."

Janna cried, "I drink from any cup I like! You can't say I'm wrong. Loving freely is a virtue among the Riding Women."

She had a shrill voice, and one of the children began to cry in response, rousing two others. Janna was obsessed by the children, he thought, but in an intense, demanding way that disturbed instead of soothed them. Maybe she would have to leave the Children's House, maybe soon.

"You're not among your precious Riding Women now," Leesann answered disdainfully. Many NewFree found the subject of the Grassland people irritating, Setteo had noted. "And there are those who think Marish 'virtues' look an awful lot like the way the masters used to behave among themselves, if you bother to remember."

Dark color flooded Janna's heart-shaped face. She set her clenched hands on her hips. "Come and say that to me outside. I don't want to thrash you in front of the children."

Setteo stepped nearer, ducking his head submissively and murmuring, "Please, Heras, may I take the diapers that are still damp and lay them out again for you? There are a couple of hours of sunlight left."

"Oh, here then, take them," Leesann growled, thrusting the pile roughly into his arms. Only with the babies was she soft and loving. Sometimes he wished he were newborn himself, to receive her gentleness instead of the edge of her tongue.

Behind him he heard Janna complaining, "You'd rather have that crazy cutboy help in here than share with other fems."

"Setteo is careful, willing, and dependable," Leesann retorted, hastening off to attend to the squallers, "which is more than I can say about some people!"

Well, he thought, *that's thanks, of a sort.*

Outside in the wide, grassy yard, Setteo set his burden down on a trestle table. He began spreading the cloths, soft with washing and patterned with the residue of old stains, in rows on the thick lawn. They kept it green inside the walled space for the little ones to crawl and scoot about, squealing and quarreling over the toys and dolls that people brought for them. Setteo had spent the morning picking up their clutter and packing it away again in the chests that lined the deep doorway.

The kits were quiet again, which made him uneasy; he was better off outside. He loved the usual cacophony in the old building even more than he loved the charged peace of the Book Room. The children's noise was almost enough to fill the place in him where the Cold Country once had been.

He furtively dabbed his nose dry on one of the diapers. When he thought of his past journeys with caught breath and quaking heart, a bold traveler in a secret place full of peril and power, he always got weepy.

His land no longer: snatched away and given instead to others.

Oh, Cold Ones, he prayed silently for the tenth time that day, please let me come to you again. My heart is too hot, it scorches me. Cool me with your cloudy breath. You let others visit now, but I was first! I have carried your messages faithfully. How can you shut me out?

Here came Beyarra-Bey with Sorrel Alldersdaughter.

(What kind of an answer was that? One of the Bears' jokes?).

"Setteo," Beyarra said, her eyes eager with anticipation of seeing her own little girl, "where's Leesann?"

"Inside arguing, Hera." He glanced covertly at her companion, who had a brooding look. He shivered with apprehension. Life could become difficult when the Heras got upset.

This one had fixed a fine, silver thread between her heart and the new little boy's. Setteo could see it gleam even now, as she turned to look around. That's what these people did, spinning each other into a complex net that thrummed and trembled with the heats of love and hatred that they sent streaking between them. A hard tug here or there set them all stumbling wildly for balance.

Beyarra took some of the cloths from his stack, saying, "As we're here, we'll help." To Sorrel she said, "Leesann finds fault with everybody who tries to lend a hand, except Setteo."

"Why?" Sorrel said. But her eyes searched anxiously about: she cared nothing about the question or the answer; she was looking for that boy Veree.

"Because she can tell him what to do, but with the Free she's got to ask nicely. Even then we're contentious."

Sorrel's scowl deepened. "Veree is in the hands of quarreling bullies, is that what you mean?"

"Oh, don't be ridiculous, please!" Beyarra said. "Leesann would die before she'd hurt any child. So would all the rest of us. Setteo knows; he spends more time in the nursery than anybody but Leesann herself. Tell her, Setteo."

He had lost track of the subject, distracted by how the shadow of Sorrel was much too long for her (now, how had she come by that?). He could only smile and hope that the smile would serve.

The young Hera didn't seem to expect a reply. With another angry stare around the inner walls of the yard, she muttered, "You keep them penned up like this all the time?"

Beyarra said, "We live within walls, here; well, most of us do. Besides, the older children are hard to keep track of. They're so active, liable to be up to trouble even when they're quiet, like eating the laundry soap.

"They play just as well in here where we can keep an eye on them as they could outside, and a lot more safely. Veree will have lots of friends in no time. It will be good for him—"

"Stop *saying* that," Sorrel said, snatching a diaper and vehemently snapping it flat. "At least in the Grasslands nobody was preparing him to be shackled up all his life!"

Beyarra said more softly, "I've got a child here to visit myself. Come and see her."

"I can see what I need to from here," Sorrel said. "Are you sure Veree's even in this place?"

"Setteo, give me those a minute." Beyarra took the diapers from him and put them on the creaky wooden table by the wall. "Now come inside with me. I want you to bring out Veree for my friend."

Inside with him she added privately, "Setti, anything you can do to reassure this visitor would be very welcome. I hate to see her so frightened for that child."

Off she went to see her own babe, which had been born with a stub for one hand and so had been a cause for grief as well as joy. In the old days the Seniors would have sent the infant to the Matris to smother. Now it turned out that some of those discarded children had been secretly handed on to people hiding in the southern swamps.

The Cold Country was a place of wonders, but the Warm World held surprises of its own.

He carried the new child from his bed, trying not to wake him. Veree generally ended up at least once a day crying himself into exhausted sleep, bawling for his "ma."

Back in the yard, Setteo sat down on a bench with Veree in his arms. Sorrel did not reach out to take the boy. This was a relief, since Setteo wasn't sure he was supposed to let her hold him, not with that big, agitated shadow of hers.

She crouched down facing Setteo and stroked the boy's forehead, which was marked from being pressed into his bedding. "He feels hot," she accused.

"Only from sleeping." Setteo kept his voice low, although the alarm shivering in her, the anxious need, filled him with tension. "I've sat with little ones who were feverish. They don't feel like this."

She straightened the curls pasted with sweat on the

child's cheek. "I miss him all the time, and he's not even mine!" Then she looked at Setteo directly. "You're the cutboy who helped save my bloodmother's life at Lammintown."

He ducked his head in assent, embarrassed and a little scared by her attention. But he was curious, too. This person had come out of the body of Alldera herself, as these nursery babies had come out of the bodies of the Free.

Despite what people were saying, he could see nothing of the Endtendant in her. She smelled rather like Sheel Torrinor; maybe the Riding Woman was really her "father."

"Veree's not happy here, is he?" Sorrel said, looking past him into the open cavern of the hall with its bundled children asleep on small mattresses, here a plump, bare leg sticking out, there a sharp-boned little back shedding its blanket.

"All the babies cry sometimes," he said, "but they laugh, too. He does the same."

"But who's going to love him here?" she demanded. "What about you? Do you like the babies?"

"I asked to help with them; only the boys, of course, of course. The little boys like me. Once this one is more used to me, he won't cry so much."

She hugged her knees and stared hard at Veree's round, dark head. "But he misses me, doesn't he? I know he does."

"You can borrow him," Setteo said, bending closer and speaking confidentially. "Take him to eat with you and sleep where you sleep tonight. People come to Midfast just to hug the babies, to take them out for a walk around the town or a ride along the river path. If they want to, they can take one overnight to their hearth sometimes."

She hissed her breath in. "That would make it worse—having to 'borrow' him! Other people have borrowed him already?"

He nodded warily. Some mothers suffered from violent and unpredictable fits of possessiveness, though not usually with the boys. He hoped he wasn't going to have to call Leesann for help. Sorrel looked strong.

She shook her head, an expression of pained bewilderment on her face. "I was raised in a country of sharing. This is so different."

"But no other mothers have come here from that Grass country," he observed. "So you are specially important to him, and he to you, isn't that so, Hera?"

"They're right about you; you're not as crazy as all that," Sorrel said with a measuring look. "I said he was mine so the Free wouldn't grab him away from me as soon as they saw him. They just waited a little and then grabbed him anyway. I told a stupid lie that didn't accomplish anything."

She stooped forward to touch Veree's fingers to her lips. "Some Motherlines are jealous over their young daughters," she mused. "They are criticized for it."

"It is a great question," Setteo said gravely, "this matter of one person owning another."

"Only on this side of the mountains. The Riding Women don't go in for that kind of thing." She straightened the neckline of Veree's rumpled gown and picked a small crust of food off it. "Can you tell the boys and girls apart without undressing them?"

An icy flash of dread shook him. What did he really know about this person? What if she were sent by the Bears to fetch them a tasty meal? He couldn't sense these things any more.

"I know every boy by sight and by name," he stammered, "and who the mother is. Everyone does."

"I bet you do know them all," she said, eyeing him with frank curiosity. "People check up on you all the time, don't they? Making sure you don't slip away and hand over some little boy to the stickmen."

Setteo leaned his cheek on the child's warm head. Sorrel squatted and tore out a blade of the thick summer grass, which she shredded in her fingers as she talked.

"Do you remember your own mother?"

"Many memories were stored in what they cut off me."

She winced. "Ugh. Is it so bad, though? In my country, gelded colts live easier lives than studs do. They don't get hurt fighting over the Mares. Is it different for men?"

"I don't know, Hera." The suggestion had been made by Hera Kobba and some others that all the men of the New Holdfast be gelded after breeding, as the swampland males were. Well, Kobba would say that! He suspected, although he could not see it with his own eyes now, that the tall fem from the mines was often ridden by the spirit of the oldest and cruelest of the Bears.

They were both quiet, watching Veree scrub at his closed eyes with his small fists.

She said suddenly, "Does Kobba come here often, to see the children?"

He shook his head. "Never, Hera. She is barred, she and some others who are always angry."

Sorrel said, more to herself than to him, "Well, at least you give me answers. *They* don't tell me anything but what they think will calm me down and shut me up. What's the use of being Alldera's bloodchild if everybody treats me like some bent-born witling?"

Something fiery and lithe, that was what she was: not a Bear or a carrier of Bear spirits like Kobba, but something else. He trembled to think of having to work out relations with some totally new set of power-beings.

He had thought the Heras were daughters of the Bears, but now he doubted this. They worked so hard, and not always to a successful outcome, like losing almost the entire acorn crop the year before last because insect borers got there first. The Bears never worked at all, but they feasted well.

"What do *you* think will happen to this boy when he gets older?" Sorrel demanded suddenly. "To all the boy-children?"

Setteo rocked the slack, warm weight of the sleeping child. "Oh, I don't think, but they talk of it all the time. Some say, put them on the stagger stick when they grow body hair."

She bared her teeth as if in pain. "Not Veree! He's not like the others, he was raised free!"

"They are all free, for now," he soothed.

"But he never enslaved anyone! He's an innocent child!"

"It could be much worse," he said, to comfort her. "At Lammintown two years ago, there was a rising, very quickly put down. Lammintown men were punished."

"Punished, how? I never heard about that."

"They all went on the stick for a while. Two leaders were blinded to make sure they never made trouble again."

He smiled, trying to communicate the humor of it: "They were very poor servants after that, naturally, bumping into things all the time."

"Don't you dare joke about such things!" she said fiercely.

He began to hum to himself so that she would see that he was crazy and leave him alone.

Beyarra came back, her face flushed with the pleasure of seeing her little Karenn (a name she had found in a book). She looked at the sky and turned toward the piled diapers on the table.

"The wind's getting up, but it's a dry wind. We'll have to put stones on the corners so these things won't blow away. You too, Setteo, don't just stand there! Carry Veree back in with the others and come help."

Returning from this errand he heard her explaining, "—never run off, close as he is to Eykar."

He hung back, listening.

"Who knows what goes on in a madman's head?" Sorrel said. "They could plot something together. You seem to give them both the free run of the place."

"Eykar's not that kind of man," Beyarra said. "You don't know him." Then she got that dismayed expression that meant she wished she hadn't said what she had said.

"And you do?" the younger Hera said. She had an odd shimmer around her now, Setteo thought, glancing back as he went to fetch stones from the dry-well at the low end of the yard. A wavering of color, reddish and fiery—ah! His breath stopped.

He was seeing that again, the soul-light that had used to glow around people when he looked at them!

He took up stones slowly, tucking them between the curve of his arm and his ribs. Then he went back, barely feeling his feet touch the earth as he strained inwardly for the scent of the Cold Country.

"—your father," Beyarra was saying. "If you spend time with him, you could get to know him yourself."

Sorrel turned toward him, brushing her palms together. "Setteo! If you met your father now and knew him as such, how would you greet him?"

"Dancing, Hera," said Setteo. "It is best to make people smile when they meet you, if you are me."

Sorrel insisted. "No, what would you say to him? What would that mean to you, to meet the man who sired you?"

He felt the blankness on his own face like a wooden mask. He dropped onto his knees, the stones he carried thudding onto the ground around him.

"I don't know, Hera. Only tell me what would be right, and I'll do it."

Beyarra said gently, "Is there any older man you feel differently about than you do about all other men, Setteo?"

"One," he said readily (for he had few secrets about such things from her).

Beyarra sighed. "Eykar, of course. Silly question. Oh, get up, Setti, please, no one's going to hurt you! You lay out the rest of these, will you? I'll be right back."

She went back into the building, to say good-bye again to Karenn, no doubt. The children were stirring now, waking and calling.

Sorrel came very close and stared into Setteo's face. "They wouldn't harm the children, not even the boys, would they? It would be evil to hurt babies!"

"Sometimes," he said, picking up and carefully arranging the fallen stones again in the crook of his arm, "the children break things, they fight, they scream for things they want. Sometimes they get smacked for it, if people are tired or upset to start with. The girls are scolded more, hit less."

"Hit," she said, her eyes narrowing dangerously. "By you, Setteo?"

"Sometimes," he mumbled. "To keep order, and to teach respect and obedience. They have to learn. The boys, I mean." He glanced at her and away again, flinching from what he saw in her face. "Otherwise they'll be punished later, harder than anyone would ever punish them as foolish little boys."

Sorrel spoke through clenched teeth. "I'm the crazy one, to even think of bringing him here! Well, I threw this rope and I can coil it up again."

Setteo saw her more clearly, all bright with danger. He tried to back away, but she grabbed his arm. "If I tell you to do something, you have to do it, right?"

"Yes, Hera," he stammered. Then he added, craftily, "If I understand it, I do, but I'm not right in the head—"

"You're right enough. I'll come see you later, and I'll expect you to obey me."

She pushed him away and strode quickly after Beyarra.

Setteo stood swaying, full of fear. He lost his balance and lurched forward onto one of the pale rectangles of cloth—which dissolved to land his foot in one of many pools of black water dotting a white, open plain.

He scrambled madly for purchase, flooded with a storm of exultation and panic. He had not looked for it to happen like this; he was ashamed to be so flustered and unready.

"Watch your step," hissed a voice, and he saw a great, white, wedge-shaped head, streaming black water, break the surface of one of the pools.

"Oh yes, elder brother," Setteo panted, stepping quickly in place to stay free, treading water, as they said. "I remember the rules."

"The rules have changed," the Bear said, grinning yellow fangs at him. "So how can you remember them?"

"Teach me then, elder brother!" Nothing but boldness could save you from the Bears.

"Why should I?" said the Bear, with an enormous yawn.

"Because I'm also changed," he gabbled breathlessly, hugging his ribs for warmth, "and you wouldn't wish to see your poor younger brother fail out of simple ignorance, would you?"

"Stupidity is more like it," the Bear said. "So listen carefully, and don't forget: the boy that has been put into your hands you must keep, until you bring him to the Sunbear."

Setteo's mind raced. A certain amount of knowledge had always to be assumed, or they would make mincemeat of you—"When is the Sunbear coming? How will I know him?"

"What color is the sun?" the Bear said. "He comes bright with blood streaks, of course, and dragging captives behind his chariot. He won't be hard to spot. You must have your gift ready. You don't want to be caught unprepared."

Then it licked its black lips with its narrow black tongue and submerged again, and there were only the stones, and the diapers, and the grassy yard.

But he had been again to the Cold Country. Whatever happened now, he had been given renewed access, without manna or the chanting of the Bear-cult men, to the most powerful allies a man could have. Let the Heras make demands of him now, any demands they liked, and the men as well: he could find the answers he needed in the place where all answers lay.

Outlaws

Daya prayed, kissing one after another the smooth white pebbles knotted in leather thongs that hung from her belt. She no longer begged for understanding. If Moonwoman did not understand her by now, no one could.

Without fanfare Daya had taken up residence in the small guest house behind the Midfast Moon's House. It was a good sign that old Kastia hadn't come around trying to roust her out again. No one had brought her food, either, but Daya was comfortable fasting. The Lady lent her strength.

She was risking so much, and could yet lose her chance for redemption. She prayed for clarity. She prayed for success with Galligan, so that the reconciliationists like Beyarra would begin to trust and respect her. Upon that base so much might be built! That was what a person who was not a warrior by nature might contribute: the crafting of the greatest gift of all, a true, sound peace.

After moonrise she heard movement outside her door. She thought at first it might be people bringing Galligan to her after his hours of display for the instruction of other men.

But the sounds were furtive. Perhaps enemies come to kill her, to prevent her from sullying the Moon's House with a man's presence? Who would dare attack her under the Lady's own roof?

Looking out, she could discern two figures only, crouched in the shadows of the little portico.

She knew them even before they pushed in past her. Beneath the dingy white moon-cloaks that they threw off were the same ragged fugitives who had fled into the Wild years ago, after the attack on Alldera in the Watchtower: skinny, homely, hollow-eyed Leeja-Beda, and Tamansa-Nan with her dark, curly hair hacked short now.

"What are you doing here?" Daya demanded, her hands fluttering in an involuntary effort to magic them away again. "If anyone saw you come—"

"No one recognized us," Leeja said, sinking down onto her heels and hugging her knees to her bony chest. "These moon-shrouds are handy for getting around. We stop at the cairns. People let us be out of respect. And we have other friends in the Holdfast besides you, Daya; they help."

"Not everybody thinks we're demons," Tamansa added. "Idiots, maybe, to have done what you told us to, but not demons."

"That's a nice way to talk," Daya said, "when you're here to beg a favor, as always!"

She snugged the door as tight shut as it would go and drew them both to the farther wall, away from the window. Anyone creeping around out there might still catch sight of them but would have difficulty overhearing.

Of all the times for them to show up! She did not need more complications. "You can't have used up your supplies already!"

Leeja chortled. "We hardly use anything at all, Tamansa is so stingy." She smoothed her smock over her flat belly. "I'm thinner now than I ever was as a slave. Freedom is grand."

Tamansa said, "We came for Galligan. We want you to turn him over to us."

"To you!" She stared at them incredulously. "What for?"

"To take with us," Leeja said. She grinned and made a pumping motion with her fist. "We're getting lonely out there."

Tamansa scowled. "It's not a joke, Leej! We want him, that's all."

"How would you manage him, just the two of you? And feed him what? Am I supposed to smuggle you supplies for *three* now? Not that you'd hold him for long, even yoked and on the stick. He'd get away and vanish into the Wild, just as he meant to do in the first place. He's not stupid."

Tamansa said, "He's fertile. We need a child. If we come home with a daughter or even a boy-cub, people will forgive us and take us back."

"You've been living in the forest too long," Daya said coldly. "I'm amazed that you got this far undetected if that's how clear your thinking is!"

"We were dumb enough to listen to you at the Watchtower," Leeja said scathingly. "But there's nothing wrong with our thinking now. You'd be amazed how it clears your mind, scrounging a living of nuts, roots, berries, and worse in a wilderness."

"You're both old for breeding," Daya said, holding them hard to the point. No good could come of yet another dreary round of mutual vituperation over the past.

Tamansa said, "We hear that Jeeyenna had a child, and she's older than I am!"

"She had help, enough food, and Fedeka's medicines to ease the birth," Daya said, ticking these advantages off on her fingers.

"We can manage it on our own," Leeja said. "We'll have to. I'm not spending the rest of my life starving!"

Tamansa looked at Daya, her clenched fist under her chin, her huge, dark eyes low-lidded. "I've said it all along: you've been forgiven, but you're not willing to help *us* come back."

" 'Forgiven' isn't exactly the word," Daya said. "Come beg the Lady's protection and take your chances openly, as I did, and you'll find out. I'll help all I can."

She knew they would not risk this, but held her breath for their answer anyway. The last thing she needed was to have the old scandal raked raw again by the reappearance of these two! Now she regretted not having exposed them years ago. Kobba would have made short work of the only two of Alldera's attackers to have escaped from the Watchtower.

But Daya had always been inclined to hoard any secrets that came her way. Moonwoman approved of prudence and foresight.

"Help, from you?" Leeja crowed. "What a hope!"

"You started all our trouble in the first place, with your angry talk against Alldera," Tamansa said.

They were a savage-looking pair, squatting there wrapped in the rags of the clothing she herself had sent them, at great personal risk. There had never been any real hope of their going to the Grasslands and fetching back Juya and her baby, as they had originally planned.

She wondered if they knew about Veree.

"Galligan is our chance," Leeja persisted. "We hear you're getting him as some kind of sacrifice to Moonwoman. Well, we want him first!"

"And I explain his disappearance how?" Daya inquired.

Leeja shrugged. "Say your Lady took him."

"You want me dragged down for trying to get some wretched stick into your bed? Then who will send supplies to you at Endpath?"

Tamansa whispered, "If we tell the Council that we came to you three years ago, and that you've kept quiet about us all this time since—"

"When Kobba hears," Leeja said, picking up on her companion's thought the way they often did now, after living together so long in isolation, "what do you think she'll do?"

One of her front teeth was black with decay. Didn't they even look at each other out there?

Daya had helped them just to spite her enemies and to have allies, even such poor ones as this. Sometimes she obeyed an impulse, confident that an opportunity would present itself later to build upon unplanned action a stunning coup. Perhaps that instinct had betrayed her.

"Don't threaten me, please," she said icily. "It doesn't help any of us." Daya breathed deeply and thought of the Lady's calming light flooding her mind, revealing all in stark brilliance and shadow.

"Look out," Tamansa warned snidely, "she's thinking."

Leeja jumped up, swearing, and padded around the little room picking things up and slapping them down again: a bowl, a lamp, a dish of soap. "We're not going without Galligan!"

"I can't give him to you," Daya said. "You'll never get him back to Endpath. You let hope cloud your reason, and who could blame you?"

Tamansa's shoulders slumped. Tears glazed her cheeks. She could still look quite pretty, in uncertain light.

Leeja's jaw was set. She was on the edge of an explosion. Something must be offered, some promise to take the place of the prize they had set their desperate hearts upon.

"I have an idea," Daya said. "Less risky, and much simpler. Alldera's child is here—"

"We know," Leeja said. "No one talks of anything else but how you hitched yourself to this girl and used her to get yourself out of Oldtown."

"When Alldera gets home there will be a reunion," Daya went on, "a settling of scores between bloodmother and child. That girl harbors some grudges, you can read it in her eyes."

"So what?"

Daya's mind raced, bright and clear now. The Lady had made a path for her. "Fedeka will bring everyone together around their meeting, under the blessing of Moonwoman. You know how the dyer loves a ceremonial fuss. We haven't had a really big celebration since Alldera's return from Endpath, and that's nearly five years now."

Leeja nudged Tamansa. "She's going to tell us to wait."

Daya said quickly, "They've already sent word that Sorrel is here. Alldera must be on her way home. It will take Fedeka a short while to whip up some grandiose uproar over the reunion of the famous mother and daughter.

"I'll make sure you're alerted in plenty of time. You'll come in the Lady's white again, and then in front of everyone you'll beg the moon's mercy and tell of your hardships, and the useful things you've learned living in the forests—"

Tamansa sniffed. "We've learned to be hungry and sick and uncomfortable, that's what we've learned."

"You'll be taken back as people strong enough to admit your mistakes and accept the judgment of your peers," Daya concluded triumphantly.

Leeja muttered, "A nice story, very grand. If I believed you for one moment—"

"What don't you believe?" Daya said. "That I'll help you? That it can be done?"

"That I'm ever going to live like a human being again,"

the gaunt fem said. Her voice cracked. "*With* other human beings."

"Don't glare at me," Tamansa cried, knocking a box of white pebbles to the floor with a slap of her hand. "The one who's to blame is right there, telling us what to do—again."

Leeja grinned a predatory grin. "The question is, are we idiots enough to obey her a second time?" She leaned toward Daya, menacing in her intensity. "Will you hide us here till then?"

Daya tugged her robe tighter around her shoulders. A chill had entered the room. "You know I can't. They say I'm out of my place here as it is, and people take note of what I do."

"So we're to go back north," Tamansa said, "without Galligan. Without anything. This is a plan?"

"Then get some of your other friends to hide you," Daya said, wondering nervously if there really were such people. "Or go ask the swamp folk to keep you with them for a while."

"The Bayo-born?" Leeja sniffed. "They had their nice little Island lives for generations while the rest of us carried the masters on our backs. We don't want their help."

"We went to Bayo two years ago," Tamansa added smugly. "You didn't know about that, did you? We found an old beached ferry and floated a chunk of the deck back north, to be our summer home. That's all we want from Bayo."

"Then go back home," Daya said, shaken to hear that they had dared so much, and without warning her: how was it that no one had heard of that reckless expedition? "Go at once, tonight! You may have partisans among the NewFree, but if any men learn that you're here, they'll bargain that information for favors for themselves."

"Stinking sticks," Tamansa muttered direly. "I'm not afraid of them."

"Well, you should be," Daya snapped. "As outlaws you're at the mercy of anyone who knows you're here. The sticks nose out secrets just as keenly as we used to, when it was us in bonds. Go back to Endpath. When the time is right, you'll find five moonstones on a thong hung in the Watchtower."

Tamansa bent to scoop up the pebbles she had spilled. A lance of moonlight lit her profile. She had an ascetic look, as if she had been pared down and purified in the Wilderness.

I could be in love with her, Daya thought, *on another day.*

"Our Watchtower signal post," Leeja said dryly. "So obvious. You're sure nobody's caught on yet?"

Daya said, "Why shouldn't I send prayer tokens to the scene of my crime? People are willing to carry them for me. They know the Lady finds this meritorious."

Leeja hitched her torn tunic together over her ribby chest, scratched herself, and thought. She was as narrow as a reed doll, all knees and elbows, but nothing of the clown remained about her. Exile had worn hardest on her, perhaps because she was the more intelligent of the two.

"All right," she said at last. Tamansa groaned.

Daya nodded calmly, as if this had been a foregone conclusion. "Take the cakes and fruit in that basket for your journey."

"Your breakfast?" Leeja said, looking under the napkin spread over the basket on the bed. "Then we'll take it, cunnie. And we'll wait—for a while."

A Family Quarrel

"No," Eykar said. "No, no, no—do you hear me, Setteo?"

Setteo stood shivering, his body speaking terror, his eyes brilliant with exaltation.

"The Hera has instructed me," the cutboy said. "And the Bears also command." His voice was too loud, echoing from the walls.

Eykar knew the signs. Setteo had lost hold of the perspective and proportions of what he called the "warm world." Something had thrown him back into the country of his madness.

"Sorrel is an outsider," Eykar said, "who has come here on business of her own. She has no right to involve you."

Nothing changed in Setteo's expression. He was beyond the reach of reason.

Eykar knew how that was, although he had never entered Setteo's personal, illusory hell. After the Fall of the Seniors' rule, Servan had dosed Eykar with manna and dragged him like a slave from one ragged enclave to another, keeping him half-poisoned with the drug. Meanwhile Servan had cheerfully taken payment for "consultations" with the Endtendant of Endpath, The Man Who Killed His Father—a mighty Oracle.

It was hard to think back to those years between the Fall of the Seniors and Alldera's return. Occasionally a word, a scent, a sound would start a train of drug-sodden images coiling, darting and bleeding into one another. Eykar's mind would drop into that painful but sometimes beautiful place informed with the twisted logic of dreams.

But nothing of those days now endured. He needed to speak that language of madness to the madman he loved, but it was gone. The patterns of reading had stabilized his brain's connections; the easy shifts and slides of insanity were gone.

Christ, he thought, *she'll get him killed serving her obsession with that child! What am I going to do?*

"Take me to her," he said. "I'll speak to her myself."

And so he made his hitch-gaited way into the night that was banned to men. Setteo, clumsy with the confusions of world-hopping, was a risky guide. In time he would regain some sort of balance, Eykar hoped, but now he was oblivious to barking his shins or stumbling over mere physical obstacles.

The way, however, was clear: they followed the riverside road past the workfloors that adjoined the quays. The sparkle of starlight on the water, interrupted by the hulking blackness of the buildings, helped Eykar keep his bearings.

She was alone, sitting on a three-legged stool and twisting rush torches by the light of a hanging lamp. This task was usually done in daylight, with the north wall of the building opened for light. Nightwork increased the possibility of fire (half of the waterfront had burned down three years before because of a workfire carelessly put out).

She greeted his arrival with a sharp look, remembered that she must speak first, and said curtly, "Can't sleep; trying to make myself useful." Then, less surely, "Nobody will mind if I use a cup of lamp oil to make torches, will they?"

The way she was tying up the resin-stiff rushes instead of twisting them, her torches would fall apart before burning very far down. He didn't think it prudent to point this out. In her long tunic and soft boots and with her hair tied back with a braided leather lace, she looked young, mutinous, and determined. She reminded him of her mother.

Oh, it was too much! Why must this ignorant, reckless stripling crash into his life and wreck its fragile peace? He almost turned around and left.

"Well, come in," she said impatiently. "You won't be bothered here. The watch have already looked in on me twice. There's a flickstone game going on at the end of the next pier, everybody's busy down there."

"Hera, may I speak?" He was going to speak anyway, one way or another, but keeping to the forms of things might let him get a little further with what he had to say.

"Why should I let you?" she said. "Men aren't even supposed to be out at night." She was getting the hang of power over others; playing with it. Unreasonably, he saw that he had expected better of her.

"I have no choice," he said, his voice harsh with forcing. He hated being here, and he hated being afraid. "You've commanded Setteo to take a hand in—your affairs. It's a mistake. You don't understand his limitations."

She bit off loose cord and tucked the finished torch into a wide-mouthed basket at her side. All work that someone would have to redo later. "I've told him to help me rescue a little boy, a male child, from slavery. Why aren't you on my side in this? On Veree's side?"

"Because it's impossible. You'll fail, and they might punish you, but they'll surely punish Setteo. Why should he pay for the mistake you made in bringing that child here?"

"You're pretty bold," she said. "Being Alldera's favorite has spoiled you, I think."

This was so unfair that it left him open-mouthed. Finally he said, "May I sit, Hera? An old injury bothers me when I stand too long."

She thrust a bundle of rushes at him. "You can size these for me if you're going to stay. And Setteo can sweep up. They use the scraps for something, don't they? They use everything."

Setteo at once searched out a handful of willow twigs and dropped to his haunches to begin brushing the rush chaff into a neat little heap. He gave the impression of being perfectly sane and capable of following instructions, damn him.

Eykar, settling onto the lid of a wooden chest, pressed on doggedly, "Setteo isn't fit to be part of your plans. He already lives at the full stretch of the tolerance that he earned, if I may remind you, by saving your mother's life."

"Helping to save her," she corrected. She regarded him gravely, and her voice lost its edge. "You took a chance for her too, that night, a big one. Why?"

"Because she was and is the most fair-minded and sensible person I know of among the Free. I thought we all had a better chance of survival with her in charge."

How she looked at him! She could not know how such a stare, from a fem to a man, would have been met in the Old days.

"Well, what about the chance you took before?" She picked up a handful of rustling stems, regarding them with a critical eye. "When you sent her out of 'Troi by herself—well, not exactly by herself, since she was carrying me at the time."

He hadn't come here to talk about his past, and he certainly didn't want to be burdened with hers. He resented her for bringing it all up. Maybe if she were still a little kit, he might have warmed toward her (on a visit to the Children's House he had found himself inexplicably moved by Beyarra's little girl Karenn, with her malformed hand).

God, what a stupid thought! This "daughter" had a terrible effect on him, with her curiosity and her probing. Who could know the truth of the past once it was gone? Even the Ancients' books contradicted each other.

She said, "Why did you help Alldera escape from 'Troi?"

"We had been thrown more closely together than either of us would have wished," he said reluctantly. "So we had accumulated quite a history by then, although by the rules of the times we should not have. I suppose I understood enough about her life to want her not to suffer more pain at men's hands."

Her glance transfixed him like a knife through the heart: this close there was no doubt that she had her mother's eyes, frank and active. Could this whole, strong, passionate young person, full of desires of her own, really have sprung from the melding of minuscule secretions of his body and Alldera's? Could something clear and straight come from so much distortion, rage, and pain?

"You took a lot of risks," the girl observed, "for somebody you hated."

"I didn't hate Alldera. I admired her then, as I do now."

"That's a joke, right?"

"No," he said sharply. "Those people on the far side of the mountains should have taught you more respect for your mother."

Her lips tightened. "Don't be rude."

She regarded him with a youthful haughtiness that he found irritating but appealing, too. It was so transparent a cover for something very different, something about feeling lost and alone in an alien land. He knew those feelings. Endpath was the only home he could claim as his.

"If I am rude, Hera," he said formally, "it's because my concern forces me past the boundaries of caution. You don't know the—the intensity of feeling that the Free have about children. What you demand of Setteo is suicidal for him, and dangerous for you as well." *No matter whose child you are.*

"Is that what Alldera would say to me if she were here? Do you offer me a mother's advice?"

"I don't know what she would say." He handed her a bundle of reeds.

"You're not worried for me. The fact is that if Setteo falls you may, too."

He said nothing.

She threaded lacing through the twist of rushes in her hands. "I've seen slave punishment here."

Galligan, she must mean. Good; Kobba was a better teacher of the realities of the New Holdfast than Eykar could ever be. "It could have been worse," he said. "It often is, when certain steadying hands aren't present."

"Alldera's," she said promptly. "Who else?"

"Beyarra-Bey, if she chooses to intervene. Fedeka."

She pulled thoughtfully at her lower lip, an old person's gesture. He wondered, fleetingly, who she had learned it from.

"Even with both of them away," she said, "would Kobba really harm Setteo for helping me?"

"Worse," he said. "Myself as well, as you say. You must understand, Hera, my privileges—and Setteo's—come at a price. A number of jealous and resentful people of both sexes would rejoice at our ruin."

She said, "Do you sleep with him?"

How much could she understand, coming from a land where a man was seen only as a demonic enemy, scarcely a human being at all? "His life has been harder than most. He has never been master of anything." His voice caught. He coughed to free it. "Sometimes we can comfort each other. I don't want to see him destroyed."

"Do you love him?"

"Yes."

"Did you ever love my bloodmother?"

"That's a very dangerous question," he said after a moment. "Fortunately, I have no idea how to answer it."

"You should call me 'Hera.' "

He said wearily, "Must I?"

A beat of silence, and another, fell between them.

"No," she said at last. "I don't think so. I'm not one of the fems who took the Holdfast. I haven't earned the honor of that title."

Pleasure warmed him, brief and startling. At that moment he hoped she was his child, agile of wit, candid, and remarkably self-possessed in conversation. Even beautiful, he thought, in a hardy, unrefined way. Her muscular limbs seemed charged with poise and energy, her hair glowed.

Alldera had never had such vibrancy. Any observable spirit had been beaten out of her at Bayo, as a matter of course. Maybe this was what slavery really meant: the visible differences between the dam and the daughter.

"You're staring," she said sternly. "Is that what happens when I say you don't have to call me 'Hera'—all the rules go? Lend an arrow and lose your bow-arm, as people say."

"She told me, your mother told me, about you," he said on impulse. "The news was not kindly meant at the time. At least I think not. I never thought I would see you with my own eyes." Alarmingly, his already faulty vision was blurred with tears.

"What's the matter?" she said.

He shook his head, wordless. He shared this lamplight with someone attractive, intelligent, and daring, and she was—maybe—the result of something bitter and crippled that had happened between himself and Alldera years before. Potentialities destroyed or closed off in both of them now lived, perhaps, in this young person.

He wished Alldera would come back.

Setteo, sweeping up dust with gentle, abstracted strokes, sneezed a string of small, pinched sneezes.

"Is it upsetting," Sorrel asked, looking away now, "to find that you are someone's father? My father?"

Father, he shuddered. What joy had knowing his own father ever brought him? He was afraid she would reach out and touch him and he would lose himself in some way that could never be remedied. Something dark turned deep down, flashing, in his heart.

He said, "You are so forthright. It must be a healthy life over there in the Grasslands; not so—complicated as here."

He could not say, I hated my own father so much that there was nothing to do but kill him. *Did he see me, in those moments before I struck him down, did he see me as I see you now?*

He only thought of Maggomas the Engineer these days in moments of ironic recognition that the Free were taking up some of the old monster's ideas and discoveries to support *their* Holdfast: like the wheatfields Maggomas had established at 'Troi to supplement the failing lammin crop.

"You don't know anything about the Grasslands," she said repressively, jerking tight the knots on another torch. His answer had angered her. "You've never been there."

"Why would I go, even if I could?" he retorted, and pressed his lips shut. It was a long time since he had spoken so to anyone female.

She sat up straight. "You reminded me of somebody when you said that—oh, Sheel, of course. The Torrinors can be very terse in conversation."

A good thing Sheel didn't hear that!

"I hope this is half as hard for you as it is for me," she said crossly. "Where I come from, people don't have conversations with their sires. You can ride a stud horse, you can even talk to him, but he won't talk to you."

A sputtering laugh escaped him.

"Oh," she said. "There. You looked like a regular person just then."

"Hera," he said wearily, "I am not a regular person. I am one of the most irregular persons in the Holdfast and always have been, as you know very well."

"Well," she said, "so am I. A lop-eared mare has a lop-eared foal."

God-son, did they all talk in proverbs over the mountains? "Which makes it more dangerous for us to talk like this—"

"Oh, I'm in so much stupid trouble already!" she exclaimed, "Trouble at home, trouble over here—that's another word for 'irregular,' I'll bet: 'trouble.' "

"Do you think much about words?" he asked, surprised.

"No," she said. Again the frown, quick and mobile, a gesture of thought rather than emotion. How expressive her features were, unlike Alldera's slave-trained impassivity. "That is, not unless a particular word catches my ear in conversation. Like now."

"Words have saved me," he said. "Words are power. The Book Room is full of the power of words. If you give up this plan to steal that boy, if you stay here and study, I could—"

No. He remembered his father dictating his future for him.

"You could come," he amended, "and find out more, if you liked. Maybe they would let you bring Veree. The children should learn—"

"They'll never let you teach the boys!" she exclaimed.

"If you learn," he said (she was right, of course), "you could teach him. It's important. Command of words, spoken or stored on paper, is a kind of magic."

She cocked her head. "Then why are you working so hard to give that magic to men's enemies?"

Dangerous ground; tread carefully.

And get nowhere. Years among books had made him cautious. She was not cautious. She shamed him into frankness.

"The Free are not my enemies," he said. "Neither are the Riding Women. Some may think that they are, but they are mistaken."

She leaned closer. "If I'm not your enemy, don't act as if I am. Don't stop Setteo from helping me."

Clever child, full circle. So make her think it through, make her see: "Even if you succeed in getting the boy back, what other place is there for him on either side of the mountains? Where will you take him?"

Her expression darkened. She swore and jerked the cord out of her crooked work, shook the reeds even again, and started over. "Back to the Grasslands. I can pull some kind of family together around us, even if we have to go off by ourselves. My foremothers made a Riding Woman of Alldera Holdfaster. I'll make a Grassland rider of little Veree; near enough, anyway."

"And if you succeed," he said, "how will he feel about it when he's grown and finds that he fits nowhere? How did that make you feel? I know how it made me feel."

"You?" she said blankly; and then, "It wouldn't be the same for him!"

"It would," he said. "You just said that that's the best you can do for him, and it's no better than what you had yourself; maybe worse." She maintained an angry silence. "The Riding Women, judging by the little I do know of them, would never accept a male. They'd kill him sooner or later."

"But he wouldn't be anybody's slave!" Now there was a look of Alldera about her again, that righteous determination that could shift stars.

He didn't care about Veree, whom he had not even seen. He cared that both Setteo and this stubborn young person would be made to pay for kidnapping that child. Setteo would die, and Sorrel's own freedom could be taken from her on account of Veree. Damn that little boy for being so dangerous!

"What is it; do you agree with them?" she said, glaring at him. "You think they're right in what they do, your Heras who chain men up? You think all males *should* be slaves, raised to it as horses are raised to rope and saddle?"

He looked down at the floorboards between his feet. "Sometimes I do think that."

"Because you are a cripple," she said furiously, throwing down her lopsided twist of rushes. "You're jealous. You'd like to see Veree on the stagger-stick so he'd have to lurch and stumble, as you do."

"Would you rather have that," he said, "or more of the same miserable history that made women into 'fems'?"

"That can't be the only choice," she said.

"It's the only choice that your mother's people see. It's the only choice that I see when I think of the Old Holdfast."

Her lip curled back from her clenched teeth. "That little boy's mother, Juya, did not cross the mountains to have him end up treated like a stock animal!"

"Better a stock animal than a monster."

"Better a human being, man *or* woman, than a master of slaves!"

Silence, except for their stressful breathing and the faint lapping of the dark river waters outside.

She said, "Are you right-handed? Is that the hand that you used to serve out poison to men sick of life when they came to you at Endpath? I bet a lot of bond fems were good and sick of their life; too bad they couldn't go to you. Did you fell Raff Maggomas with that hand, the way we club our culls down in dry years? Listen, murder-man: I don't believe that all boys have to grow up to be like you."

He hadn't meant to include himself in his condemnation of his own sex. He had begun to think of himself as a builder, a helper, in his own modest and indirect way a creator, along with Alldera, Beyarra, and other forward-striving spirits of the New Holdfast. But she was right to remind him that he had more blood on his own hands than anyone.

"The old men made you a killer," she said. "I've heard all about it. Their horrible rules made freaks of men and fems alike. Veree won't turn out like that if he's not forced to. You're not like that yourself any more, or they wouldn't let you go freefoot."

"Who knows," he said in a hard voice. "Given the right circumstances . . . The risk is always there; in Veree, too."

"Ah, the risk," she said, sitting back with her hands braced on her knees. "Every time I ride my horse she could put her foot in a hole and throw me on my head. You've already been thrown good and hard, I can see that. You're all beat-up and busted and you've done desperate things, so you're scared to take chances any more.

"But you're old. Veree is a child still. You can't keep a colt hobbled all the time for fear he might someday kick!"

He wanted to say, "It's not that I'm old, it's that you're so *young*," but that would only make things worse. She did not think of herself as young; what young person ever did? She thought of herself as grown-up and wiser than her elders.

"Sorrel Alldersdaughter," he said, "listen to me, I beg you. These Free people will kill that boy rather than let you take him away to grow up out of their sight and their control. You made a mistake in bringing him here. It's done; live with it as best you can, that's what sensible people do. Not everything is correctable."

"Who'll kill him?" she asked ominously.

"Someone, here or in the Grasslands; someone will. And if you try to defend him they'll kill you, too. You must part your way from Veree's way. Leave him to a man's life here, harsh as that may be. It'll be easier on the little one. I'm an old wreck, as you say, and Setteo, there, is a young one. Veree has a chance for something better. Let us live our lives as best we can, and you go live yours."

"How can you talk like that?" she demanded scornfully. "You just don't want anything to happen to your cutboy, a useless, crazy person who helps you with your precious books."

"Veree isn't even yours," he said. He got stiffly to his feet, impelled to do something to forestall her folly.

She glared up at him with bitter certainty. "You're going to tell them, aren't you?" she said. "Well, go on, then! Get out, leave me alone."

"There's no talking to you!" he exclaimed. "Can't you think, can't you see what madness you're planning?"

"Rape-cock," she said in a tight, deadly tone, and she pulled the knife from the sheath at her back and presented the blade threateningly. "You fucked my bloodmother when she was a slave and had no defense. I could kill you for that. No one would blame me if I took the revenge that she's too—too femmish to take."

He backed a step, bumped into the storage chest, and sat down again on it, hard. "What do you know about it?" he said breathlessly. "You were saved from such knowledge by your bloodmother. You're a child of freedom because that was her gift to you. Mine too, if you'd stop to think!"

A fierce, pleading expression transformed her face. "And I'm giving someone else that gift, is that so terrible? I'm going to pass it on to Veree. You can't stop me. Now, take your slave's slave, there, and get back to your place before you're missed."

"Why did I think I could talk to you?" he barked. He shook off Setteo's helpful, steadying hand, and limped out into the first pale shine of morning.

A Dark Room

I felt as if I were raiding Red Sand Camp all over again to lift the Hayscall Racer. But this was harder: I was alone, easily recognizable, and beset by enemies. Yet although several people greeted me, no one stopped me on my way to the Children's House.

They were busy cleaning up after the evening meal. I moved through a swirl of cheerful chaos and found Veree and a little girl taking things out of a wooden box in a corner. They were talking happily as if to each other but really to themselves, as children sometimes do.

"I get my spoon," he chanted, "my wood horse. You can have the straw horse, and Effie's red stone—"

I held out my hands and called him to me.

"I need my horse!" the child said, making a dive for the toy box. The little girl screamed in outrage and tried to shut the lid, which set him to howling and struggling with her.

"I'll make you a new horse, a better one," I told him, grabbing his hand.

Another child, darting past behind me with others shrieking in pursuit, caromed off the backs of my legs; just like a childpack in full career.

"Come on, Veree," I said. "Aren't you glad to see me?"

"I'm playing with Biri," he said. But the little girl was chasing the child who had run into me, screaming like a marsh-devil. I clutched Veree's hand and walked him toward the big open doors.

"Come on, we'll take a ride on Patch, remember Patchie? But she won't carry you if you're noisy."

"Can we give Biri a ride too?"

"Not tonight. Next time, all right? Now, hurry up."

Leesann looked up from cleaning something off the floor. I waved jauntily to her and kept going, out into the grassy yard.

I saw Setteo hurrying toward me. He was supposed to be waiting around the side with my horses. In a panic I hissed, "Where are my horses, you dickfuck?"

He smiled timidly and held out his hands. In each palm lay a toy horse, woven of dried grass and twigs and trimmed with a brightly colored string bridle.

The gates slammed shut across the yard. I pushed Setteo away and saw Janna throw the wooden bar. In the doorway to the Children's House behind me Beyarra-Bey stood with two others.

Veree, hanging back against my grip, began to whine, "Ma, let me go. I want my horse. Setteo took all the other horses and I can't find mine."

When they closed in and took him from me, I disgraced myself by bursting into tears of frustration and despair.

Leesann gave Setteo's toy horses to Veree, and carried

him back into the Children's House. I saw him looking at me over her shoulder. He waved and called good-bye, a stiff-legged little horse clutched in each fist.

Now that he was out of range of flying fists or butting heads, I tried to fight my way free. But they were too many, and because they were angry they were not gentle.

I ended up sitting on the ground with someone crouched behind me, holding my arm hiked up my back so that my shoulder flamed. Over my ringing head, there was a lot of palaver to which I paid no attention. My overworked feelings were dulled and out of reach. I had failed. It didn't matter what happened to me.

I didn't struggle as they marched me away (amid a good deal of argument still), and locked me in a storage room that smelled of dried fruit, sweet and faintly putrid.

Daya and Beyarra came at dawn the next morning. Beyarra brought a tray of scramble-fry and came inside to eat with me. Daya, hugging herself deep into the folds of her white moon worshipper's gown, stood in the doorway in silence until we had finished.

That was soon. I was starving.

Ignoring Daya, I said to Beyarra, "Well, are you going to keep me here until Alldera gets back? I won't last that long. I'll die if I spend another night shut in here. It's like being buried alive."

Beyarra said, "You can't just steal our children! To try to take one of the boys—you must have known we would never let him out of our hands! You're lucky you came out of it with no more than some bruises."

"He's never been one of your children!" I yelled. My voice sounded deafening and half crazy in that enclosed space. I tried to contain my distress. "So have you given Setteo and Eykar honorary fem status for betraying me?"

I hardly knew what I was saying; I just wanted to wound them—these fems, those men, anybody I could. I had had terrible dreams all night, although I felt as if I hadn't slept at all.

Daya said, "They were right in what they did."

I squinted balefully at her. "Don't speak to me, traitor!"

"My dear child," she went on in a kindly tone, "we would have hunted you down. Do you think you could escape us in our own country? Don't give me that hateful look, Sorrel. You don't understand my actions, but I know more about the problems of the men in our Holdfast than you do. I'm only telling you the truth."

Beyarra nodded and said in a subdued tone, "She's right. Things must change for our sons and daughters, but this, what you tried to do, doesn't help."

I leaned toward her, to exclude Daya. "I dreamed that fems were making soup. The bones in the pot were a child's bones, and I saw the head of a fresh-killed sharu in there. No Grasslander would ever eat sharu; or a little child, either."

Beyarra reached anxiously out to me. "Are you feverish?"

Daya shook her head. "They don't ever lock people up in the Grasslands. Listen now, dear child: Beyarra and I have been talking together all night."

I glared. "Why? I thought you two hated each other."

Beyarra sighed. "We talked, *and* we hate each other."

Were they allies against me? Daya maybe, but my blood-ma's bedmate? Was there no one I could trust in this cursed place? I had to stand up, but when I did, the ceiling loomed close and heavy over my head. It made me feel sick, and I sank down again.

"You people," I groaned. "Your thinking twists and branches like the tunnels of a sharu burrow. I wish I'd never come here!"

Beyarra said soothingly, "But it's good that you did. People need to be reminded that men must be made human again somehow, and your feelings about Veree are that reminder. We don't want you to go away. We don't want to keep you locked up. But you have committed an offense which you must defend before Alldera herself at least, and then maybe before the Whole Land Council as well."

Daya added, "When the time comes. Meantime it's better if you don't stay here at Midfast, near the children."

"You mean I should go away?" I said, trembling with outrage. "*You* should go away, Daya, not me! This is all your fault!"

"We'll look after the boy," Beyarra said, laying her

short, tapered fingers very gently on my arm. I threw off her touch.

Daya said coaxingly, "We don't hate the little males, Sorrel. Who could? They're just children, not that different from our little daughters. And many of us had infant sons taken from us in the old days . . ." Her voice trailed off.

Acting, I told myself angrily. *She's a born betrayer.*

Beyarra cleared her throat. "I have spoken for you as best I could; but I can't be responsible for keeping you out of trouble until your bloodmother returns. Daya is in no position to do it either, as I'm sure you understand, and no one else has volunteered. But we have come up with an idea."

I leaned my forehead on my folded arms, too worn out to fight them. Here in the Holdfast I was a worse failure than I had been back home—a useless, clumsy, impulsive fool who could do nothing but put herself and other people in danger. Someone had better have some ideas for me, because I certainly had bad ones for myself.

Alldera's child! I was lucky that my bloodmother wasn't around to see what a mess I had made of things. I was going to have to depend on other people to clean up after me, while I had no choice but to resign Veree to his fate.

I blubbed miserably to myself while they told me: Beyarra herself would escort me back into the mountains, to the place called the Refuge where Sheel Torrinor was working. If Sheel were willing—and as one of my sharemothers, she could hardly refuse—I would stay there with her until Alldera sent for me.

"Wonderful," I groaned. "You'll deliver me to Sheel."

"Don't you trust even her?" Beyarra asked sadly.

"Of course I trust my raidmother—in anything but this! She won't help me. She's a Riding Woman, she despises males."

"Exactly," Daya said with satisfaction. "She won't be tempted to let you get yourself into more trouble over a boy-child, that's the point. Then she and Alldera together can decide what to do about you."

Which was precisely how the Riding Women would have handled the problem, if it couldn't be hashed out in the Chief Tent: send the troublesome persons home to their mothers to work it through in family. In Alldera's absence that appeared to be her bedmate, Beyarra, and my treacherous aunt (for it was clear that these two were acting on their own, trusting that Alldera's authority would shield them from blame).

Well, anything was better than another night in that close, cloying darkness; I agreed.

They locked me in again and went away. I squatted on the earthen floor, sick with defeat and trying to hold down my food. I couldn't even think of Veree. I could barely think at all.

What seemed like years later, the door opened. Sunlight blinded me. I was so disoriented by my time in that makeshift prison that I could hardly stand.

Beyarra had brought mounts for two. Daya could not come with us, having given up riding as part of her submission to Moonwoman. "Besides," she said with maddening coolness, "some one has to stay and explain where you've gone to. I was a storyteller once, I'll make a good tale of it."

Of my failure, my misery, my idiocy. Was she involving herself with my fate to undercut Alldera with such tales of the Conqueror's daughter? Or to try to make amends to Alldera for past malice? Or just to establish her own importance among the Free?

I said bitterly, "I don't understand anything you people do or why you do it."

"That's all right, child," she said, "we're all in the dark now and then." Giving my arm a squeeze, she set a cushion of old sacking in the open doorway of my prison and sat down to await the inevitable questions and accusations.

Once clear of Midfast's outer straggle of buildings, Beyarra and I rode briskly toward the northern arm of the mountains. Riding my good Patchie, I felt as if I had been born again into the wide world.

Beyarra must have thought my silence was due to worry, not the slow return of my draggled spirit.

"Veree will be all right," she told me, over and over in different words. She was like the Caranaws, back home, who can't let a thing go once they've accomplished it but must talk and chew it over endlessly afterward, convincing themselves that it's really happened, and for the best.

"I'm tired of the whole subject," I said at last. I couldn't think of Veree without feeling sick. I didn't believe for a moment that Daya, or Setteo, or anyone could prevent Kobba from harming him if she felt like it. I had seen her in action on the Steps.

Beyarra said wistfully, "I wish we were just out riding together. My enemies will make a spicy stew of my doings with you and serve it to everyone."

I grinned nastily at her. "Why would you have enemies?"

She looked hurt, but went on as if I hadn't spoken. "That's what comes of reading books, they'll say of me—pride and foolishness and rash action, like some arrogant master!"

I had to laugh; anyone less like an "arrogant master" than this diffident, dainty person would be hard to imagine.

She gave me a thoughtful look. "I don't think you appreciate the complexities of the intrigues and rivalries among us. There's so much at stake for everyone, and no clear rules. Our wrangling can get very raw, even over little things."

I shrugged this off: I didn't really care. One night in that black box had darkened my heart; and anyone might lock Veree away in similar darkness if they wished to. Suppose that little girl he'd been playing with accused him of some transgression, out of childish spite?

He could never survive being locked up that way. I barely had. I felt as if I had been split apart, a person with "two shadows."

"What I can't understand," Beyarra said, "is why you didn't wait to come here at a time when you could have brought that child straight to your bloodmother."

I smoothed my horse's mane, unwilling to explain the pressure I had felt to take Veree over the mountains. "I thought I could count on Fedeka. She *was* my oathmother, sworn to come to my aid if I ask her to. I thought the Free kept their promises."

She was quiet for a moment. Then she said very softly, "Fedeka didn't betray you. She just didn't know what else to do. She had no idea of what you were about to slap down on her plate, and in front of everyone!"

"That would make no difference to an honorable person. She's my oathmother, sworn to help me," I insisted.

She answered with a kind of admiration, "You see things so simply! When Fedeka took Daya under the Lady's protection, many people were outraged. They said she was using Moonwoman to rescue a confederate from execution. They thought Fedeka might have been in the assassination plot, too, because Alldera didn't believe in Moonwoman and said so."

"Horseshit," I said, but I had no heart to argue the point.

"There was no evidence, of course," Beyarra said, "but some people are still suspicious of the dye-maker."

"I thought she was respected on account of being so close to this Moon Lady of yours."

Beyarra sighed and reached over to brush dried mud from my horse's shoulder. "Well, her motives looked a little—complicated, even to her friends. Fedeka used Daya to show the Lady's protective clemency, but you could read her actions in a worse light. Fedeka still has to be careful, for her own sake. And she'd rather die than compromise the Lady in any way."

I shook my head in bafflement. "But why do you have to *believe* in something? Besides yourself, your line, your friends and relations, I mean."

"Most fems' experience of humanity hasn't been very encouraging," Beyarra said after a pause. "We seek the reassurance of something more. And there are always those who use religion as a tool to get what they're after or as a screen to hide their real intentions."

I raised my eyebrows. "I thought you and Daya were friends now."

She wrinkled her neat, pointed nose in distaste. "Allies; not friends."

"Well, what is Daya after?"

"You knew her in the Grasslands. What do you think?" When I didn't answer, she said, "Daya says she agrees with you about the boy-children. I think she's telling the truth."

"That's what you talked about all night?" I sneered. "That must have been fun. *I* think she's crazy and wicked."

"However corrupt her motives," Beyarra went on, "she's made no secret of her dissatisfaction with the way things are between men and women. Some of us share that feeling, Sorrel."

"You have funny ways of showing it," I said.

She tactfully let the subject drop and we rode in silence for a while. Then I asked where she thought Fedeka had gone. She waved her arm.

"Somewhere out here, actually. Sometimes she just retreats from things; Alldera's done much the same, taking this trip south." She smiled a shy, conciliatory smile. "I do my hiding in books, usually."

I think that was the first time I realized she was only a few years older than I was, and I wondered uncomfortably whether Alldera ever thought of her as a daughter.

"What's that?" I asked, pointing. Ahead stood a single figure, beside a cairn of stones.

Beyarra, squinting ferociously, tugged her horse to a standstill. Then we rode forward again and she called out a greeting: "Fine day, friend, and how are you faring?"

The woman on foot ignored us although we rode pretty near. I took breath to hail her myself, but Beyarra put a finger to her lips. We pulled up and dismounted. Following Beyarra's lead, I hobbled my horse and squatted in its shadow to wait.

Beyarra put her mouth to my ear. "You know her, don't you? That's Vayonna, a First Free from the Grasslands."

I looked again, surprised. "I didn't recognize her with her hair cut short. Why is she all alone on foot in the middle of nowhere? Is she being punished for something?"

Punishment was a subject prominent in my thoughts.

"No, no," Beyarra whispered. "She's on a prayer walk. Most people go in company but some prefer to travel alone. The Whole Land Council recommended that she be by herself for a while."

"Why?"

"She's been fighting pretty fiercely with her lover. Their hearthmates were worried, and asked her to go. We are not so many that we can afford to lose anyone."

I was baffled. "You mean she might have injured this other person? You'd think everybody would have had enough of fighting in the war against the men."

Beyarra gnawed at her thumbnail. "War makes people crazy. Sometimes they stay crazy for a long time, or fall back into craziness long after it's over."

"So what does Vayonna do on this prayer walk, besides think about being not so quarrelsome when she gets back?"

"She'll make the rounds of every Holdfast cairn, giving heart offerings to the Lady at each stop."

I thought of all the cairns I had seen in just my brief travels in the Holdfast. "But she couldn't have known all those dead fems!"

"Not just people she knew," Beyarra explained. "Fedeka started this custom more or less by accident on one of her plant-gathering walks. She went all over the place with a book from 'Troi with pictures of plants in it. I had marked out some especially promising ones. She was looking for useful plants that we could raise in our gardens or gather wild.

"But people began to say that she was working with Moonwoman to lay to rest old, unhappy ghosts by remembering all the dead commemorated by the cairns. Now others walk over the Holdfast when they can, hoping to help soothe the spirits of the lost."

"That's morbid," I protested. "What's the good of winning your war if all you do afterward is walk around reminding yourself of every bad thing that ever happened here?"

"What's the good of living through the 'bad things' if you forget it all after?" Beyarra said with a trace of asperity. "Then nothing's learned."

"Maybe what you need to learn most is to forget," I said.

She sniffed. "You can only say that because you are Grassland-raised," and after that we both let it alone.

At length Vayonna finished her prayer and came over to greet us. She embraced me with somber pleasure and sat with us over tea, which she insisted on making for us from her own supplies. She did not seem quarrelsome to me, only tired and sad and introspective—which maybe meant that the prayer walk was working.

We camped together that night. Vayonna did not ask

about people back in the Grasslands. I volunteered little, for I felt that she had deliberately withdrawn from her memories of that other life. Next morning she left without a word of farewell, walking away with her saddlebags of provisions slung over her shoulder, and we continued on our way as well, heading northwest.

Compared to the Grasslands, the Holdfast even in its hinterlands was thickly peopled. Half an hour later we came upon another lone foot traveler by a rock-topped ridge.

Fedeka was grubbing in the earth under a hedge of thick green shrubs bordering a fenced field. Her figure and her posture were unmistakable, even hunched over on the ground and at a considerable distance from us.

I felt an echo of the childhood impulse to race up, leap out of the saddle, and hug her, but she had betrayed the bond of those days. Beyarra-Bey was the one who embraced her, standing slight as a child next to that solid form. She spoke so quickly in choppy Holdfastish speech that I couldn't catch more than a phrase or two. Fedeka looked past her at me and I saw her breast rise in a great sigh.

Alone in the open under the day's bright sun, the dyemaker looked shockingly old. "Aren't you going to come and greet me, my girl?" she called in such a longing tone that my anger burst out.

I shouted, "You shouldn't be out here alone like this!" And I just bit back the words, "You stupid old fool!"

"I'm all right," she said, walking toward me. "You're not still mad at me, are you?"

Her plaintive words were killing to me, but I couldn't bring myself to offer forgiveness.

Beyarra trailed after her, peering anxiously around. "Where are the Flatstone people? They're are supposed to be working these fields; their hearth house is right over there, isn't it?"

"They went off to somebody's freenaming over at Hidden Springs," Fedeka said. "They'll be back tomorrow."

"I worry about you, camping out here by yourself," Beyarra said.

Fedeka shrugged. How well I remembered that big, lopsided gesture! "I didn't help conquer the Holdfast so I could run around in nervous little fem gangs everywhere! I'll go where I like in the company I like—or no company, when that suits me better. I already told those Flatstones that I didn't want them hanging around. You know that Divviny-Vye, always trying to cadge something for nothing. They'd tell her to move on out of their hearth if they had any sense."

She laid her wide, grubby hand on my rein. "So, Sorrel my girl, Beyarra says you've created such an uproar that you're to go stay with Sheel until Alldera comes back."

The despair of my long night in the storage room washed through me in one final, cold wave and left me at last. For the first time that day I felt fully awake and alert.

Also (like Fedeka, but in my own way) I was fed up with being told what I must do. I swung down from my saddle. "I'm not going anywhere. I'm staying right here, and I'm going to build a cairn. I see plenty of rocks up on that little hill."

Beyarra opened her mouth in surprise; closed it, staring where I pointed, and said, "A cairn! For whom?"

"For Veree," I said. "For his future, his freedom, his life. For my hopes in bringing him here. You can show me how to build a prayer tower to your Lady, Fedeka. It's the least you can do."

The dyer sighed again hugely.

I turned to Beyarra. "If anyone wants me, tell them they'll find me out here with Fedeka, heaping up stones for Juya's son."

Sight of Home

In a sullen, argumentative straggle, the men trudged south. Engo and Arred were still sick, and no one wanted to face Erl's lads with their own ranks under strength. But they grew increasingly restive, recognizing signs of home in some of the vegetation, or thinking they did. Servan felt their impulse building just to keep on going until they crossed into the Holdfast at last.

No one had openly challenged his authority since that fool Blix, after their disastrous flood crossing, had reminded everyone that they could have stayed at Rock Pool living an easy life hunting wild goats in the mountains.

Of course Blix hadn't suggested this back at Rock Pool. There they had been high on the capture of women, tree-sweet, and goats. And what was the point of possessions, if not to return to the Holdfast wealthy beyond their wildest dreams?

Difficult wealth: the goats, the astonishing goats, had turned out to be mad, unpredictable, and destructive by nature, consuming shoes, belts, the sleeve of a leather shirt. Shareem said they were just hungry. Jonko said they were the true demons of the Wild.

Eight had escaped, two more had sickened and died; the big billy had drowned; and since then a young and succulent ewe had been found with its neck inexplicably broken.

No one admitted responsibility. Servan guessed from Hak's smirk that he and a few of the younger fellows had taken steps to get a meal of roasted goat. Hak was not above flexing his own authority, derived from having captained a coastal ferry in the old days.

At any rate, the band they had managed to round up at Rock Pool from the bounding, bleating chaos of the larger flock was down to four adult animals and two kids.

Still Servan knew he could reenter the old life not as a skulking outlaw but as leader of a group of hard men united (mostly) by shared adventure and richer than Erl and his cronies had ever been. It was an attractive prospect.

Not that he couldn't do fine on his own still, if he had to. He was not fixed in place yet; not old, just older. And skulking around alone was a boyo's game.

Meanwhile, effective leadership took constant alertness, and, even after almost seven years of staying alive together in the Wild, a great deal of hard work. He disliked work, but disliked even more taking orders from someone else.

He signaled a halt in a wide glade sloping down toward the clifftops, and signing to Jonko and Kedge to come along, he took a turn through the nearby woods. They slapped and swore at the biting flies that were such a torment, but that was all the life they found.

"Have the women go dig that patch of taydo before we move on tomorrow," he said, nodding at a lush-looking stand of leafy stalks. "Don't let them run the damned goats through here first, or there won't be anything left for us."

"That little brown goat is stumbling lame," Jonko said hopefully. "Did you notice?"

"Forget it," Servan said. "That's the only male we've got. If he doesn't live to grow up I'll have to put you to pronging the ewes personally."

Kedge wiped at his forehead with the back of his broad wrist. "We can send out hunters to the north later and fetch more bucks any time. We'll be giving the orders, when people see what we've brought back!"

D Layo said, "I wouldn't trust Erl's City lads to catch a goat if they were shitting goats out of their assholes. Think about having to go back north to snare new stock yourself, next time you get a yen for roasted kid."

But it might not be possible to keep the tiny herd intact as far as the Holdfast. Sometimes he thought the men lusted for meat more than for sex.

"Hey, Migayl," he said, squatting down by the little dry-grass fire that Salalli had made, "I've got a knot in my shoulder. Tell your Tarisha to come give me a rubdown."

Migayl said, "What's wrong with your Sal, then?"

Servan stretched, letting his hand come to rest, casually, on the butt of the Rock Pool gun where it rode snug and heavy against his hipbone. "She's mending my shirt. Everybody knows your Tarisha has good hands. You made a good pick there."

But he himself had made the best pick: Black Sal, the woman belonging to the top man of that miserable town; a woman not every man of the Holdfast would have had the nerve to take, either, black as she was, like the legendary nigs who had helped bring the empire of the Ancients down.

He had had a moment of terror himself when he killed their leader, a brown unman with long fingers and great glistening eyes. Servan had met this fear by throwing himself upon the woman: dive in, and let her do what she might against him. Which was little enough, it turned out. She was just a jumped-up cunt like any other, under her dark hide.

Taking her had strengthened his authority at a time when it had begun wearing thin. And he had the Rock Pool gun, a far more valuable prize than any woman.

But force was nothing without thought.

The rest of them had only their slings and knives, for that fool Ardy had taken the other weapons of the Townsmen—bows for hunting wild goats—and burnt them, saying that they were cursed and would turn in the hands of true men and wound them instead of their enemies. Ardy had been afraid that the Townswomen would get hold of those weapons and slaughter them all in their sleep, that was all. If he hadn't gone down with an infected wound taken in the fight at the Townsmen's welcome feast, the other Ferrymen would happily have killed him themselves for his idiocy.

Servan was grateful to poor old Ardy now. The gun was much more impressive in the absence of those bows; maintaining authority came first.

When he'd left the Holdfast, he had chosen young companions for their energy and resilience. Hak, the one-eyed ferry captain, had made a natural second in command. Six men had died, two of violence, the rest of hardship, heading north. The remaining fourteen were tough and lucky. Servan was now the oldest. The older they all grew, the more that mattered.

The funny part was that he had never expected to live past thirty, let alone into his fourth decade.

He smiled at Migayl, who was thirty-two or so but older-looking, aged by hardship as they all were. *I can still whip you, boy, with or without a gun.*

Hak, reclining nearby on his elbow, grinned approvingly; he too would be a Senior now by the old rules, but he seemed content not to challenge Servan's leadership. He could be an irritating commentator though, without saying a word.

Migayl growled, "Suit yourself; but your Sal will give Tarisha a bad time for it."

"They hold hard to their new men, don't they?" Servan said. "They know how lucky they are to have us."

He sat watching Salalli sew up a rip in one of her dead man's shirts, Servan's shirt now. Kneeling behind him, Tarisha rubbed into his skin a slippery goo they made from some sort of vine. The stuff smelled rank but it kept the small black flies away. Well, most of them. Hak had scratched bites on his neck until they had turned into nasty red boils.

All I have to do is keep them moving, Servan thought, arching his tight shoulder involuntarily away from Tarisha's probing fingers. *God's son, that hurt! And she knew it, the yellow bitch!*

Old Erl will shit himself when he sees these unman bitches, not to mention the goats! Let him try bossing anything or anybody after we get back!

He tried to envision their homecoming, but it wouldn't come clear. Suppose Erl had been taken down by one of his followers, suppose they'd had a wave of sickness decimate them, or fallen into a deadly religious frenzy? It wouldn't be the first time.

He daydreamed about slipping away in the night and driving the goats south, with Hak, maybe. No, Hak was sour, sad company these days, since his best lover had been killed in the fighting at the Pool Towns.

Go alone, then, never mind the damned women and their leaping, chewing, thieving goats. Never mind any of it. He could get back faster alone.

No one to worry about but himself, what luxury! It would be like the old days of doing just as he pleased despite all those huffing, snorting Seniors, and no ties to anyone.

Except to Eykar, of course; but that tie Servan had always broken at will. The Endtendant was probably dead by now anyway (no, not Eykar, who had always been too much at odds with his life for his life to let him go easily). Eykar's eyes would pop when he saw d Layo again. Blood would color his pale cheeks and he would lose his precious composure and fall, as ever, before he was pushed.

D Layo studied the backs of his own broad hands. The veins stood up under the sun-browned skin. He had a thickened, yellowed nail on the left thumb, which had been mashed in a tumble of rocks.

Not a Senior's hands. But, networked with the ingrained dirt and the scars and calluses of clawing over six years' survival out of the Wild, neither were these the artist's hands that he remembered. You wouldn't know he was rich, with his ragged clothes, his patched and shapeless shoes of beaten bark, his dirty hair, and these hands. Christ-God-son, he had grown used to stinking like a work-worn Junior of the Old days!

"We're nearly home," he told Salalli. "Smile; you'll be somebody in my country, a lucky stranger saved from the Wild."

She went on sewing. Her silence annoyed him.

"You don't think you're lucky? Whatever's left of the Holdfast, it'll still be better than those cold stone huts you people were living in. And we'll have the pick of it all."

Silence.

"Where's that kit of yours, that Liss?"

Now he had her attention; he could tell by the careful flatness of her voice. "She saw some berries back on the trail. She went to pick them. Shar took her and Luma back there."

His head came up sharply, and he felt Tarisha's hands lift from his shoulders. "You let them all go together?"

"Children need time by themselves."

His back was tightening up again. He would do more than slap her face if that boy bolted, with or without his sisters. He didn't have to say so. Despite her bold words, she knew.

He turned to Tarisha, who had a red-lipped mouth bent in a sullen bow. "My shirt."

She handed it to him, first wiping her oily hands on the grass. He restrained an urge to seize her wrists and put it to her right there, fast and fierce, in front of Salalli. Into that swollen-looking mouth, wet and sweet. Tarisha's palms and digging fingers on his back had aroused him.

Migayl would fight. Jonko wouldn't—he'd let anyone prong that slut of his—but Migayl would fight over Tarisha. Someone could get hurt, maybe killed. This close to home, where numbers would matter, it wasn't a risk worth taking.

"Get going." He gave Tarisha a shove with his foot; she hurried back to Migayl, who turned his back on her.

It angered Servan sometimes to find himself living among people all tied to him with a thousand invisible threads. Any way he turned, the threads tightened and cut him somewhere. They held him back from the swift reachings of his heart, which were as blithe and sudden as they ever had been.

"I'm going to go see what's keeping those youngsters," he said. He pulled on the shirt Tarisha had handed him and told Salalli to put up a windbreak for the night.

He walked quickly among the spindly trees and brush, glad to leave the others behind, with their wants and their fears and their jealousies. Salalli's brats were not far away. He heard them arguing in whispers before he saw them.

He stood still and listened. He could make out enough of their odd, swooping speech to guess that the subject was escape. There was nowhere to go but the ruins of their old home. And they knew that if they ran away, he would punish their mother.

He stepped quietly into view. Three tight, scared faces turned toward him.

Still warm from Tarisha's hands, he ordered Shar and Luma back to the camp with the slingful of berries they had gathered. He would stay with Lissie to gather the last fruits (*and the first*).

They hesitated. He said, "Do you want me to take this up with your mother? Do what I tell you."

Then he set to work with Lissie, plucking ripe and unripe fruit and getting stains on his hands. She tried to stay out of his reach but her concentration was a child's. When he chose his moment he was quick.

She struggled, and then she quivered, and then she wept. Her tears, so nearly silent, were to be expected; it was her first time, and she was such a skinny little thing. But pretty, with her golden skin and big dark eyes. She must learn not to spoil her looks with crying.

"You're young and small," he explained as he did up his britches. "That's why it hurt. It gets easier later on. But don't let anyone else get at you. If they try, you tell me. Not Shar or Luma or your mother: me. You hear me, Lissie?"

She lay motionless, curled on her side, eyes closed. Why hadn't her mother prepared her better? What else could the girl have expected?

He said sharply over his shoulder, "Come on, get up! Bring the fruit. Your mother will be worrying about you."

He walked back to the camp, thinking about tackling the rising headland before them next day, and what they might see from its height.

Lissie dawdled in after him. Looking back, he saw her deliver the sack of fruit to her mother and go to help Shareem and Luma milk the goats. She did not lie down with the rest of them at the brush shelter that night but sat up late, poking at the fire with a stick.

Servan saw Arred watching, a hungry gleam in his gaze. He'd had his eye on that girl for some time. They were not men of the Old Holdfast, to avoid fems out of superstition. And if Servan could take on one of the darkest ones and rule her without harm, why wouldn't others with an appetite for it think of fucking that woman's brown-skinned daughters?

Well, now they were all aware that he had claimed Lissie for himself. Most particularly he wanted the boy, Shar, to know it. That way he would understand that taking his sisters with him in an attempt to escape would be considered a theft, for which Salalli would be made to pay.

It was a fascinating game, this business of "family," rich with ways of controlling what other people did, often without even having to demand what you wanted out loud.

If the mother had said one word about Lissie, asked one question, he'd have smacked her silly; not that he was a cruel man, but hunger was no better for his temper than for anyone else's.

Salalli was quiet, but he felt her lying awake beside him. A quick, rough fuck would have given her something besides her daughter to think about. But he had spent himself completely on the girl.

"Go to sleep," he hissed. "You're keeping me up, lying there staring at the dark."

They made good progress the next morning, although bad footing forced them to swerve inland through dense brush. When they came out again onto rising ground with a sea breeze blowing over it, Servan called another halt for food and rest. He took Shareem and two of the lads on ahead a couple of miles.

He saw smaller trees of the home-Wild and then the tall ones, and then bare turf sloping toward a low drop to the sea. His heart lifted. He inhaled the wind, tasting the salt tang that toothed it. He pointed southward along the coast.

"Down there," he said to the others, "we'll find first Endpath, and then the Holdfast. We're as good as home!"

Djendery set up a wind-shredded cheer.

"Anyone would think you never expected that I'd get you home again," Servan said sourly. He saw the gleam of tears in Djendery's eyes before the other man looked away.

Hak stared south under a shielding hand. "There've been times I thought I'd be an old man by the time you did."

Shareem stood a little apart, gazing out at the far horizon and dabbing furiously at his nose with his shirttail.

"This is our sea, now," Servan said, coming up soft-footed behind him. "Yours, when you learn to be one of us."

The boy's back went stiff. The old men hadn't been crazy to take children away from their dams and their sibs. Look how knowing that Servan had had a little fuck with the sister made Shareem so sullen. He wouldn't have cared if he didn't *know* she was his sister.

Servan hunkered down beside him. "Don't be stupid, boy," he said kindly. "Someone was going to lay Lissie for the first time. I was easy on her. Will you take a little advice? Think of yourself, not your sisters. You'll soon be a man, made for fucking girls yourself, not picking fruit with them. There's a lot I can teach you if you're not too stubborn to learn."

Shar hung his head and made no answer. Servan looked at his thin, smooth neck, then got up and walked away.

He remembered a boy, the only survivor of a village they had raided west of the Pool Towns in their third year out of the Holdfast. The Ferrymen had been disinclined toward mercy or forethought about keeping women and children alive then, particularly as those women had defended their town alongside the men.

Servan had let the lads have that boy to mark their first

victory in the Wild. They were starved and exhausted and deserved something, and he couldn't have held them back.

They had taken that lad along for sex and as a taster of unknown plants that might be edible. His name had been—what?—Orry, something like that? He had finally eaten something that killed him. Servan thought he had done it on purpose.

A weakling. The Holdfast was a hard place to live, but it made you tough. He thought about what he himself had survived in the Boyhouse (and Eykar; it had been much worse for him). Orry wouldn't have lasted a week. The northerners, it seemed, had bred their boys to work instead of fight, had hoarded their harvests and sung to their goats, and had never ventured beyond their own little territories.

So Salalli's Shar was a disappointment. He had no spark of wildness in him, only barely disguised resentment and a secretive look that suggested plots and plans.

Well, he was young and pliant, with a promise of sultry sweetness if properly brought along. Maybe Erl the Scrapper would pay well for him, which would gall Black Sal. Servan could sell her too, and find something fresh for himself among Erl's younger fems.

He thought now that they should have taken other captives from those lake villages instead of wiping them out. But they hadn't been strong enough, or rich enough in supplies, then, to encumber themselves with prisoners.

On the other hand . . .

How he hated looking back! You saw so many mistakes that it would be so much more pleasant not to notice at all. Worse yet, you saw alternatives that might have been mistakes or might have been brilliant successes, there was no way of telling any more. The one sure thing about them was that the time to choose them was past.

Most of his men didn't think about the past. They didn't think much at all, actually; a man's nature was to act, not to sit around thinking.

Who had taught him to think about things? Eykar, of course.

Otherwise Servan supposed he might have turned out like the rest of them: do it (if you think you can carry it off) and figure out why after (but only if you must). He felt real affection for the ferry lads when he thought of their unreflective impetuosity and directness.

Without him they would have died, savaging each other for a root, an edible flower, or a sticky palmful of nuts. Well, maybe Hak could have held them together, but he doubted it. Hak had closed up since the Juniors' rebellion. He was not the jaunty, confident, young ferry boss Servan had met on a fateful night all those years ago.

Servan clapped his palms together and stretched his shoulders, feeling the hum in his muscles. *Not an old man yet, by Christ-God-son!*

They camped that night just outside the seaward edge of the forest and used wood blown down by storm winds to fuel two small fires. In the morning they woke in a rolling fog. They kept well within the trees as they moved southward again, avoiding the invisible edge of the cliff.

Servan's right leg stung with each step, a reminder of an old injury. What he needed—what he would have as soon as they got home—was a pepper poultice for his knee and hot mannabeer for his soul. The small stock of the drug that he had brought with him had lasted less than six months. Today he could taste the phantom flavor on his tongue.

The Pool Towns women walked in a nervous cluster, wrapped to the eyes. They led the goats on ropes, if you could call that halting, struggling process "leading." Shareem handled the two large goats that pulled the laden carts.The men swore as their clumsy bark shoes slid on wet roots, wet stone, and wet, tough grass.

They had to stop again that afternoon. The ground rose in a stony slope that was too treacherous underfoot. Instead of burning off, the fog had thickened.

Dojan's woman dropped her balanced load of baggage and he would have beaten her into a useless cripple if Servan had not intervened. He sent Dojan, Blix, and Migayl to scout ahead, to keep them occupied.

The others made a flimsy camp at the edge of the dripping wood. The men were testy and keyed up. Servan read them easily: they were afraid of getting home, now that home was so close.

What if Erl the Scrapper surprised them, somehow, and overwhelmed them, or even tricked them out of their hard-won booty? That was how they themselves had overcome the Pool Towns. They all knew how devastating a swift, unexpected, and savage attack could be, and they would be heavily outnumbered.

Vigorous young Ferrymen who had gone exploring for the hell of it were returning older and grimmer, with something to fight over, something to lose. *We did better when we had nothing,* Servan thought; once they wouldn't have cared a fem's fart for Erl and all his men.

Once, he would have come back from fucking Lissie and pronged her mother too, and then gone and played dickery-dock with one of the lads, all without strain. Once he would not have felt the fog gnawing on his knee. Someone had hit him there with a flung stone during the first village battle. Servan had never imagined that recovery included permanent pain.

If this was part of not being young any more, he didn't want to consider the horrors of actually becoming old.

The goats breached their makeshift pen before sunrise. While trying to gather them again, Garris slipped on wet rock and fell. He died down below on the pebbled beach, his head oozing bright blood onto the gray sand.

Torby caught one of the women and pressed his knife to her throat, roaring, "Your damned beasts led him to his death! We should have left you all to rot with your men, you black north bitch!"

Servan said, "Let her go, Tor. We didn't bring her all this way for you to throw her away now."

Torby pushed the woman away, his face working with shock and grief. "You give me the boy, then," he snarled, "in Gar's place. You've got those girls of Black Sal's; the boy should go to one of us. I'm left with a cold bed now, thanks to these damned witch-women!"

"You and I will talk about that," Servan said pleasantly, curling his fingers around the butt of the gun, "when the right time comes."

"Done," Hak said, putting a hand on Torby's shoulder. "Now you wait for us a little. Everybody waits while we tend to our crewmate."

They scrambled down the cliff with some others to straighten Garris' limbs, retrieve anything of value he had on him, and pile rocks over his body. It was a hard thing to have happen, so near to the end.

"Bad luck," Hak said when they came back up.

"I make my own luck," Servan answered lightly. "You know that from when I took my friend the Endtendant riding on your ferry to Bayo, on his way to find his father."

But secretly he feared the idea of his luck, turned bad, breathing damply at his ear. Although Torby came back up subdued and no longer in a mood for confrontation, Servan was careful not to turn his back on him.

The next afternoon was bright and clear. Near mealtime the scouts sent on ahead returned, tired and famished and jittery with excitement.

They had reached Endpath, they said, which lay just behind the next headland southward. They had found signs of people living there, not in the sealed-up fortress but in the wreck of an old ferry (they were in furious disagreement over which one) moored at the dock, cut down to a sort of heavy raft with a rickety cabin on it.

They had seen no one, but ashes of old fires, pits of buried garbage, and a small cache of moldy laver indicated two or three people who meant to return.

Laver from the City ponds; what were Erl's Citymen doing way out here? Something was wrong, he could taste it.

Over a meal of the toasted laver, which they had brought back with them, the men brooded on possibilities. Servan listened to the desultory talk and looked at their hollow-cheeked, sunken-eyed faces. After a while he said, "We go down there and wait, and we grab these boyos when they come back to their boat."

"They could be gone for weeks," Migayl argued, "months, even! Who cares about a couple of fellows love-nesting off by themselves at the old death house? We should march on past them, right down to Lammintown."

"Not," Servan said, "if there's a chance to lay hold of these outliers, whoever they are, and ask them a few questions first. Don't you want to know how things are at home these days, Migayl?"

Hak chimed in thoughtfully, "If Erl has died of too much beer at last and that mean-mouthed, grabby-fisted, gut-grinder Nazon Morz has taken over the City, I want to know about it *before* he glad-hands me while one of his lads knifes me in the back. And I'd want to know how many fellows are with him, and who's against him, and where they're all located."

They sucked at fragments of laver toast caught in their teeth and looked into the fire.

Migayl muttered, "Be cautious, be careful, find out first—that's how the Seniors used to talk."

Arred shook his head. "Hak's right; we'd be fools to leap without looking first." Other men nodded, or said nothing, and Migayl shut his mouth and sat glaring into the fire.

Servan sent Shareem west with the goats to a little valley where the animals could graze without their bleating giving the men away to anyone else wandering the coast above Endpath. No one needed to guard the Townsfolk. So far from their ruined villages, on the very edge of the men's country, where could they run to?

Then the Ferrymen hunkered down in the forest above Endpath and waited. It was like an attack on a northern town, only safer, since by all the signs they outnumbered their quarry—the men living at Endpath Dock—pretty handily. They submitted their eagerness to Servan's command and Hak's judgment.

Even in sight of their homeland, Servan thought they were still his men. But he knew better than to believe he could rule them unchallenged past the border of the Holdfast.

III

Bear Dancers

They invaded the Book Room, quick men with hard, purposeful faces. *This had to come sometime,* Eykar thought, and moved hastily away from his work table so that no books should suffer damage.

Arjvall stood with his arms folded, his feet spread wide by the stick between his ankles, regarding Eykar impassively. He said, "You're invited to a singing, Endtendant. Sit down. You're to travel fast and in comfort."

They shoved him into an old wicker chair, first sweeping to the floor some books he had piled on the seat, and Arjvall took up the oil lamp Eykar had been using. Then, hoisting him chair and all, they carried him to a sidechamber of the ruins. They lowered him through a trap door in the floor (he knew it was there but had never used it) and carried him through tunnels of the old Midfast water system, sections of which were unused now.

He held on to the creaking armrests and tried to remember just where he had left off in *Boardroom Ninja;* difficult, since the book was largely incomprehensible. The thought that that gibberish might be the last text he would ever read hurt him immeasurably.

Panting, his bearers shuffled down dank, rubble-strewn passages, then ducked through a huge, ragged hole in a stained foundation wall. They descended some none too sturdy steps into a long, low, painted chamber luridly lit with fire.

It had to be some Senior's private provisions cellar in an abandoned uptown villa sealed up by the Heras.

Chokky Vargindo's people were there, a dozen or so, many of them moving with the strange, wide-legged grace of the sticked. Vargindo himself was giving directions.

Eykar's chair was set down. His carriers moved away, and he dared to breathe freely again and wished he hadn't. Since the Heras liked men fresh, staying rank had become a gesture of resistance. He had given up trying to convince the hard-core haters that keeping clean was part of staying healthy.

Payder didn't seem to be present; maybe he had listened.

Close by, three men daubed each other with colored clay, striping their bodies and faces. One, a sponsored older man called Relki, was describing an improvement some men had devised for the plows used in the wheatfields.

His presence was disquieting; few sponsored men involved themselves in the risks of Bear business. Relki, wrapped up in what he was saying, drew the design improvement in clay on Jorag's back for Maddery to examine.

"Bad idea," Maddery said. "If the yield is increased, the bitches eat better."

"When they eat better, we eat better." Jorag craned his neck to try to see his own back. "At least when things go well they don't hog all the extra like the Seniors used to do."

"That's because fems are too stupid," Maddery said.

"Fuck, Maddery," Jorag said disgustedly, "nobody's so stupid they won't hoard food if they get the chance to."

"Then sharing their extra food with us must be a trick," Maddery muttered, smearing away the sketch Relki had made. "Nothing fems do is straight."

"Crap," Jorag said, with a huge yawn. "They're mostly like us, some straight, some crooked."

"Then what are you doing here tonight," Maddery sneered, "if you have such a liking for the bitches?"

"Hey, they've got a liking for me," the other man said, grinning and patting his crotch. "Once they get me to breed-bed. But I'd rather they wore the yoke and stick than me, and I wouldn't mind some help to change things back the way they were."

Relki drew an ochre line down his own thigh. "Be careful what you wish for, cockie," he said in a low voice. "You might get it."

Vargindo appeared and slumped down on a chipped sitting block across from Eykar's chair. Up close, he was smaller than Eykar remembered, a skinny, knotty-muscled man who was years younger than he looked. In shadow, beyond him, other men were busy at something Eykar could not make out.

The chamber had been cleared of whatever it had once held—there were scrapemarks on the hard dirt floor—and large, manlike shapes had been painted onto the walls. Their postures suggested set scenes from the manna-dream cycles that men of the Old Holdfast had been taught as children.

"Something's happened, manna-man," Vargindo said, leaning forward with his hands on his thighs, his sharp elbows aggressively akimbo.

Eykar said warily, "Not that I know of."

"Doesn't your cutboy talk to you in bed?"

Eykar's heart took a tripping beat of apprehension.

Vargindo smiled. "We have news from the Cold Country."

That again! Eykar said testily, "Yes, yes, someone is coming, a warrior with an army. What's new about that?"

"Setteo hasn't told you?"

"Just bits and scraps, the usual pathetic rescue fantasies, if that's what you mean."

Vargindo paused, absently fingering a nasty-looking sore on his cheek. "Your cutboy," he said, "is a problem for us. Just lately, I mean."

"I told him to keep away," Eykar said. "Is he here?"

Vargindo's hand settled hard on Eykar's knee just below the old scar, pinning him in place with a crawl of pain under the skin. "He's all right. But you're going to have to keep a closer eye on him from now on."

Eykar made himself wait without moving.

Vargindo lowered his voice further, leaning closer. "Not that we aren't grateful. He dreamed us the Sunbear. That's why you've been let be, with your books and your bitches that pretend to learn reading. Because of him, see. Setteo."

"He dreamed you the Sunbear," Eykar repeated. "You mean he had a—vision, a seizure? But all that has stopped. He hasn't done that for a long, long time—"

A sly smile curved Vargindo's thin lips. "Well, he got hold of some manna a while back—"

"He got hold of . . . ? Who gave it to him? You?"

"Shut up and listen," Arjvall cut in, stepping nearer.

"We got Setteo to journey to his Cold Country for us,"

Vargindo said, "nothing terrible, it was only half an hour. He'd been after us to let him try, so we did. When he woke up he had seen the Sunbear—"

"You mean all this—this Bear worship started with Setteo?"

"And we're grateful," Vargindo repeated, nodding earnestly. "His story put such heart into the lads, I can't begin to tell you. Well, we all know he had a real vision once, the one that took him to the Watchtower when the hags turned on their chief bitch. So when Setteo sees things we take notice, believe me."

"Unlike some visions that certain other people have claimed to be real before," put in Arjvall. He leaned forward, looming over Eykar.

"Now," Vargindo said, "other lads have learned to visit the Cold Country and carry messages. They know how much manna to drink and what to look for when they get there. But Setteo comes around begging a drink at our singings, since he can't get there on his own."

They were both silent, Arjvall staring at him, Vargindo studying his own grimy knuckles.

"And you," Eykar prompted, "don't want to send this mighty prophet on a manna dream again because . . . ?"

He stopped, looking from one of them to the other.

"Look," Vargindo said kindly, "he's young, he was born too late to learn the old chants, the old dreaming ways. He doesn't know the style we want to draw on, if you see what I mean."

"Style?" Eykar said. He wasn't used to feeling stupid. It made him angry. "What in the name of Christ-God-son are you talking about, Chokky?"

"Setteo told us, that first time," Arjvall said briskly, "that the Sunbear was coming, and that he had death-power in one finger of his right hand, and that he led men with hearts that could devour a fem and the horse she sat on in one gulp."

"Well, not exactly," Vargindo began, but Arjvall glared at him and he shrugged and fell silent.

"He hallucinated," Eykar said, "because you drugged him. What of it? People surely aren't taking this seriously."

Vargindo fixed him with a grave stare. "Yes, they are. I

do, anyhow. You do too, Arjvall, don't you?"

"Oh yes," Arjvall said solemnly. "Who'd deny such an uplifting, hopeful prophecy?"

"You mean you saw a way to use him," Eykar said scathingly. "To use his visions. And now you don't want him coming around begging manna from you—why?"

Vargindo nodded with the satisfaction of a man rewarding a slow pupil who finally catches on.

"It was all just fine, very inspiring," Arjvall explained. "But he also said that the Sunbear approaches attended by horned demons and shadow people from the Wild, which is arguable; and we don't need argument. Worse yet, it sounds a little like how the bitch Alldera came back to the Holdfast, and look how that turned out. The lads have enough doubts and fears to contend with without problems of—interpretation. And he said some other things that could confuse people."

"What things?" Eykar said. *Oh, Setti, what have you gotten yourself into here?* No wonder they had sent Setteo home with Payder that time. If Eykar still had his old, sharp sight, if he'd been watching other men instead of struggling over his books, he would no doubt have noticed a difference in the sticks' attitude toward the cutboy.

Vargindo said patiently, "Our fellows who dance into the Cold Country bring back the news we need. But your Setteo—he's a wild throw, you never know what he'll come back with."

Eykar caught the tone of calculation in Vargindo's voice.

"Ah," he said, sitting back. He could not contain his contempt. "You mean he sees truth and tells it, and you need seers who are more—suggestible."

"Reliable," Vargindo corrected pleasantly. "Hell, the lad is crazy, always has been. Who knows what kind of nightmares he might spout next time? You, of all men, know how changeable those dreams can be."

He knew. Setteo might see failure, destruction, and death for them all, Sunbear or no, and they could tolerate no more of these things than came to them daily as part of their present lot in life. He was almost sorry for them.

Arjvall said curtly, "It's better without him. Keep him out of our way, Book Man, or we'll get rid of him."

"I don't control Setteo," he answered. "God knows I try, but it's like managing the tides. I'll do what I can. Is he here now? Just send him back with me—"

"Not yet," Vargindo said, sitting back also and conveying more threat at that distance than he had close up. "You're to stay for the dancing. You need to understand the importance of all this."

Vargindo left to join the others.

Eykar sat rubbing the ache in his leg where the man's fingers had gripped. He could scarcely believe that Setteo had somehow provided, out of the world of his madness, a ritual of hope and aspiration for these men. Setteo's Bears, of all things, had replaced the gods that had been lost with the culture of the Old Holdfast.

So much for helping Beyarra to destroy the old Holy book of the Ancients (those stories of the thundering, bullying Father-God had ignited an inexpressible rage in his heart: had they not, men and fems alike, had enough of tyrannical fathers?). These men worshipped instead the Cold Country and its Bears, stolen from Setteo of all people! No, the cutboy had delivered it all up to them, in exchange for the manna he needed now to take him there, but they were refusing to pay up. They denied him a return to the land of his own madness.

A hopeless situation altogether, but there was no point saying so; Arjvall certainly knew, if Vargindo didn't. No point attacking this new religion in a room full of its adherents, either.

The rattle of sticks was becoming a rhythm now. The singing had begun. Eykar wondered which of the men in attendance were spies for the Heras: at least one, he was certain. Relki, maybe. Later there would no doubt be a conversation with Beyarra-Bey about his own presence here.

The clacking of sticks and the clink of cuff-chains made their music, with a high, nasal singing style that he supposed the dancers had brought back to them from the Cold Country.

Elder brothers, lend us power!
By trickery we were made captive.
Lend us power, lend us vision!

Our enemies are sly and cruel.
Lend us power, lend us fortune!
We will feed the bitches to you,
Femmish flesh and bone and muscle,
Femmish terror, femmish pain.
Lend us power, lend us greatness!
Let us roar with Bearish voices!
Lend us hearts of frozen steel,
Hands of granite, cocks of stone!
Elder brothers, lend us power!

In the center of the cellar, a caped dancer was turned this way and that by helpers with bulky-looking hoods of coarse sacking pulled over their heads and shoulders. They propelled him all around the cellar, winding among the pillars, with a glinting dust drifting down from them in the firelight.

It was a coarse, clumsy business. Eykar wondered where Setteo was, and how long this mummery would last.

Suddenly the two attendants threw off their hoods, revealing another covering beneath: rough masks of straw. A bowl of warm beer was passed among the spectators by the men with clay-striped skins. Eykar handed it on without drinking.

Vargindo was watching him. What did he expect, that the man who had been the Oracle would sip from that bowl and give them all a free prophecy?

Then he knew what must be coming, and the hair stood from his skin. Vargindo was watching to see if he had the guts to watch. *Damn him, and damn them all.*

The dancer representing the messenger to the Cold Country, a lad named Kurryan, danced naked now. He was crowded closer and closer by the straw-furred "bears," until they forced him down between them, lifted their kilts, and fucked him, mouth and anus, with ferocious force.

"Power, power, power!" the onlookers chanted, faces flushed and gleaming as they stamped in rhythm to the strokes of the "Bears."

That had been Eykar once, naked receptacle, "holy" victim, drug-bound Oracle. That had been him, helplessly inflamed, shiny with sweat and shuddering with the impact of his faceless assailants' lust, while others stared and rubbed at themselves under their clothes. Many of the men in the room had witnessed his degradation, recreated here before his flinching eyes. Some of them had worked him as the "Bears" worked Kurryan now.

"Power!" they chanted, they roared, they prayed. "Power!" they begged, with all the strength of their tumultuous and anguished hearts. Hopeless to hope that the shine of tears was not noticed on Eykar's cheeks. Well, let them look, then, let them see. He was damned if he would wipe those tears away. Maybe some of them might guess that he shed them as much for these ruined men and their desperation as for his own bitter past.

It all stumbled to a ragged ending in the stifling heat that had built up in the cellar. The two "Bears," panting loudly in their masks, picked up the slack, shining body of the exhausted dancer and carried him away into the darker recesses of the cellar.

The watchers murmured and sighed and coughed and quietly dispersed. Maddery took a long-handled push broom and began to sweep the stone flagging, coughing in the rise of dust and chaff that had fallen from the "Bears' " headpieces.

Vargindo, standing by Eykar's chair, said, "When Kurryan has slept it off he'll give us the Bears' message, and he'll be grateful for the chance to serve them. We're serious about this, you see." Vargindo's face loomed close, menacing. "Keep Setteo away. He could lead the bitches to us out of carelessness, he's so eager to be part of things here."

"He's not an idiot," Eykar whispered. Christ, he was tired. "And there's nothing he wants from the Free that he would betray you for. Where is he? Send him back with me to the Book Room."

"Alldera-bitch thinks she protects you," was the rasping answer. "But Setteo protects you, because he gave us the Sunbear. Now you protect him: tell him to find some other dreamland to play in."

Two men lifted Eykar's chair and shuffled rapidly back toward the Book Room with his weight balanced between them. His mind veered and skipped over the scene he had just witnessed.

That was my past. It's not just Setteo's visions. They are using my past as Oracle, thinking that its magic will create the future they want. But there never was any magic, only Servan's clever way of keeping the two of us fed in bad times.

Close to his ear, one of the carriers said softly, "Enjoy yourself, Endtendant? Kurryan was good tonight, really tranced. He's been out working near where two of his friends died in the war, and he's not been sleeping on account of it."

Eykar did not turn his head; he knew the face he would see. "Why do you hate me so much? I tried to save your friend."

"But he died," Arjvall replied, as if it had happened yesterday instead of five years past.

"I'm no prophet. I never claimed to be. D Layo's 'Oracle' was his creation; it was a farce, a swindle."

Arjvall deliberately jarred the chair as they rounded a corner in the stone passage. Eykar winced. The other carrier swore.

"What was my dead friend's name?" Arjvall asked.

Eykar held his breath through the tiny delay before fear kicked the name into his mind: "Bavell. Bavell Charkin. He had the quarry cough."

"He had the quarry cough," Arjvall mimicked bitterly. "I got it too, but I survived. He would have survived. But some bitch thought he was too sick to be worth keeping and wagered him away. One of those damned plains witches won him and killed him for the hell of it, and all because he had the quarry cough. Say you're sorry."

"I've sat with a lot of dying men," Eykar said. "I was always sorry, and I still am."

"No you're not," Arjvall snarled. His spittle dampened Eykar's cheek. "Your life-man is still alive."

"Setteo isn't my—"

"Not Setteo. Didn't you hear what we said? He's padding around in the Wild, getting ready to come home and be a hero. So what do you care if my soul's brother is gone? What can that mean to you anyway, after all the other dead boyos? You don't wake up each morning asking yourself why you're alive and the person you loved with your whole heart is dead."

"What—who are you talking about?" Some huge blade was poised to drop, severing his life in yet another place from which all things would be changed. He sweated with fear of the answer, although he already knew in his dread-filled heart.

"The bitches used to tell their stories," Arjvall said, "about runaways who would come back from the Wild and rescue them. One day it all came true. It's only justice that now it's the same for us. A brave man risked his life to go exploring in the Wild. Now he's coming home to help us.

"Only maybe he won't ever get here; or he'll arrive and turn out to be the same selfish, giddy, showoff prick that I remember, not fit to lead an uprising; but until he falls down on the job, your old heartman is our Sunbear. You see?"

Oh God oh God, his mind wailed, *let it not be so.*

Aloud he said, "Someone's seen him? You've heard from Servan, you've had a message?"

Arjvall said in a bitter singsong, "The Bears told Setteo, and Setteo told us. Vargindo doesn't want you to know yet; he wants to make it a surprise. But I want you to know. Ask Setteo yourself, if you've got the guts."

It was impossible, of course; but who knew with Servan, luck's golden lad, master of surprises?

They set him down in the Book Room. Setteo was there, had been there for some time, tied up and rolled in a blanket, singing in a muzzy whisper to the wall.

Arjvall lingered when the other carrier had left, leaning over Eykar to pin him in place in the creaking wicker chair.

"Just remember," he said, "If you say one word about what you saw or heard tonight, I'll slice Setteo's heart out. And then I'll come for you. You're alive because Vargindo thinks you might still be useful. But when even he agrees that you're all used up, Book Man, I'll come claim you."

Lovers

Daya knew which ointments to prepare although she could not read the labels Fedeka had lettered onto her pots and jars. The pet fem had not wished to learn reading, that insult to the storyteller's art. But over years in the Grasslands she had seen the old healer treat many injuries, and her memory was good.

With Fedeka out wandering, nobody else in Midfast had the nerve to forbid Daya the salves stored in the Moon's House. She had healing skills herself, no one could challenge that, and such things were the province of Moonwoman. And no less a person than Beyarra-Bey had returned from escorting Sorrel out to Fedeka's camp and had backed up Daya's explanation of that event.

All this had made people reluctant to challenge Daya, as they could not be sure where she stood. She had acquired a sort of tacit authority (at least until Alldera should return and clarify the matter) with which she was well pleased.

In effect she had won the right to keep Galligan with her until the Whole Land Council—or Alldera—said otherwise. The Council would not meet for more than a month. This late in August, the Free were too dispersed among the tasks of harvesting to assemble for formal events except in dire emergency.

As she walked coolly through the white-walled courts and passages of the Midfast Moon's House, some of the resident devotees turned their backs on her. But that was as far as anyone dared go.

She had been emboldened by their reluctant deference to command Galligan to be sent to her here for treatment of his injuries. On her insistence his yoke had been removed (otherwise it would be impossible to deal with his mashed fingers).

"Come," Daya murmured to the man who hovered in the doorway behind her. "Shut the door."

He ducked his head and shuffled in, his stagger-stick clattering annoyingly on the raised threshold. How anyone could stand listening to that chuttering of wood and metal all day long, Daya could not imagine. She much preferred the symbolic ankle cuff, which had become a form of masculine jewelry among sponsored men.

Galligan sat down warily on the bench that she indicated, where daylight fell on him from the window across the room. He had regained his voice in the week and a half since his ordeal on the Steps. He carried his left arm in a sling as Daya had prescribed, giving his broken fingers the elevation they needed to minimize swelling.

"Unwrap that," Daya said, washing her own hands in the basin on the work counter. She thought a silent prayer to the wash water as she poured it away. Fedeka would object, of course, to any such devotions attaching to business concerning a man. Daya smiled to herself, humming an old love song about how the Lady, in her guise as Ocean, carried the heroine Enka safely out of bondage to an island of love and pleasure.

Galligan mutely presented his injury. The whole hand was still swollen and discolored, but the worst of the wounds had scabbed over cleanly. Even the middle finger, which had received the heavy punch of the yoke's end when Kobba had knocked him off his feet, appeared to be healing straight.

He quivered but kept silence as she applied a poultice soaked in an astringent mixture.

"Hold that firm," she instructed.

She inhaled delicately, enjoying the acrid stink of him at close quarters. There was nothing quite like the scent of a healthy man, detectable even through the herbal odors of the room.

"Now tell me once more what you thought you were doing, Galligan."

"Nothing, Hera."

"Oh, Ganni. You hit Fandua over the head and ran for the hills. Why?"

Silence.

"Why?" she said, reaching out to run her palm over his short, fine hair. Cupping the side of his head in her palm, she pressed with her fingertips, massaging the rigid muscles of his jaw. "I need to know."

"Went crazy, I guess," he offered.

Daya leaned closer, holding his head with both hands and lowering her voice. No one passing in the corridor or outside the window must hear.

"Tell me the truth, Ganni, or—" Her lips brushed the edge of his ear. "Never again. Never, ever again."

He groaned and hunched nearer to her.

"You were trying to get away from me," she murmured. "What else can I think? Do you see how insulting that is? I took you into my own bed in Oldtown and lavished on you all the skills of an accomplished pet fem. And what's the next thing that I hear? Galligan has bolted!"

He laughed despairingly. "Just hand me over to Vargindo or Arjvall and you'll have your revenge. Picked to be some kind of Moon-witch's man! They'll kill me first."

She chuckled warmly and stroked the back of his neck. "I warned you not to spend time with the wrong cockies, my dear—the stubborn ones, the haters, the plotters. Look at the trouble you're in!"

He shrugged wearily.

"Never mind, that's all behind you now. You're going traveling again, but this time with me."

He flashed her an apprehensive look.

"I have spread the protection of Moonwoman over you just as I said I would. But that's only the beginning. Through you, we'll make a path of cleansing for all men. I'm not the only one to think that you good lads and our own boys growing to manhood need a way to step out of your chains. We are going to create that way at Endpath, with the Lady's help."

And Beyarra's, of course. A foolish woman; but useful.

Galligan was gaping at her, clearly appalled. "Endpath! Why Endpath?"

"Because that place used to be the heart of the men's religion. You and I are going to give it over to the Lady."

He looked positively green. "Endpath? You can't!"

Daya took the cloth and soaked it again in the liquid simmering over the little brazier. She wrung the rag out, refolded it, and handed it to him to apply again to his injured hand.

"Yes I can, because I'm right and because I'm lucky."

She untied the bandage about his throat for a look at the faded rope burns on his skin. "You're lucky too, my lad. Kobba *could* have killed you. Instead, she tipped you into my hands. Now I'll do the last great deed, the crown of the Conquest: wiping slavery from the face of the Holdfast once and for all."

"What? I don't—"

"You'll be a hero too, Ganni," she said. She really was very fond of him. "The first man to enter Endpath under its new ruler, the Lady—the first man to enter there and live."

"Eykar Bek went back there," he began uncertainly.

"That dried-up scrap! That's not a man. Did he open a way for other men to follow, to rise cleansed from their defeat? He couldn't do that; but you can. Between us, we'll make a better path for Vargindo's followers than his miserable Bear cult."

"This is crazy," he said with some agitation. "Endpath is miles away!"

"Our passage is already arranged," she said serenely.

"Oh Christ," he whispered, and some warning flared in her mind. She saw the shift in his eyes—his beautiful long eyelashes had first drawn her attention to him—and then he said in a hard, quick tone, "You can't go to Endpath. Men are coming, from the Wild. It was them I was trying to find when I ran off—I meant to join them. Coming from the north, they'll reach Endpath first. They're bound to stop there."

"Ah," she said faintly, her breath swallowed by terror. "What men?"

"The DarkDreamer and the ferry crew of that Chester ferryman, Hak One-Eye." He looked away bleakly. "Now I've told you, I'm a dead man for certain."

Dreams came clear like a thunderclap, errors blazed, and new paths glimmered. Her fear vanished. How wonderfully the Lady did her work! How subtly and with what delightful surprises she designed the course to her chosen goals.

"So you ran away to look for these Ferrymen?"

He nodded. "I tried to go north but I kept having to swing wide, to keep from being seen—so many people are in the fields, or out mending roofs and such. I meant to work back seaward again above Lammintown and turn north through the woods to wait for them—at Endpath."

This wonderful foolishness of men, their absurd leaps of faith! It was a wildness of mind seldom seen in women. Her own mind grew calm, seeing her way here. Not the one she had constructed, but the one the Lady had prepared for her.

"It's not just a story," he said. "We all know it's true. There've been signs. Everyone's getting ready."

"Then we'd better get ready too, Ganni," Daya said. "Shift that rag a little, it's slipping."

And she began to think.

Monument

My building project actually had nothing to do with Moonwoman. I didn't believe in her to begin with, and I needed to do more than just pile up stones in a shapeless heap, as the Free did to commemorate their dead, because that wouldn't take me long enough. I meant to spend the rest of my life building this thing. The act of stacking stones would become a monument itself, a prolonged gesture of protest impossible for the Free to ignore.

Fedeka foraged most days in this little cluster of low, rough hills for medicinal plants or dyes, or spent her time cooking, drying, and packing her finds for transport back to Midfast. We had little to say to each other, those first few days. I was still very angry with her; but I had to admit that I loved her, too. It made me glad to see that her sturdy self-sufficiency was not diminished by her years.

To me this was strange country. To her it must have been full of harsh memories. Being there could not have been easy for her. I didn't know how long she meant to stay, and I avoided thinking about what I would do when she did decide to head home.

I didn't want to be with people again. Not fems with their impenetrable politics and horrendous history, and not Riding Women (whom I had so deeply disappointed) either. I could just stand being with Fedeka, sometimes.

She would come stumping back to camp of an afternoon

with a full belt pack, or bent under a cloth-wrapped load on her shoulder. Her posture was perpetually canted now by a tenderness she complained of over her right hip in back.

She was very impatient about this. I thought she was crazy not to see that a person who carries burdens fit for a horse should expect some effects from abusing her body this way.

She was not always grouchy.

"You know," she told me one evening, "this is like old times. Your mother came to me out in the Grasslands after a bad time in the Tea Camp. She lived rough in my tent for a while. She found her strength during that time."

As I had heard it, Alldera had found her strength in the months she had spent alone and on foot, stalking wild horses on the plains, which was not the same thing. It was in Fedeka's camp, after she came back with those horses, that she and Daya had became lovers. That was surely not what the dye-maker meant by saying Alldera had "found her strength." Their affair was probably something Fedeka preferred to forget, in the light of Daya's treachery.

Despite her initial reticence—her shame, as I saw it, over failing her oath to me—Fedeka had a lot to tell me. It's amazing how talkative your basic hermit can be, given an audience. She would have told me the entire saga of my mother and the Free Fems at calm, interminable length if I had been willing to sit still for it.

I wasn't. Nobody had told me anything of any damned use to me for some time now, so I was not in a trusting mood. And Fedeka had still not apologized to me. In fact I was barely civil to her, although I never mentioned Veree's name or actually challenged Fedeka over her betrayal. Let her figure it out for herself, I thought.

Working with the rocks gave me a sort of respite. My mind was freed to serve me up thoughts that I could turn over in peace while my hands were busy.

But even out there people would not let me alone. Riders on their way to their harvest work at Hidden Springs stopped by to assure me that things were fine in Midfast, that Veree was flourishing in the Children's House, that this one or that one had taken him home overnight to her hearthmates because he was so sweet and funny. This was something that had seldom been done before with the boys, only with the girls, they said portentously.

These reports filled me with relief, liberally mixed with jealousy and distrust of those who were enjoying the company of my little boy.

Visitors always watched what my hands were doing, which gave me satisfaction. I was quick to explain what my work was and how it was intended to rebuke them.

I tried to use as a model what I had seen of the Free Fems' stonework in the Grasslands: the granaries they had built at the Dusty Season wells. But what I was building was a stone tent. I mean a Grassland tent with a taut-stretched roof and flanking wings, but raised on slim stone pillars instead of poles. The side wings of the tent were a problem, since these should curve inward toward the roofline, like stretched, sagging leather.

At the cost of pinched fingers, scrapes, and bruises from failed efforts, I learned to stack my stones in thin flakes, rows and rows of them wedged tight with smaller chips, to create a very shallow and gradual curve, just a hint of a curve really. I wedged my pillar stones too, making the seams as tight as I could to reenforce the height of the completed stack.

It was going to be a misshapen tent, absurdly tall and narrow, like something drawn in the dirt by a child. Stone is not felt or leather.

But how to do the downward dip of the roofline, between the stone "poles"?

One day Eykar Bek came out with Beyarra and some other people bringing supplies. They would take back to Midfast Fedeka's treated herbs for storage at the Moon's House there. They all acted as if it was a regular sort of visit.

But there was that pale man, driving a loads-cart behind the femmish riders. They settled down to talk with the dyer. He limped over to look at what I was doing.

"I think you want a keystone," he said after a while, and explained to me what this meant, scratching a drawing on one of my stones with a sharp-edged chip. "That's how the Ancients of the Ancients built a stone vault."

I pointed out that this meant making the roof arch upward, instead of sagging downward in tent-roof style. He said he knew that, but that maybe the technique would work inverted. I said I didn't think so.

The voices of the others drifted over to us. There was no way to escape except to leave my work, which I refused to do.

Beyarra-Bey and a spectrally thin NewFree called Muvai (she had spoken at Galligan's trial on the Steps) told Fedeka, over tea, how this or that sick person was doing, and about some quarrel over a new wheatfield near Lammintown, and how people wanted Fedeka to come back to Midfast to help keep Daya in line.

The Free, Lora-Lan had told me, tried to avoid the insult of issuing orders to each other as male masters had done to femmish slaves. It was not so surprising that in the absence of both Fedeka and Alldera, nobody but Kobba seemed prepared to command the pet fem back to Oldtown, and Daya simply ignored and avoided the big miner.

Fedeka said loudly, "Talk to Marajee-Mai, she's your councillor. Don't come whining to me. I came out here to get away from all your complaints!"

The voices went low and coaxing again. I saw that Beyarra was not engaged, though; she had her eye on me and my "father."

"If you plan this to be a structure where people can sit safely where we sit now," he said, "you'll need at least three butresses along this long back wall. Hera."

"Tents don't have 'buttresses' "

"No doubt," he said shortly. He was different from the last time I had seen him—more tired and strained. "Do you mean for this thing to stand or fall?"

" 'Hera,' " I reminded him.

He pressed his lips tight in irritation. "Hera. Stand, or fall?"

"Oh, don't be stupid," I hissed, bristling at his insolence. "I mean it to stand, of course! You've never seen a Grassland tent, you can't understand." I drew a picture in the dirt.

He hunched forward to look, then said thoughtfully,

"It's like the tents once used in the desert countries far east of here, over the sea."

"No one lives over the sea," I said. I had not seen the sea and had no wish to, but I knew it was a sterile waste that could conceal no life. The very idea made me queasy.

"I meant in Ancient times," he answered, "as you could discover for yourself, if you learned to read what is written in books."

"I'm a Riding Woman," I retorted. "We don't have books and we don't read, but we've never been slaves nor made slaves of other people."

That quieted him for a time, but he could not keep from offering advice. "If you think of a tent as a—a soft house, it might go along better."

"How much stone building have you done?" Really, he was insufferable.

"None," he said stiffly, "but I have read about it."

"Fine," I said. "You've read about building houses. This isn't a house. It's a tent."

He lowered his voice. "I'm sorry about Veree. I couldn't let Setteo get involved in stealing a child."

His apology sounded genuine, if forced. I said, "Of course you had to run and tell someone. I can see that a slave has to do what will protect his own neck; or his lover's."

I saw the mutinous glint in his eye, but he said nothing. His silence provoked me.

"Spoiling my exploit probably saved my life and Veree's too," I said angrily, "but don't think that's a debt you can collect on, all right?"

He watched me work. After a time I asked him if he had something else to do, some duties for Beyarra and the others while he was here.

He said, "Being lame, I am permitted to drive that cart, drawn by an old, slow horse, and provided the cart is carrying other, more useful things as well. It's work, driving a very old, slow horse. I'm allowed to rest when the opportunity offers. This is my rest. Besides, the Heras don't want me overhearing their conversation. Hera Beyarra will tell me later what she wants me to know."

"You probably know it all already," I said. "Like all you slavemen. That's what the fems say, anyhow."

I did my best to ignore him as I sorted stones by size, stopping now and then to try splitting a big one if it looked likely to break into usable pieces for building. I used a round-heeled hammering rock that so far had held together and a rag of leather wrapped around each hand.

"I have heard," he said quietly after a bit, "that Alldera is on her way home."

I split a stone.

He said, "You could go to meet her out of courtesy."

"I'm busy," I said.

He ran his fingers over the inner surface of the long wall. "This won't go anywhere, if you decide to leave it for a while. No one will dare to interfere with it in your absence."

"There isn't going to be any absence," I said. "You've got a nerve, you know that? What do you care whether I'm out here banging stones together, or back at Midfast acting ridiculous and getting myself locked up like a sharu in a plugged burrow over a child who isn't even mine?"

He squinted at the distant mountains, as if searching for signs of danger from there. "Some people find it strange that you spend your time making a shrine to that male child. Your mother may agree with them when she hears. Your absence from Midfast, on top of that, might upset her more than you intend. Do you want her to be already angry when you two meet?"

"That's her problem," I grunted. What right had *she* to be angry, or he to care? "Alldera can come to me if she wants to. I've waited long enough for her."

"Maybe she's afraid," he said, "of meeting you again, after so long."

I laughed. "Alldera Conqueror, afraid? Why?"

"Why not?" he said. "I was."

He spoke to me just as if he were another of my sharemas. And to think that he had sired me—if he had—by force upon the body of my bloodmother! I could scarcely look at him. His very appearance was an affront. He ought to look like a monster, not a tired, worried cripple of middle age with silver in his hair. Everything about him seemed to me to be offensively wrong.

"How many deaths are on your hands?" I asked.

Gaze lowered, he answered, "As official executioner at Endpath, a thousand or more. I have thought about it a good deal. Considering that to the sick men who came there I offered mercy, and that I can't know what the death drink meant to any of the rest, I try to avoid feelings of guilt."

"You could have refused to do it at all."

"Then the four Rovers who were my guards would have broken my neck and run up the flag to signal that a new Entendant was needed. Or I could have taken the death drink myself, as most of my predecessors did. But I was determined to find my father—you know that story?—so instead I ran away. Not a brilliant solution, but better than some."

"Don't you dream of their ghosts, all those dead men? And him too, your sire?"

He scratched at his twisted thigh through the skirt of his tunic. "He needed killing; ask your mother, when you see her."

I didn't need to. I knew what Eykar's blow had spared the fems who were slaves then. I regretted my question, but did not say so. People in the New Holdfast did not apologize to men.

He added, "My life in those days wasn't so strange, Hera, compared with the lives of other men. That was a brutal, murderous world, running on the fear and rage of aging men at the prospect of their own inevitable deaths."

"The Riding Women say they were just crazy."

He answered sardonically, "That's another way to put it. The Juniors replaced their rule with a milder system—"

"Not for you," I said. "I've heard about how you became their 'Oracle.' "

"Well," he said, looking down again, "I wish you hadn't. Still, although unlucky in some ways, I was also very fortunate. At least some of my actions seem to have prevented even worse things. Not everybody is given that."

"And you have your books," I said. "Do you bring some with you when you travel?"

"Oh no," he said, visibly shocked. "They might get lost, or damaged."

I said, "Why are you here?"

"I asked to speak with you," he said.

"You mean Beyarra wants you to tell me to leave," I said.

He did not smile. "Going home to your Grasslands might be better than staying out here with no companion but Fedeka."

He spoke very intently. I stopped hammering to listen.

"There's unusual unrest among the men, a sense of . . . anticipation. They report dreams of revolt, of upset, of heroes appearing from the Wild. There's always been an undercurrent of resistance. This, now, may become something more."

He lowered his head, creating a more intimate space between us. I saw the thinning of the hair at his crown. "You are too exposed out here."

I said, "To what? A few dirty, drunken men shambling about with wooden bars fastened between their feet?"

He tapped the ceramic cuff around his ankle. "Once you would have been the one wearing this, not I. The history of the Holdfast teaches, Do not to underestimate the lowly."

I caught his hand and turned it and laid my other hand next to his, palm upward. His resistance was automatic but quickly checked. My hand was a good deal dirtier than his. His skin was warm and dry; touching him seemed perfectly natural.

"Not much alike," I said, letting go. "Maybe you shouldn't care about another man's daughter being 'exposed' to danger. Your brothers on the stick wouldn't appreciate your concern for me anyway. Fedeka says the stickies would like to kill you for teaching the Free to read."

"I can worry about what they'd like to do to me, or I can read," he said. "Life is short. I read."

I laughed, and I thought I saw a little flush of pleasure in his pale cheeks. Then he ruined the moment, the way older people will do, by falling into coaxing me to return with the others to Midfast to meet Alldera.

I interrupted, indicated the visiting fems with a jerk of my shoulder. "Beyarra told you to say that. Look, Midfast is that way." I pointed. "The Grasslands are in the opposite direction. Which is it? Never mind, it doesn't matter. Wherever I decide to go—and it might be on to join Sheel Torrinor at the Refuge—I'll leave when I'm good and ready.

"So you can tell your Heras they won't get anywhere treating me like some feckless girl, sending my . . . the only one of my parents who's around to whuffle and nudge me toward where they want me to go, like some nervous old mare with a straying foal."

He took a split stone from a pile I had made and turned it in his hands, his thin fingers exploring its surfaces. He repeated, "Go home. Our quarrels aren't yours. Take the child back or leave him, but go, go soon!"

His intensity unsettled me.

"*Hera,*" he added, and then Beyarra called him. They were ready to leave.

He rose with some difficulty, using my wall as support. I heard stones shift. Maybe he was right about the buttresses.

He held out the flake he had taken from the loose pile. "If you see a place for it, Hera, would you build this into your monument? In memory of a friend of mine, long dead now. The sight of your horses would have given him great joy."

"Oh," I said. "Captain Kelmz."

I looked down involuntarily at Eykar's scarred leg; I had heard that story from Alldera herself back in Holdfaster Tent, of the Rover captain who had chosen to take the deadly worst of the blow which had crippled Eykar Bek. This man was one whom another had sacrificed his life for; I felt a shiver of nostalgia for the romance of those old tales, in which I could not find a way to place this battered slave before me. Trying made me dizzy.

Eykar placed the stone in my hand and lightly curled my fingers around it. "And you might try wearing your headcloth pulled over your face for this work. Breathing stone dust can harm you."

Beyarra was watching us, but she didn't come over. I had to appreciate her tact. I was beginning to understand what my bloodmother saw in her.

"You can't stay here much longer," the dyer said to me,

looking after them as they left. "I'll be going back myself soon. I don't like what I'm hearing about Daya, that scheming bitch. Giving her Moonwoman's protection was a bad mistake."

"Well," I said, "everybody makes mistakes, that's what people are always telling me."

"They brought other troublesome news," she said, ignoring my sarcasm. "Some people seem to have decided not to wait for Alldera to bring back word from the Bayo-born on pasturage. A group of hotheads working at the salt pans near Bayo have driven some horses into that Bayo-west country. People are angry. Some want to go drag them back, even if it means a fight."

"Another mistake, I guess," I said. This new trouble must involve Raysa and her friends, which made me nervous. I didn't want to talk about it.

Fedeka squinted at me and shifted her ground. "I don't like this stone thing of yours. It's not even a proper cairn for people to add tokens to. It's all yours and yours alone, a selfish thing, Sorrel. What did that man say about it?"

I shrugged.

She made a disgusted face. "Told you how to do it better, no doubt. He's stuffed full of notions gleaned from the Ancients' books. It's comical sometimes.

"Beyarra shouldn't have brought him around to talk with you. She thinks too much of that man and too much about the men in general; I don't like it, and I don't think the Lady approves, either."

For the sake of peace, I ventured no opinion.

In the middle of the night I woke thinking about stacking up stones inside the walls of the tent and then jamming the roof stones tightly together in a horizontal plane across the top of the whole pile till they were tight, making a solid shape instead of a hollow one. Then I could remove the insides and leave the roof stones to stand alone—or to collapse on top of me.

If I died in a crash of rocks and rubble, what difference would that make to anyone? Even Veree would forget me in the Children's House.

Sometime later I started up again, ringing with painful clarity like a struck iron: men like Eykar Bek were guilty, no matter how fair they might speak, because they had owned and abused fems. But all little kits were innocent, never having harmed anyone. Slavery should not be something boys were born into, but a punishment for crimes against the Free.

I should have ridden into the Holdfast carrying that banner and proclaiming it everywhere, with Juya's son as the clear sign and pledge of my determination, not with his sex disguised. Then I could have met my bloodmother proudly when she came home; I could have deserved Raysa's regard.

Even if I'd lost, I could have shouted out what none of the Free would say aloud, not even Beyarra, not even Alldera herself: that no child should suffer for the sins of its fathers, not even a father's son. I had been so wrapped up in Veree that I hadn't been able to see past him to all the other sons of the Free, and their innocence that also demanded acknowledgment.

My stone tent was a monument not to Veree but to my failure of Veree; and of myself.

Bug Bites

Bites," Beyarra said, "so many terrible bug bites!"

"Well, you spend a few weeks in the swamps and see if you don't come back covered with them too," Alldera said, glancing at the angry-looking welts on her arms.

Once upon a time, she wouldn't have let herself notice. The Seniors had held that *all* the beasts of Ancient times had died in the Wasting, so no one could acknowledge the existence of insects. You killed the ones you could and kept quiet about the rest.

She laughed ruefully. "The Bayo-born never had the option of pretending that insects were gone; the 'skeetas' down there could fly away with you. Honestly, sometimes when I look back at the idiocies we went along with—"

Roona snapped, "Better a live idiot than a wise corpse."

Some fool, goaded by Roona's complaining, had commented to her that morning that in the Old days few fems had lived long enough to suffer from sore joints; which had not sweetened Roona's temper.

"Agh!" Alldera said, shrugging hard in place of scratching her shoulder blade. "Thanks, Bee; now that you've drawn my attention to them, they're starting to itch again."

Beyarra said, "Sorry, sorry! We brought back some things from Fedeka's camp—maybe Kastia can cook up a salve for you."

Alldera, wallowing in hot water, reluctantly noticed the opening Beyarra had made for the necessary question. "How is Sorrel doing out there?"

"Fedeka says the child is working off her angers."

"Child? She's no child by now. How does she seem to you?"

"Young," Beyarra said with wistful humor. "Earnest—well, glum, and no wonder. She's made a situation, bringing that boy-cub here, and she doesn't know how to fix it."

So it's for me to fix instead. Alldera grumbled, "If she'd come by herself, that would have been complicated enough."

"She's like you," Beyarra replied with a little smile. "She doesn't do things the easy way."

Alldera laughed despite herself. "Poor kit! I wouldn't drop that curse on my worst enemy." She shifted in the tub, swirling the water. "There's no time to go out there; she'll have to come here. The Council has postponed a whole list of things which they could easily have handled without me—"

"They like to have your opinion on the touchier matters," Beyarra murmured.

"Naturally. But it's made a bundle of knots for me to try to untie, from silly little snarls to great big snarls. Like these Breakaways riding off south. I half wish I hadn't come back at all. And I don't like what I'm hearing about this 'Bear' business. It needs firm handling, or it could grow into something much worse."

"That's why it needs your personal touch." Roona always defended decisions made by Marajee, who was an old holdmate of hers. "Anyway, Bear-craziness is nothing compared with some people driving horses away south."

Beyarra sighed. "Some people got impatient."

"Who?"

"Some of the First Free, that's who!" Roona said with relish. "They want to be back in the Grasslands, living on meat and tea and playing pillo. Gardening and farming is *work.*"

Beyarra lathered Alldera's hair with firm fingers. "Do you know that they had special hair-washing soap in the Ancients' times? 'Shampoo,' they called it."

Alldera, who had been distracted by a sudden memory of Nenisi patiently explaining to her how "real people" gathered the grain they needed rather than tying themselves down to one place to grow it, fell back into the present with an incredulous laugh. "Shampoo? That's a word? Is that the kind of thing your books are stuffed with?"

Hurt, Beyarra said, "You know what we found in the books about growing wheat and making paper. I didn't think that was so silly."

Nenisi, who would die before she would stoop to tilling the soil—that keen dark face like a stream-polished cobble of fine-grained black stone—

"So," Alldera said with a sigh, "what about this new wheatfield that Ebba-Basarr and her hearth have been working? It's not the worst problem I've come home to, but so far it's the loudest."

"The same old thing," Beyarra said. "People of Quartz Rocks Hearth run horses on the higher ground, which is too stony to farm. But they don't keep the fences up—they couldn't, they say, with Pannamin on the Council and Chuletti-Chai sick with fever all last spring. I think they just don't like penning the horses up. They are mostly First Free up there now.

"So the horses get into Ebba's field and what they don't eat, they trample down. Which, the Quartz Rocks say, wasn't a problem before the Basarrs got greedy for more farmland and made that field there, out of stony pastureland. Ebba says she worked that area when she was bond, weeding manna for the men. She knows that soil and can make it produce, so why let it go to waste when there's plenty of pasture if the Quartz Rocks would just move their horses and build a new fence higher up?"

"That sounds like ordinary Council work," Alldera said.

"Well, but there are lots of personal complications," Beyarra began, and Alldera held up a soapy hand to stop her.

"I'll hear more than I ever wanted to know about every kink in that string all too soon," she said. "Tell me what Kobba's been up to; she went for a runaway on the Steps, I hear."

She got a detailed account of Galligan's trial.

"He should never have gotten loose in the first place," she said blackly at the end. "How can people be so careless?"

"Some people are saying," Beyarra said reluctantly, "that we need to be harder on them, that it was a mistake to sponsor so many off the stick. We've missed your voice in this."

"Get used to missing it," Alldera retorted, wondering what Daya might be up to, stealing Galligan. Well, it was someone else's worry; she stayed out of Daya business. "I'm not immortal, you know. They say, 'Stick them all up,' every time one of these aging boyos gets into mischief; and it's always the same people saying it, too. They think they're being tough, but in fact they're scared witless of a beaten enemy."

"This Bear cult has the men stirred up," Beyarra said. "Two of them nearly killed each other while you were gone."

And they can't work it off driving horses down south for a new start as we can, Alldera thought. "We aging warriors," she said, "both sexes, are more alike than not: a restless, quarrelsome bunch. Two bunches, men and First Free. Thank the stars for you NewFree, Beyarra; you're younger, cooler—"

"From the outside," Beyarra said primly. "And we would still be slaves, if not for certain of you 'aging warriors.' Please don't talk today in Council as if men and First Free are alike. You know I agree, but it drives some people mad."

Alldera sighed for the peacefulness of the Islands of Bayo swamp, bugs and all. "I never say such things in public, Bee, any more than you do." She paused, then asked, "How's Eykar?"

"I don't know," Beyarra said, frowning. "Sometimes I can't make him out at all. He's been keeping to himself, tearing through books like someone pursued by demons. I had to tell him I couldn't spare any more oil for reading at night. He looks terrible. Haunted."

Alldera had seen that look. "Maybe meeting Sorrel upset him."

"Maybe," Beyarra said doubtfully. "I thought he handled it well, myself."

"I probably should have been there," Alldera admitted. She was infinitely glad that she had not been. She folded the washcloth and slapped it down over the edge of the tub. "But really, people have to manage their lives without me. I'm not the damned Woman in the Moon, with nothing better to do than to watch over everything and everybody!"

Roona, laying out clean clothes for her on a chest at the foot of the bed, told her not to curse.

Alldera dragged her mind away from trying to imagine Eykar Bek meeting Sorrel. "So, this Galligan who bolted—freckles? Lots of freckles? Yes, I know the one. Edeez-Ea thinks she got a daughter off him two years ago. He's never been any trouble. Kobba gets more extreme the more peaceful our lives become. She didn't cripple him, did she?"

Beyarra shook her head. "His hand is healing cleanly, from what I hear." She hesitated. "He's over there with Daya at the Moon's House. Some people don't like that. I think Fedeka has stayed out of Midfast to avoid the fuss."

Roona brought a large tan towel. "You stayed away too long yourself. You can't turn your back for more than a minute on Daya, haven't you learned yet? Imagine the gall, showing up in Midfast clinging to Sorrel's shirttail! One way and another, your daughter has thrown this whole place into an uproar. You should have been here to control her."

"She's grown," Alldera said tersely. "Adults control themselves."

"I'm just telling you what people are saying," the old fem replied in an offended tone. "If you think I'm too stupid to talk to you, I'll go away."

Alldera caught Roona's knobby hand briefly with soapy fingers. She had seen Roona shine with power once: during the battle at Oldtown she took a man prisoner before Alldera's eyes. It was painful to find the old fem so shrunken, plainly shuffling on her way toward the ultimate defeat.

"I didn't mean that. It was your scalp the masters took, not your brains! I'm just on edge; all these problems, before I even wash off the grime of my journey."

"Well, you asked about people," Roona said.

"You're right, I did."

"At least your daughter has made us focus on the next generation of men instead of their elders, for a change," Beyarra said.

"It's a pretty child," Roona mused. "That Veree boy. I saw him playing with two little blonde girls yesterday—those twins of Kenta's—very lively and happy together. Belett had made dolls out of some old leather cuttings, and the kits hummed and burbled away with their heads together, acting out some story or other with a lot of chasing in it. At first I wondered whose little girl he was."

She sighed heavily. "It would all be so much easier if men were born as ugly and nasty as they grow up to be, so you'd know how to feel about them right off."

Alldera, barely listening, rinsed soap from her chest with clean water from a small basin on the floor. She found a creepy familiarity in the facts of Sorrel's arrival: a lone person making the strenuous and dangerous crossing between the Grasslands and the Holdfast with a child; and the child being taken into the life of the people she found on the other side of the mountains.

It had happened before, only the traveler had been herself, pregnant with Sorrel and crossing in the opposite direction, from the Holdfast to the Grasslands; an untried youth with nothing in her head but fear and a crude concept of freedom.

Full circle, she thought; *how strange.*

Beyarra said, "Your bath's getting cold," and went to get more hot water from the kettle on the hearth.

Roona leaned near enough for Alldera to see the yellow of her teeth; but how her faded eyes gleamed! "Take many baths with such loving help while you were in that swamp country? I hope your Bee, there, doesn't hear about it if you did."

"Lady hold your tongue!" Alldera said.

"Don't gossip, Roona," Beyarra said, hurrying back with the steaming ewer. "What's she been saying about me?"

Roona sat back, out of the way of the splashing water as it poured. "Told her you've done nothing but bury yourself in books since she rode out of here, that's what. You and that Eykar, whispering and scribbling like a couple of Seniors divvying up the fresh lads from the Boyhouse!"

"I wish you wouldn't talk like that," Beyarra said unhappily. "It puts wrong ideas into people's heads."

"Not as much as those books do," the old fem said, gathering herself to rise. "Ferries that fly through the air! Tiny little animals living inside people's bodies and making them sick! No wonder the Refugees went crazy, if they read that kind of thing for amusement. Put this round you, there's a chill in here."

There wasn't—the morning was already warm—but Alldera took the towel from her and stood up. She imagined the looks on their faces if she were to drop the towel and reveal a skin laced with red and black swirls from nape to tailbone. It would almost have been worth it.

She remembered Sinduann's dazed expression and trembling limbs as the girl walked unsteadily away to bathe her fiery skin in water. Well, no, it wouldn't.

"Thanks, Roona," she said. "So you're keeping an eye on our two scholars."

"Oh, it's not just us two any more," Beyarra said with an eager smile. "Shibann is teaching a reading class herself. She turned out to be very quick, after a bad start." She hesitated, then added, "I thought she might go and read some stories to the little ones, see how they take to it."

"You thought, or Eykar thought?" That was unfair, and Alldera regretted it at once. Sometimes she had to wonder whether she was a little bit jealous of the ease between Beyarra and Eykar Bek. "What stories?"

"We found some about animals."

"Talking animals," Roona scoffed. "Of all things!"

Alldera bent to dry one foot braced on the tub's edge. "Well, the Riding Women tell stories like that, about horses and sharu and even Keeoties and Hairs, that haven't existed for generations. It hasn't addled their youngsters' brains."

"We'll have to get Council approval, though," Beyarra said.

Alldera heard resignation in her voice. She thought of all the talking and haranguing that she had missed during her absence. They had decided early on that just falling into the old ways (skewed to favor fems instead of men) was not good enough; and how they had congratulated themselves on that!

But it meant that every decision had to be weighed and considered, often more than once, twice, or three times. While she'd been gone she knew there had been no pause in the endless palaver that it took to keep the New Holdfast running.

Might as well ride home to Stone Dancing and settle myself in the Chief Tent for life.

"Put it on the slate, then," she said. "Reading stories to the children." Yes, but which children? Just the girls? Which stories? She could hear the questions already.

"Oh, and Bee—you'll want to look at Chisti's notes on the Bayo-born," she added, stepping out of the tub onto the cool stone flagging. "I'll answer any questions I can. Other Free Fems will travel down there I'm sure, so if I forget things or get them wrong it won't matter."

"We'll start as soon as you have some time to sit down with me and talk," Beyarra said. "No one sees exactly the same way anybody else does, and we all miss things."

So eager to fix the flying moment, Alldera thought, noting the incised metal cuff Beyarra wore on her earlobe, hiding the lump of scar tissue there (*who gave her that bauble while I was gone?*). It was as if the pretty NewFree had caught "history" from breathing book dust with Eykar.

"There aren't enough of those wicked old books, she has to make new ones," Roona sniffed. "I'm off, before Beyarra starts lecturing us about paper and ink."

She pulled the door to with a thump behind her.

Beyarra blotted moisture from Alldera's neck with a fold of the towel. She murmured, "Maybe you want to rest before the Council meets."

Alldera caught hold of the towel. "I missed you," she said, and drew the rough cloth over her shoulder until Beyarra's hand came with it. She turned and crushed her cheek and lips on that smooth, warm skin with the delicate tendons beneath.

There was a fragrance, a light musk. She had missed that scent when she had embraced a certain Island girl with a fine filligree of Memory tattooed on her hands and feet. And if Chisti-Chai let slip anything about that, Alldera would murder her for troubling Beyarra, whose sweet weight now slid eagerly against her like warm, dense water.

"What else," she asked later, "have people been arguing about, that's not up on the slate?"

Beyarra lay with her head pillowed on Alldera's upper arm and talked in a contented voice about rumors, quarrels, grudges, and mistakes. But no more about Sorrel; and Alldera could not bring herself to ask.

Nothing on the slate or off it got discussed at that afternoon's Council session. A NewFree rode from the north with news that turned the meeting into a tumult: a strangerman had entered Lammintown.

The Council session went on and on, circling around the basic paucity of information beyond the barest facts. Alldera left them still arguing at moonrise. She found Eykar limping up and down the reading room. One small lamp burned. By its light she could make out his rumpled bedding in the chamber beyond.

"Where's Setteo?" she said.

"Somewhere," he said in a painful gasp. "I heard you were back."

"What's wrong?"

"Cramp in my leg."

"Lie on your back and put your feet in the air. Sometimes it helps."

A glare from his good eye. "Thank you. I'll walk it out."

She sat down on a table against the wall, first shoving stacks of books aside. Thunder, she was tired. "I hear you met my daughter."

He nodded. "A handsome girl with a mind of her own."

She ignored his sardonic glance (*Just like her mother*, it said). "Is she in danger here, Eykar?"

"How can she be the Conqueror's daughter and not be at risk?" She didn't like the way he suddenly would not meet her eyes.

"I meant some new problem," she insisted, scratching the bites on her elbow. "Some fancy secret plans of the men?"

He moved haltingly across the flagged floor. "I wouldn't know. Ask your spies."

She had believed that he shut his eyes deliberately to the ever-creeping tendrils of the stickmen's vengeful hatred. But now one of those spies had reported that Eykar was involved. Of course, spies were not reliable where Eykar was concerned, because of the mixed feelings of the men about the Endtendant.

She said more lightly, "Found anything world-shaking in the books while I've been gone?"

He shook his head, visibly relaxing. "Fatness," he said, "an ungodly number of books about food and fatness. The Ancients were fat and worried about becoming fatter."

They looked at each other in shared puzzlement.

"Well," she ventured, "Elnoa was fat; it made her dependent on others. Senior Bajerman was rather fat. The Ancients were richer than either of them so maybe they were fatter, too."

Eykar said, "Are there books down there at Bayo?"

"It's too damp; things rot." On the same breath she added, "Someone sneaked into Lammintown from the Wild. Who was it?"

His eyes widened. "Lammintown? When?"

Gauging the depth of his surprise, she thought she glimpsed some bedrock of pre-knowledge not far beneath the surface.

Ah, Eykar, you liar, she thought; and she felt keen regret for the frankness on which they had built their unlikely alliance years ago. Only a shadow of that candor remained between them now, for to be a slave is to be a liar.

"It was a man, going freefoot and softly," she said. "We might never have known he was there, except that he attacked Ila-Illea. She fought him off. He ran. It seems he was a stranger."

Silence. He shook his leg and put tentative weight on it.

"You know, Eykar. Tell me what the men say among themselves."

His mouth set in a stubborn line.

"I should beat you bloody!" She shoved away from the table and stepped up close to him. "You think you can hold yourself apart while we scramble for a footing here? Whatever happens will happen to *all* of us. If you've heard something, tell me! You know the stakes!"

His eyelids lowered, hiding every spark of consciousness from her. Amazing, how fast new slaves learned slave skills.

"If the Bear-men have something planned," she said harshly, "and we lose one life, Eykar, because you haven't spoken honestly to me, I will burn your books in front of your face, one by one and page by page."

He stood, a stone, saying nothing.

She returned to the table, willing her heart to calm. Well, she was acting like a master and getting as far as a master would get. Slaves were not the only ones who learned their roles quickly.

She forced her thoughts back to how it felt to be helpless and hedged about by threats. It made you feel numb, suspended on a thread between one moment and the next. The mind shut down and you endured until—one way or another—some relief arrived, an interval of rest or an ending. Eykar was good at endurance: she would draw nothing from him.

She turned and strode out to meet with the riders she had called on to spread news of the Lammintown intruder to every hearth, camp, and outpost. She must remind them to carry word to the Island towns, although she expected no aid from there. The Bayo-born would melt back into their swamps rather than risk a fight. That was their way, and it had worked well for them.

It was a good half-dozen years and more since the Free themselves had had to fight; and now some of them were away southward, playing at being Riding Women on disputed lands.

Thinking again of what she had said to Eykar, she felt angry with herself. Whatever Eykar knew, Vargindo and his crew must have threatened him if he *did* talk, probably with exactly the same consequences she had promised if he didn't. But what else could she have done?

Sharemother

Sheel Torrinor paused to study the animals grazing in the hollow at Fedeka's camp. At the sight and scent of her own animals—small, sturdy Grassland horses she had collected from New Forge where Sorrel had left them—the fat-bellied Holdfast horses set up a nickering and head-tossing of greeting.

Fedeka's shelter was little but sturdy sticks and skins greased against rain, the weather being intermittently showery. Plants lay on ground sheets wilting in the sun, and hung in bundles from poles. Close by stood the thing everyone kept talking about, a stack of rocks roughly the size of a small Grassland horse, head down to graze and solid from the spine to the ground. A tent, they said she called it. It was nothing like a tent!

What could the child be doing?

Sheel off-saddled and unloaded her packs, hobbled her horses, and walked slowly around the stone heap. It was nothing like the cairns, with their stark, haphazard form that signaled, "Here occurred a disaster that cost someone her life."

The cairns were a clumsy substitute for proper memorialization in the self-songs of friends and relations. But few people sang self-songs here any more ("Marish boasting," they said, a dangerous custom dividing First Free from NewFree).

This structure had some other purpose. She hoped Sorrel had not fallen into the femmish fantasy of a great god-woman living in, or perhaps actually *being*, the moon. Some Free people said the cairns drew moonlight down among the stones, recharging the earth with energy.

The things people said here! She never ceased to be amazed.

She squatted by Fedeka's tent to wait, drawing up her headcloth against the afternoon sun. Fedeka wouldn't mind finding Sheel Torrinor taking her ease inside, but it wasn't good traveling manners to enter without permission.

Sheel liked to set a good example. When the First Free died off, who would keep their children from disgraceful behavior inherited from slave times? If adults acted properly now, the children would learn; if not, then not.

People said that Sorrel had grown up a decent person although prone to moods; as who would not be, given her unique background and her inability to start a family of her own. She had always managed to be away when Sheel traveled home, probably because she was ashamed of her own barrenness.

"I wouldn't come to you, so you've come to me?"

A young woman stood a few yards away. "Well, I'm glad to see you, raid-ma," and she came to give Sheel a quick embrace.

"Child, I hardly knew you," Sheel said. "You are taller than I remember! You should have your headcloth on, and your shirt, not just a breast-wrap. How many times do people have to tell you, the sun eats skin like yours—"

"Don't scold, I'm too old for it," Sorrel said, smiling. "You're the same, just the same as I remember."

"Am I? Holdfast rain must wash away my wrinkles, then."

This young woman saw her with the eyes of fondness, to see her as unchanged. Tears stung; was this all it took to turn a seasoned warrior into a sentimental old woman, affection from her sharechild?

Sorrel said Fedeka was collecting herbs for the soup pot. She herself had been looking for stones for her construction, having used all the suitable rock from the nearby ridge.

She said this last casually, but the challenging set of her head made it plain that she meant to have this creation of hers noticed, not passed over in silence.

"I've heard about your building project," Sheel responded, glancing over at the structure. "I've been tending to a much older house, myself. Did they tell you where I was?"

"Doing something at this Refuge place."

"Something!" Sheel said. "A very particular something. I went with those Rois cousins and a stick gang. We had the men clean out every last corner of that cowards' hideout. It will never be usable again when we're done with it."

"I heard it was a whole underground city," Sorrel said. "I would have liked to have seen it."

"It's a wicked place," Sheel said. "The Wasters of the Ancient world hid down there from the destruction they themselves had caused. You taste evil with every breath.

"But what about you? I want news, I want to know how things were in the Grasslands when you left."

Sorrel looked down. "I'm sorry I avoided you on your last visit, raid-ma."

"Good," Sheel said. "I'm glad you said that." *Say the rest.* "In all honesty, Sorrel, I wasn't anxious to see you either. But we should clear the air between us."

The young woman studied the ground in silence. Sheel went on: "You must have been angry over being left behind, first by Alldera and then by me. Do you understand better now? The Holdfast was—*is*—a very dangerous place. We both chose not to put our sharechild at risk."

"Oh, it's all been explained to me a hundred times," Sorrel interrupted. "By Nenisi, especially."

"I can imagine," Sheel said with a chuckle. "It's not much good being a Conor, which means you are always right, if nobody knows just how right you are."

Sorrel laughed, then sobered. She had shapely, expressive eyes and brows. "I was pretty furious."

"Are you still?"

"A little."

"Do you forgive me, or must we work out a debt here?"

"I wouldn't have forgiven you then," Sorrel said slowly. "Maybe I wasn't grown-up enough to go to war, but by this time I must surely be grown-up enough to forgive you."

"I'm very glad to hear it," Sheel said, immensely relieved. She dug out a carefully wrapped knot of tea from a corner of her much-mended saddlebag. "I've missed my home, my families, my friends and relations. There's never enough time to sit and talk on my visits back there, except about this place and what the Free and their damned men are up to.

"So tell me news from our tent: did you ever get the Hayscall Racer back from those Golashamets? Surely that horse is too old to bother stealing!"

"Oh, that was a grudge raid," Sorrel said, and launched into the history of some complex quarrel with the Golashamet line. Sheel knew most of this, but she enjoyed the youngster's animated account. They talked a long time, drawing an invisible tent about themselves within which Sheel found herself deeply at ease.

Fedeka walked in after sundown carrying a lumpy sack over her shoulder; she had been harvesting the white fungus that sprouted like magic among these hollows after rain. On her way here Sheel had seen many such round, pale shapes dotting shaded slopes. They could be dried and shredded into good tinder for a live firebox, Fedeka said, and made clean dressings for wounds.

She dropped some leaves from her belt pouch into the stew pot and settled on her bedding. Quietly chewing a twist of Sheel's tea, the old dyer was no more part of their talk than the horses were. When the evening clouds melted away, she got up and walked off into the darkness. She didn't bother inviting them along, for which Sheel was thankful. They heard her sing her prayer to the moon upward into the deepening sky.

Sheel cocked her head toward the sound. "Moonstruck yet?"

"Their Lady is nothing to me. Does Alldera—?"

Sheel shrugged. "Not last time we discussed it, but who knows? I still can't read her very well, even though we get along better than we used to."

A quick, bright glance: "Really? You like each other now? Was it going through the war against the men together?"

"We've had our moments," Sheel said. She was reluctant to go into it. Young people should respect their mothers' privacy once the share-tent was struck. She redirected the arrow of inquiry in a direction chosen to rebuke Sorrel's curiosity: "Has Fedeka taken you into her bed yet?"

A blush stained Sorrel's cheeks, visible even by firelight. "I didn't come here for that," she protested. "And if I had—well, she's old! She has a prickly temperament, too."

"Still no family of your own back home?" A mistake, she knew it as soon as the query left her lips, for Sorrel visibly drew in upon herself. Sheel retreated to less sensitive territory. "You were very close with a Soolay girl when I left, but that must be long since over."

"Yes, Eelayenn Soolay might be missing me."

A dull lot, those Soolays, but there was a rider for every horse. Sheel said, "Don't be modest. You've left many broken hearts behind you, I'd lay bets on it."

The flush again, but this time Sorrel held her head high and didn't try to hide it.

"I'm not fresh out of the childpack, raid-ma, to need advice in my loves and friendships," she said with a fetching combination of forthrightness and embarrassment. "And I have weightier things on my mind."

Sheel would have preferred to have avoided the "weighty things" longer. Everything happened so fast in this country!

"This Veree, now," she said, jumping in first. "You shouldn't have brought him here. No, hear me out. I'm the one who sent Juya-Veree over the mountains in the first place. It would have been a favor to me not to get people here stirred up about this wretched kit of hers."

Sorrel frowned at the fire. "I still don't think I was wrong, whatever anybody says. I've known him since he was born, Sheel. He's just a child like any child, a little person, so open to the world and so full of possibilities."

Sheel wanted to protest that a male child was no more a "little person" than a litter of sharu-get were "persons." But she kept quiet while Sorrel talked, and watched the gleam of firelight on the smooth bole of her sharechild's throat.

How surprising that Alldera's blood daughter had turned out handsome (could that Bek man have contributed this refining and rebalancing of the runner's plain features?). You could glimpse something still of the child: bursts of energy, storms of gloom, deathless loves like grassfires blazing up on a breath of wind. Thank the founders, you could still see it.

"Veree's not just somebody's property," Sorrel ended, defiantly.

"Well, you must let the Free decide that," Sheel said, "now that you've put him in their hands. Actions have consequences, Sorrel. You're an adult, you know this."

"What I know is that people you trust betray you," Sorrel said bitterly. "I mean, I walked into it with Daya—she must still hold a grudge against my blood-ma and was taking it out on me—but Fedeka! I still don't understand that."

"Have you asked her about it?" When Sorrel shook her head, Sheel said, "I have no doubt that she did the best she could see to do; she's that kind. As for Daya—I still maintain that that creature is crazier than Grays Omelly. Nothing she does is about anybody except herself, when you get down to it.

"She's not the least bit interested in you or your doings, including that child; she was just using you to get back into the middle of things, run Fedeka off out of her way, and build herself toward taking over the whole Moonwoman cult."

Sorrel said, "But Beyarra seems to trust her, a little."

"Beyarra's a softheaded NewFree who shares the pet's delusion that men are real people," Sheel said. "All I can say is, she'd better watch her back!"

Sorrel sunk her chin on her knees, saying nothing. There seemed little point in pursuing matters that just distressed and divided them. Sheel waved her hand at the stone structure, a hunched shoulder dark against the starry sky. "What's this thing you've made?"

"It's for Veree," Sorrel said morosely. "So they won't forget him when he's grown and they've chained him up to be just another slave."

My fault, Sheel thought, wincing. *If only I had thought of the possibility of a son instead of a daughter, before I sent Juya-Veree to the Grasslands! Actions have consequences* . . . But how could she have foreseen this, coming from a people to whom no male child had ever been born?

"You should see the stonework at the Refuge," she said, stretching her shoulders. "It's that false stone, gray, massive, ugly—they poured it as thick as a horse's barrel. Not like this work of yours. This has a nice pattern to it, like hard basketry."

Sorrel explained that the inside was going to be pulled out again, once the roof was tight, to make a hollow shelter instead of a solid lump.

Sheel smiled. "I've been at just that task, my girl: emptying out something. The Refuge was a shelter too, though it only sheltered mad folk; what you are rides with you no matter how the trail winds about. We explored as much as we could, but it's dangerous. Whole sections are leached out with water and could collapse without warning."

"I wish I'd been there!" Sorrel's eyes gleamed with interest.

"Not much to see, just chambers and corridors stuck onto each other for miles. There are acres of shelves and bins full of shiny discs. Beyarra says she read in a book that these are a kind of book too, but there's no way to read them. She's upset that I used some to trim my best bridle.

"We had to rig torches to see our way and unblock the ventilation shafts just so you could breathe down there. What a job for a Grassland rider! I must have been crazy to go."

Sorrel gave her an amused look. "Oh, you like busying yourself in these people's affairs, good-ma."

About to exclaim to the contrary, Sheel was caught by a quiet assent in a corner of her thoughts. She sometimes found herself imagining what her own responses to Holdfast life might have been, had she been raised here. It was like growing another life inside her mind, another self totally unlike all other Torrinors who had ever been or would be. Just a game, nobody else's business.

She said, "The Roises like the Refuge. They stayed behind to finish up. It's a Rois failing, this unhealthy appetite for new things."

Fedeka came padding back out of the dark and settled by the fire with a blanket pulled around her, thinking dour, Holdfastish thoughts in that heavy old head of hers, no doubt.

"What with planning it all and making sure the sticks didn't smuggle anything useful out of the place," Sheel went on, "it took ages to finish the job. We should have had more men, but there are only so many healthy ones. You don't want to be too much outnumbered by them, either.

"We tried to collapse the weakest sections, but it was too risky. So we had those cockies fill it all in; dump dirt, pack it tight. They had to dig a good-sized hill down to do it."

She sighed contentedly. "In a few years, grass and trees will cover the whole site. No one will be able to find it, which is how it should be, and no loss, either. I expected great halls, sinister statues, bloody altars—some trace of the grandeur we've stumbled on from time to time in our own country; oh yes, we have, though we don't make much of it. But this was nothing but broken-down underground rooms full of trash."

She looked into the flames, seeing again by torchlight the dreary maze of dusty, rubble-strewn corridors and chambers.

"Now that I think of it," she added, "we could have left it as it was, a monument to the fools of the past."

And she looked sideways at Sorrel's stone structure that looked more like a horse than a tent. Sorrel said nothing. She probably did not appreciate the implied comparison. Well, let her reflect on the uselessness of buildings. People should bring life into the world, not things.

Fedeka yawned loudly. "We have enough hulks and ruins hereabouts, and that's not counting the live ones rattling around the place."

She cleared her throat and sang a song with a clapping chorus about a fem with a rash on her face who had such bad luck in love that she flew away to the scar-faced moon and lived there with the Lady, spitting down cold light on the heads of the people who had spurned her on Earth.

Sheel didn't trust any song that wasn't about a real person's life. Still, the fanciful ditties of the Free appealed to her; few self-songs had ever made her smile.

"I like that song," Sorrel said. "I heard a good one on the boat from New Forge, too. Does Beyarra write down songs as well as stories, so they won't be forgotten?"

Fedeka said very dryly, "No, she only wants true things."

Sorrel stared into space. "*He* says some books were made by the foremothers of the fems."

"Well, *he* would say so, to you," Sheel said. "So what? He can tell you anything about all that paper and ink, and you wouldn't know any different."

"Maybe I should learn to read for myself, then."

"Some can learn, some can't," Fedeka said. "Alldera herself went south to get away from books because she couldn't learn to read them."

Sorrel flared, "She's the Conqueror of the Holdfast. Does she have to read books too?"

Good; a daughter should stand up for her mothers. Sheel said amiably, "It's all sharu-scratchings to me too, and I don't think that makes me a lesser person than anybody else."

She tossed the dregs of her tea out to her right for the ancestor-mothers' use in making their spirit tea. "Time to sleep. Tomorrow we ride. You too, Fedeka, if you'll sit a horse's back for once, to save your friends anxiety. Things are too uncertain now for people to go wandering. Alldera's heading north to Lammintown tonight. I've been asked to travel there with you and Sorrel to meet her."

What a look on the younger woman's face: anger and apprehension. "Is it really too much for her to make a swing inland to meet me first, since I came so far to meet her?"

"Not at all." The child was as touchy as her blood-mother was—used to be, anyway. In some ways they bred true to line after all, these double-blooded people. "She meant to, but word came from Lammintown: there's trouble up there—men, they think, living in the Wild. Alldera's gone to help sort it all out. We're to follow."

"Well, you took your time getting to the point!" Fedeka exclaimed. Sorrel was silent, probably trying to think what this might mean for that kit she had brought with her.

"I'm hasty sometimes, but I don't like haste," Sheel said. "I wanted to get to know you a little again, child, out here where we could have time together without busybodies hanging on our every word."

Fedeka made a rude noise.

"I won't go to Lammintown," Sorrel burst out, "not with Veree still penned up at Midfast! I told them, I've told them a hundred times, but nobody listens!"

Sheel sighed. "Now *you* listen. Men may attack Lammintown. If you want to be heard about that little boy's future, you've got to earn that right. You'd better show yourself willing to defend your blood-ma's country."

She didn't say, "Show yourself as willing, and as able, as your bloodmother," but she saw by Sorrel's offended glare that the thought had run between them without words.

"Or you can return to Midfast," she continued. "I just thought that you might rather go meet trouble than wait for it to come find you changing diapers in the Children's House."

She saw inward struggle reflected in Sorrel's face, and she waited quietly, thinking, *This girl will never forgive herself for missing a fight against men because of a kit in Midfast.*

"Well?" she prodded. "Will you come to Lammintown with me?"

Sorrel turned to Fedeka. "Oath-ma, I'll give you another chance to honor our bond. Will you take it?"

Fedeka scowled, and Sheel thought she would argue that she didn't think she had failed her oath. But the dyer said, "You know I'll give you any help I can, child, as soon as I can figure out what that help might be."

"You don't have to figure it out; I'll tell you," Sorrel said. "Don't come to Lammintown with us. Go back to Midfast instead and keep watch over Veree for me. Tell him I miss him and I'll come back as soon as I can."

Sheel could have laughed out loud at Fedeka's look of consternation. That would teach a Free Fem to take on a mother role that was made for the Grasslands! Oath-ma, indeed!

Trust Alldera's bloodchild to throw challenges in everybody's face; just like the runner herself in her younger days.

Well, not *just* like.

Reading the Signs

We cut northeast across country using landmarks Sheel knew as well as any of the Free—fenced fields, gardens walled in stone to keep out wandering horses, hearth houses, and storage buildings. The countryside was also marked with cairns, a depressing lot of them, in fact. I asked about some, but Sheel professed not to know their stories.

It was a strange land, neither plains nor forest. At the jointures of fields and tracks grew stands of skinny trees. Sheel said the Free cut them carefully, to be able to go on using them for everything from tools and fuel to weaving furniture, instead of having to go out to the Wild for wood.

All along the ditches or other lower ground beside trackways or fields, swathes of long grass lay drying. Some had been done up in odd little constructed heaps, "stacks," Sheel called them, to be stored later as winter feed. I said it was silly to gather up graze and carry it to penned horses rather than loose the horses and let them graze for themselves. Sheel pointed out that the femmish way made sense in this small, crowded country of fields and gardens.

Everyone we met asked for news. Rumors flew, of course, but I was surprised at how the basic facts had already gotten around in roughly the same form to everyone.

Sheel explained, "Some people here and there can read. The same written messages go everywhere in the pockets of riders like us."

She herself carried a grubby scrap many times folded and rattling with crumbs, with black loops and slashes of ink running across it in crooked lines. I could see that it had been written on before, then cleaned and used again, like Eykar's flagstones.

"They make this stuff up by Lammintown," Sheel told me. "It's a long process with lots of rinsing, worrying about the temperature, and such. Once it's made, they get all the use out of it they can."

"These people are crazy," I marveled. "So much work for such a tattered, stained result."

"These people are frugal," Sheel corrected me. "They say that waste is what the Ancients did to show how important they were. They're serious about such things. You'd be amazed."

I was amazed, to hear Sheel speaking of the Free so temperately. But I listened with only half an ear. Ahead, cupped in a great rise of stony cliff, lay Lammintown itself, still hidden from us by the shoulder of the hill.

Straight out to the east stretched the long blue line of what I guessed must be the sea. The sharp, moist wind blowing steadily toward it had given me a little ache in one ear. I wadded my headcloth on that side of my head for protection.

"There," Sheel said, pointing up the steep and barren slope rising ahead of us, "is the Watchtower, where Daya and her pack did their pathetic best to murder Alldera. Do you want to see?"

I hesitated. The roadway we were on, beaten down by a summer's traffic of hooves and cartwheels, curved around the base of the hill, over a grassy rise, and out of sight. Sheel had drawn me a map in the dirt when we had last stopped for fresh mounts. This road entered Lammintown from the south, edging the beach at the foot of rising cliffs.

What difference would it make if we rode in a little later in the day?

"All right," I said. "Let's take a look."

Our horses plodded uphill on a path branching off the main road, a mere trail of balding sod. Sheel pointed westward, inland. "Over there runs the stream where we found Tyn Chowmer passed out from drink, drowned in two inches of water. I'll never forget it. Ray Rois and I were looking for new arrow shafts. I told her we wouldn't find anything up here that grew straight enough for arrows. Instead we found Tyn, the first and only Riding Woman to die in this country and not even fighting against men. Now, there's waste for you."

Although Tyn Chowmer had come with us on my maiden raid, I could not now picture her clearly, only the heavy built Chowmer Women I had last seen in the Grasslands.

I said, "Why do you stay, Sheel? You have bad memories here, and people miss you at home."

She looked at me. "How can I make you understand? The place grows on you in spite of everything. Ray and Gayala Rois keep coming back, too. It's exciting here, they say. Everything's in motion all the time, people and events and ideas shifting about like bubbles on a running stream.

"Of course sometimes it's just plain incomprehensible. People argue about work as if it were the main thing in life—how so-and-so gets to be crew chief of a harvest team instead of someone else, and for how many seasons running. Whether everyone should bring wood for the signal beacons on the hills, or whether the Wester-Hearth people should do the wood in exchange for having their gardens tended; swapping unlike tasks, which is looking for trouble if you ask me.

"It's all things nobody would need to think about at all if they would just follow their horse herds like proper folk! But the ones who want to live that way—First Free, mostly, who learned right behavior from us—are scorned by the house dwellers and gardeners, who are mostly NewFree.

"Now some brave souls have taken horses south to live properly down there, or try to, and what a row that's started! With this business at Lammintown, it's true they couldn't have picked a worse time. But it's always chaotic here; nothing is ever settled enough for the year to make a normal round."

"It's all new still," I suggested, embarrassed for my femmish kin who still could not live like sensible folk.

"Ha," she answered, "that's because they keep making it new; never satisfied, these folk. It's like a dozen games of pillo going on all at once on the same flat, but the winning score keeps getting advanced so nobody can ever reach it. The confusion is vast. But the Roises are right: it's also entertaining."

We rode up past a weed-grown tumble of building stones and stopped, looking down from what seemed an enormous height at the edge of the land.

I scrambled off my horse in a hurry. What if she stumbled, what if the cliff gave way? I was afraid I—or she, with me on her back—would fall into all that space, turning and spinning helplessly till we smashed on the rocks below.

Sheel squatted down next to me. Our horses fell placidly to grazing behind us.

"Northward," Sheel said, "just visible on a day without heat haze, is Endpath. It looks like a little spit of land from here but up close it's a sizable headland. They'll have to go and take a look, of course, now that Ila-Illea has been attacked. She's not one to make up stories or to mistake drunken dreams for reality."

My heart quailed at the thought of people riding up that rough coast of forested bluffs. If enemies appeared in those woods there was nowhere to go except out into the empty air, and then down to the rocks and the bright surface of an endless reach of crawling water.

"Will you go to scouting to Endpath?" I said.

Whenever Sheel Torrinor came home on a visit, Women went around afterward sharpening their weapons and checking the fitness of their horses. They made maps in the dirt and stood over them talking about holding the passes, and where to set ambushes against invaders from the Holdfast.

Now Sheel, squinting away under her hand, gave a satisfied grunt. "They've got a watch posted. Kobba's here, I'll bet. Scouting will be her job." She lowered her hand and flicked my cheek lightly with her finger, as she had used to to when I was a child. "Don't look so shocked. I've had my fill of warring for fun. Besides, if things should turn out, badly, someone will have to ride like lightning and warn our Grassland kin."

I shivered. The idea of men attacking the Grasslands was unbearable.

"Who else is here with you now?" I said. "Besides the Rois cousins, I mean."

Sheel tossed pebbles over the edge. They clicked faintly on the way down. I shut my eyes, but that made me dizzy.

"Well, last time I visited home a Torrinor cousin and a Salmowon I'm related to both said they would come back here with me. My cousin got thrown in a race and broke her leg. The Salmowon had an evil dream and decided that her foremothers were warning her, so she didn't come either."

She clapped me on the shoulder. "So it's just those Roises and you and me, Sorrel, to uphold the honor of the Riding Women and look after our interests in a foreign land. The Roises stayed up at the Refuge to oversee the last of the work, so we're it for the moment. Now, my daughter who takes famous horses from under the noses of their owners, shall we go track down this bloodmother of yours?"

I stood and looked at the Watchtower ruins. "It happened in there?"

"Yes," Sheel said, glancing around as she swung up onto her yellow gelding. "There's not as much to see up here as I thought, except the ocean."

I had heard often about the widening nest of curved streets that made up Lammintown, inlaid on the face of the long slope like string after string of a pale stone necklace looping down a giant's chest. We rode two abreast, descending along the broad streets and the lanes that cut downward from one to the next. Rows of stone facades stood on the inland side of each street, and on the seaward side rooftops stepped down toward the shore.

"Where is everyone?" I asked.

"Oh, these outer buildings are deserted," Sheel replied. "See how the windows are blocked up? Now, the first thing they made the men do here was level the lamminworks down near the water. People work the lammins under canopies now, in light and air; in smaller batches, too, because the take is less these days. It's much pleasanter work, I'm told.

"The second thing was to fill these outer villas and halls, room by room, with stone piled in as high as it could be stacked; good, hard work for breaking down any rebellion left in the stickmen. Now no one can hide away or stash stolen supplies or meet secretly in these unused places. It's like what I've been doing at the Refuge, come to think of it. Even in broad daylight these dead streets are spooky, aren't they?"

Our voices and all the sounds of our movements seemed magnified by the stillness. I was glad to get down to where the buildings were occupied, and voices and footsteps could be heard and curious faces turned to watch us as we passed.

"Where's the main palaver, Bellana?" Sheel called to a fem who stood leaning in a doorway, wiping grayish dust from her face with her long apron.

"They've all gone down to where Ila-Illea was jumped," came the answer, "because Alldera and some Council people wanted to look. Not much to see—is that Sorrel Alldersdaughter? We've heard you'd be coming!"

Smiling widely, she stepped into the street and patted my arm, leaving a powdery handprint on my sleeve. She clasped Sheel's hand briefly too, which surprised me. I had not thought of Sheel having friends here.

There was so much I had not thought of.

"Flour," Sheel said, brushing her hand clean as we rode on toward the noise echoing up through the stony ways. "This grain they farm gives more seeds than our wild grass at home, but the flour's not as good. The noodles have no taste unless you salt them to death.

"This is a bad time to have trouble, right in the midst of harvest. They bind themselves tight to their earth's life, these people. But they're learning how to make it work."

"You didn't use to talk about fems like that," I said.

"I never knew the fems in their own home country, only as troublesome guests in mine." She regarded me a little sadly. "Do you remember me as such an intolerant person, that I wouldn't admire good in people where I found it?"

I said, in some confusion (that was just how I remembered her), that everyone had always known how she felt about the Free Fems. I was surprised to find that my raid-mother, whom I had idolized as a child, cared what I thought about *her*.

The noise was coming from a clutch of people at the water's edge. They were clambering over the rocks below the dark cliffs that bounded the northern end of the beach.

The tide was out, Sheel told me, which meant that smooth sand sloped down a long way to the water, glistening brightly.

"You should hear how the waves crash on those rocks in a storm," she said with relish as we rode over that shining sand. "The backflow pulls on all the pebbles at the foot of the cliffs and makes this sucking, chattering sound, like people dancing with big rattles. You'd have to hear it to believe it."

She spoke with enthusiasm, as if of great horse-lifting raids or deep Grassland disputes generations old. I wanted her to say something about Alldera but she talked about rocks and water, her thin face bright with pleasure.

I felt as if I were dreaming one of those vivid dreams that burns itself onto your mind's eye forever, even though it makes no sense at all to your waking thoughts.

People turned and pointed us out to each other. I knew Alldera at once. Why not? It was only a half-dozen years (and a world-changing campaign) since I had seen her last.

She stood on a low crest of rock, one hand shielding her eyes from the sun's glare on the twinkling sea and gleaming sand. The ends of the sash knotted around her waist snapped and spiraled in the breeze.

While I gaped, she jumped down onto the sand and trotted toward us. Her feet and legs were bare, femmish-style, below the hem of her belted tunic: solid limbs, a little knock-kneed, with broad feet and a sure, slightly inturned tread.

It was as if she had never been away. I saw the same sturdy build and wide-boned face, light brown hair tied roughly back with wisps fluttering wildly all about, decisiveness in every step. She was not coming to meet me on a rush of ungovernable emotion but on determination.

Then she was at my horse's shoulder, looking up at me. I saw no joy in her eyes, no relief that I had arrived safely or even anger that I had come.

"Sorrel," she said. "Thank you for leaving your cairn-building to come here. I should have gone to you, except for all this."

Well, I thought, *that's supposed to make up for everything?* But in my heart I felt grudging approval, the more so because she pitched her voice for only me to hear, and maybe for Sheel. Her greeting was not some grand gesture for all to admire.

Reluctantly, I surrendered the advantage of making her look up at me. I slid down from my saddle and stood facing her, surprised to find myself a couple of inches taller than she was. How tall does a hero grow in the tales of her exploits?

Now I saw the deep lines around her eyes. Her lips were chapped from the wind. White strands, not gray but bone white, threaded through her hair. I thought, *But she's not old!*

A pucker of pale scarring along one side of her neck reminded me of one event that had aged her; her hand too, when she took my shoulder in a weak and crooked grip.

They had hurt her permanently, that cowardly pack of assassins.

"I'm glad you're here," she said, giving me a little shake with her scarred hand. She smiled up at Sheel. "Have you filled her head with gossip about me, Sheel?"

Sheel chortled.

"I ought to have come sooner," I said. My voice cracked a little and I covered this with a nervous laugh.

Her eyes were not green as I had remembered, but hazel, her gaze clear and direct. Her smile showed strong, square teeth yellowed with tea stain. "We can exchange reproaches and apologies later, is that all right?"

I mumbled that it was; what else was I to say?

She said, "Now, come with me. We can use another good head."

She let me go and turned, hesitating a moment before leading the way back to the black rocks. I thought she had meant to put her arm around my waist but changed her mind. We walked together up to the rocky spur, with Sheel riding alongside and leading my horse.

Alldera said to the others gathered there, "Friends, this is Sorrel Holdfaster, born to me but raised by her sharemothers in the Grasslands. I hope you'll all be kind to her for my sake while you get to know her better. I have to get to know her myself, to my shame."

Then she made introductions to people whose names I immediately forgot, except for Kenoma—I remembered her from Holdfaster Tent years ago. Each person took both my hands briefly, in the way that people often did here when greeting each other, and murmured a word of welcome.

I had been stared at before in the Holdfast. Now, with Alldera close by and Sheel as well, it was much worse. I wondered how much time must pass before people stopped measuring what they saw in me against what they saw in my mothers.

"Right here," Alldera said, striding ahead of me to a small inlet where the sea had made a pool in the rock, "is where you lost track of him; right, Ila?"

A short fem with gleaming black hair pulled back in a horsetail nodded energetically. "Yes, he went into the water there. It was dark. I didn't see him surface again. But I know he did, because I found some wet patches on the rocks over there, where the sea doesn't reach except at high tide. There wasn't enough to track him by, though, not in torchlight.

"He was heading up the coast, toward Endpath." She grinned. "Cassara thinks he was limping."

A pale person with a figured blue headband added, "They were footprints, not just splashes and drips, and they were uneven. Ila kicks hard."

Ila shrugged. "I felt it connect, all right. That was your training, Alldera—all that kick-fighting practice that some people don't want to find time for."

Another fem made guttural sounds and flashing hand signs.

Alldera translated this handspeech, ostensibly for those who didn't see but probably also for me: "Oleeyot says the kick worked because the man grabbed for you from behind, Ila. If he'd banged you over the head, it would have been different."

"If the sky fell down, we'd all be this tall," Ila said equably, holding her thumb and forefinger an inch apart.

Oleeyot made the Lady's circle sign on her chest with her closed fist. Others did this, too. Alldera did not.

Ila-Illea had been on watch up at the old rock quarry, original source of building stone for Lammintown. Now they got stone, ready cut and dressed, from the closed villas on the upper streets. The old quarry was where each night they penned sticks and freefoot men traveling without their hearth sponsors.

"You can see the path, there," Alldera said, "leading off the end of the street with those pointed roofs, going up over the rocks to that roof frame built high on pillars. That's the shelter at the quarry.

"So, Ila was coming off her watch by herself—even though nobody's supposed to trot around alone at dusklight—"

I saw a blush stain Ila's swarthy cheeks as another in the group said, just loudly enough to be heard by all, "She was on her way to meet Bessolay at the sea caves. Then there'd be two together."

Ila called out good-humoredly, "Oh, shut up, Tuja, you

old beady-eye! You think you know everything!"

"So," Alldera continued, "she descends to that point right there, at the pier where the lammin boats are moored. A man jumps up behind her and grabs her, and he says—"

"He says," Ila said, in a mock growl, " 'You're coming with me, bitch.' So I gave him the back of my head in his face good and hard, which made him let go. I whipped around and slammed my foot into his knee, and down he went with a yell and a splash."

I wanted to kiss her, right there in front of everyone. Just arrived, and I was in love again!

"I rushed down to the water, but he was gone," she ended.

Alldera said, "He must have escaped up the Devil's Stair, which we blocked last year. Well, we thought we did." She stepped back for a better view upward, feeling for her footing on the smooth black rock. "If he got away over the top of the cliff, hurt knee and all, he's pretty strong."

Ila also stared up the jagged fall of rocks from the cliff above. She was frowning, perhaps for the first time seriously considering how it might have gone. I was ready to pray thanks to the Lady myself for her good fortune.

Sheel said, "Find any bloodstains up there?" She rolled a shoulder in Ila's direction. "If she bashed him in the face, he must have bled."

People shook their heads, no. Ila said soberly, "I had his blood in my hair. We were too excited to think of looking for a blood trail. Too bad you weren't here, Sheel Torrinor."

The Riding Woman ran an appraising gaze up and down the steep tumble of broken blocks that comprised the Devil's Stair, climbing high above the narrow beach. "I wouldn't have been much use; I have no head for heights. So you think he was one of those Ferrymen nobody's seen for years?"

Ila nodded. "First thing we did was check the quarry. We hauled them out in the middle of the night and counted every stick. No one was missing or had fresh bruises. We sent riders to Oldtown and Midfast right away, asking for a special check on their men for anyone missing or injured, and to have the signal beacons lit along the way. No one's reported a man missing or wounded. This was a stranger."

She hesitated, then added, "Besides, he smelled different. Different from our men, I mean. No, not better, Oleeyot, just different." People laughed nervously.

"A different diet," Sheel suggested. "When I go home to visit, Women say I smell odd. It's from eating so much farm food and less meat."

I wondered if I smelled funny to these people. I knew there was no way on this earth that anyone or anything could have persuaded me to tackle climbing the steep and precarious jumble of the Devil's Stair, either escaping or pursuing.

Around me they were talking about edible fruits, nuts, and root plants found in the northern Wild in summer. These were often left unharvested because, with the fields producing so well, they weren't much needed. But could a person, a renegade man, say, subsist by foraging?

They got onto the subject of harvesting acorns, with some heated exchanges about people claiming ownership of certain heavy-bearing trees, but Alldera called them back to the point: if d Layo and his Ferrymen were back, they could probably sustain themselves for a time in the woods while making quick, limited raids like this one.

Sheel, squatting on the rocks and gazing out to sea, said suddenly, "Where am I, in the Chief Tent? People should go and find out. I thought that was already decided."

It was. The group broke up. Sheel took our horses to look after. This freed me to go with Alldera. She needed to choose maps for the scouts' search of the woods between us and Endpath.

I looked back once from the edge of the beach and saw them all gathered around Ila-Illea. I envied her and wished that it was I who had met an enemy and sent him scurrying away again with a bloody nose and a sore leg!

But no, I was Sorrel Alldersdaughter who had showed up bringing an extra problem no one needed; who had ridden out of Midfast in a temper when she couldn't have what she wanted; who had spent her time since then piling up rocks in a pasture. A warrior's daughter who had never fought men.

Everyone must be thinking the same. Alldera must be thinking it.

It was so unfair that I should care what she thought or didn't think.

The Ice Stair

Setteo would have done anything for them. It was difficult to retain his old caution, to which he owed his survival in the Cold Country, because he was so eager to confirm the Bears' renewed trust in him.

Other men had visited the Cold Country safely by throwing away caution and acting boldly. But they were whole men. The rules were different for them.

And besides.

He had no doubt that those interlopers were riding for a fall, which was of course the only way that men could ride at all, the Bears said (a typical Bear joke which those men would not understand). And the Fall was coming, you could feel it in the air.

The Bears had not really accepted these "dancers," only let them in so as to reap a greater harvest of lives when the Bears' cold breath at last blew full blast into the Warm World. Which was already preparing to happen. He could tell by the breeze tonight, coiling down from the north.

The Endtendant had been hard at work in the Book Room since the beacons on the plain had raised the alarm. He rapidly took down books and wrapped them, one by one, in scraps of oiled fabric or soft, worn leather he'd been hoarding.

Now he limped off again, heading for the old kilnyards where he was stowing his treasures for safekeeping. That was his task, the true work of his heart. Setteo was afraid even to offer help. A fanatical gleam lit Eykar Bek's clear eye. He had, in that hour, no love to spare for a mad cutboy.

There was reason for all this activity, as there was reason for everything. To learn it Setteo must enter that white land again; Eykar would have no answers. He never did. The

Bears had cast a film over the eye he had once trained on their world, and the other eye saw only this one.

It saw what he hungered to see: books, print, words. Wise as he was, the Bears and their doings were invisible to him.

Setteo withdrew silently. No one would trouble about him. They expected him to be with Eykar. He would be, too; he would come back to Eykar and the books, if he came back at all.

You never knew. Which was why you had to find out, because ignorance was kiss, the kiss of death, the hiss of breath, the Bears' black breath that could suck a man's soul out of his nostrils on a single sigh.

He paused to stuff his own nose with plugs of earth before following the swirling breath of the Bears, not by scent but by taste. He walked open-mouthed, eyes shut, along the broad sweep of the old Market Arc, which was empty now. He tasted the acrid breath of the Bears on his tongue, taking the changes in the flavor as his guide.

Little was left of the labyrinthine City ruins he had known so well. Much had been pulled down, smashed and washed away into the river, or else broken up to mend holes in Midfast streets, roads, and the pathways along the river.

No one challenged him. The Heras were out guarding the horses and the stone cellars where the men were penned, yoked and chained to heavy metal staples sunk in the walls. People worked hard and quietly to shift stores of food, fuel, and weapons to secret locations prepared against just such a time of threat.

Between one step and the next down the middle of the broad, empty street, the mantle of the Bears' interest flowed over him and hid him like a shroud. Chilly and damp against his skin, it drew him inexorably forward and—up, suddenly, steeply.

He mounted cold steps into that sky which no true sun ever lit. He breathed lightly, straining the air between his teeth so as not to swallow too much of the Bears' deadly breath.

The taste of the air got sweeter. He opened his eyes.

He walked on an arch made of fused ice blocks, each block the size of a horse. Their curve rose high above a glittering plain. Star-shine illuminated the translucent steps under his tread.

There were faces inside; no, whole men, frozen in twisted postures—sly Chokky Vargindo, angry Arjvall, Jebbie Kanga who said he was a tough man like the Hemaways of old and had cut their symbol into his skin. The scars glowed on his breast now.

Men he had seen as Bear dancers were here, faces distorted with terror. Their fingers clawed, their fists pounded at the enclosing ice in nightmare-slow movements. They stared as he passed above them. They screamed—inaudibly—for help, and struggled on in their slow, doomed way.

"Meat keeps better in the cold," said someone.

Setteo felt the chill of breath on his bare calves and knew now why the curve of ice vibrated slightly under his feet. A heavier being trod the crooked steps behind him. Trembling, he led the way up into the star-pitted dark.

"Greetings, elder brother," he said over his shoulder. "I feel safer on this narrow way in your wise company."

"I feel hungrier," said the Bear behind him, "in yours."

"You tease me, elder brother," Setteo gasped. The air was thin up here. "If you eat now and grow heavy, your weight could crack the path and drop everything to the warm earth below."

Silence. The bridge of men in their enclosing ice shivered and creaked under his feet.

"How may I assist you, brother?" he ventured, trying not to plant his heel squarely in the center of Relki's pleading, ice-bound features. "If there is anything I can do, you know I'll give you all the assistance that I can."

"One warm body can melt all this wealth of food so that we can reach it," said the Bear. "The bodies of children burn very warm, and to be given these men by their children would please us and make us laugh. You may have noticed that we do not laugh much. We are short of humorous happenings here."

How they lied, the Bears! It was the children they had decided to devour, not the men. He had seen this coming, of course, when the first infant was born to the Heras. Now the time foreseen had arrived. It seemed obscenely sudden. Tears quivered in his eyes, blurring the image of Maddery's profile underfoot, scarred across his nose where Vargindo had cut him in a grudge fight.

"No child could be carried up here without crying in fear," he said, "and the shrill sound could crack this path to bits while you yet climbed it."

But where were they going, that they climbed so high and needed such supplies of meat? His ignorance made him panic, and he felt his hastily set foot slip. He froze, tottering—an arm or leg thrust out for balance could be snapped off immediately in the mighty jaws of the Bear that followed him.

Teetering, he tried to think of some way of dying before hitting the warm ground below.

Rough, chilly fur brushed his leg. A heavy body shouldered him straight, keeping him on the stair.

"That's how much you know," remarked the Bear. "You've been away too long. The young ones burn so hot and high, they will run up this bridge all on their own to get cool again. All you have to do is bring the hottest one to the lowest step, which is called 'Sunbear.' If you really want to help, that is."

"Oh, always," Setteo said hastily. His mind raced. "Then I can teach this child to come visit you too, and do these little jobs that a Warm person can do as tokens of esteem for you and your brethren."

"Only birds fly in these skies," the Bear said with a chuckle, and Setteo looked up and saw them: white, triangular shapes blazing past like arrows of ice, bright and pure. "And there are only so many favors we require. Why clutter the place up with more Warm walkers? You leave all that to us."

"Naturally," Setteo said. "Naturally, elder brother. I would not choose otherwise even if I could."

"Run along, then," the Bear said, shoving him behind the knees so that he lurched forward. Ahead, the bridge sloped sharply down again, back toward the earth. He had his foot on the block that was the keystone and summit of its curve.

Inside that central wedge of ice Eykar Bek curled with one arm over his eyes and the other thrust out—thrusting out—fingertips already free, in a dimpling of melt-water where the ice had flowed away—

"Run or fly," the Bear said. Setteo ran. Down he fled, sobbing with terror as his legs scissored wide and wider, carrying him in huge, jarring bounds over the steep, hummocky ice of the Cold Country itself.

He misjudged his footing and fell with a cry.

No thick fangs tore his flesh. Air warm and moist and faintly milky smelling enveloped him, with a tang of . . . sewage? He picked himself up in the grassy yard of the Children's House, where torches leaning in brackets on the walls lit a scene of frantic activity. Janna strode by with a blanket-wrapped baby on each hip. One child hiccuping quietly, gazed back at Setteo with big eyes.

They were emptying the hall, taking the little ones to a safe hiding place down among the stumps of the old docks. Years ago he had collected wood-ears among those decks and pilings. Boats were stored there now, for escape on the river if need be.

People rushed about carrying children, food baskets, folded cots and bundles of diapers, blankets, and clothes. They brushed past him, paying him no attention.

"A stupid idea!" hissed a NewFree called Kazy, her front swelling with an obvious pregnancy. "Why should I be locked up with the children as if I were a baby myself?"

Belett tried to propel her forward with Ambalay, who was more pregnant still, saying angrily, "We can't risk losing you to renegade men, not with a child in your belly!"

Kazy twisted free, protesting, "Let me be, I'm not your slave! I never wanted a baby anyway. It's because Muvai's daughter died. I was going to name mine after her."

"The little ones need us," the other young one urged. "Come help, Kazy."

Kazy said bitterly, "I should be out riding patrol, but who'd have me, all puffed out like a dead horse!"

She stamped in ahead of them, shouldering past Leesann, who emerged holding one sleepy toddler by the hand and carrying another astride her shoulders.

A Bear's voice husked, "You can claim a favor from me later for leading me to such tasty snacks."

"What are you doing here?" Leesann said, blocking the way.

"Help," he said, in a desperate voice. These children

were warm, very warm; just what the Bears were looking for.

"Good, we can use all the help we can get," Leesann said. "But if you come with us, you stay with us until it's all over. I won't have you wandering off to blabber our secrets to our enemies."

"Men will never taste them," whispered the Bear. "They will be fed to us first, a feast instead of a snack."

Setteo whimpered and hugged his own ribs, cherishing his scrawny body as it vibrated in the chill of the Bear's ravenous breath. They were not discriminating about their food.

"Shouldn't he be helping with the books?" Belett said severely, pausing with an armload of blankets.

"To hell with the books," Leesann retorted. "Let Eykar Bek save them if they're so important. We're shorthanded with those deserters off playing at being Mares. Get going, Setteo. There are still some kits to bring along."

He hurried inside, anxiously scanning the torchlit chaos for the telltale heat that he had been sent here for.

Behind him someone said angrily, "—Lammintown, for the Lady's sake! It's too soon to fly into a panic down here!"

"—no chances," replied another voice as someone pushed past hugging a sputtering infant in her arms, "of those Wild Ferrymen getting their hands on—"

There: a glow of energy that could melt any amount of blue-green ice.

Setteo caught Veree up in his arms. The boy, sweaty with sleep, squirmed and whimpered. Setteo loosened his grip, and the child reared back to look at him, breathing snuffily.

"Where's my ma?" Veree's eyes were huge. "I have to go with my ma."

Setteo saw his own reflection in the child's pupils: there were yellow fangs pushing out his upper lip. He whispered, "It's all right, Veree. I'll take you to your ma."

Kazy marched up, lugging a heavy jug of drinking water in each hand and still complaining: "Just what old Erl used to do with us when other men came sniffing around: lock us up for safekeeping!"

Ambalay, similarly laden, panted, "You're just scared that Leesann will kill us herself if there's a chance we might be captured with kits in our bellies!"

Kazy swore and shoved her into Setteo, who skipped back out of the way. Ambalay swung weakly at the other Hera with one of the water jugs.

Kazy snarled, "Coward! You'd be the first to beg a man for mercy!"

"What are you two waiting for?" shouted Leesann.

"Grouchy old Matri," Ambalay mumbled under her breath, which made Kazy laugh. They hurried on together.

"Snacks," whispered the Bear's voice, "and then courses."

Setteo hiked Veree up close and kissed his soft fingers. *You are not mine,* he thought, his lips warmed by the touch of that soft child-skin; *no one like you can ever be mine. You belong to the Bears because they have claimed you. I will deliver you to the Sunbear, and he will make you one of them—a painful process, sucking the tender skin off you and gnawing the sweet red meat in order to build you stronger muscles out of stone and a skin of ice and fur, like theirs.*

But not yet, not just yet.

He set off quickly with the child already heavy in his arms, moving away from the others, away from them all in the summer dark.

There would be no mercy for him if he were caught, of course. But as it happened, no one stopped him.

Naturally not; the Bears looked after their own.

Migayl's Raid

The two fems stood shivering, clutching their rags about them. Skinny Leeja, whom Servan remembered from Erl's femhold in Midfast, dared to show hatred on her long, sharp-nosed face, although she had quickly learned to keep her gaze lowered.

"I have more questions, bitches," Servan said. He stood aside so that they had a clear view of the tub on the deck, filled with scummy water from the foot of Endpath Spit.

At this, dullness quenched Leeja's clever face. She made

no attempt to evade Laxen, who limped close behind her and lashed her wrists together at the small of her back. She was preparing herself, trembling, for another round. How did she do it? She kept breaking, as anyone must break, and then gathering her shredded strength around her again for Servan to destroy again.

He would continue until she was finally too shattered to ever recover. The Pool Towns women should see the ultimate futility and price of courage in a female.

The other one, Tamansa, was already moaning and trying to scramble back to their cage of saplings, which swung, open, on a rope beside the worn decking. The two captives spent their days inside that cell, lowered to place them within reach of the daily tides that soaked them.

Tamansa, easier to deal with from the start, could barely speak a coherent word any more. Well, send her off, then, for what she was good for. She was still pretty in a bruised, mad way, with her wild dark hair and staring eyes.

He nodded at the lads and they dragged her down the decking to the aft shelter and disappeared inside with her. Other men gathered outside, joking together while they waited their turn. The fem's wails were stopped.

Servan took pains to wring every drop of information from the captives over and over again. Perhaps he was misinterpreting what he heard; more likely, they were lying. He kept hoping to hear something different, something—*possible.*

How could the Holdfast have turned into every man's worst nightmare just in a few years? It was like a conjurer's trick, a fever dream.

Torby and Arred walked around silent, like men asleep, and the rest of them argued and raged continually. He often felt them watching him, waiting for a solution. If he didn't come up with one soon, they would look among their number for someone else who could.

So he worked on knowing more. He could not see what else to do, or how to do it. In any case the men were too shocked to act against him yet, no matter how some of them blustered.

He himself had never believed in the supposed incapacity of fems. His own experience had enlightened him, although he had kept his heretical opinions to himself. But even he had never expected such an upset.

He remembered Alldera the runner, of whom these captives told such unwelcome news. He could all too easily credit—sometimes, anyway—that she had indeed done all that the two fems reported she had.

At least he had learned some facts that might be useful: summer's end was still harvest time in the Holdfast, although the crops were different now. (Maggomas' wheat, of all things!) Bringing in enough food for all was difficult. It would be best to attack soon, when it would be hardest for the fems to muster their full numbers for a fight.

It was the numbers that paralyzed him: what *could* they do, fifteen men and their handful of captives against ten times that many fems, armed with bows they knew how to use (damn Ardy forever for his fanatical destruction of the Towns' weaponry!) and riding these horse things? When he thought about it, he fell into a numb, incredulous rage.

Now Migayl had run off somewhere. He had spoken to no one of his purpose in going, or no one was admitting it if he had. There was nothing to be gotten from Tarisha but stark, gasping terror.

They were all raw with nerves. The men showed it in the way they threw themselves into abusing the two captives, even those who would normally never touch a female. They did it out of bitterness, and to reassure themselves and each other.

Tonight, again, they needed to see Leeja beaten down into a mindless, cringing wreck like Tamansa. Hell, he needed it, too.

Yet he was distracted. At this moment Alldera herself might be directing her people to press information from Migayl just as Servan was doing with these outlaw fems. He did not doubt that if caught Migayl would talk, despite the men's professed belief to the contrary. Anyone could be made to talk.

And if Migayl was captured and revealed everything to these "free fems," then what?

All I have to do is turn my back for a second!

He seized Leeja, jammed her against the side of the tub, and forced her head under the water. She twisted, strong with desperation. Her resistance made him long to hold her face under until all the life bubbled out of her.

He glanced up. Salalli held Luma against her and would not let her look (have to have that out with her later; they were *there* to look). But Lissie was watching, and so was Shareem. Death had lost much of its shock value for them, but torture could still hold their attention.

He heaved Leeja out again, wrenching her streaming face up toward the stars. She choked and retched.

"How often do Alldera's riders patrol these woods?" he asked. "How many, and how often, in summer?"

"They never," she gasped. "Any more—never—"

She coughed in heaving spasms that made it hard to keep hold of her. He loathed the greasy feel of her hair in his fingers, the chilly clinging of his own clothes that were sodden from her splashings.

Imagine, two bitches strolling up the Pilgrim Way to Endpath as if they owned the place! And then imagine finding out in fact that they, and all their kind, *did* own the place.

But he found no real pleasure in tormenting Leeja tonight. He wished he had never seen her. It might have been better just to march into Lammintown, strong in ignorance, and play things as they came.

He let go and stepped back, wiping his hands on his pants. "Jonko. Give her a turn in the deckhouse, see if she'll say anything new."

She staggered down the deck like a spastic, kept upright only by Jonko's hard hands. The waiting men closed in behind them.

Later, he lay in his bedding thinking about these "free fems." He could hear a few men still shouting and laughing in the deckhouse, dealing as they pleased with fems no longer free.

In his mind he went over the numbers, the implacable, hopeless numbers. Alldera had taken the Holdfast with a ludicrously small force. Their "New" Holdfast held some hundred and twenty-five fems, masters now of seventy-two defeated men. There were also some young children, born since this "conquest." Leeja gave different numbers every time.

Worst of all, there were completely new elements to contend with, barely imaginable additions to Holdfast life: distance weapons, horses, and mysterious foreign warriors.

And Eykar, that sturdy weakling, that mournful murderer, that prim, reluctant sensualist, was still alive. He was tougher than a cliff-clinging tree; Servan had always thought so, and now it was proven.

He wedged his hand between his legs and began to squeeze and stroke, groaning softly, until a sweet, straining spasm burned through his nerves. Then he thought he caught the scent of Leeja on him. He inhaled deeply, hoping the odor of her fear and dirt would buck up his wilting flesh for another shot. Instead he drifted off to sleep, his hand still tucked warmly over his groin.

Salalli woke him. "She's going out again," she whispered. "Tarisha, the same as last night."

He gripped her wrist in the dark, hard enough to make her wince. That was for not telling him about it last night. Then he got up quietly and followed the furtive sounds of Tarisha's progress through the night woods. She went inland and southerly off the Pilgrim Way.

Blix, supposedly on watch, was asleep, his snores whistling audibly through his open mouth. *Deal with him later.*

Was it being near the Holdfast border, the New, femrun Holdfast, that dulled everyone's wits? Servan could hardly believe that Tarisha would be so stupid as to try to steal food from the storage pit. But that was what she was doing.

He caught up with her, grabbed her arm and twisted it behind her back, clamping his free hand over her mouth. She froze, making small squeaking sounds of pain but not daring to bite.

"So, where are you off to with that sack?" he said into her ear. "Are there more of these 'free fems' lurking out here for you to give our food away to? Then why don't they come rescue you?"

She sobbed and tried to shake her head.

"It's not for yourself, is it?" he said, giving her a shove that made her gasp. "You wouldn't dare. So it's Migayl. He's back, isn't he? Show me where he's hiding, and no games or you go into the cage too."

He let her go. She stood panting, her hands on her knees. If he didn't need her, he would have killed her. You could never forget that the fact that they said yes and did as they were told did not mean that they could ever be trusted.

Come to that, though, he had only ever known two entirely trustworthy *men,* and one of them was dead.

Stumbling along ahead, Tarisha led him a winding way to where a fallen trunk, wedged aslant among standing trees, supported a crude wall of dirt and twigs blown against it by the wind. The hollow within was empty.

Tarisha's step rustled among the dead leaves. A voice came out of the darkness above them.

"Tarisha?" someone whispered. "Don't make so much noise!"

Servan pushed the woman aside. He looked up into the lower branches where he could just make out a dark, hunched figure.

"Miggs," he said quietly. "Come down here and talk to me. Give me a brilliant explanation for all this, and I might not kill you for the treacherous little cuntsucker that you are."

He heard Migayl's breathing now, stertorous and labored. For an instant he thought he might be wrong, that it was someone else—who, Christ-God-son?—a trap of some kind? He eased the gun loose in its holder.

Migayl's voice said plaintively, "I'm coming. Back off a little, give me room."

He descended slowly, grunting with effort. "Let's get under cover at least," he said. "There's room for two. Tarish, get out, make space there."

Inside the lean-to, he lowered himself to sit with one leg straight out (*like Eykar, with that game leg of his*).

Servan squatted next to him. "Talk."

Migayl scrabbled about stuffing something, rags or earth, under his extended knee. He sighed heavily and sat back.

"I went to see for myself," he said truculently. "I didn't believe those two bitches. You said, 'Wait, they'll tell us more,' but what good is that if it's all lies to begin with? So I just went, that's all."

"Do you believe them now?"

Wind gusted past. Migayl coughed. "Have to. I saw the things they told us: chained men, driven at their work by fems. Horses—they're big, and fast, you wouldn't believe it!"

He stirred restlessly. "Fems were having foot races on Lammintown beach, like lads sporting away a free hour. Only it was part of something else, some kind of sparring with kicks and twists and jumps. Fight training. Fems!"

"Did you talk to the men?" Another sound of movement. "I can't see you, Miggs. Was that a nod?"

"Yes. No. I mean, no, I didn't try to contact the men. The fems might have seen me. I couldn't have outrun those horse things, even before I hurt my knee."

Servan struck sparks with his flintstone, lighting a little heap of dry leaves and grass he had been quietly scraping together. Migayl raised a hand to shield his face, but the bruising was impossible to hide.

"Somebody's broken your nose, my boy," Servan observed. This premature contact with the fems might have ruinous consequences, for which he would make this fool pay when the time came. For now, though, it had its funny side. "Don't tell me she broke your leg, too?"

Migayl put his hands protectively over his knee. "I fell."

Deliberately, Servan jarred Migayl's injured leg with his foot. Migayl whined, clutching his knee.

"Tell me what happened, Miggs. I'll decide how much of it to pass on. Now, while we have a little privacy, I want to know just what we're really up against. You're a better witness than those two cunts in the cage. So tell me everything, with no lies and no improvements to make yourself look better."

There was depressingly little difference between Migayl's report and what the two captured fems had revealed.

"How did you get your war wounds?"

"I wanted to bring back proof that I was there," Migayl said. "Well, would you have believed me?"

"You just couldn't resist," Servan jeered. "You thought, 'Never mind that they're the masters now, I can take one down any time I feel like it.' Didn't you, cockbrain?"

The prize Migayl had come upon—he thought it was a

fem he had known in Midfast, a sound young creature with a naturally cheerful disposition—the prize had smashed his nose and nearly dislocated his knee as well.

"I've stayed out here to watch my back trail for trackers," he finished bravely.

He'd stayed out here because he was too ashamed to explain his injuries. Well, let him keep some dignity for the present. That left him something to lose.

"It didn't occur to you," Servan said, "that if these 'free fems' caught you, they could find out all about us? How few we are, and what we have that they might want for themselves?"

Migayl glowered sulkily at the little flame Servan had lit. "I wouldn't have told them a thing."

Servan thought about ducking Migayl's head into the scummy water instead of Leeja's. He thought, *I could kill him right now. He doesn't even imagine that I might, the idiot!*

Kill him, dump him, tell Tarisha to keep quiet, and nobody would ever know. It was what he deserved. And he was dangerous now, although he didn't know it. Men might follow a man who had suddenly shown initiative, even if it meant deserting a leader who had brought them successfully through hell.

Cut him and stick his head on a stump for disobeying orders and jeopardizing everything.

But there were many "free fems" down there, and their men-prisoners might be in no shape to fight or might have no will to any more. He couldn't spare any of his own lads. Store this disobedience up for later, among other scores to be settled.

"It took nerve to go scouting on your own," he said. "So I'm not going to break your nose again for you. Stay here tonight. I'll send someone to help keep watch just in case. In the morning, you and Tarisha come back to camp.

"Smile, you've got your way after all: now that you've given those rebel fems our scent, we'll have to make our move before they make one of their own."

Padding back through the woods, he worried about which men might line up with Migayl if it came to a challenge. And he thought about Alldera. How galling, that she slept in his home country somewhere tonight, and she was not afraid! Well, she would learn to be.

She must be a dried-up hag by now. He looked forward to meeting her again.

By Christ-God-son, she would piss herself with shock when she saw him!

It bothered him, though, that five years ago it would have been him, not Migayl, who slipped into the Holdfast on his own. Only he would have brought his chosen prize back as planned, and it would have been Alldera herself.

He would get his hands on her sooner or later, he promised himself. He must think of something better than the water barrel for her, something very slow and dramatic for everybody to watch.

Meanwhile, he had the perfect task for Salalli.

Envoy

I sat in the chamber made from a natural cave near the cliff's summit, a place called "Cliff's Eye," from which other hollows and passages spread through the bluff above Lammintown. I knew from femmish stories that Cliff's Eye was connected by these tunnels both to the town below and the Watchtower ruins on top.

Alldera had pored over maps for hours, conferring with Kobba, Kenoma, and others about where best to set patrols and who might be spared from essential work (most of it concerning food or horses) to staff them. And then there was the question of who should go to Endpath—on foot.

They would take no chances of losing horses in the Wild, not with men out there who might capture them. A captured fem could try to defend herself, but a horse was helpless. And, as I knew from coming over the forested mountains, mounted archers would be at a disadvantage because of treacherous footing and tree-masked perspectives.

I was uncertain about what was expected of me. Alldera, seeing my hesitation, asked me to stay and eat with her.

Her eyes were puffy with weariness, but she ate vigorously and watched with approval as I cleaned my plate of the light meal–with–tea customary in the afternoon here. She said nothing, in the femmish way of dedicated food consumption.

The silence made me uncomfortable, so I said (to say something), "Sheel's changed, hasn't she? She's not very eager to go after this outlander man."

"Sheel knows we can take care of our own affairs," she answered, dabbing a bread crust in the salty oil on her plate. "Also she has a long-standing liaison here that tends to take precedence when she's in Lammintown."

"A lover?" Ha! And she had been so inquisitive about *my* love life.

"One of the NewFree. It started with archery lessons. I think Sheel only rides off somewhere now and again—like the Refuge project just now—to show her independence from Shanuay."

"You mean she's staying in the Holdfast because of . . . ?"

"Partly, though she'd deny it if you asked her." Alldera rolled her eyes. "Don't tell her I said that, would you? They've been together for two whole years but they're both a little sensitive about it, each for different reasons."

"What reasons?" I said, fascinated.

"For one thing Shanuay likes sleeping with men, too, like many of the NewFree. After the Seniors were kicked out, the Junior men weren't so hard on their fems, so NewFree tend to dislike men less than First Free do. This makes for tensions among us, as you can imagine—I shouldn't be gossiping about this."

A broad grin transformed her face. "With the Lady's help, I'll stop—in a minute!"

"Sheel said you don't believe in Moonwoman," I said disapprovingly. "So why do you talk like that?"

She shrugged. "Just a way of speaking; you'll pick it up too if you stay here a while. What was I saying? Oh yes; frankly, I think Sheel gets a kind of thrill from Shanuay's . . . mixed tastes. And, though your raid-ma wouldn't say so, I think she's come to appreciate how strong it can make people, to stick with each other as a couple. Still, she'd probably turn back into a Grassland free player if she went home."

I saw a speculative glint in her eyes: Are you free-hearted? How do you run your love life, child of the Camps?

None of your business, I thought, warming to a quick, groin-heating flash of Ila the hero. But as she was NewFree too, she might prefer men. Sheel might find that intriguing, but I didn't. The idea made me feel queasy.

But there was Raysa, the guard who had come down the river with Galligan. If people would just let me get on with things my own way, I might have a love life of my own here.

Thinking of lovers I said, "Is Beyarra in Lammintown too?"

"No, she'll come up from Midfast in a few days."

She poured only tea, not beer. I had forgotten that she drank no liquor. They said that during a bad time in the Tea Camp once, she had nearly destroyed herself with drink.

"Beyarra's been nice to me," I said.

"Good." Alldera got up and walked to the window and back, fiddling with the knot of her sash. "I hoped that you two might become friends."

"That's not a replacement," I began, and stopped. *No replacement for the long lack of your friendship, blood-ma,* I meant.

She paced, eyes averted, and I knew she understood the meaning of my words and smarted from it. Now I noticed a hitch in her gait, a tightness that shortened her step on one side. The strong, balanced stride that I remembered so well was gone.

A fem brought in a plate of moist, grainy cheese and a pitcher of fresh tea. I was startled to recognize Emla, with her shock of white hair. Once Alldera's enemy in the Tea Camp, she was not my idea of someone to make into a companion—or even a bedmate, in Beyarra's absence?

She may have sensed my feelings; she did not stay.

When she had gone, Alldera raised an eyebrow inquiringly. "Don't you believe that people can change?"

"You always hated that person," I said. "For good reason, I heard. Sneak attacks aren't the kind of behavior that people grow out of."

She shrugged. "At least she never tried to kill me outright. And she learned good things from Elnoa the Green-eyed as well as bad ones. It turns out that Lammintown runs more smoothly if Emla has some authority here. Besides, if I don't have a deep rubdown from her once a month or so, I get too stiff to walk."

I said, "I hope you take your massage with a knife in hand."

"Come sit with me a minute."

I accepted a cup of salty second brew with thready noodles floating in it. They liked their noodles thin and quick-cooking on this side of the mountains, I had noticed, preferring them thick and hearty myself. She sat down across from me on a bench carved into the wall under the windows.

The cushions on the seat bore stitched designs. My blood-ma was reputed to have become something of a craftswoman even with that damaged hand. The stitches were large, I saw, and the designs bold and simple, not fine work but pleasing.

The chamber smelled of the dry splits of pine propped on their ends in the hearth, ready for the evening fire. I felt as if I were sitting with my bloodmother inside the fragrant skull of some long-dead wooden giant.

"Will you go north with the scouting party?" she asked, as if my doing so would be the most natural thing in the world.

"Are you going to lead them?" I countered.

"I don't think so. Younger people need to take charge of things. Everyone says so, anyway." She hesitated, then added, "We've had some deaths here since the Conquest, mostly First Free, and not from old age. Sometimes I think my leadership may not be so good for peacetime.

"Destroying old ways is easier for us than creating better ones." She grimaced. "I don't like to think so, but sometimes I do. We were so eager for children that we discounted the dangers to older mothers. People died; some babies, too. I fault myself for not foreseeing those terrible births."

"How could you have stopped it?" I knew how fervently the Free Fems had spoken in the Grasslands of having daughters to raise free, and how touchy they had been at any suggestion of restraint on their hard-won liberty.

"Oh, who knows; somehow." A haunted look dimmed her gaze. She looked into her tea and took up a writing pen to stir it with. "Anyway, I try to make space for new leaders."

I felt her interest beat toward me, warm with—hope? *Will you one day lead these people?*

My impulse was to say, "No," to see if it would hurt her to hear that. But it seemed such a cold, bald word—up close like this, alone with her, no matter how *she* had hurt *me*, no matter what she owed me, I couldn't say it.

She rose abruptly and paced the room again, holding her cup in both hands. "Curse it, why does everything have to happen at once? I need to spend time talking with you. I should have gone back to the Grasslands with Sheel last time to see you."

I grunted. "I dodged Sheel when she came back, and I'd have done the same to you. Pretty childish, actually."

She brushed this aside. "I have so much to tell you." She laughed, a light, joyful sound. "You're good-looking, Sorrel—who would believe a homely old creature like me could be your blood-ma!"

"You're not homely," I countered sharply. Why did she have to run herself down so? Was that where I got that habit from? "Or old. Maybe you looked bad when you were a slave, overworked and badly fed, but you look good now.

"They've told you about Veree, Juya's son?"

My bringing him up cooled the emotion warming between us.

"Oh. Yes. The boy who you claimed was yours, but who turned out not to be."

I blushed with embarrassment, but I felt defiant, too. She must see why I had tried to throw the protection of my name over that poor little mite.

She said, "I have to confess, I don't understand: what interest can you have in Juya's child?"

"His blood-ma died," I said. "His sharemothers more or less abandoned him. If I hadn't stepped in, he probably would have died. He's like a little brother to me."

There, I saw understanding register in her face: *They abandoned him as I once abandoned you.*

She moved right on: "Not like a daughter?"

I shrugged. "Sometimes that too."

"So you protect him."

"I've tried to," I said, and to my horror my eyes filled with tears. "I mean, I meant to."

"It's not always possible." She sighed. "My 'best' for you wasn't as good as it should have been, either. I'm sorry."

What could I say to that? I wasn't a little girl any more to break down in wails and reproaches, or turn away and sulk. If I had had just this one mother I might have been more overwhelmed by my feelings. But I'd had my other mothers to cuddle me and play two-hands-on-top and pinch goop out of my nose.

I wasn't spurned, like Veree, by my Grassland kindred but welcomed with love. A great deal of my adolescent torment over my abandonment now appeared to me as foolish and self-indulgent at best.

"I haven't come to put myself forward as some great warrior, or anybody special," I said. "I just wanted to give Juya's son a better life than he could have had in the Grasslands."

She looked down at her scarred hand, spreading and contracting her fingers. They did not make a proper fist. "I left you in the Grasslands so you wouldn't have to be a warrior at all. Intentions don't go nearly as far as we'd like them to in this world, do they?"

I opened my mouth to put words to the wave of sympathy I felt, but nothing came out.

Then Emla hurried into the room again, stammering with excitement. "They want you on the beach, Alldera, right away!"

"What now?" Alldera shouldered past me to stare out of the window. She turned back at once, her annoyance changed into alertness, and pressed Emla's hands. "Stay here and watch. String your bow, Emla."

To me she said, "Will you come?"

I followed her.

On the way back down through the streets we caught up with two fems hurrying ahead of us. Alldera plucked one by the sleeve and said, "What are you doing? Plenty of people are already on the beach. Go up, ride the inland perimeter and see that its stations are held."

They both turned back at once to do as she said.

I had trouble keeping up with her. Even with her limp she was fast, and her wind was good.

A squat, broad-shouldered person who looked very familiar to me met us by some lammin bales stacked for loading. It was Forrenz, one of Galligan's guards on the Steps at Midfast.

"A stranger's been sighted," she said excitedly, "coming south along the beach—alone, we think."

"No signs of an attack elsewhere, while we're watching this visitor?" Alldera asked.

Forrenz shook her head.

We hurried out onto the sand. I held an arrow nocked to my bowstring. I hoped that if I had to shoot, my shot would be straight and steady.

Four Free people stood spaced across the breadth of the beach, bows drawn, facing a single figure. This person approached them on foot along the tideline, empty-handed so far as I could see. At first I thought it was one of the Rois cousins. The skin was of a deep hue found only among the Riders of the plains. But she was not tall enough to be a Rois.

Before I or anyone could prevent it, Alldera broke out ahead of us and trotted toward this unknown arrival. I saw the tension in every fem, the bristle of weaponry, the taut determination.

No wonder the men had fallen to the Free.

I turned and scrambled up on top of another stack of lammin bales for a better vantage point, bow in hand.

Alldera advanced twenty feet and stopped. The archers behind her shifted so that they could fire past her at crossing angles without endangering her. No one spoke.

The newcomer's hair coiled in tight black ringlets around her face. Her colorless rag of a shirt was tucked into calf-length pants tied about the waist with a cord. Over one shoulder she carried a pair of shapeless-looking shoes. Her long, bare feet stepped flat, with splayed toes.

She had a big-boned body with nothing like the gracile slimness of the Roises; more like my share-ma Shayeen Bawn, who was Indin by blood. But this person was darker than any Bawn.

If she had a weapon, it was hidden.

"Stop there," Alldera called.

The dark person paused and spoke in halting, accented Holdfastish: "My name is Salalli. Servan d Layo sent me to tell Alldera the runner that he would like to speak with her."

Someone uttered a low but heartfelt curse.

Alldera said after a moment, "The Servan d Layo I knew would have come himself."

"He says to tell you," said the newcomer carefully, "that he sends me to you in honor of the changes you made in his homeland. He says that I am to answer whatever you ask."

"Then tell me where he is."

"He and his companions have returned from the lakes and forests of the north," said Salalli readily. "They are rich men now. They camp by Endpath."

"How many men has he?" Alldera asked.

Salalli replied, "Of the Ferrymen who followed him into the forest, thirteen, and one young man, still a boy really, who comes from the Pool Towns. Of women and young girls from the Pool Towns, nine."

My breath came fast. What "Pool Towns," where?

Alldera regarded her in silence for a moment, then asked, "And these all call d Layo their leader?"

"Yes. But we weary of life in the forests. So he wishes to meet with you, Alldera Conqueror, to talk of the future."

"When?"

"Tomorrow morning."

"Or else, what?"

The stranger opened one pale palm toward us, placating. "Or else some other time, at a place of your choosing; you have only to say. He has brought home goods that he would like to trade."

"Trade!" Alldera laughed incredulously. "The Dark-Dreamer would like to trade?"

Salalli swept her hand in an arc, taking in the watching Free. "His men are too few to fight you. But this is still their country, that they struggled to return to, as well as yours."

"That," Alldera declared, "is debatable."

"He says fems of the Holdfast are not as they were when he went away, but he and his men are not as they were either. So, he says, people should talk."

Alldera folded her arms across her chest and said dryly, "Has he changed so much?"

"I only know him as he is now," said the emissary, "so I am not one to say. He says you yourself must hold hard feelings for him because of old troubles and bad times, but he was a great deal younger and more foolish then than he is now."

"He's still an optimist, I see. He wants to meet at Endpath? Well, that won't do. You can go back and tell him to come down here. Let him bring what he has to trade, and we'll talk on this beach under open sky as you and I talk now."

Salalli nervously licked her heavy lips. "Then I should leave now, to tell him your answer."

"Since he sent you here to answer questions," Alldera said, "stay the night with us so we can ask some. If he's as interested in conversing with us as he says, he'll wait for your return. And to tell the truth, I'm in no great rush to see him again soon."

"As you wish." Salalli took one shy step forward; every arrowpoint dipped slightly, trained hard upon her. She checked herself and added in a strained voice, "He would want me to stay with you if you desire it, as surety of his goodwill. May we go where we need not shout against the wind? Also some water to drink would be very welcome."

Alldera warned her gravely, "It's a risk. He could attack us while you parlay in good faith. The DarkDreamer I knew wouldn't hesitate to sacrifice his best lover to serve his interests."

Salalli lifted her chin. "I am his chosen woman. His trust honors me. I do my best not to shame it."

I felt the strangest mixture of revulsion and curiosity: did she mean some sort of voluntary slavery? How did my blood-ma feel, to be addressed this way by "his chosen woman," who must have felt the DarkDreamer's weight and thrust in sex as Alldera once had in her own bondage?

And how was I to feel? If this stranger had any children by d Layo they might be, in Holdfast reckoning, my little sisters.

As for the DarkDreamer himself, I knew of him as a clever and ruthless killer, closely connected with Eykar Bek and—perhaps—connected with me. I had assumed him to be dead. I didn't want to meet him, either.

It was unsettling enough to see Eykar Bek as my father. Why did this other man have to show up and muddy those waters again?

Alldera stood considering for a moment longer, then turned to walk back the way she had come. We all jumped, seeing her turn her back to the newcomer. She paused and glanced over her shoulder. "Well, then, come along please—Salalli."

But where had the creature come from? Even Servan d Layo could not create fresh human beings, fully formed and matured, out of the trees of the Wild! Sheel would not be pleased to learn of other survivors out there, particularly if they had truly allied themselves with the wandering Ferrymen.

As for me I was scared, but happy and excited, too. It looked as though my luck had brought me home to my bloodmother's land at a fine time after all.

The View from the Watchtower

Alldera sheltered herself from the late wind behind a fragment of curved stone wall. She always visited the remains of the Watchtower when she was in Lammintown. Out of habit she poked at the ground with the toe of her boot, looking for a stone to add to the structure.

For her, as for Beyarra, the tower was a cairn marking the death of Tezza-Bey, who had tried to run away with a boy she had thought herself in love with. He had died, too, that night, at the angry hands of Daya's ring of conspirators; but it was for Tezza that the free placed these stones.

Down below people moved purposefully about, raising rubble ramparts at the outer ends of the streets and avenues of Lammintown. Nearly all the Lammintown men had been collected and put on both yoke and stick.

When one of the sponsored men asked why, a tongueless First Free had answered in handspeech, "Because your hero is coming, and we want you kept quiet while we smash him to bits."

Chokky Vargindo was heard exhorting the men to be patient and prepare for the victory of their "Sunbear." Spies said that not all of the stickmen had received this news with smiles. But to Vargindo, d Layo had acquired the status of a god. How on earth did the DarkDreamer do it? The spirit of drama itself must arrange his flamboyant life for him.

Not that he could do the sticks any good at the moment. The majority of the men were now headed south in stout wooden cages on wheels. They were also deprived of their most troublesome leaders, who remained here. If, Lady forbid, the Free were defeated in Lammintown, the older men caged at Midfast could be dispatched and the younger ones passed on to the swamp folk, to be dealt with as they saw fit, before d Layo could reach them.

This harsh resort had been planned against the return of the Ferrymen or any other Wild-wandering men: "Better no men than masters again," people said. She hoped they all meant it.

To the west lay the wastes and mountains patrolled by the Riding Women; to the south, the Bayo-born; to the east, the sea. The potential threat had always been from the north.

"We should have sent riders out with your orders," Kobba said, "not runners." She had just finished checking the sentries again. The excitement agreed with her; she fairly glowed with it. But she was no youngster any more. Alldera hoped she wouldn't wear herself out too soon.

"We should have driven the rest of the Lammintown horses south too," the tall miner continued, "keep them out of the DarkDreamer's reach, same as the cockies."

"We don't give up superior speed and mobility unless we have to," Alldera said, "and we have few enough horses up here now so they can be easily guarded."

But oh, Lady, how stretched and strained she felt—and the challenge had just begun.

The plan had been arranged long before. Her price for returning to the Whole Land Council after Daya's attempt on her life had been immediate preparation of defenses against attack. Plans, made with comments and ideas from all the Free, had been put in place for just such a moment as this. It heartened her to see those much-debated ideas turning so swiftly to well-drilled action. In a way it was helpful of d Layo to return now and test them.

That busyness down there near the Lammintown laundry pools marked the transfer of essential supplies to central storage. At the same time small caches of food, drink, blankets, and weapons were being placed along the outer walls for defenders to use if they were cut off or needed supplies to carry with them, either in withdrawal or pursuit.

Not enough of the harvest was in—six wheatfields still stood ready to cut, and the autumn horse culling had not yet begun—but it would have to do.

Ila-Illea squatted with her back against the broken Watchtower wall, knotting menstrual plugs with nimble fingers as if nothing untoward were happening. She was by nature a calm, self-contained woman, her movements fluid and economical, and Alldera wondered briefly why she had never felt drawn to this capable young person.

Ila was too young, perhaps, too self-confident, and reputed to be not much interested in the love of women. She would have to be a conquest.

Maybe I've had my fill of conquest, Alldera thought wryly. *Maybe I'm just getting old and lazy.*

Ila spoke from the level of Alldera's thigh.

"This Salalli," she said. "Suppose she's here to keep us busy while he mounts a sneak attack? Let some of us head north now, while he thinks we're all huddled in awe around his pet bitch and her news. We could find him and flatten him like a midnight hailstorm."

Alldera said, "If he's gotten inside Endpath itself, he'll be hard to get out."

"Maybe not," Ila answered reasonably. "He has nothing to eat but what he's brought with him, and that can't be much or his slave wouldn't talk about trading. They're sitting up there scratching their skinny bellies and smelling the cooking fires of home. I bet some of them would abandon the DarkDreamer for a good meal. They were always a practical bunch, those Ferrymen."

Kobba grunted. "Make him come to us; remember how we took the City? Now we *are* the City. We must force a meeting on our ground, not his. And we should draw these Pool people out of the forest onto territory they don't know, in case they choose to fight against us, too."

Ila said with cool scorn, "They'll fight us. That Salalli

thinks d Layo 's men will beat us even though we outnumber them ten to one. You can see it in her eyes. Those people will fight us out of fear of their masters."

"We'll have a better idea of what she thinks when I've spoken more with her," Alldera said. *How quickly we learn to despise those whose bondage we no longer share.*

"We should have questioned her right away," Kobba said, "while she was still hungry and scared."

Alldera pushed away from the wall and rubbed her hip, feeling scar tissue pull. "That's how I'd treat Ferryman, Kobba. Salalli should be rested and fed when I talk with her. I want her to know that we're doing well enough to offer an alternative to d Layo's band."

Kobba said impatiently, "Waste of time. Ila's right, Salalli's too scared of her masters to change sides. What do we need with a bunch of black-skinned people from the Wild anyway? That one is like a ghost of the unmen, out of men's legends."

So that was what was bothering her.

"I hope her people are all dark-skinned," Alldera answered warmly. "Do you believe those Old Holdfast lies about evil nigs and blackies helping to bring on the Wasting? I don't. Look at us, Kobba; hardly anything but blonde hair, brown hair, light skins, light eyes. We're free, but our bodies are still cut to the pattern our masters chose for us."

Kobba shrugged but was silent.

"We can change that now. The DarkDreamer has brought us the means in these Pool people. I want a wider world for my daughter than the narrow one his kind tried to lock us into."

Ila said, "My little girl is darker than most of us. The men of the Old Holdfast would have killed her. Would you kill her, Kobba?"

Kobba still said nothing. Alldera guessed she was thinking of Nenisi Conor, Alldera's lover among the Riding Women. Nenisi was as black as the stones of Devil's Stair. Kobba had never approved of their liaison.

Oh my best beloved, shall I ever see you again in this world?

Alldera wondered if her longing flew west into Nenisi's dreams, a faint farewell after years of separation; and she shivered. *I have not done well there,* she thought.

Kobba said finally, "They and their children would always look different from us and ours."

"And so?" Alldera said. "Do you look at our horses and see bays and grays and sorrels and say, get rid of the bays, they don't belong?"

Ila said, "Some say white-footed horses have weaker hooves."

Alldera said, "Maybe horses with white feet are also smarter or give better milk. Maybe a herd with horses of many colors is better able to meet the unexpected than a herd of, say, all gray horses."

"Sounds like something from Eykar Bek's books," Kobba said dismissively. "You listen too much to that man."

Alldera said, "We're all gray horses here because our masters made it so. We knew that without Eykar's books."

"Well," Kobba said stubbornly, "we haven't done so badly. We haven't missed having this Salalli and her kind with us."

"But," Ila said (she could always speak on all sides of a question, a valuable but irritating trait), "we NewFree did a lot better after foreign people came to us from the Grasslands, didn't we? You could say that we gray horses were penned up tight until a bunch of piebald Grassland ponies came back with some of our own strays to break us all out."

Kobba twitched her wide shoulders in annoyance. "These are strangers, not our own come back to us. All we know about Salalli is that she serves the DarkDreamer and his men. How could we ever trust her?"

"Can we trust each other?" Alldera retorted. "We've all taken orders from masters at one time or another, and we all switched sides, Kobba."

No one spoke for a moment. They heard some shouting from below, but no alarm sounded. *Gray horses,* Alldera was thinking. *Wild horses.* An idea was forming, a plan shaping around a memory. "I don't think d Layo will attack tonight. He gave up the advantage of surprise in exchange for whatever he hopes to gain by sending Salalli here."

"He sent her to spy on us," Kobba said at once.

Ila said, "From what she says, he knows a lot already. Maybe they've been spying on us for weeks."

Alldera watched the shoreward crawl of the waves below. Could an attack come by sea? Servan's men had crewed the coastal ferries of the Old Holdfast, after all. She hadn't enough people to guard all sides of Lammintown. If pressed from the coast, they could retreat toward the mountains and beg for help from the Riding Women. That would have to do.

If she was right. If she wasn't overlooking something crucial, or mistaking her man, or Salalli and her folk.

She said, "He may not know much. What he has found out he wants Salalli to tell us, to scare us into thinking he has informers among us and to weaken us with suspicions and fears."

Kobba turned restlessly. "I should have gone south with the cages. I should be there to make sure that if he gets to those stickmen, he finds nothing but corpses."

"And miss a fight here?" Alldera said. "With d Layo himself? You know you'd rather jump off this cliff!"

Kobba laughed. Her laughter, seldom unleashed, could be astonishingly rich and throaty. Alldera had known people to fall in love with that laugh.

Ila said, "He could be heading west right now, meaning to skirt Lammintown and strike straight for Oldtown or New Forge."

"No, that's too . . . *big*," Alldera said, groping for the word. "Too complicated—too many people, too many plans and contingencies. He was always best with quick, limited action that doesn't depend on other people. I think he does intend to go softly at first—meet with us, talk with us, get a better feel for the situation. When he sees a way to slip past our guard, he'll attack on the spur of the moment, counting on surprise and luck to bring him success. That's his way."

Ila said musingly, "Yes, he was like that when he used to drag the Oracle around and sell 'prophecies.' An opportunist, not a strategist." She coughed and added, "Sorry."

Alldera reached for her shoulder and gave it a reassuring squeeze; a sign that she wasn't sensitive about talk of that terrible and demeaning time in Eykar's past.

"He'll come after you," Kobba said bluntly, turning toward Alldera. "You above all."

"Let him come," Ila said equably. "We've won some fights since the Old days."

"So has he," Kobba growled. She kicked angrily and repeatedly at the wall behind her, like a restive horse. "How else did he capture Salalli and her folk? He's an experienced commander now."

Alldera had a vision of an army camped in the woods between Endpath and Lammintown: a hundred men, two hundred. She said, "Where are the men of those north towns, Salalli's men? Have they joined d Layo?"

"They're dead," Kobba said. "He's killed them."

Ila said, after a moment's hesitation, "I think so, too. It would be too risky to take in defeated enemy-men, extra mouths to feed that might turn and bite you. And he didn't know he'd need an army, did he?"

"Agreed," Alldera said. "Salalli said he's wealthy. D Layo doesn't create wealth, he hasn't the patience. If he's rich, it's through taking things from someone else. The Pool Towns women are his wealth. He's killed the men to take the women." She gave a snort of angry laughter. "He probably wants to trade his captives for food."

She stretched and yawned. *Nerves more than fatigue,* she thought. *Because I'm afraid of him, afraid I don't know him any more. What if I'm wrong about what he'll do?*

Maybe she should send Kobba back down to Midfast; was there too much command power concentrated here in Lammintown? No, too many people were on the move already, with too many chances for confusion and error.

She pushed herself away from the wall, wincing at the twinge in her hip; those old wounds got worse, not better, with time. "I'll go talk with Salalli. Hope for a quiet night."

"I'm off too, then," Ila said. "I'll check in again before dawn." She left them, and in a moment they heard her riding west down the slope toward Chowmer Stream.

Kobba said, "What about Sorrel? You should send her home, out of harm's way."

"Didn't you see the shine in her eyes?" Alldera said with a sigh. "Harm's way is just what Sorrel is looking for, to show me what a fool I was to leave her behind in the first place. If I told her to go, she'd refuse."

"You can't be sure," Kobba began. "You could tell her

you need her to carry a warning to the Riding Women—"

"She didn't come here to take orders from me, and she knows I've already sent word. Don't worry about her, Kobba. That's my job."

She went to Salalli's guarded sleeping space in the Cliff's Eye complex. It was an inner room, windowless, with a claustrophobic feel to it. There was a draught hole high over the doorway.

The dark stranger had finished the meal that had been brought for her. She had neatly stacked her plate, mug, and utensils on their tray and now crouched by the stone fireplace in a corner of the chamber, warming her hands at the flames.

She looked up warily as Alldera entered. Her skin shone smooth as polished wood. "I have three children," she said. "Their father is dead."

It twisted Alldera's heart to recognize the plea in that simple declaration. Three children by a dead man. Three hostages in d Layo 's capricious hands. Salalli was a slave, all right.

"I hope your children are well." Alldera folded her headcloth under her and sat down. "So what else does Servan d Layo want me to know?"

That got a glimmer of a smile. "He wants you to know that he is strong and confident. He wants you to know that he remembers you well. He says he respects you and is ready to deal with you as a leader in your own right."

"No surprises so far."

"He also wants you to know that he won't make trouble about the men you have cast down. If they couldn't hold their own against you, then they have the fate they deserve.

"But he and his followers are different. They have never been defeated. He demands that you deal with them as equals. After all, he went to another land and won from it what he needed with hardship and struggle, as you yourself did."

Alldera stared at the fire, thinking of the father of Salalli's children, his death doubtless just one incident among many such during d Layo's sojourn in the wilderness. "Did d Layo make you memorize that speech?"

No reply. Alldera regretted speaking so bluntly. She no

longer knew how to conduct an easy conversation with a bond person. Too much freedom had happened for her.

Close up, d Layo's emissary was not much like Nenisi Conor's line. Nenisi's hair was much more springy and dense. Nenisi's smile was wide and dimpled, not taut like this woman's. Nenisi had never been any man's "chosen woman." The two dark people might as well have come from different planets.

So, to business: "Did he leave any of your people alive in your towns?"

"All that survive are here," Salalli said. "That life is over. He has made us his—dependents."

She had spirit enough for a bitter gibe at her own subjection. Alldera said, "You could become our allies."

"Thank you," Salalli said, "you are too generous. We were work-hardened in the Pool Towns, not battle-hardened. We're not like you."

"We were all very much like you, once. We've learned to fight, but we haven't forgotten how to work."

Salalli looked steadily at her for a moment, then turned away again. "He told me that you were—that fems are lovers of fems here. Is it true?"

"Yes," Alldera said, surprised; and seeing how Salalli's lips parted in an involuntary grimace, she added, "Not everyone is, but mostly yes." She studied the dark woman carefully for her reaction. This time there was none.

"How was it in your northern towns?" she asked, trying to disarm the unease that she sensed in the other. "We know from books that among the Ancients men and women were paired off together by custom, supposedly for life. Was that the Pool Towns way?" As there was no reply she added, "We in the Holdfast have always found it more natural for men to cleave to men and fems—and women to women, like to like."

Salalli looked as if she regretted having raised the subject, but having done so she went on, murmuring, "I don't know how to answer you. We had some people that were sexy-versy, but it was not approved of. One of my sisters . . ." A heavy, tremulous sigh, and silence.

Alldera said, "We don't need to speak of such things

now. The answers to such questions are probably not as important as people think."

Salalli responded quickly, "If your numbers were as small and as uncertain as ours are—were—you wouldn't want people loving with those who could give them no children."

"When life is hard," Alldera replied slowly, "people take comfort where they can find it without too much worry over costs and rewards; haven't you found it so?"

The dark woman's teeth showed briefly in a frightened snarl. "Have you come here to take some of this—comfort?"

"No," Alldera said, folding her arms and trying to keep the anger out of her voice. "I can see that he's told you some lies about this. You know what a liar he is."

Salalli studied her intently, then turned back deliberately to the fire, her hesitation clearly resolved. "Here's something he doesn't want you to know, not yet. He has a gun. Do you know what that is? I've seen none here."

"I know what that is," Alldera said. Her heart beat heavy and hard. She remembered Maggomas' men, shooting at rebellious Juniors from the terrace at 'Troi. A few such weapons had turned up after the Conquest. Ila-Ilea and others had argued for keeping them, for defense. Alldera had wanted no weapons the stickmen might get their hands on that could outperform a good, stout bow.

She had won the argument after an eager NewFree had tried to fire one of the guns and the thing exploded and blew half her hand away. The guns had been melted down for trade chain. Alldera still had a gunmetal bracelet as a memento.

Maybe Ila had been right.

"It was our gun at Rock Pool," Salalli was saying. "My husband Gaybrel kept it in case of enemies." She wiped her eyes. "An enemy came and now he owns it, with the bullets my husband had made for it. He can destroy you."

"With one gun? No," Alldera said. At 'Troi town all those years ago, the men with guns had been overwhelmed by the sheer numbers of their opponents. Still, the cost in lives had been immense. They had no lives to waste here.

"He can destroy you," Salalli repeated, staring into the

fire. "With the gun or without it. He has only to look at a person and he sees how to ruin them. He is a terrible man."

"I think you've slipped back into telling me things he would want me to hear," Alldera said gently.

"You think I'm weak to be so afraid of him."

"I was his property once myself, Salalli. Your caution is only good sense, in your position."

"You think you can beat him. I don't think so. I can't take the chance." A bitter smile. "As he knows very well."

"Because he has your children. Boys?"

Salalli lowered her head so that her hair hid her face. "I don't want to talk more about my children."

Alldera almost spoke of her own daughter. But it might seem arrogant to mention a child raised free and unbroken to Salalli, whose children were in all probability neither.

"Why only one gun?" she said.

"We had others. Some were taken by men who went exploring. They never came back," Salalli said. "Kasheyena threw one into the sea after one of the boys shot her little girl's eye with it by mistake. We meant to make more, but life was busy, and there was never a need. A gun isn't as good for hunting wild goats as a bow is. You have to get very close, and if you miss, the noise scares off the whole flock."

"What are 'goats'?"

Salalli shook her head, gazing into the fire.

"Having more guns wouldn't have helped us," she said at last. "We were sure of ourselves and proud of our hospitality. I told Gaybrel, I said to him, 'These ghost-people have betrayed us in the past, be careful!' But *he* said, 'You women think too much about old times. Memories make you timid. I'm not afraid of white men. Do you think I am weak?' And so . . ."

She pressed her lips together. Dark teardrops spread silently on the hearthstone by her knee.

Alldera said, "How did your ancestors survive the Wasting? The end of the Ancients' world, I mean."

Those eyes, so dark with the black irises and dark brown coloring, turned upon her again, narrow with anger. "Why would I tell *you* our secrets? White, you are white, like him! We survived. That's all."

She would make a fighter, Alldera thought. She already was one, to have endured and kept her children alive.

"Join us, Salalli! We'll help you get your children back and set you on the road to your home."

Salalli answered harshly, "I have traveled a long way with d Layo and his men. I know the power of their bodies, their cruelty, their will. I've seen how they use that power. I want to be standing with them, not with you, when they use it here."

"Do the others from the Towns feel as you do?"

Salalli shrugged. A chunk of wood cracked and spat sparks, and she hissed and brushed them off her thigh. "Will you let me go back tomorrow?"

Alldera thought. "Yes. Here's what you can tell him from me: he will not be allowed to reenter the Holdfast. We will not meet with him or trade with him."

Salalli looked hard at her for a moment, her own expression carefully blank. "I think you knew he was coming."

"Yes," Alldera lied, keeping her face relaxed. "The men here have dreamed for months of his approach, and informers among them have told us of their visions. We're already watching him. He can't make a move without us knowing. And if he tries to come here, we'll stop him. You and your people are welcome, but he and his men no longer belong here. Tell him I said so."

When she left Salalli, she climbed to her office in the Cliff's Eye, lit the meeting lamp, and set it in the big window. Kobba came at once with two runners. Alldera sat down with them over her maps and explained what she intended. It took a long time to work through the possibilities. She thought they were not convinced of the soundness of her plan.

It was not sound; it was a gamble, like all war plans. And this was war, however slow and circumspect. The runners left, one of them first making the Lady's sign very solemnly.

"Does it bother you?" Kobba asked curiously, catching something in Alldera's expression. "When people put their foolish trust in Moonwoman?"

"No. I'm glad they've got someone to believe in besides me."

Not long after lying down to rest at last, Alldera was wakened from a light sleep by footsteps at her door. She threw on a shirt and unsheathed her knife.

Maybe Salalli had fooled her with lies and the Ferrymen were here—but all else was quiet.

The footsteps were Beyarra's. She brushed back the curtain, a lamp flickering in her hand, then stumbled and dropped the lamp with a low cry.

"What's wrong?" Alldera sprang up and embraced her in the dark. "You weren't to come till tomorrow."

Beyarra spoke into her shoulder. "They said not to wake you, but I have to tell you—"

Alldera covered Beyarra's mouth with her hand. "Wait. Let me kiss you first." She did, and then moved back, out of Beyarra's convulsive grip. "Now, tell me."

"Setteo has taken the boy Veree and vanished," Beyarra said wretchedly. "No one has seen them since the rest of the Midfast children were tucked away safe in hiding."

Alldera closed her eyes, her mind ringing with shock.

"We'll have to tell Sorrel," Beyarra went on. "We can't keep it from her—other people who came up from Midfast know. If only I'd thought—she'll hear it from someone. I brought Eykar Bek with me so nobody down there would punish him for Setteo's betrayal."

"Bloody, awful hell!" Alldera exploded. "Where are we supposed to put Eykar? We've already got Arjvall and Vargindo locked away up here. How many secure places do you think I have to play with, how many people to spare for guarding men?"

"I'm sorry," Beyarra wailed softly.

"No, all right, just tell me what happened," Alldera said.

"Despite all our drills, there was a lot of confusion when word came to secure the town; and of course they're missing the people who went south. Leesann-Leesett thought the cutboy had come to the Children's Hall to help out."

Alldera retreated to her bed, skipping and swearing when she stepped in the hot lamp oil that spread silently on the floor. "Well, it's done. We'll have to make sure everyone is warned to watch for the pair of them. I'll find someplace for Eykar. What else?"

Beyarra gulped. "What?"

"What other news from Midfast?"

So while Alldera found and lit another lamp, Beyarra reported on the consolidation of stores; the deployment of weapons, fighters, and horses; the messengers despatched to Oldtown and New Forge, lighting the beacons alerting outlying work teams as they went.

"Fedeka?" Alldera said, when Beyarra paused for breath.

"Barricaded in the Midfast Moon's House with two devotees who want to help her defend the place. No one could budge any of them. She's praying, she says. I think she wants to die."

"What? Fedeka wants to die?"

Beyarra gulped a sobbing breath. "Sorrel charged Fedeka with that boy's safety. Now he's stolen. Fedeka was helping fortify the Moon's House instead of watching over Veree."

Alldera nodded wearily. "And Daya?"

"On her way back to Oldtown." The younger woman hesitated, then added in a rush, "I sent her there to keep her out of people's way, but I hear she took Galligan with her."

Alldera sprang up.

"Shit!" she spat, striding up and down. "That man's untrustworthy, and so is she! What a shambles! Do I have to be everywhere at once?"

Beyarra stood mute and miserable. Alldera swore some more.

"Our first real challenge since we took over here, and we lose track of the people who most need watching! Oh, Beyarra, don't snivel, please. There's no time for it."

Great keening sobs now, worse and worse; they angered Alldera and at the same time made her want to cry too in exasperation. She sat Beyarra on the bed beside her, holding her hands, trying to communicate reassurance through her grip.

"I'm sorry, I'm sorry, you can't take every word I say to heart. You've done your best, you brought me word. It was right to bring Eykar, too. Look, there's blood on your sleeve. Are you all right?"

"I don't know; it's nothing." Beyarra scrubbed ineffectually at her stained cuff. "Mother Moon, what's Sorrel going to say?"

"She'll say it to me, whatever it is, so don't worry." She gathered Beyarra's stiff, resistant body close and smoothed her wild damp hair. "Give me a hug, do you think I'm made of stone? Now I've got things to do. No, you stay here—rest. Sleep here tonight. I'll wake you myself when you're needed."

She kissed Beyarra's forehead and left her.

How in the world could this news be given to Sorrel?

She brings her child to my country—as good as her child, as good as my country—and the first thing we do is lose that child to a madman, with worse men pressing at our gates.

I never thought I could live this long and still be such a fool.

Clearfalls

The currents of Holdfast life poured together in a whirlpool of activity through which Daya swiftly passed. Having lived for half a decade as an unofficial non-person, the pet fem had learned to use eddies of cross purpose and miscommunication to further her own aims.

She knew, for example, that Beyarra would turn a blind eye to her departure from Midfast with Galligan. Beyarra believed in improving the status of sponsored men and was persuaded that Daya's plans to dedicate this man to the Lady would further that aim.

Home again in the Moon's House at Oldtown, Daya paused to collect personal items for her further travels; her greatest journey was begun. She met there with two First Free with plans of their own. For Daya's small hoard of trade chain they took her and Galligan, with two wagonloads of fibers bound for the paperworks, northwest toward Clearfalls. On the way they saw beacon fires burning high but they did not turn aside to investigate.

Tara-Toann and Falsha talked, when they talked at all, about joining the Breakaways in the south. They needed trade chain to buy horses to take with them. Down there, they said, people could do the work that Riding Women did, not the slavework of digging food out of the ground or the sea or the forests while Alldera and her special friends read books, fondled their sponsored men, and traveled for pleasure.

Daya stayed out of such discussions. They were unjust to Alldera, but Daya was hardly the person to point that out. Personally she felt that the Lady disapproved of fems trying to live like Riding Women. But bringing religion into their conversation might offend them. She needed no more enemies.

As they traveled she had strange, lurid dreams that she awoke from sweating and breathless with fear. She prayed every night to the waning moon. She studied the reflection of her face in every cup of water, searching for some mark of destiny, doom, or transcendence, for she sensed her life narrowing toward some climax. But her scars masked her even from herself.

Clearfalls was the place from which she would reclaim her pride and her reputation. Galligan was her instrument, although no longer in the way she had described on the Steps in Midfast. His revelation of d Layo's return had changed everything.

They avoided two foot patrols on the border and passed unhindered into the higher forests, moving at the slow pace of the cart-horses up the steep road. On a still, warm afternoon they reached their destination: a dank clearing surrounded by tall upland forest.

"There's no one here," Galligan muttered, looking nervously around at the big square cabin of cross-piled logs, the lean-to with its canvas awning lashed down over the tubs and tables of the paperworkers. Against an outside wall head-high stacks of firewood aged for winter use.

"All the better," Daya replied composedly, although she was uneasy herself. She had not expected the place to be so primitive. That it would be deserted she had dared to hope.

The making of paper required cold air and cold water, so Clearfalls was never fully staffed until autumn. But there were repairs to make, summer plants to harvest for inks, sizing, and caustics. People should be working here.

Falsha said tensely, "Those beacons we saw—something's up; they've gone. You'd better come on to New Forge with us."

"No, with thanks," Daya said, directing Galligan to drag her bundles out of the wagon. "We are under the Lady's protection."

"Come with us," Falsha said again when they had unloaded all their cargo into the storage rooms. "No free person should be left alone with no company but a damned stick, and a runaway like this one, at that."

Galligan lowered his head, cradling his bandaged fingers in his other hand. He hardly looked a threat.

"I'm safe enough," Daya said.

Tara-Toann, whose fortunes in love Daya had told with uncanny accuracy by scrying the face of the moon, made the Lady's sign with her closed fist at her chest. She lowered her voice. "If you mean to sacrifice that muckie to the Lady, won't you need some help with him?"

Daya assured her that she would not. "He's the Lady's already," she said, enjoying Galligan's ill-disguised alarm. "He'll do what I tell him."

After helping Daya drive a thick staple into a foundation log to lock Galligan's stick-and-chain to at night, the two riders left at last, driving the empty wagon up the forest track toward New Forge at a rattling rate. The clearing grew quiet again, except for the pouring of the nearby stream from one washing pool to another below. The golden sunslants had begun to vanish from among the trees.

Daya mixed a porridge of cracked wheat, herbs, and nuts to cook on the cabin's hearth. Galligan built sticks and tinder into a fire, favoring his injured hand. He muttered, "I hope your Moon Mother can protect you from ghosts."

She chuckled. "You ran off into the Wild. What were you going to do against ghosts?"

"They'd be men's ghosts up this way, the dead of Endpath," he said defiantly. "They wouldn't bother me."

He took the heavy kettle and hooked its handle over the crosspiece in the hearth. Crouching by the hearth to strike a fire, he said in a strained voice, "Do you mean to sacrifice me to your goddess, as that Hera said?"

"No, Ganni," she said.

He blew on the embers. "Then why come here, if you don't mean to do some moonish ritual at Endpath?"

"I never intended any such thing," she said. "That was just a story for Beyarra, to get her help in slipping out of Midfast with you. You wanted to join up with Servan d Layo out here in the Wild, and so you shall—because I want you to. I'm joining him, too. You're going to take me north with you to meet the Sunbear."

An anguished groan of protest broke from him.

She smiled, feeling the inspiration of the Lady dancing in her blood. "Stir the pot, Ganni, stir the pot. You're my servant and Hers for a little while still, so earn your keep!"

He set down the pot lid with a clang. "Don't play with me, Hera! I'd rather have Kobba crush me with her red right hand than be toyed with like a straw doll!"

Easy to say when Kobba was miles away and fully occupied. She sat down on a warped bench by the hearth and patted the space beside her. Sullenly obedient, he sat with her while the food cooked and she told him part of the truth.

"I have my own reasons to seek out the Ferrymen. Can't you imagine what they might be? Can't you believe that I might be drawn to d Layo like a nail to a lodestone? He's bold, strong, unbroken, like the men who were my masters when I was a pretty young pet fem."

Anger darkened his face; good. A little jealousy would keep him on his mettle. A jealous man could be a fine tool if a fem were clever enough to manage him.

"The moon has driven you crazy," he growled, reaching out to stab a long wooden spoon into the pot. "I don't know where to find d Layo. We'd just be blundering around in the woods. Even if we do stumble on him, he won't grab you for his bed. He's the Sunbear, the punisher. He'll kill you."

No, she thought. *I will kill him; I, the spoiled pet fem who has never struck a blow against a master!*

He went on, earnest, almost pleading. "Once I've fought

beside him against the fems, he'll respect me. I'll be able to protect you. But I can't help you if we both go to him now, when you're a renegade bitch and I'm just a miserable slave."

"You can help me by telling him something he'll believe from you, but not from me," she said, leaning against his side. It had been a long hike up rough country. "You can tell him how I became Alldera's enemy. Tell him what I've done against her, and how I was treated for it, and how you've used my hatred of her to bring me over to the men's cause."

He sighed and rubbed her shoulders with his good hand. "I don't believe that myself, and he won't either." He kicked at a coal of burning wood that had rolled out onto the hearthstone. "No fem would choose to be a slave again!"

"Oh," she said in a teasing tone, "is that so? You haven't heard about certain Free folk who play love games with whips and chains, where someone is the master and someone is the slave? Come on, Ganni, you all know. You men make jokes about it."

He laid his big, unhappy face against her hair. "But that kind of thing's a game. With d Layo, it would be real. He's got a cruel streak."

"Everyone has a cruel streak, if you scratch them deeply enough," she said. "Here, give me a taste—I think it's almost ready."

She scraped a clump of mush out of the spoon's bowl with her front teeth. The mixture had cooked too fast and was dotted with dry lumps. She ought to scold him for his carelessness.

"You can't do this," he said. "Go to Lammintown instead. They'll be glad to see you there, they'll need you to call your Moonwoman for them."

"No," she said. "We go north."

"I don't know where to find him. He could be anywhere."

"His lads are Ferrymen. They'll keep to the coast and make for Endpath. That's where we'll find them, you and I together."

He hunched his shoulders, keeping his head down and

chewing a mouthful of the food, and would not answer.

Daya thought of Tamansa and Leeja-Beda up at Endpath. They were clever, living there undetected all this time, but now—they could hide in the woods and take care of themselves. Anyway, she had warned them to go to the Bayo-born. They should have listened. If people didn't listen, they must pay the price.

"You're an arrogant man, Ganni," she said, "to think you'll be of use to d Layo even with that hand." She caught his wrist, checking his skin for telltale marks of poisoned blood. There were none. "Well, I can be of more use than you can."

"He'll kill you!" he shouted, jerking away from her. "He'll send your head to Alldera!"

"And she'll rejoice that a traitor is dead at last," she answered, pleased; he really did seem to care.

"I don't understand," he groaned, "why you want to do this."

"It's not for a mere cockie to know why his Hera does this or that, is it? Go scrape the pot out, and mind you wash it downstream of the rinsing pools. The paper crews get very cross if they find impurities in there.

"Then we'll curl up here tonight and make for Endpath in the morning. The DarkDreamer may be there already. We want to arrive in daylight so he can see us coming."

She kissed him lightly and sat back again to look at his face. "I can read your thoughts, Ganni. Yes, you could probably get loose tonight and run off. But I've been to Endpath, I'll find my own way if I must. I'm going to your Sunbear. If you love me as you say you do, you'll help, not hinder."

They made love on a bed of drying-felts piled together. He cried afterward, sitting in the dark with his back to her and striving to muffle the sound.

She had sorrows of her own, which she kept to herself. Much as she enjoyed the kisses and the touchings, the salty lickings, the slippery skin, the act of intercourse itself had become painful. She had been taught, as a pet, to expect this if she lived long. She had made a study of Fedeka's herbs and medicines in order to concoct unguents to ease the raw stinging in her vagina after fucking. But she was losing ground even so.

She lay quiet, waiting for the burning sensation to fade and making a small prayer to the Lady against the ravages of time. She had already done all the crying she meant to do for the loss of youth. Soon she would become a respected elder, a woman with the blood of a mighty and dreaded enemy on her hands.

It would not be Alldera who avenged herself on d Layo, the DarkDreamer, the Sunbear. Daya would do it for her, in reparation for that terrible night in the Watchtower. Everything would change then. No one would dare to say that Fedeka stood closer to the moon's heart than Daya stood, in the flesh or in the spirit; or closer to Alldera either.

And if Daya had to give her life to accomplish the deed, why, that was well enough: Alldera would raise a cairn to her memory with her own two hands.

A Promise

Alldera told me herself about the stealing of Veree. When I thought of this later, I had to give her credit. She didn't palm the job off on anyone else but told me the bad news herself first thing in the morning.

I was sleeping in a tent on the beach with Raysa, who had turned up at the Lammintown horse pens and shown herself a very warm companion. I was lying there divided between the sensual call of the two little moles on her shoulder blade, which I had spent some time kissing the night before, and the question, "What if our life is a dream, and I'm dreaming you?"

Raysa snugged her behind deeper into my lap and muttered, "Then I'd be dreaming you too, wouldn't I? And what kind of a question is that?" And then Alldera called my name and said she needed to speak with me.

I was embarrassed and felt ridiculous and angry at being made to feel embarrassed; why should it matter that Alldera found me in bed with someone? She had long ago seen to it that this situation must mean less than nothing to either of us. So how come it seemed to mean something after all?

Grouchily I replied, "Just talk to me. Raysa won't run gossiping to the whole town of anything she hears."

Alldera said, "You'll want to hear what I have to tell you in private, Sorrel."

So I knew it was bad news; and I suspected something of it at that point but at once turned the unbearable suspicion out of my mind. While I lay there fighting panic, Raysa grabbed her shirt, murmured, "I'm off to the squats before I burst," and ducked outside.

Alldera came in. Sitting on the bedding with her muscular legs crossed, she told me that Setteo had taken Veree from the Children's Hall and vanished with him.

I was seized by a horrible plunging pain, which froze at once into cold anger, like a boulder of ice in my belly. I was glad of the anger: in the face of something so strong, no evil would *dare* befall my sweet-skinned boy.

I let my anger fly.

"I *said* it was a mistake to put him in that place," I yelled, yanking on my clothes. "So now I'm proven right, and what are you doing about it?"

"Everyone has been alerted to watch for them," Alldera said.

"Your people should be out searching, not just watching in case they should happen to amble by!"

I could not see her eyes in that shadowed light, but her lips were thin and bloodless. "You know that with d Layo on our border and a dozen good riders gone south to the Bayo pastures, I have no one to spare for a search."

"Your people brought this about," I flashed back at her. "You owe me more than asking them to keep an eye open for Veree in the midst of everything else they're doing!"

She stood up, stooping under the sagging tent roof cloth like someone bent by age, but her voice was vibrant with urgency. "Everyone's at risk right now—including all the children, not just your foreign-born boy. Don't ask the impossible, Sorrel."

"Well, you wouldn't care, would you?" I said. "Children are nothing to you. You had little enough use for me when you carried me in your belly, and not much more once I was born."

She said steadily, "You're a grown Woman of the Grasslands now. I claim no authority over you. If I offer you a part in our defense, will you accept it?"

I pulled on my boots, feeling too sick with dread and rage to answer. Her words brought home to me the hopelessness of Veree's position: stolen by a madman in the midst of the frenzy of battle preparations.

"What 'part'?" I spat.

Smoke has been sighted at the paperworks. We've had no lightning storms to set a fire up there. It could be a diversion by d Layo. It could be Setteo, if he's been traveling on horseback. He's never been completely bound by our rules, and he has a relationship of his own with the horses.

"Or it could be something else. But we need to know. Will you ride up there with a few others to find out?"

"Maybe," I said, though I knew I would. I just needed to spread my suffering around a little. "If I decide to, I'll come find you."

She left. I threw myself down on the rumpled bedding still redolent of love, wept, then stuck my head outside the tent and vomited, unsuccessfully, on an empty stomach. Raging, I threw my clothes on and raced to the bakery, Lammintown's general meal kitchen during the emergency, to snatch a bite in hopes of settling my roiling guts. I didn't plan to linger where Raysa might come and commiserate as I was in a mood to strike out, not to accept sympathy.

I spoke to no one. Few people were there; everyone looked grim and ate fast.

Raysa found me there. "I heard," she said, and kissed my cheek. "You'll be off to look for Veree. I can't go with you. Kenoma and some others see the splitting of the main horse herd as a raid. Some people want to chase after the Breakaways, some want to warn them and help them keep their horses. But we can't spare anyone, not with d Layo on our doorstep. We've been fighting among ourselves over all this."

"Your friends couldn't have picked a shittier time to sneak away," I growled.

She nodded unhappily. "No, they've cocked it all up. The idea was to to put a few head of horses down there, a token really, to make our claim on that pasturage *before* Alldera got back with a refusal by the Bayo-born. Well, we guessed they'd say no, as they do to anything new. I said I would stay here and make our case to Alldera and the Council. But hotter heads have prevailed, and they've run a sizable herd south."

Alldera had asked her to go at once, she explained, and persuade the Breakaways to return and help fight the Ferrymen.

"They'll come," Raysa said, but I saw an anxious tightness around her fine eyes. "I can't imagine that they would refuse, not with d Layo on our border. Anyway, I'm off toward Bayo in an hour, and I don't know when I'll be back."

So I kissed her, and drank her taste into my memory, and we parted as I suppose lovers have always parted in wars and troubles.

My thoughts returning to Veree, I went to find Eykar Bek.

This was not so easy to do. Some people I asked were clearly puzzled, saying that all the men had been taken to Midfast the day before. Others seemed to know where he was but wouldn't tell. The presence and whereabouts of the Endtendant were being kept secret.

I found him at last penned in, of all places, the Lammintown Moon's House, which was otherwise nearly deserted. I told the guard who I was and pushed past her.

He was locked up in a whitewashed cell containing a bucket, a pitcher, and a straw pallet. When I strode into the room, he whirled from the small, high window, a hectic, eager blaze of hope lighting his pale face.

"He's been found?" he said, obviously meaning Setteo, not Veree. I wanted to kill him right then and there.

"You knew, you bastard!" I screamed. "You knew that DarkDreaming man was back, or you wouldn't have come out to Fedeka's camp with all that talk about me going back over the mountains! If you'd only told me what was happening I could have ridden to Midfast, I could have been there to save Veree from that maniac you sleep with! Damn you, now he's gone! You knew what was happening, and you didn't tell me!"

I felt slammed forward by the wind, mindless as a grass fire. Before I knew, I lashed out and my fist connected at the jointure of his jaw and throat. He pivoted wildly on his stiff leg and fell headlong. I heard the back of his skull thud on the stone floor.

For a moment I hoped I had killed him. The strangest mixture of fierce triumph, loss, and resentment of that loss rose in me. Cursing and shaking my sore hand, I knelt beside him. His skin was ashen under the silver stubble of his beard. His eyelids, blue-shadowed, fluttered.

What a weakling! And I was a hotheaded fool. I loathed us both.

He came to and looked up at me like a different man, a much older one. That alert, inquisitive face seemed blurred by a caul of shock and hopelessness.

"Sit up!" I grabbed his shirtfront and yanked him into a sitting position. He was heavy. He sagged forward, breathing stressfully. I felt in the short hair at the base of his skull. He flinched from my probing fingers.

"No blood," I said, sitting back on my heels, "just a lump. You'll live." I wiped my palm hard on my headcloth.

He sat bent awkwardly forward, his hands over his face now.

"They're not found?" he said in a muffled voice.

"Of course they're not found," I snarled.

"Ahh," he groaned. His hopelessness enveloped me like a cloud of cold, damp smoke. I sat on the floor with my back against the wall thinking, *This is how I'll feel if Veree dies.*

I said vengefully, "You should be glad. They'll kill that cutboy when they catch him!"

He did not respond at first. I saw how the foot of his crippled leg lay curled a little, deformed by years of offsetting the crookedness of the leg above. No wonder they didn't bother putting him on the stick.

Then he whispered, "What have they told you? Do they say that I've had a lot of pain in my life? I have. Do they say that a little more doesn't matter, that you get used to it after a time, you come to like it, to crave it even?

"It's lies. I don't want any more. I don't want any more. For Christ's sake, he's a crazy man who sees visions! Is he so valuable to anyone else in the world that he has to be taken away from me?"

I pitched my voice low in case the guard was listening. "Tell me where he's likely to be. If Veree is all right, I'll just take the child back and let your life-man go—"

"Go where?" he cried. "Setteo isn't fit to wander about on his own. He—is—mad. It's not an act. He was better for a while, but this Bear-cult business has pitched him back into his 'Cold Country.' He's not in the real world at all."

I said, "I don't care where he *thinks* he is. Where might his feet actually be carrying him while he's imagining himself to be traveling in his cold place?"

He bent his good leg and hugged his arms around it, resting his cheek on his knee. His eyes closed. I saw him wrench his emotions into control. I hope I never have to watch someone drag herself up from such depths again.

"He could be anywhere," he said finally. "It depends on where he thinks he'll find his 'Bears.' "

"Why has he taken Veree?" I demanded. "A child from over the mountains has nothing to do with your cutboy's madness!"

I read from his silence that he knew or guessed the answer to my question, and was deciding not to tell me. I moved to crouch by him, my hand on the haft of my knife.

"Listen to me, Murder-Man," I said, between my teeth. "That child is as good as my own and I'll do anything to get him back, understand me? So you talk to me right now. Otherwise by the life and honor of all my mothers and their kin I will stick this knife into your eyes, one after the other, and leave you in darkness for good—no books, no reading ever again."

I could no more do what I threatened than melt stone with my breath, but he couldn't know that. I laid the flat of my blade against his cheek, pressing it there so that he would not feel the tremor in my hand.

His dark lashes made his eyes seem paler than they were, ice-gray rather than blue; I thought, with a shiver, of the Cold Country. Was this where Setteo had first glimpsed the wintry reaches that occupied his mind and commanded his miserable body?

Eykar lifted one hand, closed his thin fingers around my wrist and gently pressed my knife hand away.

"You don't have to do that," he said. "I'm used to taking

orders, I've done it all my life. I don't know where Setteo is headed, but I would imagine that he thinks he's going to meet the Bears. He's carrying the child with him as either an offering—wait, let me finish—or perhaps as a sort of apprentice; you understand? Someone to take his place as a link between the Bears and the Warm World—us."

I disengaged his grip and sheathed my knife. "Either way," I said, "you're telling me that he took Veree as a kind of sacrifice."

"Either way."

"How can I stop him?" He stared at me hopelessly I tried again. "If you could search for him, where would you look?"

His posture loosened and he sat quiet, looking into distances invisible to me. After a moment he said, "For him, all places are subject to sudden transformations, from ordinary patches of beach or road or field into the Bears' country. I think that his experiences have sanctified some special sites for him in the real world, where this happens repeatedly."

"What sites?"

"The place where he first saw the Free Fems might be one, west of 'Troi somewhere. And maybe where he brought me to meet Alldera after she took Oldtown. I remember waiting on a little hill near the City; that's Midfast, now. I wouldn't know the place again, but Setteo might.

"There must be other locations, tied to events I don't know about. The Watchtower, because of that terrible night . . ." He looked through me for a moment. "Endpath. He used to spend hours communing with the sea there."

My mind ranged among the many possibilities he raised, and the ones he hadn't. Setteo might have hidden Veree someplace and gone on to one of these mystical destinations on his own; or Veree might have given Setteo the slip—I had lost him in the uplands myself, that time. The child could even now be wandering alone, hungry, and frightened, in a strange country under siege.

I said, "What about this 'Sunbear'? Maybe Setteo is trying to take Veree to an imaginary being."

Silence again. He massaged his temples with his thumb and fingertips.

"Not imaginary," he said at last. "The Sunbear is Servan d Layo, returning from the north."

I jumped to my feet, charged with energy again. *Smoke,* I thought, *at Clearfalls—on the northern border inland. You might stop there on the way to Endpath, if you wanted to avoid alerting Lammintown.*

Without looking up at me, he said, "Don't kill Setteo."

My revulsion at that moment wasn't about Veree at all. It was fury that this *father* of mine, a person of stature in some odd way, should be sitting bowed at my feet, begging.

No grown person should be in a such a position; no share-ma of mine. Not for any reason. Gray hairs are tokens meriting respect in the Grasslands by virtue of surviving a lifetime of dangers. I looked down at the bent back of my body's sire and I felt as if my world had been split and gutted.

I swallowed hard. "In the Grasslands it's wrong to hurt mad people. I wasn't raised here, I was raised there."

Not that I knew for certain that I could refrain from killing the cutboy when I found him; but proud speech felt good, and very little else did. My feelings were in such a turmoil of hope and alarm that I scarcely knew what I was saying anyway.

But I was determined to find Veree.

The Demon

Salalli walked swiftly, keeping well to the inland side of the partially overgrown path. She was nervous of the cliffs after Garred's fatal fall. The coast at Rock Pool had been low-lying. She had known every knob, dip, and split in the rim of the land there.

If she were home now, she and the children would be out looking for ripe beach plums to dry for winter. The men would have gone inland to the lakes to harvest wild rice and trade with the Lake Town people. Lost harvests, lost folk; would the ache for them never grow less?

She should have grabbed the children and hidden be fore the arrival of the "guests"—but Gaybrel knew better,

Gaybrel wanted to attract this "new blood" by showing off the confidence of a thriving community.

We could have hidden until they left and then scavenged enough to live on. Axinter and those wives of his hoarded supplies. The southmen never found any of those stores, but we could have. And Shar is old enough to hunt goats.

But the southmen could have come back. It all could have turned out just the same. Or worse. She knew she was just daydreaming, her imagination sparked by these bold-talking fem people in their cliffside city.

Pale, homely, they were d Layo's kind; and they were doomed. He would kill them or catch them, like the two caged at Endpath. *They will fall as we fell,* she thought, ashamed of the bitter-tasting satisfaction she felt. *They think they're too strong and smart to be whipped; so did we, and look what happened!*

No, don't look, don't look back.

Into her unwilling mind came not the lost joys of the life left behind but the things she had never imagined she would miss: the winter storms that pinned people in their homes for days while sky and sea met in a frenzy of destruction. The coughing fevers were left behind too, that came after the storms and brought waves of winter deaths. Damp, bone-biting cold, mildew, sand in everything all the time—only an idiot would miss such things.

Well, maybe her life now was the life of an idiot.

The woods were different here than at home: less tall pine. She spotted a clump of berry-laden bushes where the trees had been knocked down by one storm-broken trunk, letting sunlight stream in. *Blackberries,* she thought, hesitating; *boil them up, dry them in sheets of fruit-leather to chew or to flavor winter porridge.* She had been taught to make the most of good provender when she came upon it.

Best not to stop, though. Best to give him no excuse for anger by dawdling or delay. Somehow, just in these last few hours, it had become even more important not to die.

What a strange thing—a land of women living free and forthright with no men above them! And, in the place of what d Layo and his men had expected, how satisfying! To see these savage men find their world turned more upside down even than her own had been felt positively celestial.

No, they must have fooled her somehow, those women. She should go back and look at them again. The further she hurried from the cliff-cupped town of the people who called themselves "free," the more she wanted to go back there.

They had stores of food. She had seen sacks being carried, barrels rolled, bulging baskets lugged away in preparation for trouble. They had served her the roasted meat of "horse," a creature much bigger than any goat.

What a good thing d Layo had learned of the men's fall from those two captured wretches! Otherwise Salalli did not think that she would survive her report of the shambling male slaves she had seen loaded into a prison wagon and driven away.

Alone in the forest, thinking about that, she laughed, and quickly covered her mouth.

Her glance shifted constantly, warily. The southmen talked boldly and familiarly about this trail, "the Pilgrim Way," as they called it. But she had noticed how, because of their fear of ghosts, they had looked with furtive respect at Migayl, who had journeyed this way to Lammintown and back all alone.

No adult normally gave credence to ghost tales, but the trail beneath her feet had been a death march for these people; and who could be sure of the protection of Sallah, so far from home? She breathed again each time she noticed something familiar—mushrooms cresting an elbow of dead tree roots, acorns ripening on a hefty oak.

If only she could be sure of who was going to win, she might find some way to shelter her children for the future. Suddenly she glimpsed the possibility of there being a future, one not so bleak as she had thought.

False hope, wild dreams, take care, she told herself, *or you'll be made to pay. Or the children will.*

"Hey, Black Sal!"

Kedge, perched cross-legged in a high tree-crotch, grinned down at her. "Nice visit? Don't let those bitches give you any smart ideas. d Layo can read rebellion in your eyes. He'll slice your heart out and make one of those girls of yours roast it for his supper. You should never have taught them to cook!"

Silent, she waited to be released by him.

He threw a twig down at her. "Go on—he's waiting!"

D Layo was with the others outside Endpath, that great black berg of a building, trying to pry it open. The doors stood firm despite the men's deep-voiced work chant with the power-shout at the end, despite their straining backs and sweat-slick skins.

"Leave it, lads," the DarkDreamer called, seeing her. "We'll come back to it again." He had been overseeing their effort, judging the placement of the wedges and levers they had made—green wood, much of it, slippery and unreliable. It was a wonder no one had been crippled.

He strode jauntily down the spit and swept her along with him up toward camp, his arm warm and heavy across her shoulders. He was full of excitement, whispering hotly in her ear, "So, Salalli, what can you tell me? Did you speak to Alldera? She won't come to me, will she? Arrogant cunt! Is she still ugly? Did she try to touch you, kiss you, pull you into her bed? That's what the women are like in my country, did I warn you?"

That was what he said, he who had undoubtedly been screwing Laxen after she'd left for Lammintown.

"She sent a message," she said woodenly.

"Good girl, then, Sal!" he answered, nuzzling her ear playfully, nipping like a goat. "Come and tell me. You don't have to cook today, Lissie's doing it."

Him with Laxen's sweat on his skin, Laxen's spunk casually wiped off on his shirttail. Her insides surged with revulsion.

Where were her children? She glanced frantically around the group of shabby shelters. He answered her unspoken question. Shar, he told her, had gone to help keep an eye on the goats and on the two Townswomen who were tending them. d Layo liked to pretend that Shar had come over completely to the side of the victors. He knew how Salalli hated that.

Luma was with a group digging what they called taydo root.

Lissie squatted by the fire, baking meal-cakes on a flat stone. With a solemn expression that might mask any sort of feelings, she served d Layo, then passed Salalli a cake and the pot of watery gruel.

"So what's the message?" he asked, sucking juice from his fingers.

Heart in her throat, she told him: Alldera would not meet with him and wanted nothing he had to offer. He and his men were not welcome in the Holdfast. That was all.

His eyes narrowed. She thought he would hit her. But he said, "Now tell me what you observed for yourself, Sal."

Salalli told him everything that she could remember, but none of her thoughts, her opinions, her questions about the Holdfast women. He was so eager in his questioning, so attentive to her answers, that she could not help but warm to him a little, baited by these glimpses of the good-tempered, cheerful companion he could choose to be.

Then she caught a glimpse of Lissie's face, so dull and inward in expression, and cold hatred for the southman uncoiled again under her heart.

He squatted on his heels, thinking, watching her eat. "I thought she would suggest meeting somewhere else. It's not like her to turn from a challenge. What do you make of her, Sal?"

"She treated me courteously," Salalli said cautiously. "She seems confident. She takes time to think about things."

He nodded. "Yes. Whether that's a strength or a weakness depends on circumstances, though. Did you like her?"

Was he determined to entrap her, to make a reason to punish her? Salalli said stolidly, "I don't know. I just wanted to get back."

He hummed to himself, watching her mop out the pot with a scrap of cake that crumbled in her fingers.

"So did you see the daughter, Alldera's child? She'll be much less pretty than your girls, of course. You saw how homely the runner is."

She was supposed to say something but she was thinking about how Lissie had not greeted her. Lissie must blame her for going away and leaving her at the mercy of this man.

"Be good," he warned, noting her inattention. "Don't provoke me, woman."

"Not pretty," she croaked, and took a sip of water to open her throat. "The daughter is a wild-looking person with a—a bold face and a severe gaze."

"Does she resemble me at all?" he asked casually.

She blinked at him, confused.

"Never mind, it's not important. What did they talk about among themselves, these 'free' people?"

"Some child of the daughter's, but I never learned why the child is important," she said, putting it together in her mind.

Alldera Holdfaster was his bedmate too. Sorrel must be his get, or so he thinks. Why else ask about a resemblance? If Sorrel is his, then her interests are pitted against those of my children. He shows me this to keep me divided from Alldera when I carry his messages to her.

"Well, well," he said thoughtfully, studying a scabbed-over scratch on the back of his hand. "A child of a child, so fast. Life is full of surprises." He stretched. "That sleeve of mine ripped again. It wasn't very well made, your Gaybrel's shirt. You can sew up the sleeve for me while you recover from your time among the 'free.' "

He stood, darkening her with his shadow.

"Will there be an answer to take back to her?" Now she felt tiredness in her legs. It had been a long walk.

"Let her wait," he said, turning away. "I haven't decided yet. Maybe I'll send one of the girls next time."

He probably didn't even mean this, but it amused him to remind her of his power over her children. She imagined Alldera slicing his guts as he himself had sliced Gaybrel's. She moved into the shelter of the lean-to and fell asleep immediately over the sewing he had left for her.

Angry voices—men's voices, of course, no Townswoman dared speak in anger these days—jarred her awake. They were gathered in the big brush windbreak, men sitting or crouching or sprawled on the ground, speaking in aggressive tones that she knew all too well.

She sat slumped, eyes shut as if still sleeping. By the warm stroke of sun on her cheek, several hours had passed since her return. She listened.

It wasn't a complicated argument. It never was, with them; nothing about how the best men of Old Times had gone to the stars and left only their rubbish behind on Earth, nothing about how the climate changed over the generations, or what those joined loops of tough, whitish plastic were that drifted up on the shore all the time—the kinds of topics once raised in the houses of Rock Pool. She could have wept for the companionable buzz of men's voices, the laughter and the exclamations, the ruminative, many-voiced evening talk in the town.

When there had still been a town.

These southmen never talked about what might be, or how things had come to be the way they were. They occasionally spoke of their past, those who had known each other before, but the future was a coarse vision of timeless triumph.

She remembered d Layo laughing so hard he had nearly choked when Hak One-Eye told him that some great elder of theirs, Ravmagmus, had been tricked by a rival into thinking somebody was his son who really wasn't, which error had apparently led to an uprising of young men against old in that country.

"Why didn't you tell me that before?" d Layo had cried, flushed and sputtering with mirth.

Hak smiled and said, "I wanted to wait until you needed cheering up."

They liked jokes, the crueler the better.

Most of the time they talked about going home rich men. They talked about who was stronger, and who was pronging or getting pronged. Or, as now, they argued about what to do next.

Kedge, back from his watch in the forest, said they should attack tonight, make Lammintown their base, and use fems from there as hostages to force the capitulation of all the rest. Move now, while the bitches were still in a tizzy of surprise. Take the initiative; Migayl had had the right idea, he said.

D Layo pointed out in scathing tones that Migayl had come limping home hurt and empty-handed, having revealed their presence and gotten nothing in return except confirmation of what they already knew.

"All the more reason to move right away," Kedge insisted. Salalli saw how he stared around at the other men with his wide-set, little eyes, challenging them to support him.

"There are fourteen of us," d Layo said. "I think the world of you lads, but I don't seriously believe that fourteen men can take Lammintown from forty fems on their guard against us, or hold it against three times as many once we had the place."

"So what are we going to do, then," Hak One-Eye inquired, "sit and starve?"

"Other ideas?" d Layo said blandly. Someone guffawed. Salalli wondered how many of them realized that he was picking their brains for a plan, which he would then take the credit for himself.

"I've a thought," Arred said modestly. They should stay where they were on the edge of the Holdfast and build up their strength. Trade with these renegade fems, get them used to having free men around, and meanwhile steal some horses for themselves: gather bows, male runaways, maybe a few fems tired of playing master and starved for a good fuck. And then, when things looked more promising, attack.

"That makes sense," Torby said. "We've got the brains and the muscle. All we need is to wait a while."

This raised a derisive snort from Dojan. "*They* won't wait."

Torby nudged the man next to him and said nastily, "Looks like Dojan isn't so eager for a fight if it's with a whole pack of fems instead of just his N'deen, eh?"

Dojan gave him a fuck-you sign.

Jonko shifted his thick body and spat on the ground between them. "If we've got brains, let's use 'em, all right? The bitches won't let us sit on their border gathering strength. They'll strike at us first. And we can't beat them in a battle, not even up here in the forest. There's too many of them."

Jonko was smarter than he looked, and he had the gift of bluntly persuasive speech. Salalli did not think that she and her children would prosper under his rule. She leaned closer to hear better, squinting through her lowered eyelashes.

Jonko continued, "All we could do is kill some of them and then run for it; and that's how it would go until we were all hunted down. In a few years we'll be down to a few scrawny baldheads creaking around in the woods boasting to each other about the great trek north we once made and drooling over the smell of food cooking on the Lammintown fires."

D Layo cut through the somber silence that followed this with a few claps of ironic applause. "Fine," he said, "but I missed the part about what we *should* be doing. We didn't take the Pool Towns on rhetoric. We took them on hunger, speed, and nerve."

"We took them," Jonko said, catching Salalli's eye as he spoke, "with treachery and surprise." He gave a brief, yellow-toothed smile and turned his gaze from her again. "That won't work here. Ex-slaves won't trust their old masters. They'll come for us."

"So," Kedge said impatiently, "what's your plan?"

"They know we're here, so let's be somewhere else. We cut ourselves some good barge poles and float that bit of ferry decking down the coast at night. We land well south of Lammintown, and strike inland for the City as fast as we can go. That's where we'll find most of the slave-men, I'd bet on it. Cut them loose to join us right in the heart of the Holdfast, and maybe we'd have a chance."

Engo hooted with disgust. "Sure, if we don't get pulled away on a riptide, or smash up on the Lammintown rocks for the bitches to pick up and chain with the rest of their slaves. We were Ferrymen running our boats past the pylons on a fast line, not free-floating sailors."

Hak murmured, "All this time by the water, and Engo still can't swim!"

Jonko raised his head and stared at Salalli again. She froze, caught looking and listening with the torn shirt in her hands. He said, "They had a boat; her people. They must have traveled free on the ocean."

D Layo said, "Then maybe you shouldn't have stuck your knife in the last man standing at Rock Pool, should you?"

"What about the boy?" Kedge said, looking around. "Shareem must know about boats."

Salalli could not breathe. If they asked her whether Shar knew how to sail on the sea, which answer would give him the best chance for survival, yes or no?

"Sure he knows," d Layo agreed. He glanced at Salalli

but made no summoning gesture. "Their older men shared their skills with the boys, just as our Seniors used to share with us."

That raised a few derisive chuckles. Hak looked out at the water. He said regretfully, "We don't know the coast between here and Lammintown, and neither does that cub."

D Layo nodded. "Any other ideas, besides trying to pole a raft across a sea-tide under the captaincy of a prisoner whose father we killed?"

Blix, who had said nothing that Salalli had heard so far, now clapped his palms down on his knees and said, "Yes."

He stood up, a calm, homely man with wide, rough hands. He had grown very quiet since the fever had left him, and he spoke quietly now. "Judging by everything we know now, the fems have the Holdfast firm in their grasp. They rose up and took it as we took the Pool Towns. I say, leave it to them."

Jonko shouted, "Traitor! Sit down, Christ damn you!"

"We left the northtown country empty behind us," Blix went on steadily. "We could go back there, repair the houses, hunt the hills for goat hides and meat. These women would help; they don't want to starve. What the Pool Towns men did we can do."

D Layo said contemptuously, "Live like savages in stone huts!"

"Live free," Blix said composedly. "Our sons would grow up never seeing a man yoked or chained. Later, when there are more sons, if they think it's worth the trouble they can come south to fight or trade. But Arred's right: the Holdfast belongs to the fems now."

How could Blix, whom she had seen butcher two men of Rock Pool that night, understand what a homeland was? How could he glimpse the possibilities of living in the north? Salalli saw that by speaking this way he had moved away from the others; but some of them looked half minded to follow.

Maybe d Layo would shoot him dead with the Rock Pool gun. Against all reason, this thought disturbed her. Blix had done murder with the rest of them that night, but he spoke of the north country with something like warmth and he had shown no further brutality on the journey south. Of course, he had been sick part of the time, but still.

I should have been taken by him, she thought.

D Layo raised his voice. "Who wants to trek back, cross the rivers, climb the steeps? Who wants to wrap the northern chill around his bones and grow old shivering on a rocky shore?"

When no one replied, he said, "I'm Holdfast-born and bred, and I won't abandon my country to a pack of renegade bitches."

Blix replied, "The Holdfast is a scrap of coast with a bad history. Now that I've got wind of it again, I'm ready to turn my back on it for good. Who's with me?"

"Before anybody accepts," d Layo warned, crossing his arms on his chest as if utterly easy about the outcome, "let's be clear that none of our supplies go north. What we have we won as a crew, working and fighting together. Anybody who quits us now is on his own."

They all watched as Blix and his woman from Sand Pool, a gossip and mischiefmaker named Melnie, picked up their few personal belongings and walked away.

Oddly, Blix caught Melnie's elbow to steady her when she stubbed her foot on a root. They walked close together and shared their loads, meager as they were. Something had happened to them while she tended him in his fever that Salalli, filled with her own stratagems and anxieties, had not even noticed.

Now she felt lightheaded and afraid, watching them go. She felt parted from a last chance. She envied Melnie.

One of the other men made a move as if to follow the deserters. d Layo gave him a look, and he turned back as if he had never meant to go.

"This weakens us," Jonko said sharply. "Even one less fighting man signifies when there are only fourteen to start with! We can't let him go."

Hak said, "Do you want him covering your back in a fight, feeling the way he does? Not me. Let him go, man."

"So what are we going to do?" Laxen said, scratching with his toenails at the fresh scar on his other calf where the floodborne tree had ripped him.

D Layo said, "We're not going north, we're not going to sea, and we're not going to commit suicide in an attack of thirteen against fifty. That's settled, right? What we are going to do is camp here a while and watch for a chance to change things in our favor."

"Like what?" Torby said.

The DarkDreamer hunkered down with them, conspiratorial, sly. She had to strain to hear him. "Like the opportunity to get hold of Alldera herself. She's their leader; and she has a child of her own. What would they do to get those two back?"

So that was how he gave Hak's plan his own flavor and claimed it as his.

Jonko looked disgusted. "And just how are we supposed to grab them without the suicide you were just talking about?"

"That's what I'm going to work out," d Layo replied easily, "now that I know who's with me. Or would you like to take over the job, Jonko?"

He strode away before Jonko could reply. The others scattered, silently or in murmured conversation. She saw d Layo looking pensively after the man who had at first made as if to follow Blix, saw him weighing the chances that their number would be at least one less by morning; or that it ought to be.

One-Eyed Hak, trailing him toward Salalli's shelter, remarked, "It'll take a better story than that to keep these lads steady on the winch. I remember you telling a real rouser back on my ferry. The lads would have followed you through Hell's asshole then."

D Layo grinned over his shoulder at him. "Hell, man, we've already come through there!"

Later that day the men were making another attempt on Endpath itself—this time trying to throw a grapnel on a rope to catch on top of its walls—when a woman bolted out of the forest screaming an alarm.

It was N'deen, who had been tending the goats with Shar. Two strangers appeared from the trees behind her. One was a man in a tattered smock belted with rope, his right hand wrapped in a dirty bandage. The other was a thin woman with high-piled black hair, wearing a pale, grubby robe which she held raised delicately above the muddy ground.

"Galligan?" Engo cried. "Is that you?" He ran to embrace the male stranger in a smothering hug.

The stranger-woman stepped past the two men and called in a bright, melodious voice, "My master Galligan has come to join the great Sunbear d Layo. Which is he?"

Someone pointed at d Layo. She floated up to him and sank gracefully to earth, her hands set out palms up on the turf and her long neck curved downward to his startled gaze. Salalli now saw the boniness of the strange woman's neck and back, the gray imperfectly darkened in her hair.

"I put myself in your hands, good master," this woman said in a sweetly chiming tone. "Not all fems of the Holdfast place themselves above their natural lords. Some of us have only been waiting for your return, while we endured the insults and incompetence of the slave cunts who have stolen your authority. Your word rules this fem."

"Do I know you?" he said, looking down at her with perplexed amusement.

She raised a face of fine-boned beauty, cruelly scarred, a demon-face. "Daya the pet fem asks only to serve, please you master, and to add her poor, weak hands to your effort to set the Holdfast right again."

"What an excellent idea," d Layo cried, clapping his hands together with energy. "Get up, come talk to me. Galligan! Where have you come from, man?"

Dismayed, Salalli thought, *He is intrigued by that creature. Will I have to fight her to hold my place?*

The newcomer was looking at her from the corners of her eyes. Salalli fearfully read in that liquid glance a knowing awareness of her own thought. *Oh great god of the sea,* she prayed, *protect me! Have I lost so much and come so far only to fall into a new struggle?*

With her elegantly submissive words and postures, this stranger had set into motion a dance native to this southern country, of which she surely knew every step and turn—while Salalli knew none at all.

Stalkers in the Forest

Servan talked late into the night with Galligan: a solid if unimaginative fellow as Servan remembered him, from the days when the City belonged to Erl the Scrapper. This "Sunbear" story of his was a startling turn of events: what was it but the result of the reckless misuse of manna—DarkDreaming, in fact? That sort of thing Servan was well fitted to cope with, perhaps even to turn to significant advantage.

The men had offered Galligan a cool welcome. They were uneasy with a man who had submitted to the bondage of femmish masters, and muttered among themselves that they could have used a dozen stout fighters rather than one injured man with a scarred pet fem in tow. Servan could hardly blame them.

He had indulged himself with the pet fem, over Galligan's vain protest; what could be denied to the Sunbear, after all, and it made a good test of Galligan's professed intentions.

Yet there was a constraint here too, and a warning: if Servan acted outside what the slave-men had decided were the rules for the Sunbear, he might lose them. Hell, he might never gain them in the first place!

There were so many factors to consider, with the men's grip on the Holdfast broken; it was a dizzying change. He remembered Chokky Vargindo as a sly, ambitious man, not the sort to meekly step aside even for the "Sunbear." He would use d Layo for his own purposes if he could. Servan did not remember Arjvall at all. The prospect of jumping into the intrigues among these people was less amusing than it would have been once: less like play, more like work.

While Servan was still trying to shake off a thick sleep the next morning, the camp erupted over not one missing man but two, Engo and Djendery. Kedge reluctantly admitted that he had encouraged the pair to make a predawn sweep of the surrounding forest in hopes of laying hands on femmish spies (following, he implied, in the wake of Galligan, their agent).

Before long a trail was found and then the place where one of the pair, Djendery, swung suspended, head-down, from a tree limb, gagged to muffle his cries for help.

"They were waiting for us," he gabbled, sitting on the ground and rubbing his sore ankles, "four of them. They took Engo. They said if we catch one of them, they won't come after her. They'll let her die rather than be lured into a trap."

"Big talk," Jonko scoffed, "from renegade bitches!"

Djendery said intensely, "You weren't there! But they're here, Jonko—listening, watching. Watching, that's their orders. If they find us by ones and twos, they'll grab us like they took Engo. Otherwise—they'll just watch."

Servan said, "I recall fems having more mischief in them than that; what else?"

"Also," Djendery said, "if there's edible stuff anywhere around where we are, they'll grab it first. If there's shelter, they'll pull it down. They'll leave us nothing at all, until the Wild spits us out once and for all. Meantime they'll keep track of where we are and what we're doing and make sure Alldera knows all about it."

"How?" Jonko said. "Are they mind-readers now?"

"They're runners," Djendery said. "*She* trained them. And she's taught them that kick-fighting they do that we used to burn them for if we caught them at it, remember? How do you think they took me and Engo down?"

He showed a huge bruise on his ribs.

"They carry only light provisions so they can move fast. I'm telling you, it's a whole system. You'd think they'd been practicing for us."

Of course, Servan thought, *they probably have. This changes things. Again.* Events were moving with alarming speed.

No one wasted breath objecting that mere fems could not organize such a defense. Dogma was no weapon against armed and determined opponents.

"They're stalking us, see," Djendery explained. "Engo and me didn't see them or hear them. They know these woods, they've been cutting fuel and picking nuts and such here for years."

"Where are the demons of the Wild when you need them?" Hak asked, raising a too-hearty laugh from the others.

"We didn't find any demons," Torby replied grimly. "They didn't either, so they've quit being scared."

"Well, there are demons now," Servan said; "us, lads." He held in his rage at Djendery and Engo: what a pair of fools!

"Fems are watching us right now?" Migayl said, glancing quickly around at the trees.

Servan laughed expansively. "I hope so! Let them come sneaking around, that's what we want. We're rich, remember? We have women, we have animals of our own. Let the Free have an eyeful. Greed will get the better of them, curiosity will get the better of them, and sooner or later we'll have them!"

He thought it best not to mention the Pool Towns gun. Against more than a few Holdfast fems it would be little use. Its chief significance now was as the tool with which he enforced his authority over his own men.

When they returned to their scrubby camp of brush shelters and crude cooking pits at the root of Endpath Spit, he confronted the pet fem, who was patiently filing her fingernails with a curved stone.

"What do you know about all this?"

"Nothing, please you master," she said, her eyes humbly downcast. "This poor creature knows so little of anything, but there is a story—please you—may this fem tell it to you?"

She told how Alldera had gone out into the plains beyond the mountains, alone and on foot. She had tracked and harried a herd of wild horses until they were too weary, footsore, and hungry to run from her any more.

"It is an old horse-catching method of the Riding people," she finished.

"Men aren't horses," he said, and left her.

No fems crept out of the forest that day to free the two wretches locked into the willow cage. Only one of the captives showed signs of life, but still, if the Free were indeed watching you would think . . .

After the late meal he gave Salalli a packet of dried kid's

meat and a small plate of precious tree-sweet to be carried to Alldera with a promise of more in trade, and the return of Daya the pet fem as well, to do with as she chose.

Salalli came back a scant hour later. "Your gifts are on their way. I was stopped, and they were taken from me."

"And this pet who says she was once Alldera's own love?" he said. "What did they say when you told them we have her?"

She stared at the ground. "They said, she came to you of her own free will; let her stay with you. They don't want her back."

Well, he was disappointed but not much surprised. Daya had spun him a tale about being Alldera's enemy and paying the price for it; apparently it was true. And looking like that, the scrawny thing—no wonder they didn't want her back!

He made a joke of it to the men, but he saw by their faces that they understood: *They don't want us back either.*

He told Salalli that evening not to give the pet any more of their dwindling food—she was no damned use to them, why feed her? Salalli obeyed without a murmur. Divide and conquer; it never failed.

The pet fem only said, "To stay with such a great master, this pet will sustain herself on roots and dirt."

Of dirt there was plenty, but she would have to be quick indeed to find any edible roots before Salalli and her friends did. Servan did not believe that the Free were in fact stripping the area. Why should they? Servan's own people were doing that job themselves with desperate efficiency.

On his orders they moved well away from Endpath the next day and camped inside the forest, not without considerable grumbling. The sultry end of summer might break into autumn storms any time, and the men had hoped for decent shelter inside those sheer black walls. But they had been too exposed on the rock spit, imagining watchers everywhere.

He took Leeja with them, leaving the other's corpse for the fems to find in the willow cage. The half-mad, skeletal figure of Leeja would keep the men's spirits up. Daya, humble as dirt on your shoe, took charge of her and led her along after them. But there was some scheme going on behind the pet's fright-mask face, he was sure of it. She kept turning up at his elbow, handing him his water bag, crouching nearby for hours in perfect silence and composure.

Servan found her intriguing in a morbid sort of way, with her nightmare features and her curious impersonation—that was the word that kept occurring to him—of an old-time slave fem. She kept herself clean somehow, and she was a remarkably good fuck for old, spoiled goods.

Galligan had to take seconds. Still, he kept slipping the creature part of his own meager ration.

No one came for the goat they left tethered by tumbled-down shelter along the Pilgrim Way. They heard the animal bleating all day. Despite all Servan could do, the fems were not going to come to him. He sat up late thinking about it, unable to sleep.

That same night Torby and Migayl slipped away taking the goats, two Townswomen, and Shareem.

The first the others knew of it was when they were wakened by a burst of jeering whistles and yells from among the trees. Servan, half awake, fired the gun before he could stop himself. He thought he saw a shadow move, and if he could just bring one femmish bitch down in front of everyone . . . All that happened was that he wasted two bullets.

A moment later an arrow flew into camp, wobbling in a high, harmless arc. It carried a scrap of cloth on its shaft, a rag torn from Torby's striped shirt.

So they went tracking again, and found—absence. The spoor ended in a trampled clearing.

Servan stared down at a scatter of goat droppings and a confusion of hoofprints in the soft earth and suffered a moment of vertigo: *Am I blacking out, losing minutes, hours, whole days?* He caught the scared skitter of Laxen's eyes.

The deserters had been heading north along the coast, back the way they had all come. They had apparently meant to join Blix. But the fems had got them.

Shareem they discovered by the goats' watering hole, bound and bundled into a length of what looked like old carpeting from some rich Senior's villa. The goats, he said, were gone, scattered into the woods. He sat bowed with grief and shame, his big, adolescent hands hanging between his knees, while the men raged and argued over him.

Kedge tried to get hold of the boy's shirt and drag him to his feet, but Djendery shoved him away. Instantly the two Ferrymen were on top of each other, grunting, butting, each trying to get in a good swing at the other.

They were no longer capable of focused action, though action was their only recourse. Servan saw that they were beaten.

He shouted at the two brawlers to stop, the weight of the gun reassuring at his hip. "Save your strength for tonight," he went on. "Though I'm glad to see that you're ready."

Kedge stopped punching, rubbed at a bruised elbow, and squinted up at him from the ground. "Ready for what?" he asked suspiciously.

Christ-God-son, did I really take this scared old man to my bed from time to time, while we wandered in the Wild? And some of these others, too. But they were all I had.

"Ready to give these 'watchers' the slip, and nip into Lammintown to catch Alldera by the heels," he said. "We'll *make* them deal with us—if they want their leader back alive."

"There!" Galligan cried. "The Sunbear speaks!"

At first Servan thought he was jeering, but no, tears brightened his eyes, a great, gawky fellow like him! Even with his obsession with that skinny pet fem with the goblin grin, he might be of some use.

"We're going to be invisible, or what?" Hak inquired mildly.

Servan shook him by the shoulder. "You think I don't know Lammintown like the lines of my own palm, man? I was a DarkDreamer there, I was the man the Seniors couldn't catch."

"That was then," Hak said.

"We can't all go on the attack," Djendery said. "Somebody's got to stay with these northern women or they'll run away. Look, that boy Shareem has already taken off again!"

And so he had, in the confusion of the fight.

"Shareem is wherever his goats have wandered," Servan said confidently. "He'll be back. His people won't run away. Their share of the food won't see them home. Go get some rest, lads. I have it all worked out."

Kedge lingered, rubbing at his split lip, as the others left. "This plan of yours better be good, man. Migayl is a real loss. The lads are fed up with quarrels and hunger and playing hide-a-seek in the woods with a pack of jumped-up bitches—and Galligan's wild-eyed crap about the 'Sunbear,' whatever that is, just confuses them."

Servan patted his pocket, the one on the left side that Salalli had stitched up yet again. "I have something here to steady everybody down—manna, picked by my own hands. We'll rouse their courage up, and then by Christ we'll give these 'Free' a night they'll never forget."

Kedge said skeptically, "I saw some growing at Endpath but I left it. Can't be good for much, fresh-cut and raw."

"We don't need much, only enough to put heart back in the lads. I don't want Rovers. I want the good, hard boyos who took the Pool Towns."

Kedge gave him a stare bleak with misgiving, but turned away without further comment.

That was what being a leader was: having the others fall back for you.

That evening they crowded around the big pot for their servings of watery gruel, with their last leather shirt stewed in it for at least a flavor of meat. There were nine Ferrymen left. He felt a great affection for them; gratitude, even, for their trust; nostalgia for their Great Adventure together.

Deliberately he shed that feeling, distancing himself from the miasma of disintegration and failure that hung about them. Why had it taken him so long to see how bad it was? By no reckoning could this tiny, desperate, quarreling crew follow his instructions well enough to gain even a meager victory. Hungry, scared, demoralized, all they could possibly achieve was death or capture.

He did not intend to share that ignominious end.

As they drank their thin, rank soup he spun them a plan he had created, using his memories of how Lammintown was laid out, what he had learned from the tortured fems and from Daya and Galligan, and what Salalli had reported to him. It was a brilliant plan of attack; it impressed even him (fires to spook the horses, flooding of the passages in the Lammintown cliffs by diversion of the stream on the backslope—one grand idea after another).

He had not been sure that he could still construct such fantasies and make them sound reasonable. But the men were past reason. Even Kedge and Jonko waxed enthusiastic: they would hang that cunt Alldera in a cage and take turns pissing on her, they would—

"A little celebration before we set out," Servan said jubilantly, "something to strike sparks in us for the greatest fight we've ever faced."

He poured each man a splash of the brew he had been heating in a nest of coals by the side of the main fire. The manna was weak, as Kedge had warned, but Servan mixed in other things. Certain red berries that the dead Lake Town boy had shown him brought visions as strong as manna (and made you incredibly sick afterward, but that was no longer d Lay 's concern).

He moved among the men singing one of the old hero-chants (he had lost some of the words, but no one would notice) and touching them, coaxing them, drawing out the dreams he saw in them. He could still do that, he still had the gift.

They sank gratefully into stupor under his hands. He touched them with a valedictory touch, a salute to all they had achieved together. Not that they would remember his farewell caresses, but that was all right.

Hak still held his bowl, untasted. "Is this for dreaming, or for dying?" he said, looking Servan in the eye.

For answer Servan took a sip himself.

Hak nodded. He took something from his shirtfront—a twist of root—and stirred it into his dose with a twig. "You can't beat the fems," he said in a conversational tone. "Not with this crew. Anyway, nothing will ever be the same. The bitches know they can stand up to us now."

"You mean we know it," Servan said, watching in fascination as Hak drank, grimaced, and upended the bowl over his open mouth to catch the last drop.

Then the Ferryman said, "No. *They* know." He leaned

back against a tree trunk. "I should never have gone with you. I shouldn't have let you onto my ferry, what, twenty years ago."

"Why did you?" Servan said. How clearly he remembered the glitter of lights on the water, the vibration of the boards of the pier under the footsteps of the pursuing Rovers and their master, Senior Bajerman.

"Kelmz was with you," Hak said. He coughed. "All us Juniors respected that man. And we were on the edge of rebellion by then. It felt good to spit in Bajerman's eye. And you were so beautiful . . ."

He sat down, hard, at the foot of a tree, sagging weakly to one side. He mumbled, "Damned fem will ever be *my* master." His eye drooped shut.

Servan took the cup from his slack fingers. It smelled of the bug-killing oil Tarisha had used on his shoulders that day, but very strong. A brief wrench of loss and panic caught his breath. A door swung quietly shut somewhere behind him, closing off another rich, glorious time in his youth.

"Have you poisoned them all?"

He spun around, dropping Hak's cup. Salalli, a ragged blanket clutched about her shoulders, stood watching.

"Hush," he said sharply, "keep your voice down. They'll wake again. I've sent them into their own dreams, that's all." Not all would wake. Hak's lips oozed a bloody foam.

"You're leaving them," she said, her hand to her mouth.

Before they leave me. He shrugged and took up his pack.

"Where's Shareem?" She came closer, as if he had the boy tucked into his pocket and could produce him in an instant.

"Out searching for his damned goats."

She gestured toward the pack. "You're taking the food?"

"Enough for one," he said. He had taken all but a half-full sack of moldy meal that was too awkward to carry.

"What about us, me and my children?"

She was a good-looking creature in a flat-faced, animal-like way. She had been warm company, except for the worst nights when he had felt her lying beside him in the dark, awake and grieving. He was sorry for her now that that was all over (another door falling shut).

"The fems will take you in," he said, stooping to tighten the rags that held his shoes on. "They've already got your two friends who ran off with Torby and Migayl. Or you can head home, if you like. You're on your own, Sal; free."

"Let us come with you," she pleaded. "Don't you want us?" He saw the pink of her tongue, moistening her full, dark lips. "You prefer that—that scarface?"

She jerked her chin disdainfully toward where the pet fem sat beside Leeja, that gaping skeleton with sunken eyes. They were like two carved figures, the tall and the small, two gargoyles sitting side by side on a boulder and communing with the night.

"Daya's not coming with me either," he said. "No one is."

He needed badly to be away from here, to leave behind the stink of failure.

A low droning sound was coming from Hak's sagging mouth. Servan moved away from him.

Salalli followed. "But your comrades will blame us if you go. When they wake, they will blame us and punish us!"

Hand them their freedom and all they did was raise objections and complaints! "Don't wait for them to wake," he said. "Go find your son, head north after Blix. You'll catch up. You know as much as we do about living off the land. Use your brains, you'll be all right."

He finished binding on his tattered shoes, and he left her, left them all, trotting across the clearing toward the silent night woods.

When he glanced back, she was crouching to enter the shelter where her girls were sleeping. Other Townswomen were drifting over, gathering, with fearful glances over their shoulders. The firelight gleamed on the gaping faces of the sleepers who lay scattered around the fire. Someone lifted an arm and shook his fingers at the stars, bawling out a blurred chorus of one of the Chants Commemorative.

Servan paused to savor his success at another hairsbreadth escape. What he felt was sadness.

But he knew the signs: there was no choice. A clever leader did not try to lead people on beyond their destination. It was time to be again what he had always truly been: one alone, quick, silent, and decisive, a user of others rather than their admired chief. A survivor.

It was a little frightening, all this sudden freedom. He smiled as he made his way through the darkness of the trees. He never minded fear. It kept him alive and ahead of the pack. It kept him young.

Setteo's Fall

The little boy rode behind Setteo, hugging the cutboy's waist and whining. "I want my ma. You said you'd take me to my ma."

Setteo, clumsily steering the horse by the lines from its mouth as he had seen riders do, spoke endless streams of reassurance. Lies, of course, but what was he to do?

It was Veree who had crept up to a herd of horses and coaxed one out to carry them. Setteo could not have done that; he knew all about being a horse, but not about being a person with a horse. Veree knew that.

"I just do how they do in the childpack," he had said. Veree's voice was sometimes doubled, the child-voice echoed by a rumbling growl from the Cold Country. Setteo did what the voice told him, but he listened to Veree himself about the horse.

Not that this was the first time Setteo had ridden. On dark nights, out drifting peacefully with the herds, he had sometimes pulled himself up and lain back to be carried, his feet dangling and his back stretched along the horse's spine so that he nearly drowned in the slowly moving stars overhead. He had hoped that the horses would wander into the Cold Country and take him there with them. They never had.

Riding was forbidden to males, of course; he had never been caught at it. Now he was protected by those he served. Had he not been told to deliver the boy to the Sunbear? The chilly and treacherous protection of the Cold Country shielded them both.

"Where is she?" the child mourned. "Why doesn't she come for me?"

"I was sent for you," Setteo said, "instead."

"I don't want you," Veree sobbed. "I want my ma."

Setteo said craftily, "She told me to get you away and take you to her without anybody knowing. So if you see anybody you must tell me, and we'll hide. Watch now, and let me know."

The horse walked in that long, plunging way they had. The boy sniffed. Then he said, "Like Seeyanat Fowersath, after she killed the two Bawn sisters over the river crossing? My ma told me that story. Is it like that?"

"Just like that," Setteo said. Maybe it was.

He followed the cold, pale glow thrown off by the speeding stars as they fled north, north, pointing the way for him. Clinging to his back, the boy told him this Fowersath story, which was all about where horses belonging to different skeins of people were allowed to eat and drink. It didn't make much sense. Then the boy drowsed, and then—when the directing stars faded at dawn, and they had to hide in a storehouse full of tea brick—he began to say that he was hungry.

Setteo, fed full on the shine of those pointing stars, stopped to pick him some long beans to eat. They were rank and tough. The child first threw them down in a tearful temper but finally consented to chew some, and then asked for more.

At full sunrise they stopped and put the horse with a herd pasturing nearby, to graze and rest. Then some Heras came and drove the herd away south. Setteo carried the boy on his shoulders until Veree said that he saw riders. They hid in a field of manna plants standing ready for harvest. No one was harvesting today, and they were not discovered.

Tall sunflowers grew in the weedy banks around the field where rain had run off the enclosing stone wall all summer. Setteo showed the boy how to eat the flower seeds, making a counting game of it. They lay on the sunwarm earth between the manna rows, their hunger quieted, and talked about the clouds.

Veree told him a story about a white horse in the sky. Setteo squinted but could not make it out. They became very thirsty, but Setteo heard riders going back and forth on a nearby track, calling to each other. He was afraid to leave the cover of the plants to search for water.

When all grew still again he heard water running, and he told Veree to wait while he went to see.

What he had taken for a storehouse for manna plants was not a house at all, but a strange pile of flat, dark stones, stacked up solid like a small hill. He set his ear to the stones and heard trickling sounds inside. When he opened his stoppered gourd, water dripped out over the stones for him to collect.

The structure was an altar to the moon—the Heras had dotted their country with these, although he had seen none like this one; and it shed tears for him, out of sorrow for the nature of his errand. He brought the gourd back full, and they both drank. Setteo wondered anxiously what price would be asked for that sweet, cool water.

They played hand games and word games as the bright day wore on. The boy lay with his head pillowed on Setteo's bicep, his arm folded across his eyes. "Am I like you?" he asked.

Setteo chuckled at the naïveté of such a trick question. "No. I am no prince of the Bears."

"Am I a prince?"

Gently chiding, Setteo said, "Am I a skinny cutboy with half his wits gone?"

"What is a prince?"

"One who is carried on the shoulders of others."

The child squirmed and kicked his heel repeatedly into the dirt. He said, "Leesann carried Biri on her shoulders when we played pillo. Is Biri a prince?"

Riddles reminded Setteo of deadly Cold Country questions. He wished the Bears would come and take the boy themselves where they wanted him to go. Probably they had given Setteo the job just to see him fail at it.

He decided, cunningly, to answer question with question. That often worked. "Is Biri a gift to the Sunbear, as you are?"

"What's a Sunbear?"

Fearful of falling into some trap, Setteo said sternly, "Go to sleep."

"I'm hungry."

"We'll be there soon." They would. He could smell the dry, woody scent of the Sunbear's breath diffused in the warm air around them.

"Will my ma be there?"

"Mmm."

"If she isn't, can the Sunbear call her?"

"Yes. Go to sleep."

"I'm thirsty."

"We just had a drink, and we ate a little while ago."

"But I'm thirsty."

The child began to cry. He was plainly unhappy more than hungry or thirsty, and Setteo was afraid to go back to the waterstones again. He lay quiet, dreaming, and after a little he rose up out of his body and saw that Veree slept curled against his side. The leafy hemps sheltered the child's tender cheek from the hot, late sun.

Setteo held up his transparent hand and called, and a spirit horse drawn out of a body horse somewhere nearby came up and bowed its head. He got on. In his spirit form he mounted with an effortless spring from the ground.

The horse, which he saw now wore the white-furred skin of a Bear's head over its long face, leaped away, cantering up the air into the afternoon sky. Setteo, clutching at the horse's coarse mane, looked down and saw that there were ice blocks underfoot, like the bridge he had climbed before.

But this ice was black and impenetrable to his sight, and he couldn't look at it long. The horse growled. He thought it was laughing at him.

There were trees far beneath him, and then the Lammintown cliffs all abuzz with activity. Forested clifftops fled by below, with a half-obliterated track laid through them. It led to the dark block of Endpath, gnawed round the base by the creamy teeth of the sea.

He smiled to see the slanted walls rising from the spray-wet rocks, and the parapet from which he had fished for ghosts. The terrace where Eykar Bek had raised herbs and vegetables for the kitchen was hidden in shadow now, but he had a fine view of the flat roof where Alldera Conqueror had sat wrapped in blankets, recovering from the wounds of treachery.

The sun was setting behind Endpath, to the north. No, the sun was not setting but hovering, half-hidden, shooting out crude rays like lines drawn in sand by a child's hasty hand.

So sly, the Bears were! As if he would be fooled by this into thinking he was being shown a drawing instead of the real thing! These were not rays but fangs in the mouth of a great golden head with smiling, gaping jaws.

Poor Veree, he thought. Trembling, he said into the horse's tufted ear, "I think I've seen enough. You can carry me back now, if you wish."

"You have not seen enough," the horse snarled, flashing him a glare from its shining eye. "But you will. You will."

A black, wet eye, a pool into which your foot might sink and be drawn down in a second into the dark. The horse meant to carry him to the edge of the world and on from there, forever.

"I can't accept your kind offer," he stammered, "much as I long to see all that you want to show me. Not until I take the little prince where he is expected."

"You can't do it anyway," the horse said contemptuously. "You haven't danced with us, as other men do."

"I can do it," he said. His eyes smarted. "Let me try, at least. *I found you first!*"

"You've got no balls," the horse taunted.

Setteo, stung to recklessness, reached forward and twisted the horse's right ear hard. He shouted into the hollow of the ear, "That's why! That's why I was the first!"

The horse uttered a roar of laughter and shook free with a twist of its neck and shoulders that flung Setteo off.

I have fallen before, he thought, shutting his eyes and spreading his arms and legs wide as he spun in the air . . .

"I'm hungry," Veree whispered. He lay snugged to Setteo's heaving ribs. Above them, the sky was gray with morning clouds.

"Let's go," Setteo panted. "We'll find some food."

He pried the child off him and sat up with a groan. The sinews of his neck and the back of his shoulders were so taut that he could hardly turn his head.

You never came back unmarked from an encounter with the Bears.

Setteo picked spears of juicy yellowstalk, and this time Veree made no objections to eating rough, strange food. He didn't look well, Setteo thought, studying him covertly. The plumpness of his cheeks showed spots of hectic color.

An old gray horse with loose-hanging lips appeared and followed them as they moved on. This was the stone water-altar grown animate, shining with moisture at nostrils and eyes. Because it was made of many pieces cunningly fitted together, it could move like a living animal. It was, he realized with anxiety, the cairn built by Sorrel Holdfaster, now risen to carry this boy. As such, its intentions were suspect; but no other mount presented itself.

Filled with misgivings, he mounted the stone horse and pulled Veree up behind him. It plodded forward, carrying them slowly up rising country into forested hills. They saw no one, although once Setteo thought he heard shouts, distant and interrogative, and twice he saw the flames of beacons burning with the Heras' news.

Veree stopped asking for his mother. Slumped against Setteo's back, he made no more demands except to ask now and then to get down and pee. There was a sweet, resigned air about him. Warmth from his small, hot body seeped along Setteo's nerves and loosened the sore places in his shoulders.

No wonder the Sunbear wanted Veree. He attracted horses of both flesh and spirit, knew stories and games, and only complained when he was afraid or ill.

In the Children's House he had shown a robust and cheery will. He would need that will again soon. It couldn't be long now. The laws of the Cold Country were merging at last with those of the Warm. Setteo had no doubt which would prevail.

That day the boy slept secured to his back with a makeshift harness of cloth. Setteo rode in only his ragged kilt. Insects bit him relentlessly in his passage through the moist dimness under the trees. He occasionally caught the musty smell of winter, a season that was the gift of the Bears.

He spoke softly to the plodding stone horse: "How could I have doubted? Other men may dance their way into the Cold Country, looking for its secrets. The Bears trick them and fuck them, and then laugh when those foolish men fall back into the Warm World no better off than before."

The stone horse stumbled, recovering with a flurry of lurching steps. He knew by its silence and its heavy, jolting gait that it was not one of the Bears. It was the moon's creature, a being of stone and water, making the Warm World's humble, wordless argument by its presence. This argument he ignored as hard as he could.

"Maybe you laugh at me, too," Setteo said, stroking the slaty neck. "But when I do this task, my Great Ones will accept me as their true younger brother and wash me in black water to heal my hurts and sorrows. I'll grow a fine pelt of long, dazzling fur. And I'll never have to return to the Warm World again."

Tears chilled his cheeks.

"I'll glide through the black water under the ice and gobble down the snails that live there, great sleek creatures with whiskers as long as your arm. I'll read the future, the past, and all secrets in the flights of the soaring birds that fly and fly without ever ceasing.

"The whole time, I'll be watching for Eykar Bek to come looking for me. I can't let him see me there. I was his and he was mine, but what I had I gave up. There's always a price. The Bears never give anything free."

The horse halted with a great sigh. The stones that had been fitted together to make up its body slithered apart with a roar and sank in a disintegrating heap, straight down under him into the ground.

Setteo leaped clear. His feet struck the hard earth of a path. He stood whimpering, rubbing at one stinging heel. Voices sounded, soft cries nearby. He looked wildly around.

Half a dozen people, crowded together only a few yards away, stared back at him in alarm. He had not seen them because they were dark, like rocks. A little way apart, two small ones guarded some low, pale animals with big bellies, stick-thin legs, and long ears drooping from their narrow, bumpy-looking heads.

Sure enough, the moon's horse had betrayed him, bringing him here to these beings! Setteo tensed himself to flee.

One of the pale animals bleated loudly, and Veree, half-waking, called out, "I want some! Don't drink it up, Biri!"

The two voices, call and answer, stopped Setteo. In a panic of indecision he hesitated, dancing from foot to foot.

The strangers talked among themselves, gesturing, a clutch of dark, female stone people, beating hearts of the Warm World. One had a small girl clinging to her waist. The child pointed, speaking rapidly in a high, clear voice.

The girl was handed something and nudged toward him. She came cautiously forward, holding out a wooden bowl. Inside it he saw the wobbly reflection of the curved moon, high and bright. The other people watched, silent now.

Behind him the sea said softly, "Pay what you owe for what you drank." He remembered the water that the stone altar had wept for him, back by the hemp fields. "Pay!"

"I will," he cried. He clapped his shaking hand to his mouth, but the words were out: he was not going to do the Bears' bidding with Veree. Therefore, his life was over.

The relief was immense. He had known from the start that going to Endpath meant death. If he gave Veree to the Sunbear, it would consume the child's flesh and batten on his feverish spirit. Now here were these stone people, reminding him of that debt of water given. With a choice offered, he could not go and feed the child into the great Bear's golden maw.

His stomach cramped with terror.

He eased the knots that bound Veree to him and hiked the slender, hot-skinned little body around to rest against his front, clasping his own hands under the little boy's bottom to hold him up. Turning, Veree could reach the wooden bowl held by the little girl.

He took the bowl from her hands and drank noisily.

Setteo cleared his throat and addressed the strangers.

"If you good stone people will take Veree," he said, "I'll go on alone to the Sunbear, which must be fed. Let me just wrap myself in this child's rags so that I'll smell like him. They don't notice much when they're hungry.

"Don't worry," he added, for they had begun to talk urgently among themselves again. The little girl backed away, toward her mother. "Part of me has already been eaten, so the rest will be no great loss."

He was shivering uncontrollably as he peeled the sticky gown off Veree. The child, hot and droopy, helped not at all.

They shouted at him now, and his heart sank a little, for it was obvious that these strangers did not appreciate the trick he was preparing to play on the Bears: a last, exquisite, futile trick, but stone folk could not be expected to know that.

You can't give up someone you have played two-hands-on-top with to a blazing, pitiless, endlessly hungry monster. You don't want to, so you are not going to, not when there are earth-dark people of the Warm World standing right in front of you, with children of their own and companion spirits who speak to the child you have with you. So you do something else instead.

His course chosen, he was impatient to get on with it before his courage failed. He waited with thudding heart for them to come get the boy. Then he realized that as female beings, they could not be expected to take orders from him.

He stepped forward, holding Veree out toward the foremost one of them, who clutched the little girl close at her hip. They did not retreat, but made no movement toward him either.

"Take him!" he cried in desperation. "Do you want the Sunbear to get him?"

The woman made a vehement exclamation, disengaged herself from the little girl, and advanced firmly to lift Veree out of Setteo's hands. Veree's head drooped, his pale arms settled comfortably about her dark, smooth neck.

Oh, the relief of giving up that small, sweet weight!

Setteo knotted Veree's shirt loosely around his own neck and turned toward the red, shimmering gullet of the Sunbear as it rose from the sea at Endpath. He took a deep breath and with tear-blurred eyes he ran up the path to meet the blazing fangs, the boiling throat, of the Sunbear's devouring rage. Already he was deafened by the deep drumming of its angry heart.

The drumming changed to a brief, high whine of astonishment as a blow at his back threw Setteo outward, high above the shifting, seething Cold Country on which he need never again set his bird-claw foot. Great pinions sprouted, searing down his back and along his outflung arms. But the pain was already fading, it was nothing, for he was flying.

Up and up, beyond the reach of heat or cold, he soared, into a clean and tranquil sky.

D Layo's Woman

With a sigh Beyarra said, "So it's true—d Layo is not among the Ferrymen back at your camp? What have we done to deserve this? Are you sure?"

Salalli said again, "I told you, we left only the nine of them there, drugged or dead, in the woods. And I can't find my Shareem! He didn't come with us, he wouldn't come!"

The girl Lissie clung to her side, huge-eyed and silent when she dared look up at all.

Beyarra, shaken by her own resonance to their distress, thought, *How can I convince the Townswomen that they're safe now, with us?* This was what Alldera had instructed her to do, before she herself had ridden off to join Sheel at the Ferrymen's camp. The whole of Lammintown, below, rang with calls and signals as news of unexpected events spread.

The Rois cousins, having seen the smoke of an alarm beacon, had come galloping in from their work at the Refuge and then had set out again at once through the forest toward Endpath, intent on rescuing the Ferrymen's captives. They had assumed that these dark-skinned people were some lost cadre of their own line. Sheel had gone with them.

Then back the Roises came that same night, with the dark-skinned people they had gone to find—but without Sheel. They brought the dead body of Setteo the cutboy, Sheel's green-ringed arrow still jutting from his back; and the child Veree, sick with a fever that had crusted his eyelids and his nose nearly shut.

Sorrel was with the boy now, and Alldera was off to see about these drunken Ferrymen. The rest of the Ferrymen's captives were down in the old boatyard under careful surveillance (for Emla had spread her suspicion that it was all a trick, and that the dark women would themselves somehow treacherously attack the Free of Lammintown).

Here in the writing room, Beyarra set about untangling the confusion; but first she must calm Salalli, who was agitated over the safety of her children.

"What will your people do with my Shareem if they find him?"

"Nothing bad, honestly," Beyarra said. "You saw how carefully we handled Veree." And Setteo's body, too, although that was obviously not something to bring up now.

"He is one of your own," Salalli said, "not like my boy. Where is Alldera?"

"She went to see these dream-dazed men you tell us of," Beyarra said. "Your other daughter's name is Luma, isn't it?"

At this Lissie burst out hotly, "*She* went to look for Shareem. *I* might get lost in the forest so I can't go, but *she* goes running all over screaming, 'Shareem, Shareem,' until the trees split with the noise!"

"Be quiet, you're making a terrible fool of yourself!" Salalli snapped, tugging the girl down again onto the bench beside her. To Beyarra she said, "It's true, Luma disobeyed me and ran off looking for her brother. For the goats, too. They've been a comfort to her through a bad time, our goats."

She looked desperately around the room. The comforts Beyarra always found in this wide, airy chamber, lit by soft morning light, were clearly lost on her in this state.

Beyarra's eyes hurt from lack of sleep. Alldera had sent Salalli to her to give Beyarra something to do besides brood about having allowed Daya to slip out of Midfast with Galligan and vanish. Sitting at the thick-timbered table Beyarra felt too weary to straighten her bowed back, let alone carry on a conversation with this stranger.

Weavings masking the walls stirred faintly in the breeze

from the windows. Salalli got up restlessly and craned out of the nearer opening.

"What can we see from here?" she muttered.

"Word will come up at once when they find your boy," Beyarra roused herself to answer. "You'll know as soon as anything happens."

The hot tea and baked nut pudding she had asked for sat in clayware vessels by the fire. Beyarra got up and brought the food to the table.

"Come on, take some refreshment," she coaxed. "You have had a difficult night. Let me talk a little while you eat."

She told Salalli about the Ferrymen captured earlier and sent south at once to join the rest of the sticks in Midfast. She pointed at a sheaf of pages tied between boards, on the table. "We know these boyos, of course. We have records of things said about them by fems familiar with them from the times before they went wandering with d Layo. For justice's sake, we will ask you Town folk to tell what these men did in your country. How can we encourage your people to speak freely about them?"

Salalli tasted the pudding cautiously before passing the dish to her daughter. "Just ask them," she said.

"Maybe you could ask for us?" Beyarra said. "The others seem to respect you, and d Layo did send you, not any of them, to talk with us."

Salalli smiled sourly. "Oh, better not depend on me in such a business. I have been d Layo 's woman. Some people may take pleasure in refusing me anything they can, now. You understand? Captivity and hardship drew us together at first, but as time went on they pushed us apart as well, although we had never been quarrelsome people."

She shook her head in grim wonder. "Would you believe it, we could barely get going out of that camp last night, with all the chattering to go this way or that way, or even just stay put till those murderers woke up again!"

Then she added in a softer tone, "And I was Gaybrel's wife, so by some I am blamed for his failure to protect our town. What you want to ask the others, you had better ask for yourself."

"Will you kill the men in the camp?" Lissie interjected.

Beyarra thought, *Without hesitation, if you were mine and*

they had so much as put one finger of one hand on you. Shaken by the force of her own feelings, she stammered, "There are no simple feelings about such matters. I think we would rather tame the men than kill them."

This made Salalli smile. "Here is what I would like to do. I want to be the one to tell them how their mighty leader drugged them all so he could slip away and save himself! That should break their proud hearts!"

Then Salalli startled Beyarra by adding, "Some of the ones sleeping their drug dreams up there are not so bad. Don't be surprised if they have defenders among us." She ran one finger thoughtfully over a broad, shiny scar on the back of one of her thumbs. "We have all endured many hardships together."

Beyarra remembered striving side by side with a man called Relki back before the Conquest, when masters and fems of Squires Company saved most of a storm-battered hemp crop. That had been good, hard work, something achieved in concert. Largely on the strength of it, she had spoken up years later in favor of sponsoring Relki off the stick.

Lissie took another slice of seedcake, an intent expression on her dirty face.

Beyarra got up and rummaged on a shelf behind a hanging for a pot of ink, some pen-reeds, and a sheaf of blank pages. She must make very careful records at this critical time in the history of the Free. It was, she felt, her one chance to be remembered as the sensible and clear-eyed person she was, not a fool who had become tangled in Daya's mad intrigues.

Seating herself at the table again, she said, "I hope you can tell me a little about last night while it's fresh in your mind."

Salalli explained how the Townswomen had frantically conferred, whispering against the comatose snoring of the drugged men, about the dangers of fleeing homeward with no supplies. And if they did make it, what would they find to eat when they got there?

Or should they go south to Lammintown, where there was food but no surety of a welcome, and perfect surety of horrible death if the Ferrymen should take back the Holdfast?

"We have seen them do the impossible before," she said with angry admiration. "It's not so strange that some of us feared to come to you."

"No, it's not so strange," Beyarra said. She wanted to pat Salalli's hand but held back, thinking wistfully, *Alldera loved a black woman in the Grasslands; perhaps one as attractive as Salalli.* Instead she said gently, "We were all slaves of those men, except for these last few years. Few fems escaped in those days. No one here can reproach you."

"So," Salalli said, "at last we came down that path, and we stopped to rest—"

"*You* wanted to go back," Lissie corrected, "for Shareem, but N'deen and the others didn't want you to. I would have, if you didn't stop me. Luma went anyway. She's so dumb, she's probably lost by now."

Salalli hugged her closer as if even now she feared to lose this youngest of her children. "We were arguing about the lost goats and Shareem and Luma. And then this skinny person with the child—we thought at first he was a woman, you see, a very thin woman with her little one, so we didn't run away.

"He made a long speech that nobody understood. We saw that he wasn't just flat-chested, he was a man. He didn't look like much, but we were afraid, we didn't know what to do.

"You see he began pulling, he pulled the clothes off this little boy, and I thought—the way these southmen do with each other—we thought he meant to do some terrible sex thing with this child, right in front of us. Now they tell me this fellow wasn't a billy at all but a wether—gelded."

She paused, hissing in her breath in confusion and distress.

Beyarra said gravely, "Men here used to impose themselves on boys, Salalli, but that has changed, believe me. We won't let any child be abused by predatory elders."

The brown woman made a shaking-off movement and a grimace of distaste. "It turned out he was just taking the child's shirt as a memento, I suppose, before handing him over to me. It was all very strange—but not as strange as what happened next."

With great animation and expressions of astonishment, she told how Sheel and the Roises had come riding up the pathway from Lammintown, and how Sheel had fired the fatal arrow that halted Setteo's flight. Salalli's dark eyes flashed. "They were beautiful, the two black riders, and then that pale one with her bow raised just so, and she shot—"

Lissie broke in imperiously, "My father could shoot better. These White men couldn't even make a bow. But Shareem was going to show them how. He told me that then they would have to treat him like a man."

"Hush, child, we don't need to hear about your brother!" The mother's voice shook. "My boy is very confused about these things."

Beyarra was looking at Lissie and thinking, *She gave Veree water, Salalli said. What happened to Setteo, right in front of her eyes, could happen—she thinks—to her brother. She's watching me to see if I would kill Shareem for wanting to help d Layo's men.*

People went by in the passage outside just then, talking loudly. Lissie jumped up and opened the door to look out. Salalli rose anxiously, but Beyarra-Bey moved first and with firm hands marched the little girl back to her.

"Don't worry," she said gently. "Nobody else is getting lost or hurt around here."

"That man d Layo," Salalli said tartly, "will murder us all if he finds us."

Beyarra took her sinewy hand in a firm grip. "I am no warrior," she said, "but I swear to you that Alldera Holdfaster would die before she would allow Servan d Layo to do you or anyone any further harm."

"I have to go help Luma," Lissie announced suddenly. "The goats won't let *her* catch them."

"You sit," her mother said. "Be quiet and be grateful."

Perhaps it was too soon to ask more questions, not with Lissie there, agitated and unsure (and Salalli would obviously not be parted from the child without a fight). The slaughter at Rock Pool might be willfully blurred in the child's memory already, but she had seen Setteo killed before her eyes only hours ago.

If this were my child, my Karenn with her curled stub of a hand, I would put my impatience away and go gently, very gently.

"Your goats sound as if they know how to take care of themselves," she said to the girl.

Lissie said proudly, "They can open anything, and they can climb a tree higher than your head. They won't all come to Shareem, or Luma either; some of them like me best. I have to go find them."

Salalli caught her by the arm: "No!"

"Let go!" Lissie cried, trying to twist away from her. "You don't let me do anything!"

"I'm only worried for you," Salalli answered, smoothing the child's springy hair with her free hand. Beyarra thought of Karenn's hair, so silky, and how she hated to have it combed.

Lissie lunged free of her mother's hands. "What good is worrying," she shouted, "when you can't do anything about it anyhow when bad things do happen?"

Beyarra saw, with a stab of anguish, that the Ferrymen must have molested these girls. She had suspected but had not known how, or whether, to ask.

"Your brother will bring the goats, Lissie," she said, trying to sound comforting and failing, she was sure. How did free people talk to children who had already had some of the life crushed out of them?

Lissie stared at the floor. "He won't. He doesn't want you to kill them and eat them, like the southmen did."

Killing again. The child's view of the world might be irrevocably stained with blood and pain.

"We can't hurt the goats," Beyarra said, "even if we wanted to. They're yours, not ours."

"Those men said things like that," Lissie accused. "But they killed our best milkers and the breeding buck from Sand Pool for their stupid feast. You never saw anything so stupid!"

"Yes," Beyarra agreed, "it sounds very stupid!"

Lissie nodded emphatically. "Stupider than anything," she said, and that seemed to complete the conversation to her satisfaction. She drifted over to look out of the window, counting something that she saw down below and marking the sill with spit on her fingertip

Salalli relaxed in her seat. "And so," she said quietly, carefully not harking back to the death of Setteo, "we told these strange riders how we had left those drunken men back at our camp—"

The door opened and Ila-Illea walked in.

"Well," she said gustily, throwing herself onto the couch, "I'd like to say we've found d Layo, but we haven't, not yet." She picked a twig out of her hair and looked at it. "Walking in a forest is messy. Anyway, we'll find him."

Salalli said, "But you have the others?"

Ila said, "We may have missed a couple, but we'll get them. We woke the dreamers up with a bath of seawater." She burst out laughing. "Oh, you should have seen them, dripping wet and stamping around in their ropes and chains, sputtering threats and curses—a sorry crew! d Layo was probably relieved to leave them behind."

"No one got hurt?" Salalli said. "They didn't fight?"

"A few made a fuss, but that didn't stop us." Ila gave the Townswoman a curious look. "Were you slaves to your men, in these Towns of yours?"

"Of course not!" Salalli replied, offended. "We were their wives."

"If you'd ever been slaves," Ila said, with a glance of shared understanding for Beyarra, "you would have learned to anticipate getting hurt without letting it interfere with what needed doing. A few of us are bruised, but those men are all yoked and sticked."

Salalli answered fiercely, "But *he* is free, and he has a gun! And if the others join him—that fellow Galligan only pretended to drink d Layo's potion—"

"Galligan!" Beyarra stood, trembling. "*Galligan* was there?"

"I never saw him," Ila began, frowning.

"No, that's what I'm telling you," Salalli said urgently. "This Galligan only joined d Layo's men at Endpath, him and that pet person. Last night the two of them slipped away, right after d Layo drugged the others and went off alone. They took Leeja-Beda too, and followed after him.

"I think that pet person is mad for the DarkDreamer. She hasn't had enough abuse, she must run after him for more and drag that moon-eyed fool Galligan with her besides!"

"Daya's been with you?" Ila said, sitting up straight. "That's where she disappeared to with that runaway stick?"

"Oh yes," Salalli said, sarcastic now. "So you understand a little, maybe, why we are not so certain of all this femmish courage and resolve. That Daya creature couldn't get close enough to d Layo no matter how he maltreated her! Now she's gone to him, wherever he's hiding. If there are 'Free' people like that among you, a man like him can still make himself king here."

"Not on my watch," Ila said firmly; but Beyarra, frozen by fresh realization of her own naïveté and guilt in permitting Daya to slip out of Midfast with Galligan, had nothing to say at all.

V

Fever

Veree breathed hot, heavy breaths much too loud for his small body. I saw his eyes jump and dart behind the thin, closed lids. His dreams, I was miserably sure, were not good ones.

Sheel came in, untying her headcloth and stamping dirt from her boots. "Fedeka hasn't come yet?"

"She can't. The Midfast children have fever too. He probably caught it from them in the first place."

She clicked her tongue sympathetically. "I've seen sickness sweep through the lot of them in a week. They keep those little ones shut in too much."

"Fedeka's sending medicine," I said. I couldn't help whispering and I wished that Sheel would too, although there was no sign that mere talking could waken Veree.

My raid-ma came nearer with her bowlegged rider's amble and squatted down. "He's had a wild ride of it. When do you think you can move him?"

I stared at her. "Move him where? What do you want me to do, lock a yoke on him and throw him in with the sticks?"

She gave me a level look that made me feel ashamed of myself. She stood again. "I meant, when will you send him back to the Children's House. He's in as much danger as anyone up here, with some of those wild Ferrymen still on the loose."

"He couldn't be better guarded anywhere than he is here!"

"The Lammintown Council arm doesn't think so," Sheel said. She went over and poured herself a mug of tea from a pitcher cooling on the windowsill. "Not with all of Lammintown already at full stretch. The first job isn't to mind your boy-kit, there, but to catch these rogue men."

"You'd think these people would be satisfied," I muttered, "with the ones they found drugged and puking up by Endpath."

"You know better than that," she chided. She gestured at me with her cup, and a little tea slopped out onto the toe of her boot. She didn't notice. "This d Layo wasn't among them. I'm used to thinking of you as the Book Man's child, but you might be this DarkDreamer's."

I made a sound of disgust.

She sipped meditatively and smacked her lips. "A stud sire is a cleaner business," she agreed.

"What was Daya thinking of, joining up with that bastard's crew?"

Sheel snorted contemptuously. "I guess her moon lady watches out for her after all. These northern women say that Daya and that great gawk Galligan—he didn't drink d Layo's manna cup, he only pretended to, and then he and Daya ran off after d Layo. Galligan loves Daya but she loves d Layo—tragedy, or a big, dumb joke?"

I said, "Just nonsense."

"Worse," Sheel said lugubriously. "According to Salalli of the Towns, Daya marched up to d Layo with the declaration that she had come north to make him a *present* of herself. I've said it before and I'll say it again: Kobba should have killed Daya and Galligan both, on the Steps in Midfast. I would have, if I'd been there."

That was an image to bring me up short. "Maybe Salalli is jealous, and is telling lies about Daya."

Sheel grunted. "Everything she said sounded just like the pet fem to me."

I wrung out a wet cloth and laid it on Veree's forehead. He whimpered in his sleep. "I heard that Daya and Galligan have been lovers. Maybe she really did mean to bind him over to Moonwoman when she started north. Then she got wind of d Layo's return and . . . changed her plans," I trailed off, uncertain what on earth she could have taken it into her head to do instead that would put her voluntarily in the DarkDreamer's hands.

"You're defending her now?" Sheel said.

I muttered, "She's still my auntie, Ma Sheel."

"I wish I knew how she does it," Sheel said, strolling

around the room with her cup in her hand. "People cut her whatever slack she needs, when they ought to be yanking a noose tight around her neck. There must be magic in that spoiled smile of hers. Nobody can resist it."

"You can."

"Well, somebody has to! You realize that Beyarra actually helped the bitch leave Midfast with Galligan? Of all things! She swallowed Daya's tale of doing some kind of moon magic at Endpath to bring men back into the human fold, as if such a thing were even possible. Beyarra's NewFree, she's soft, she's indulgent with men, starting with this father of yours. She behaved like an idiot, and she's carrying coals barehanded for it now!"

I didn't want to argue about this. I just wished she would take herself and her Grassland relish for gossip and retribution out of there.

Instead she thumped down onto the couch, leaning forward with her elbows on her knees and turning her empty cup in her hands. "At least we got your boy back for you. Not that any thanks are due, nothing like that; after all, Setteo did it all himself—took the child, returned the child. A totally useless exercise, like so much that goes on in this country."

That made it pretty hard to say the "thank you" she was angling for. I reminded her that Setteo had been crazy.

"Maybe he thought he was protecting Veree," I added, curling Veree's limp, damp fingers and uncurling them with my own. He moaned, so I stopped and just held his hand again, wishing I could pick him up and comfort him against my body. But his skin was so sore with the fever that this only made him fret.

Sheel looked bored. "Maybe. Salalli thinks he imagined he was handing the child back to its mother. Well, how was I to know? There he was, a fugitive, a clear target, so I shot him. Salalli almost dropped your kit, she was so astounded."

My heart softened toward Setteo, who had caused me so much grief and anxiety. I said, "It's too bad, though. You might as well shoot an Omelly for brewing tea from sharu shit."

"I thought you didn't like crazy people," she said. "I never before heard you say anything positive about the Omellys, for example, in your whole life."

"Maybe I was stupid before," I said angrily. "Life is too straightforward in the Grasslands. Maybe it doesn't make a person think enough."

"Maybe." Sheel lifted one foot and pulled off her boot, peering inside. "Alldera's fit to be tied, anyhow. She says the cutboy never should have gotten that far north in the first place, not if people were keeping watch properly. Kobba heard about this, of course, got roaring drunk last night and tried to beat up a tree, which I guess means she accepts the blame. She's got broken knuckles on her right hand. Your blood-ma is pretty mad about all that, too."

I had to laugh, although this was a bad time for any femmish fighter to be injured.

Sheel took off her other boot and began twisting her right foot in slow circles, an exercise she did to work out the stiffness of an old break. She made a self-mocking face. "If I'd had any idea how much trouble this child would cause, I never would have sent his blood-ma over the mountains. I guess I've lived here too long. It's made me think, all right, but it hasn't made me any smarter."

There was a quick knock on the open door and Alldera hurried in with a stoppered jug in her hands. "Fedeka sent this by relay—something made from willow bark, she said; tastes terrible. Maybe he'll drink it in some sweet tea."

He did, although we had to give it to him in tiny sips. He soon sank into a quieter sleep, and his fever abated.

"Well, we've secured things as best we can," Alldera said, sitting down heavily at the small table by the window. "And that girl of Salalli's has turned up, bringing those goats to her mother." She smiled. "It's a good day for finding lost children. No sign of her Shareem yet, but maybe soon."

She looked very tired, and picked up and turned in her hands the things on the table in a mechanical way: the stone inkpot with its clay cap, the cut and uncut reed-pens, the dish of sand, the oil lamp with a reflector made of Ancient plastic rigged to throw light downward on a page.

"Is this working out all right?" she asked, and I assured

her that it was. Beyarra had insisted that I stay in her writing room with Veree because it was close to Alldera's room.

Sheel lay back on the couch with her hands behind her head. "How is Beyarra?" she asked lazily.

"Fully occupied in writing down whatever the Townswomen will tell her," Alldera said, with a quelling glance. "It's a story full of wonders, and it makes me feel extremely foolish. Ila wanted to explore up north last year, do you remember?"

"I remember," Sheel said. "You thought she was too young."

"I thought it was a waste of time. Now we'll have to go see what else is up there, if anything. Maybe we've been keeping our sentries too close to our borders."

Sheel sniffed. "That cuts both ways. A deeper sentry line means fewer of the Free on each patch and fewer hands to tend your fields. Also, if d Layo and his men had stumbled on a small party of scouts out beyond Endpath, they might have arrived at Lammintown with real hostages, not a couple of wretched outlaws nobody will miss."

I remembered what I had heard about Tamansa-Nan, whose brutalized corpse had been found at Endpath. Leeja was still missing. The Townswomen claimed to have lost track of her in their scramble to get away before the drugged Ferrymen woke up.

Alldera said to me, "I'll watch here a while, if you want to go stretch your legs."

I shook my head. She looked exhausted herself, and besides, Veree's peaceful sleep was balm to my soul.

"Well, I'm off," Sheel said. She took her boots and padded, barefoot, to the door. "I'd ask my sleep for dreams to heal him, child, but the foremothers wouldn't send that for a boy."

The room was quiet after she left. Alldera closed her eyes and leaned her head back against the wall.

"You must be worried about the DarkDreamer being on the loose," I ventured. Despite what I had told Sheel, I was very curious about the man. I wanted to hear what my bloodmother had to say about him.

She said, "He's only a man, no matter how the sticks talk him up. No, it's these Breakaways that are on my mind;

maybe Raysa told you something about them? They took some horses to make a camp like a Grassland camp, but down south.''

''She told me,'' I said.

''Why did all that have to blow up now?'' She rubbed her eyes. ''If only people would just stop making trouble for a few days!''

We talked about this a little. I was worried about Raysa, and how the desertion of the Breakaways, who were her friends, must reflect on her. I could see that the subject fretted Alldera badly, but I was too tired myself to cast far for a better topic, and ended up doing worse.

''What about Beyarra?'' I said.

''In the doghouse,'' she said flatly. ''She's young and silly sometimes, but I can hardly believe she fell for this horseshit of Daya's about giving Galligan to the Lady.''

I said, ''I can believe it. She wants some other possibility for her daughter than growing up to be a master of slaves, and Daya seemed to be at least making an effort in that direction.''

Alldera got up and began walking up and down, swinging her arms in wide, slow circles to loosen her shoulders. ''It's true, Beyarra looks further ahead since her child was born. Do you still like Beyarra? I hope so; she'll need all the friends she can find, after this. More tea?''

''Stars, no,'' I said. ''I'm sloshing as it is.''

She set the pot back down and came to gaze down at Veree. ''These fevers come and go without reason that anyone can see.''

She sounded so grave that she frightened me. ''He's not dying, is he?''

''I've seen sicker kits come out of it bright and kicking.''

''Do you want him to die?'' I said. I was upset and too tired to handle it well. ''It would make life simpler for you, but do you really want it? Listen, I've made a decision, and you should be the first to know: if Salalli's people decide to go back to their old home in the north, I'm going to send Veree with them. Maybe I'll go too.''

She only rested her hand on my shoulder for a moment and then turned and went to the door. ''I'll stop in again later. We still have a couple of stray Ferrymen to round up.''

I thought, *The Council will never let those people go home and raise free sons in the north. Poor Salalli.*

I caught a glimpse of Emla, conferring with two well-armed Free out in the hallway. They saw me watching, and one saluted me with the short lance in her hand. I didn't have to ask what they were doing there. Alldera's daughter and a sick little boy would not be left unguarded, not with d Layo at large.

My body began to feel stiff and achy, and all that tea had to go somewhere. I called in one of the people in the hall to sit by Veree's bed and I hurried down to the toilet, where I sat huddled over with my eyes shut and tried to ignore the smell of the place. No one was attending much to public hygiene just then.

I went out to stretch my legs—the sun was bright and hot, despite clouds piling high to the north—and I kept to the shaded walkways and porticos. I hardly saw anyone about, which suited me. I had had enough commiserations about Veree.

And then I found myself at the Lammintown Moon's House, halted at its white outer gate. I suppose I had it in mind to go speak to Eykar about Setteo. Eykar's cell now held several other men as well, securable spaces being inadequate to the supply of prisoners.

Remembering the dark little storeroom where I had been penned at Midfast, it seemed to me no more than justice that troublesome men should be shut up too. I was only sorry for the guards, who in a sense were shut up with them. This was not decent work for good people.

Last time I'd gone in there, I'd lost my temper and hit a crippled person, which shamed me in my own eyes. What could I say to Eykar now, with Setteo dead despite my promise?

I turned away and climbed the steps back into Cliff's Eye, to Veree.

Malice

Eykar had heard voices he knew and voices he did not know hailing the guards outside his door: "We found him, Sorrel's boy! The North Townwomen have him, safe and sound!"

But no one had said they had Setteo too, and the window was set too high for him to look out of and beg for news. Eykar couldn't stand on his toes, not with his bad leg. He shouted himself hoarse at the door, but no one answered.

Then they locked Arjvall in with him for an hour and Arjvall told him that Servan was at large but that Setteo was dead.

"How many people do you think we've got to watch them?" Kenoma had shouted angrily at the departing escort, ignoring Eykar's questions. "Why doesn't anybody ask before loading us up with more damned sticks down here?"

When they were alone, Arjvall asked if Eykar had heard the news: the Ferrymen had been found in a manna stupor in the woods. Setteo, trying to join them, had been shot dead with an arrow on the Pilgrim Way. Sorrel had shot him down because of Veree.

"They train them well over the mountains," Arjvall whispered. "Her shaft went right through the cutboy's throat, missed the cub's eye by an inch and a half."

"I don't believe you," Eykar said, pressing his back into the corner, trying to melt through the wall into some other place where this conversation was not happening. "Sorrel would never risk hurting that boy. She loves him."

Arjvall just lifted his shoulders in their heavy wooden yoke and said, "Fems don't love males."

"You didn't see it happen yourself." He couldn't stop himself from pressing, pressing, knowing that he could not change the meaning of what Arjvall had said. "How do you know?"

Arjvall coughed dry little coughs. "They were boasting

about what a good shot Sorrel Alldersdaughter turned out to be, much better than her famous dam."

"I don't believe you!" he screamed.

"Think what you like."

They came for Arjvall some time later. He was sent south caged with the Ferrymen, the Free having decided to cart them all out of Lammintown so that d Layo couldn't get at them.

Not Eykar, of course. They often forgot that he was a man, but that was natural. He was only the ruins of one.

He crouched in a corner with his hands clasped on the throbbing base of his skull. His eyes were sore from spilling tears, endless tears.

His miserable eyes. His old fear surfaced, making him groan aloud: that someday his eyes would give out entirely, only now he would not have Setteo to help him, Setteo to depend on. He would not feel those sensitive, nervous fingers on his wrist or hear the cutboy's compulsive humming under the breath as they made their way along.

So, it was only selfish needs that made him grieve for Setteo? A lie.

How had that skinny, awkward creature with his anxious eyes and eager face come to be so important? How had Eykar been so weak and foolish as to let him?

Slaves don't have lovers. Any fem could have told him that in so many blunt words. No doubt Alldera had, in her devastating commentary on femmish life all those years ago, when they had been thrown together as captives of that pompous old bastard Bajerman.

The light from the high window turned dusky. Food was brought on a tray shoved at him across the floor. No one had time for him. He had no function here, no significance. What could he have said to any of them, anyway? Curses and accusations, pleading and rage.

After a while he ate: it wasn't much, just some steamed leaf-rolls with boiled grain and nuts inside. He ate every scrap, including spilled bits retrieved from the floor. They might forget he was here, they might let him starve. He didn't care, but his body did, and he was too dulled to fight the ineradicable greed of his flesh.

Some new commotion began after sunset, the signal horns blatting, people riding by shouting to each other. He lay down on his straw pallet and wadded the blanket up around his ears. He woke in the pit of the night to hear someone running outside.

Then came a low burst of speech, laughter, an exclamation, and silence. This was followed by an urgent whisper outside his door, and the door opened and closed again, softly, in the dark.

"Who's that?"

"It's me," someone panted, crossing the room toward him with quick steps. "Don't you know me, Eykar?"

He knew that excited whisper; and the scent of the man, he knew that too, or imagined that he did. Maybe he was imagining the whole thing, maybe he had only dreamed that Setteo was killed—no, that was real. Eykar crushed his cheek back onto the blanket. "Go away, leave me alone."

"Not a very gracious welcome," chided the newcomer, still breathless.

"Go away, Servan. They'll catch you if you stay, and then I'll pay for it."

"They're much too busy at the moment," d Layo answered. He sat or squatted down close by and took a huge breath. "Close thing, though! I wouldn't have even tried, but some foreign ferry has arrived and everybody's down at the shore, watching. It's an odd-looking craft, light, with a sail—no line, no tie to land. Any idea where they might come from?"

From Bayo, Eykar supposed, or rather the Islands to the south of it; no matter. "Go hide, or they'll get you."

"I'm safe enough right here," Servan said. "Nobody knows Lammintown better than I do—don't you remember us lurking around down here the night Kelmz caught up with me, and we all shipped out together with Hak One-Eye, right under Bajerman's nose?"

Captain Kelmz caught up with you, Eykar meant to say; *and if he did, others can.* But it was too much effort, and besides, d Layo went right on: "Hak came north with me, did you know that? He's dead now, but he told me a secret, a very interesting secret, that I'll pass along to you if you give me a better welcome, Eykar."

Eykar pushed himself up and propped his back against the wall. "What do you want?" The question came out in a querulous groan.

A quick sound of movement, the slide of air past him and the fall of deeper shadow before his eyes; Servan's hand touched the scar over his eyebrow. Eykar jerked back. Any touch was obscene, because Setteo was dead.

"My poor old friend," Servan said sadly, "you seem a good deal the worse for wear. You should have come with me into the Wild."

You didn't ask me, Eykar thought, *not that there would have been much point.* At the time Eykar had been a drug-sodden wreck of Servan's own making, no use to anyone in the Holdfast or out of it; the ridiculous Oracle, abandoned by its maker and master. It occurred to him that he wouldn't mind being a drug-sodden wreck again. He wondered whether Servan had manna with him or had used it all on the Ferrymen in the forest.

"Well, I'm not any younger and shinier than I was then either," Servan chuckled companionably. "Here, I'll show you."

He stood up, quietly closed the shutter, and lit a small oil lamp, which he set on the floor between them. He sat down cross-legged on the stone flags and, taking something from a leather wallet at his waist, took a bite and began chewing while he serenely endured Eykar's squinting inspection.

His hair was sunbleached so that it looked almost as golden as it used to be. His broad, handsome face had gone ruddy with weathering, and he was leaner—ropier, less chunky. Hard living in the Wild had shaped him into a sunbrowned forest spirit, a godling of confident, lawless Nature.

"So," he said cheerfully, "here I am; it really is me."

"Why?" Eykar asked wearily.

Servan smiled. "I've come to see my friend and to make some plans."

Was he mocking, apologizing, lying? Eykar squinted harder. His sight was especially unreliable in poor light. And you did not take chances with Servan d Layo, not if you could help it, not ever.

"Where are the guards?" he asked fearfully.

"Oh, here and there. Luck favors me, it always has. Besides, I have a trusty confederate. It's not impossible to lure even one of these sharp-eyed fems from her post, if you go about it the right way."

He grinned and confided, "The weakness of these 'Free' turns out to be, surprisingly enough, discipline."

"You wouldn't think that if you'd seen them fighting five years ago," Eykar muttered. He rubbed his eyes, which only made them ache.

Servan cocked his head consideringly. "War sharpens people, but peace—well, everyone grows slack in peacetime. Do they feed you here?" He stretched out his hand, offering something. "Try this. Goat meat. You've heard about our goats? I wish I'd had some of this to bolster my strength when I was carrying you and Alldera upriver on my shoulders."

Eykar gazed at him mutely, amazed that Servan would willingly hark back to that cruel time in all their lives.

"Goats!" Servan said wonderingly. "Who would have thought there were creatures still alive in the Wild—and people, brown people, Eykar: unmen, Bajerman would say. I never expected to find such marvels."

He poured something pale from a flask into Eykar's empty drinking cup and held it out. Eykar was much thirstier than he was hungry, but he could not find the will to raise the cup and drink.

"But then I never thought your homely little Alldera would grab the Holdfast out from under us, either," Servan rambled on breezily. "Or that I would come back to find Erl killed and his lads all dead or shackled. On the other hand, I'm only a poor DarkDreamer struggling to keep body and soul together. You're the Oracle, not I."

Too late, Eykar thought with sudden savagery. *Damn you, why have you come back too late to save that sweet, mad boy of mine?*

"Aren't you going to ask me where I've been, what I've done?" Servan said. He popped into his own mouth the plug of dried meat that Eykar had ignored. "We have a little time before it's safe for me to go. I notice a strange lack of enthusiasm here. It's a sad thing to be replaced in your lover's affections by a man with nothing in his purse."

Affections! As if d Layo knew the first thing about affections! "What do you want?"

"Don't snarl at me," Servan said. "It depends on you. What do *you* want, Eykar?"

The Endtendant sipped numbly from the cup, half-hoping that he would find himself drinking mannabeer strong enough to burn his brain out once and for all. But it was some strange, sour brew that puckered his mouth. He coughed and spat.

"Not that, eh, at any rate?" Servan said with a grin. "Give it here, then, I'll drink it. Goat's milk, mildly fermented. Delicious, once you get used to it. You'd be amazed what I've learned to consume, and smile while I did it."

His voice playful and sly as ever, although of a deeper timbre than Eykar remembered, he told a long story of starving, freezing, falling sick, scrounging desperately for fruits, nuts, roots, and fungi that sometimes sustained him and his companions, sometimes made them deathly ill. He told of men quarreling and supporting each other through years of nightmare wanderings.

They had discovered a few scattered settlements far to the north. There were desperate battles, shelter won, food taken, women and children acquired as part of the loot, and unexpected wealth attained: goats.

Eykar had encountered goats in his reading. Tough, social animals, they must have been well able to fend for themselves during the Wasting while lesser creatures—and greater ones—died out. The northerners had apparently captured and tamed some again.

But animals that those men could take from the mountains and domesticate could be taken by other men in turn. And so the Ferrymen were home again, steeped in blood, victorious, and rich with looted livestock.

"Hell of a joke," Servan said, pouring himself some more of the sour drink, "to find everything turned topsy-turvy here! Topsy-turvy," he said again with relish, shaking his head. "And *they've* got animals, too—bigger, faster, stronger animals from over the mountains! 'Mine is bigger than yours,' eh, Eykar? Not to mention these foreigners arriving by sea—now there's an entrance for you! Pity old Hak missed that.

"All in all I'm shown up for a fool, which is what I suppose I deserve for playing at heroics, as if I were—oh, some staunch, selfless, thoughtful fellow like you. And ten years younger besides."

Setteo is dead, so "selfless" is right, Eykar thought; *I am left without my self. He took with him the self I had even begun to love a little.*

No, he must stay with the present. He sat up straighter, trying to rouse his mourning mind and body. Setteo was dead, and this damned man, this weather-worn and coarsened version of the beautiful lad Eykar had once adored, was about to make demands on him.

He never talks to anyone unless he wants something from them. It's all still there in his voice, same as ever.

"Now my lads are taken or scattered," d Layo said, sobering. "And these busy fems have my prizes—women, children, goats, and all—leaving me as empty-handed as I was when I set out into the Wild six years ago. Except for you, Eykar."

"What do you want?" he shouted.

"Sshhh!" Servan warned, leaning closer. "I want to turn the tables, regain what's lost! Why should fems rule here? We're men, we can take what's ours."

"You can't," Eykar said. "You're crazy."

"They'd kill me as soon as look at me, of course," Servan agreed. "Or tell any lie to lure me into a trap. Unless—unless I have something precious of theirs, something valuable enough to make them cautious with me.

"I need to lay hold of something—or someone—that I can use to make these women listen when I speak to them. They have to be made to deal with us instead of hunting us like animals."

"Us," Eykar said bitterly. "You haven't been here. Nobody's been catching you, killing you. You don't know a thing about it."

"No," Servan agreed, giving Eykar's arm a friendly squeeze. "That's why I need you to tell me what you can, Eykar, before I make my move."

"Then I'm not to be your hostage?" Eykar said.

"What?" Servan scoffed with affectionate scorn. "A broken-down wreck like you?" His voice sharpened. "If you wanted to be important, you should have accepted your patrimony from your father instead of striking the old bastard dead on the spot!"

It was said as a gibe, but at that moment Eykar caught a glimpse of the spite that lay beneath. Servan begrudged Eykar his rejection of the power that Maggomas the Engineer had offered. The offer had been to both of them, the prospect great, although fashioned out of pure insanity. Servan had not forgotten nor forgiven Eykar for his answer, not even after all these years.

That was part of what creating the Oracle had been about, Eykar saw: vengeance.

"I thought I'd take Alldera herself," Servan said in a ruminative tone, "but she'll be difficult to reach, being such a high personage these days. There's this daughter, though: her child. Yours too, I hear. Sorrel, isn't that her name?"

Servan stretched, and Eykar saw a glint of metal on his hip. He knew at once what that was even though he could not see the whole shape. Trust Servan to find such a weapon and bring it back with him.

"You could get to Alldera with that gun," he said.

"No, she's to be left in place for the time being," Servan said regretfully, drawing the gun and turning it in his hand so that it caught the lamplight. "She's got the brains to try to outthink me instead of fighting me, and that gives us a chance; because I can outthink *her*—with this to back me up." He pointed the gun at the window and mimed firing it, the imaginary recoil driving his arm up sharply.

"So I'll take her child," he went on, "which itself has a child, I hear. We'll take all the bitch-spawn of this 'Conqueror' and then we'll see how things go."

Setteo was like a child, Eykar thought. *But he's dead, and she killed him. She said she wouldn't, but she did.*

"Veree isn't Sorrel's child," he said.

"Oh, that doesn't matter," Servan said airily, squinting down the gun barrel at Eykar. "He's very, very valuable to Alldera no matter whose he is. Her people need sons, fast-growing sons to breed kits from so they won't have to keep a bunch of scheming ex-masters around for that any more."

Or keep a mad, leftover cutboy who could never sire one of these "valuable" children. Of course she killed him. Oh, come back. Come back to me, somehow. Servan wants only to torment me. That was always his idea of love.

"Help me get hold of them," Servan was saying, "this Sorrel and the little boy. Then watch what happens!"

"You don't know what you're talking about," Eykar said.

Servan shrugged (so familiar, that light, elegant shift of the shoulder, stirring a ghostly thread of traitorous desire). "I'm a DarkDreamer, Eykar. I've never known what I was talking about, but it has always turned out all right."

"This—kidnapping, it's a stupid plan."

"That's only part of it," Servan said. "The rest is, I get decent terms in exchange for my hostages, and I give myself up." He smiled beatifically and dangled the gun from his finger by the trigger guard, as if offering it to imaginary captors.

Eykar said nothing, waiting for Servan to move on to the clever explanation that must come next. Had he always been so predictable?

"Let them toss me in with their 'sticks,' " Servan said with contempt. "I'll find the ones who are still men, who aren't afraid of risk, of action. The Sunbear will arrive among them to lead the revolt from within, just as their visions foretold."

"It's not that simple," Eykar warned. "The Free will slaughter the lot of us rather than be beaten back to the old ways."

"They may try," Servan agreed lightly. "But we'll win."

Eykar tried to explain. "There aren't so many of us as when you left, and we have factions among ourselves: leaders. They won't want you, however much lip service they pay their Sunbear. Besides, the toughest fighters have died, fighting. It's the tough talkers who are left."

Servan sat looking at him, chin on fist, smiling indulgently.

Eykar tried again. "They have informers among us. I know of three at least, and there are others I don't know."

This got through.

"Men run to tattle on each other to the cunts?" Servan said, and whistled soft amazement. "The Seniors were right; we're not the men our sires were, are we? What a disappointment."

"We're not above doing what fems did when they were slaves, no," Eykar retorted acidly. Servan should have been able to work this out for himself. He wasn't thinking; he was dreaming, and his dreams could cost other men their lives.

"And they're not above doing what we did when we were masters. They're just better at it. It's no surprise that there are men willing to buy a little more freedom for themselves by cooperating with the fems."

"You're not giving me enough credit, Eykar," Servan said in an injured tone. "I'm the man who got a whole crew of Chesters to float us south to Bayo once, at considerable risk to themselves."

"They did that for Kelmz, not for you," Eykar corrected.

Ignoring this, Servan went on, "Now I'm the 'Sunbear,' the awaited one, the saviour. I can rally these 'stick' figures."

"It's not some thundering tale out of the dreaming cycle," Eykar said harshly. "You're up against an armed and watchful nation. You'll lose, and everybody connected with you will pay the cost."

"You don't think I'm the stuff myths are made of? That's sad."

"Myths are best disembodied. You'll never raise a successful rebellion as things are now."

"I see. Well, then, what do you recommend?"

Eykar thought. "Say you had your hostages. What reasonable demands could you make in exchange for giving them up?"

"I wouldn't give them up," Servan countered. "I'd only *say* I'd give them up."

"What would you ask for?"

Servan assumed a faraway stare. "I could demand Endpath, for starters, to use as a base. A few good men, to live there with me. I could create a little kingdom of free men and their women—and there'll be some women, believe me. I've already got one. The smart ones know this regime of upstart females can't last long, and they can smell a winner."

"So you see yourself as a ruler now?"

"Oh no," Servan said, with a broad grin. How he enjoyed all this! "You'll be the ruler; I'm only grand vizier material, you think I don't know that? Kingmaker, not king. Look, a crown, Eykar, offered for the second time. Are you going to turn it down again?"

Eykar hunched his shoulders, thinking, *Well, I have gone mad at last, or he has.* But another part of his mind said, *It's not a crown. He's offering a chance for revenge. Why shouldn't I taste revenge before I die? The fems have feasted on it, and see how they thrive!*

"I can take you to Alldera's daughter," he said, "if you get me out of here. But how will you take her from Lammintown?"

Servan gave him a triumphant grin. "I have a boy called Shareem. When he drapes a blanket over his shoulders and tilts his head, like this, he looks just like his older sister, Lissie. He's already led your guards astray, pretending to be her. His mother and his sisters will find us some transport and some supplies. They do as I say because I have Shareem."

"Supplies," Eykar said. "Supplies for what?"

"For Endpath. You do know a way in, Endtendant; I know you do, and I'm counting on you. We're going to occupy Endpath and deal with these femmish renegades from there. You're not afraid of ghosts, are you?"

"No," Eykar said. "I have learned to be afraid only of the living."

He was being played, he knew, by a master. Servan had been angling for entry into Endpath all along; he had only meant to impress with all those flourishes about infiltrating the stickmen and rousing them to revolt.

He could not know that Eykar had reasons of his own for going along with his scheme.

Eykar's heart quaked at the enormity of what he was about to do. But Sorrel had killed Setteo; let her pay.

He should have foreseen it, of course; he himself had killed his father just as Old Holdfast belief had warned.

Despite the tentative warmth between himself and this young woman Sorrel, she too had acted on that iron rule and, being prevented from murdering Eykar himself (by fear of Alldera, perhaps), she had struck Setteo down instead. It was the root pattern of the Holdfast, bred in the blood. He should have expected it.

What did he owe her, or her mother, or any of them, after that?

I've gone mad, a corner of his mind mourned insistently; he pushed aside this message and opened the floodgates to the hot rage pouring through him, rank as fresh-spilled blood.

"I'll show you where to find them," he said.

D Layo leaned over and kissed him—he barely felt it, it was nothing—and then sprang to his feet, aglow with anticipation. "I've got preparations to make, but next time you see me, you'd better be ready!"

"I will be," Eykar said.

If there was anyone who could exact full payment and more for Setteo's death, it was Servan.

Taken

I knew his step in the hall, the sound of the dragging foot. I got up and stood by Veree's bed.

"What are you doing here?" I whispered when Eykar Bek came into the room. Someone down below should have stopped him.

"I came to see if I could help."

He didn't know about Setteo yet, I decided with relief. He leaned to look past me at Veree's bed. "I've dealt with fevers among the men. May I look at the boy?"

Thunder, he was a wreck, with his gaunt face, his glazed eye and crooked stance! He looked worse than the fems I had seen as a child in Holdfaster Tent, people who had been abused by careless masters for decades before they escaped to the Grasslands. How dangerous could he be?

I moved aside. The last of my fear vanished when I saw

how he sat down on the edge of the bed slowly, not to disturb or frighten Veree, and how deftly he drew down the covers and touched the child's forehead.

He might even be better here than Fedeka, more knowledgeable in the case of a male child, more tender. Veree murmured and moaned as he was lifted into a drooping sitting position, his chest and back tapped while Eykar listened, his breath sniffed, his soft little neck delicately probed.

"Here," Eykar said softly, "he has swellings on both sides of his throat. I'd say he's got an infection in the lungs, a very wet infection. If I may suggest, Hera—" He eased Veree back down into the tangled bedding and carefully tucked the blanket around the knobby little shoulders. He stood up, with effort. "There is a medicine that might help, something used for the quarry cough."

"But he's not coughing," I said.

"Fluid is building in his chest. He'll start coughing soon. I mixed up a batch of this syrup not long ago. Hera Emla took charge of it. We could go to her quarters and ask?"

"You go," I said. "I can't leave Veree. What if he wakes?"

"He didn't wake just now," he said. "And I'm not supposed to wander these upper galleries at this hour. But you can go where you please. It's not far—we'll be back in a moment."

Veree had given a couple of bubbly little coughs in his sleep; he gave one now. I had seen two baby girls die of lung fever just the winter before in the Grasslands.

"Come on, then, hurry up," I said.

I saw only one of the sentries. She was leaning out a window farther down the corridor.

"Where is everyone?" I asked her.

"Out hunting those Ferrymen," she said, sparing Eykar barely a glance. "Or talking in Council, about the Breakaways."

"What about them?"

She said someone had come up by boat from Bayo to complain, more or less, that instead of going home the Breakaway fems had dug in on their new pasturage and wouldn't budge. The Bayo-born did not like it one bit. At any other time I would have been fascinated.

Now I interrupted to explain what I was looking for.

"I know where Emla keeps some medicines and things," she offered, clearly reluctant to leave her observation post at the window, "if you want me to show you?"

"You would save me some hobbling about, Hera," Eykar said. "But Hera Kobba would be angry to find this passage unguarded."

She lowered her voice, ignoring him and addressing me directly. "She is in a terrible mood, with her broken knuckles and her thirst for the DarkDreamer's blood! I'd better stay put. Look in the cabinet right across the room, that's where Emla keeps her rubbing oils and things."

I hurried ahead to the rooms where Emla lived in the south wing of the cliff passages. The Endtendant's footsteps scuffed behind me. Two lamps burned low in Emla's private room, which was littered with a disorder of papers and books. I was surprised; I hadn't imagined her as a reader.

"There," Eykar said, pointing to a painted cabinet. "But if she has left it locked—"

"Let me," I said, thinking, *If it's locked, I'll break in*—an intrusion punishable by who knew what horror if committed by a man. I strode over and knelt to open the doors.

A wad of cloth was clapped to my face, my hands were grabbed, and as I tried to stand someone hit or kicked me in the ribs. I jerked forward involuntarily, right into the pressure on my face, gasping in the strong smell of . . . something that made my brain spin and float away from my body.

The rest was a nightmare of repeatedly drowning in that smell, surfacing for a few moments, drowning again.

"—not want her hurt," someone panted in my ear as he dragged me backward up a passage with his arms locked under my arms, his wrists pressing painfully into my breasts. My hands were lashed together in front of me. Another man followed haltingly after, holding a light.

It was Eykar. He saw me looking at him.

"She's awake," he said, and he stepped close and pressed the drugged pad over my face again.

The next time—we were outside in a whipping wind, with damp sod under me—I kept my eyes closed. The other man, fussing with something close by my head, muttered, "He won't like it that we've left the child behind."

Something trailing lightly from his hand brushed my face. I remembered the voice now: it was Galligan, with the bandage on his injured hand raveling loose.

"The boy's sick," Eykar answered curtly. "He'd be nothing but a liability. She's the valuable one."

I uttered an angry grunt that was meant to be a shout. Down came the pad. Out I went, thinking, *They left Veree behind. That's all right.*

Then there was a brief time of jolting through the dark on Galligan's back, with him swearing in a frightened voice and Eykar telling him to keep quiet. They had gagged me with a twist of cloth that tasted of clay. Tears of humiliation and rage ran down my face into that cloth. Looking back, I just made out the stub of the Watchtower against the stars before Eykar used the pad again.

After that I found myself being jostled along on the floor of a creaky cart, with the men's feet crowding me against the side. There seemed to be three men now. I heard the slap of reins on a horse's back. They had spread heavily packed sacks on top of me. My nose tickled from the dust.

"—smoother road to Endpath," Galligan complained. "The Pilgrim Way is nothing but a trail now."

"Why would the Free bother keeping it clear? It only goes to Endpath." Eykar, the treacherous bastard. I fought to free my hands. The ties did not give.

A third voice, high and youthful, said surlily, "I thought it was going to be just us, just men."

"Hey, who's there?" came a cry from up ahead, and we stopped. The voice was female, and my heart leaped. There was a scuffling and whispering among my captors, and then the floor jolted as someone got down.

I heard the high voice, cranked even higher, answer, "I'm Salalli's daughter, Lissie. My mother sends me to the Ferrymen's camp, to make a fire and a prayer for those who didn't live to escape with us."

"At night?"

"For your moon-Lady to see," the youth said earnestly, "so she will know that we are her children also."

A few more comments were exchanged—I was quiet,

for fear of being knocked out again—and then we rattled on, jouncing over what felt like raw forest ground at some speed once we had picked up "Lissie," who had to be Salalli's son Shareem.

I heard this person ask anxiously about the reason for holing up at Endpath.

"You can shut yourself in," Eykar explained, "and hold the place against an army. The Free will try to starve us out, but your mother has pulled together a good load of provisions for us here. We'll have enough."

"And we'll have her in there with us," Galligan added, and by the shift in his voice I knew he was looking down at me. "That changes things."

For the first time I had a clear enough mind to be afraid.

The cart lurched again. Someone swore, staggered, and stepped on my hair. I gurgled in protest. The pad came down on my face.

There was another waking, but nothing stayed in my memory of it afterward except that the sacks had been shifted so that something that had been poking me in the hip poked harder. I passed out again without regret.

Then I lay still, in darkness. I was sprawled on a straw-covered stone floor. Someone knelt and lifted me to brace my back against a cold wall, untied the gag, and gave me water to drink. I meant to spit it back at him, but finding that I had a thirst like a grass fire I gulped it all down instead.

Galligan's voice said, "I'll send you something to eat. Stay on the pallet for a bit. You could take a bad fall if you try to walk around too soon. The drug will make you dizzy for quite a while."

"Why pretend you care?" I said. My voice broke.

"Daya cares," he said.

"Daya? What's she got to do with this?" My head was spinning, my tongue felt thick, and I realized that I needed badly to pee.

"We follow the Sunbear," Galligan said, and I heard the small sounds of movement as he rose to his feet. "Daya and I. You're in Endpath, with us. She doesn't want you mishandled. She's fond of you."

"Cut my hands free at least!" I yelled after him as he

moved away in the dark. "What can I do with my bare hands? You took my knife. What can I do?"

I heard a door open. "Who knows what the daughter of Alldera Conqueror can do? Free yourself, if you can."

The door shut with a thick, ugly sound, and I was alone. I slumped down and wept. I thought of Veree and whether anyone had gone to check on him, whether anyone back in Lammintown was looking after him. He was going to have to get along without me for a while.

Some time later, I smelled hot food. Two figures entered my cell, bringing light. Daya handed the lamp to her companion and set down a tray in front of me on the floor. The person behind her, a skeletal figure wearing only a rag around her hips, made whimpering sounds and dabbed with her wrist at her nose.

"That's Leeja-Beda," Daya said, matter-of-factly, as she helped me to use the corner drain that was their toilet, and led me back to my straw bed again. "She's harmless."

She fed me lukewarm soup with a wooden spoon. I remembered names I had heard in connection with the attack at the Watchtower. I squinted at the one who stood there like a sapling with a lantern hung on one branch, except for her continual sniffing.

"Leeja," I said, between mouthfuls. "She ran off after the assassination attempt! But where has she been all these years?"

"Here," Daya said. She touched the side of her own mouth lightly and then looked at her fingers. That was when I saw how bad she looked. Someone had been beating her.

"Where are we?" I said.

"Endpath; our little space in it, which is more than any fem has ever had before. We are historic visitors, child."

Leeja moaned and muttered to herself; the light swayed.

"Keep steady," Daya commanded her, without effect.

"She's been with d Layo all along?" I asked. I felt more confused than frightened. The soup was delicious, and it was hard to think about anything but the next spoonful.

"Oh no," Daya said. "She and Tamansa were hiding up here with my help. He found them when he and his crew came back. Tamansa died. Leeja"—she sighed regretfully—

"well, you can see for yourself. She was homely, witty, clever; not a combination a man like d Layo values. He mined her for information. This is what's left."

Even by that fitful light I could see that Leeja was a broken ruin with eyes in constant, terrified motion and a rocking, damaged stance. She made a mewing sound and opened her mouth. There were no teeth, and something was wrong with the tongue.

I closed my eyes.

Daya left me for a moment. I heard her say loudly to Leeja, "Sit there. Don't put the light down until I say so."

When I looked again, Leeja had made herself as small as she could. She looked like a cord of firewood propped on end against the wall. One of her breasts was gone, replaced by a massive crust of scab and livid swelling. I gagged.

Daya nodded. "Now you see what life here could be like for us in the Old days. It's not something you can really *explain* to someone, don't you agree?"

Her eyes glittered. She added softly, "Even I had forgotten just how—I didn't really imagine—" She took a shuddery breath. "Well, here I am, and I know better now."

"But *why?*" I said. "Did Galligan force you to come?"

"Oh no," she said. "I forced *him.*"

"Why? What are you doing here, Aunt?"

She adopted a secretive expression. "I have reasons."

This was getting me nowhere; she was insane, I told myself, moonstruck and raving. I held out my hands. "Can you untie these knots for me? My hands are hurting."

She used a bit of rag to wipe my mouth, and then she worked at the cord around my wrists. But she didn't untie it, only loosened the tension a bit. My captors wanted me tied, so I would stay tied.

"Tell me what's going to happen," I said.

"Not now," she answered, holding a mug of water to my lips. "That would spoil it."

I turned away. "What do you mean, spoil what?"

"You'll see," she said. "The Lady has had you brought here for a purpose, surely you understand that? So that you can see. She has brought us all here. Don't forget that."

She moved away from me, gave Leeja the soup bowl to

suck up the dregs, and settled down by the lamp. She used a corner of her hem and the water I had refused to clean her own face, working gingerly around the scrapes and bruises.

Now I made out two more pallets of coiled straw rope pushed against the walls.

Leeja held the bowl over her face and pressed the back of her head to the join of two walls behind her. *Hiding herself,* I thought, *or perhaps just trying to envelop herself in the odor of food.* Her ribs stood from her side like the edges of stacked platters. I wished I had left some soup for her.

"You can't help her," Daya said, following my gaze. "They have broken her so she can't be mended. She has paid the price for others' freedom."

"I don't understand," I said, exhausted and appalled.

"Of course not," Daya said, pressing away a sooty smear from over her eyebrow with the rag. Where her tunic rode up, I saw bruises on her thin thigh. "I think you've forgotten everything you ever heard in Holdfaster Tent about life here in the Old days. I don't blame you for forgetting.

"That's why we have stories and keep telling them: not to forget. Ask people to tell you our slave tales again. The First Free, mind you, not the NewFree. We know; they think they do but they don't, not really."

She nodded at Leeja, who was making a whining sound into the bowl, perhaps a song.

"She knows now; but she can't tell you."

"How do I get out of here?" I asked. My voice, thinned by fear, sounded alien to me.

"Don't ask me that," she said tranquilly. "You're not leaving, because I'm not leaving. A pet fem stays close by, ready to please her master. Once taught, you never forget."

"But in the Grasslands, Aunt, you learned other things," I said, close to tears of panic.

She held up one grimy hand. "A dream," she said. "That was only a dream." She tilted the cup, trying to see her reflection in the remaining water.

"The only reality for us is here," she murmured, "not over the mountains in another country."

In despair I thought, *She's crazy after all, as mad as Leeja; and d Layo has only just begun with her.*

What can he make of me?

Shivering with cold, exhaustion and terror, I fell asleep.

Demands

It looked as if this was going to be an all-night session. The envoys from the Islands—a bent-legged older woman called Sheh and an attendant geld—had no interest at all in the men who had come from the north.

Alldera sat on one of the great timbers from the old shredding sheds. The baulk had been planted in the sand as an archery target. She was infinitely tired, and she disliked being stared at with mild but unmistakable reproof by the envoy.

Sheh was here because Alldera had failed to prevent the Breakaways running their horses south. Now that they were there they refused to return, saying they would take as their charge the defense of the south.

Alldera had tried to explain to Sheh that the rest of the Free were occupied rounding up dangerous male renegades, and that once that was done, other pressing tasks must be attended to. They could not simply ride south to collect the unwilling Breakaways, and in fact would be most grateful for help *from* the south—from the Bayo-born themselves—against the Ferrymen.

The envoy listened politely and said, "You are great warriors, as everyone knows. Why should we worry that a few male scraps come drifting back here from some boyish expedition? You will manage them—look, you have already recaptured most of them and freed their prisoners."

And on and on, endless compliments of doubtful sincerity, while people shifted restlessly and craned their necks for a better look at the boat.

Alldera would have liked a better look herself. She had only seen small swamp-floaters while visiting the Islands, reeds bundled and lashed tight to float high in the channels between the swamp grass thickets.

The vessel on which Sheh had arrived had a sizable hull of wood and reeds, with a single square sail that the crew had now folded neatly away. The boat rode quietly at the long pier, larger than any of the lammin tenders built years ago by the men. Some people were saying it was the size of the old coastal ferries, but this was an exaggeration.

The Islander was not here to show off the seafaring skills of her people. She had come with objections to the presence of horses on the hills and meadows west of the swamplands, and she stated them repeatedly at grave, ornate length without any sign of fatigue.

She had touched several times on the fears of the Bayo-born that horses inland of the swamp would foul the Bayo waters with foreign wastes; that the presence of horses would increase the population of biting insects that lived on blood, thus deepening this affliction for the Bayo-born themselves; that the horse herders might, in venturing even further south in their search for increased pasture, run into other as yet unknown settlements whom the Bayo-born might thus be forced to deal with; and that the herders might, in lean years, come to be a burden on the ordered life of the Islanders, who kept no surplus with which to succor indigent strangers.

Kobba growled resentfully under her breath, "Why do they think we'd want to keep our animals—or our own skins—close to them and their miserable biting insects?"

"Wait till the swamp folks start trading with those Breakaways for fresh meat," Kenoma grunted, mopping at her nose. It was sneezing season again for her and for several others similarly afflicted. "They'll change their tune."

Alldera whispered, "If we go exploring the coast for other settlements like Salalli's, wouldn't you like to have a boat like that to travel in? Don't you think it's worth a bit of talk to get them to lend us a boat with a crew to sail it?"

The envoy was talking now about plants for food and medicine that the Bayo-born had gathered from the inland hills for generations, and the fear that horses would eat these plants or trample them down.

At her next pause Alldera stood up and held her hands out, palms up, in the Island gesture that meant a request to speak. The envoy sat down, folding her skinny legs neatly under her in that easy way that Alldera had never mastered.

"Everyone here knows my own opinion in this," Alldera began, adopting the stately pace native to the Islands. "I've often said in the Council and in private that I think it's too soon for the Free to spread out too far. I'd like to see us supporting ourselves more comfortably here in the Holdfast before we consider expanding."

A low surf of comment shushed among the listeners.

She raised her voice a little. "But we are indeed free people now. The Bayo-born must realize that we few, gathered here just now, have no power to command our sestern to ride south and bring those people and horses back.

"However, perhaps our Breakaways might change their plans. It is my thought that they may be persuaded to consider a seasonal journey to the south, rather than year-round residence there. Or some other arrangement may be worked out, possibly including some interchange of our peoples, the Bayo-born to learn more about herding and using horses, our own folk to study the sailing of ships."

And so they went off in circles. A number of the Free staggered to their beds worn out with listening.

Few were left when from the mouth of Bakers Alley Salalli rushed to fling herself on the sand at Alldera's feet.

Something bad, Alldera thought, checking in midsentence. She bent over Salalli. "Do you have news for us?"

Salalli whispered, breathless, "For you. Your daughter is taken by your enemy, and it is all my doing."

Alldera stood struggling to reclaim her breath and her voice. At last she said weakly to Sheh, "Our talking has only begun, honored visitor. Shall we speak again tomorrow?"

"Certainly, tomorrow," the envoy said, casting a sharp, inquisitive glance at Salalli. She retired to her boat. Her eunuch took up a watching post on deck facing the shore, a lamp illuminating his round, calm face.

"People, go get your rest or take over your watch," Alldera told the others. "You'll know what there is to know very soon."

They dispersed sluggishly, with murmurs and uneasy glances. Alldera took Salalli's arm and walked with her into the nearest shelter, a lammin works redolent of iodine and salt. She leaned against the wall thinking, *If I sit, I may not have the strength to stand up again.*

"Tell me," she said.

"That man, d Layo," Salalli said, unable to meet her eyes, "said that to keep him from killing my son, I must get him a cart and steal foodstocks from you to put in it, supplies for Endpath. Now I find that he took not only the stores of meat and grain I found for him, but your daughter Sorrel, too. She is gone, and with her a man, Eykar, your slave. They drove north on the Pilgrim Way."

Alldera saw the agonized, dead face of a fem called Paysha who had been impaled on a post by the river during the war of Conquest. Men's vengeance took frightful forms when they had captive fems in their hands.

Her skin clammy with sweat, she coughed hard, trying to find moisture in her throat to speak with. Beyarra and Kobba moved closer, trailed by a few others.

Sweet Lady of Night, protect my child! All men can be devils, and that one hates me. Protect her, protect, protect her—I'll do anything—protect her, Skymother, oh please!

Alldera pushed their hands away. She braced her splayed fingers on the scarred end of a long, narrow chopping table and gulped breaths of the sea-tainted air.

"I told you," Kobba said bitterly. "I warned you."

Alldera said, "He'll be at Endpath, waiting for me. Saddle a horse for me, someone. Pack me a traveling kit. Beyarra, will you do that? Kobba, come with me—and Ila—" She looked around at their shocked faces. "Everyone, move back, let me be. I have to think."

She could think only in patches between tides of panic. One of the things she thought was, *This is how Salalli must have felt.* Out of just this storm of feeling she had agreed to help d Layo, out of terror for her children.

Kobba had firm hold of the dark woman, who stood among them with her head bowed, making no resistance.

"Salalli comes with me," Alldera said, "to Endpath."

They rode the Pilgrim Way north.

"These are fresh ruts," Ila said, jumping down from her

horse to examine them. "That's why our mounts stumble. Someone drove a wagon here tonight."

They paused, listening. They heard the shushing of the sea. Alldera said, "Ila, ride ahead, and Kobba, trail us—they may have set an ambush for anyone following them."

But nothing interrupted their progress, and they sighted Endpath at dawn.

Alldera had never thought to see that black tomb again. Approached in the soft light of sunrise, the building had a morbid beauty. Its inky walls of perfectly fitted basalt blocks rose in a slight convexity to make a flat-topped pyramid with low, round towers at the corners. If wind and salt water had marred its smooth facing, the damage was not visible from here.

Had she really spent a winter there, wrapped in blankets, fighting fevers and the pain of her slowly healing wounds, while away in Lammintown and Midfast the Free set about establishing the New Holdfast? Maybe it had been a blessing, after the strain of the war, to be left out of the initial bickering and jockeying for influence.

It was colder up here, with a stronger scent of fall in the air. She tugged her headcloth tighter around her ears. Her horse, a bay called Champer, had gone lame on the left foreleg.

"Look, a flag," someone said—Shanuay, her hand raised to shield her eyes. "Or something. See that, flapping on the mast?"

"What is it?" Beyarra said fearfully, squinting into the sunrise. "Would that man raise a banner?"

They drew rein on the rise above the Endpath Spit, with the forest massed black and still at their backs.

"It's not a banner," Kobba said. "It's that beaded vest that Raysa gave Sorrel before riding south."

No one spoke for a moment.

Then Shanuay said so softly, so regretfully, "She's right. I can see it."

Alldera got off her horse and sat on the ground. She needed to feel the supportive earth beneath her. Others dismounted and crouched close, not touching her, not speaking. With a shaking hand she took small sips of cold water from Kobba's bottle, trying to calm her roiling stomach.

Kobba rubbed at the bandage on her knuckles. She said, "He can't hide her away anywhere. Not while we're watching."

"But he has her," Alldera said, her eyes fixed on the scrap of clothing shifting in the wind on the Endpath mast. "He's thinking over what he wants for giving her back."

"He'll send your Book Man to tell us," Kobba said, baring her teeth in disgust. "I've never trusted Eykar Bek."

"So what do we do?" Ila said. "Just wait?"

Beyarra diffidently reminded them of the tale that some Junior men had gotten into Endpath once by swimming up the underwater pipes to the central chamber. Unfortunately, no one present could swim or knew where the outlets might be.

Could the banner be meant to decoy them from quarry hidden elsewhere? Why not ride up to the doors and let these outlaws know that the Free would camp outside until whoever was inside came out? They offered whatever ideas they could: distractions, kindly meant.

Alldera said, "Listen. His quarrel is with me." The sun was up. Her head had begun to clear. "Other matters need attending to, while this man and I play out our game here on the edge of things. I don't want panic, distraction, rumors.

"Shanuay and Emla must go back to Lammintown and tell them how matters lie. Set up relays for messages between here and Lammintown, and get riders ready to carry news on to Midfast, Oldtown, and New Forge. But what's most important is to get started culling the herds for winter, and make sure the last of the ripe grain is cut and stacked and the second barn at New Forge finished."

"There are still some Ferryman unaccounted for," Emla said, biting her thumbnail and staring accusingly at Salalli, who till now had ventured no comment. She had required help to get down from the saddle.

Alldera nodded. "You'll have to organize the work and keep watch against them too. It's in your hands."

"But who's to stay with you?" Emla asked, her eyes flicking from one to the other. She would need Shanuay to steady her, Alldera thought. They would need each other.

Shanuay said, "We can't leave you with nobody. And Sheel will want to come up at once, when she hears."

"Do as I ask," Alldera said. "And keep Sheel away. Ila stays with me. Beyarra and Kobba, you stay too. Leave us the two grays, the black horse, and the buckskin."

Kobba did not ride, but she could cover the ground at a great rate with her long legs.

"What about her?" Beyarra said, cocking her head at Salalli.

"She stays," Alldera said, and caught a grateful glance from the Townswoman. She would not be treated gently back in Lammintown. They would forget that her son was also in the hands of the DarkDreamer, or else discount the danger to Shareem because he was male.

When Emla and Shanuay had gone, Kobba took a position on a knob of rock from which she could see not only the black building but the dock in the inlet below, where supplies for the Endtendant had once been unloaded. There was a bargelike bit of decking tied up there now. The smashed wooden cage that had held Tamansa's corpse floated forlornly alongside.

"They'll be in the upper level," Kobba said. "The living spaces that the cisterns serve."

"I didn't know you knew this place," Beyarra said. She herself had spent months there with Alldera after Daya's attack.

Kobba said shortly, "I know every defense we have."

"They might be anywhere," Alldera said, "inside it or out. d Layo doesn't do the expected thing."

Kobba said, "Are we sure it's him in there?"

"I'm sure. Sorrel's vest is a taunt, a boast, aimed at me."

Oh my child, you should have stayed with your better mothers, who brought no danger to you. She shut her jaw hard to hold in a scream, a sob, a howl.

Ila made a fire and heated water, acorn flour, and dried berries for breakfast cakes. Alldera could find no energy to offer help. She took her portion half-cooked and began to chew, although she could taste nothing. *This may be the last food for a while,* she told herself; *eat.*

Salalli, refusing any food, said to her in a low voice, "He

will make demands. He will require possession of some other women, perhaps of you yourself, with your daughter's life forfeit if you refuse."

"Not yet," Beyarra said. "He'll start with small things and promise to free her. But when the small demands have been met, he'll ask for something bigger."

Kobba called, "There's someone, a man, on the roof, looking at us. Just looking, the bastard. Out of arrow range." She could not have shot at him with her injured hand, but she leaned forward, visibly quivering for his blood. "He's gone."

Beyarra looked at Alldera with beseeching eyes. She did not say what must be on her mind—that Daya was probably in there with d Layo, and it was in part Beyarra's doing. She said, barely audibly, "What will you do?"

"What I will not do," Alldera said, "is sell any woman of the Free as a slave in exchange for my child."

Beyarra was weeping now, with bitter, hopeless sobs. "You can't just give her up!"

Ila, with the coolness under pressure that was typical of her, carefully stirred noodles into the pot of tea. She said, "She has sharemothers too. They'll hear of this, and they won't let you resign their daughter into enemy hands."

"No?" Alldera smiled thinly. "You don't know Sorrel's sharemothers. You're talking about Sheel, Ila; Sheel and people like the Rois cousins. Do you think *they* would give d Layo what he wants as the price for my child? Sheel would say no, accept her loss, and then hunt her enemy down and take the cost out of his hide, not out of her own heart. She could do that because the Riding Women were always free. They bow to no one, for any reason.

"Now we are free too. I have no right to sacrifice anyone's freedom to an enemy—and believe me, this man is a worse enemy than you ever imagined—to have my daughter back."

"It doesn't have to be like that," Beyarra insisted tearfully. "We can pretend to acquiesce, just until we get her back—"

Alldera barked, "That's how slaves talk, and it's how

they think, and it's how they become slaves in the first place and stay slaves forever."

"No!" Beyarra cried. "The true slave is the person who lets a master turn her into a stone instead of a mother!" She held out her arms as if a body lay across them, someone very light and very precious. "Are you ready to get her back piece by piece for your refusal? He could do that, and worse things!"

Alldera bowed her head. "Yes." She could not say this while looking into Beyarra's face. "He may do any number of terrible things to my daughter because of me. I will not give him the right to do those things to any other woman."

"You couldn't talk this way if you really—" Beyarra bit back the cruel words. She was the mother of that little girl at Midfast with the crippled hand, a child who would not have emerged alive from a Grassland childpack (and rightly, Sheel would say). It was the mother who spoke, the friend and lover of Alldera who stopped speaking.

Salalli, also the mother of a child in danger, looked silently out at the sea and rubbed at her saddle-sore legs.

Well, maybe I don't really love Sorrel. Maybe I just hate d Layo. Maybe it would be better if she and I never do come to know each other well and find out whether we can love each other or not.

Alldera got up and walked off toward the drop to the root of Endpath Spit. Through tear-blurred eyes she saw the leather vest flap twice and furl itself around the mast.

She hurled away the water gourd in her hand. It shattered on rock and flew in pieces into the clear morning air. No matter what happened now, that was her soul, splintered apart and scattered forever.

Why could this foolish girl not stay in the safety that was found for her? Why does no battle stay won?

She wished now that the Riding Women had left her on the border to starve all those long years ago, for she could think of nothing more horrible than Sorrel in the hands of Servan d Layo.

Kobba, behind her, said, "He'll drag it out, to punish you."

Alldera said, "Kobba, promise me something. If I

weaken, if you see me waver, stop me. Do whatever you have to, but don't let me buy my daughter back from that bloody-hearted man, or we'll all pay and pay and pay for the rest of our days. Don't let me do that."

Kobba folded her arms. "I won't."

Heroes

They're just waiting," Galligan said, striding back and forth on the terrace. Eykar thought he was an excitable idiot. "Why don't they attack?"

"How?" Servan said reasonably. "They can't get in. You saw what trouble Eykar had finding his own secret entrance, and this was his home for years."

Eykar smiled. *My home.*

"Well, what are we going to do?" Galligan demanded for the twentieth time. His agitation seemed to make his hair bristle and his eyes bulge, as if his body wanted to fly apart. Eykar found watching him perversely calming: here was the end of the road, but he didn't have to sputter and stamp about like a fool. Let Galligan do it; he had a talent for it.

"But they just wait!" Galligan cried, meaning that he was finding himself unable to wait.

"Good, Ganni, that's what they're supposed to do," Servan said, and Eykar saw Galligan wince at the mocking use of Daya's nickname for him. "One thing at a time."

The DarkDreamer slouched at the long, narrow table from the old Rovers' dormitory. They had dragged the table and the trestles out onto this gallery on the landward side of Endpath, three stories up. There was a fine view of the rocky spit joining them to the land, and of the forest-capped cliffs along the coast on either hand.

By the parapet of this ledge Eykar had years ago taken his exercise, sheltered from rain by the sloping slate roof and from the sea winds by the bulk of Endpath at his back. The stone slabs underfoot were worn to a gently undulating surface by the pacing of a long succession of Endtendants before him.

From this place he had once watched men trudging up the Pilgrim Way toward their deaths, men in trances of pain, rage, resignation, or drugged ecstasy.

Death thou art, to death returneth, he thought, and wondered if he had caught a trailing ribbon of thought from Setteo's hovering soul. It was the cutboy's style of mixed and mismatched quotation. He had never let Eykar teach him to read, but what a memory!

Eykar sat next to Servan on the bench, having set out on the table around him the contents of the writing kit he had found in his old room. Two sheets of paper lay under his outspread fingers; a nippy little breeze was at play out here.

A dozen times Servan had begun dictating and Eykar had begun to write, but each time Servan had stopped him—a warm touch just long enough to still Eykar's hand and then lifting away again, a tease, a promise.

"Wait, that's no good," he would say. "I've got another thought."

He kept rephrasing his demands, which he had chosen to send in writing as soon he heard that Alldera Conqueror could not read. Servan couldn't either, but that was beside the point.

"I can't ask too much all at once," he said, "or she'll just give up on the girl, won't she? We shouldn't be greedy. I just want to open the game, set the pattern of us asking and her giving in. We'll see how far we can go from there."

Eykar remarked dryly, "It hasn't the feel of a lengthy journey."

"Mmm," the DarkDreamer murmured, "so sarcastic! Oracles are supposed to be witty, not scathing."

Servan's cheerfulness on the subject of that nightmare period in both their lives was amazing. Eykar said in the same tone, "Forgive me, I'm out of practice."

Had he really imagined that the DarkDreamer would have changed? Something in himself must have blurred his expectations into such foolishness.

Perhaps he had not reckoned sufficiently on the effect of being back at Endpath. His skin was chilled as if he were already a cooling corpse. He felt remote from everything—

voices, colors, smells even. He seemed to hover half outside his own core, taking it all in but without much immediate impact.

Or maybe he was numbed by the absence of Setteo.

"I mean," he explained, "that I doubt you have the patience, Servan, for an extended and subtle campaign."

"I've learned patience, wandering in the Wild."

Galligan said, "It's not just us, you know. All the Bearmen need is word that someone's working on their side—"

Eykar cut him off. "Forget them. Their brains are rotted with the self-deceptions of defeat and with manna dreams. Besides, they expect their 'Sunbear' to do all the heavy lifting. Subtlety and patience mean nothing to nineteen out of twenty of them, and another three are informers. I told you, Servan, you're too late to spark an uprising here. Deal for yourself. It's the only real choice you have."

The DarkDreamer leaned back against the wall, tipping the bench he sat on and stretching his muscular arms over his head. His expression was one of judicial consideration of what Eykar had said, but he was posing, luring.

Eykar pushed away the writing sheets. "In any case, you can't really expect Alldera to let the men loose and load their chains on the Free just to get one youngster back from you."

He expected a mocking response, but Servan folded his arms, brooding. "No," he said, "probably not. I thought it would be easier than this."

He swung his leg over so that he straddled the end of the bench, facing Eykar with a caustic smile. "So just what are you suggesting, my oldest, dearest friend? Should I use the girl to win myself some luxurious post in this New Holdfast, something like yours, oh Underlord of the Writing Table?"

Servan was flirting with him, provoked, no doubt, by Eykar's detachment. His roughened beauty was still attractive. But there was this distance . . . distance, anger, and grief. Here was d Layo, not Setteo, because Setteo was dead; and Eykar had come for revenge, not for love.

"Master of Letters, Protector of the Pages," Servan mocked. "Would you offer me Setteo's place now that he's gone to meet his Bears? The fee is a bit steep." He patted his crotch and grinned.

Eykar turned away. His temples had begun to throb. "You were going to ask permission to live here at Endpath, I thought."

"Here?" Servan looked around disdainfully. "That was before I got into the place. Nobody could live here, not for long. Even you had to get out in the end. This is a tomb, and I'm not dead yet!"

Galligan snorted a laugh. Shareem, who squatted on the terrace playing a string game, seemed not to care one way or another. An enigma, that boy: *were we ever as young as that?*

"Then ask," Eykar said, "for safe passage north, back the way you came. Make her release the best of your Ferrymen, as many as you think you can get away with, to go with you. Then give the girl back and run."

Servan looked thoughtful, but Eykar was certain that he had already made up his mind to take Sorrel with him or kill her in the end, no matter what plan he chose now. Frustration over the spoiled triumph of his return had made him vindictive. Gone was the unpredictable generosity once as characteristic of him as his unpredictable cruelty.

"She can't cheat and send people after you," Eykar added, "not with so much harvesting still to get done. So go, take your chances on finding another pocket of civilization, further inland maybe, where they haven't heard of you yet."

"I could almost believe you're on her side," Servan said, tilting his head reproachfully, "trying to get rid of me!"

"The Free want you dead," Eykar said bluntly. "They've got enough bitter men on their hands. We can't die off fast enough for them, now that they have sons from us. Why would they want to bring you into the fold? You might raise other men against them—a forlorn hope if ever I saw one. But their fear isn't any more rational than Galligan's wishing; both exaggerate."

Galligan muttered something derisory under his breath but kept his face turned inland.

"Such flattery!" Servan began slyly.

Eykar said, "Oh, shut up and listen, for once in your life!"

That dour bruiser Jonko, squatting in the the shadows and examining a scab on his palm, spoke up suddenly: "We shouldn't have come back. We should have stayed north."

"That's a new song from you, Jon," Servan said unpleasantly. "What do you think, Shareem?"

The boy shrugged, not looking up from the string pattern held taut by his slim, dark fingers.

"I've changed my mind," Jonko said. "I've learned some new words down here: 'Hera,' 'yoke,' 'stick.' No use pretending things aren't different. We could go away, find some people. Build an army, then come back." His gaze skittered past Eykar, the Endtendant, steward of death here at Endpath in the Old days; how well Eykar knew that look. "Anything's better than staying here."

"You're insulting our host," Servan reproved him, "and you have nothing to complain about. There's drinking water in the cistern, though you have to pick dead bugs out of it. We have food, we even have women, for those with a taste for them."

Galligan's neck went red but he did not turn around or speak. Eykar was sorry for him in a dispassionate way. With his obvious attachment to Daya, the fool was an easy mark.

"Three women, or anyway two and a half," Servan amended. Eykar resolutely closed Sorrel out of his thoughts and kept his lips pressed shut.

"Not enough food; shouldn't have let that horse get away," Jonko growled, glaring at Galligan's back. "We could have lived off its meat for months."

A sore point that the man refused to let go of. The carthorse had refused to step onto the rocky spit. Fighting them, it had reared and fallen on its side. They had cut the traces to avoid losing the wagon and cargo into the ocean. The horse had at once heaved itself up again, shaken off their grasping hands, and trotted into the forest.

"You try controlling a fear-crazed animal with feet like hammers when you've only got the full use of one hand," Galligan retorted, waggling his bandaged fingers in the air.

What are these people doing here? Eykar thought. Endpath on a bright, late summer afternoon felt suddenly homelike, a shelter he never should have left to venture into a senseless world. He wished he had time to just walk the parapets alone again in peace and look out on the shifting sea.

The men—Galligan, Jonko, even Shareem—had all followed d Layo here seeking direction, hope, and power. Eykar, seeking none of these things, was bored and repelled by the pack of them. The situation could not be resolved too soon for him. He really didn't care how, so long as Sorrel paid for killing Setteo.

A stupid idea; nobody could pay for another's death, nobody's pain could cancel his own pain and desolation. But Sorrel would feel pain of her own and then death; he would see to that. His one regret was for Alldera, whom he knew had borne her share and more of suffering already.

He was not bothered about what would happen to himself afterward. He had a vague idea of jumping off the walls of Endpath before the Free could lay hold of him, an ending squarely in the tradition of worn-down, crazed Endtendants in the past.

Endpath to Endpath, and why the hell not? He knew he could count on Beyarra to look after the Book Room.

"Lunchtime," Servan said decisively. He jumped to his feet and threw his arm around Galligan's shoulders.

"Come on, let's go see what they've cooked up for us. While we eat we'll come up with the perfect message to bring Alldera to the Endpath gates on her knees."

Eykar packed his writing materials away in their case. He did not follow the others, but stepped aside onto stairs that led him down into a small storeroom.

This was where he had left it—a crooked little flask half-filled with fluid, the poison supplied to the Endtendant by the jarfull; when added to the manna drink, the color turned from delicate gold to oily brown. This was the private store that he had inherited from the previous Endtendant (a man who had chosen to jump to his death instead). Eykar had put the flask aside for himself.

He held it up to the light from a vent in the outer wall. Bits of sediment floated in suspension. He hoped it was still potent.

He slipped the flask into the pocket in his shirt, left the little cell, and limped down the dusty corridor, taking the long way because he liked being alone. He missed the quiet of the Book Room.

In stormy seasons he had found this passageway slippery with water that had forced its way through vents and cracks in the walls. All of Endpath had shuddered under the impact of heavy seas. He had had the laver bales moved to an upper room to keep them dry, only to find that the Rovers were stealing from him, breaking off chunks to chew like tree-gum.

Sounds were coming from behind a locked door (barrels of leaf-curd in there once.) He heard effortful breaths, scrapings, grunts.

Ghosts?

Sorrel. This must be where Galligan had stowed her.

He did not want to hear her weeping. (She was not now, but might; who wouldn't, in her position?) He moved on as silently as he could. He must stand aloof like Justice himself, sometimes pictured on the Seniors' painted walls as having immensely long legs so that his head was in the stars, the light of which blinded him to all but sacred principle.

Shareem was loitering at the head of the stairs.

"Are you following me, boy?" Eykar said.

"No."

"Well, what are you doing here, then?"

"Nothing."

The drooping shoulders, the big, high-arched foot poking aimlessly at the base of the doorpost, affected Eykar. Shareem had found his way to Endpath with Jonko, after Daya and Galligan too had come knocking on the gates.

"I'll show you a way out, if you want to leave."

"I'm not leaving. I'm with d Layo." He spat the words.

"He killed your father," Eykar said, taken aback by the boy's ferocity.

"My father was stupid," Shareem said passionately. "My father should have killed him first. My mother's a coward, she can't do anything, and my sisters too. It doesn't matter, they're only girls. We're going to beat these fem people, because they're unnatural, they suck each other's cunnies. We're going to put them back in chains where they belong."

Eykar reached out without thinking, pain to pain, but Shareem jerked back.

"Leave me alone!" the boy yelled, his skinny fists raised. "I'm not your damned cutboy! I'm nobody's boy!"

He darted into the shadows.

Daya had been sent to cook in the old mixing room, a small chamber sunk two steps below the main hall. The walls on either side of the wide-mouthed hearth were stacked with crumbling billets of soft brown coal, brought down years ago from 'Troi for the Endtendant's use. Daya had found cracked and battered vessels to cook and serve in, fresh-mended with tarry residue from the chimney flue.

The men were gathered at the center of the hall, where light fell strongly through a high, pierced skylight. If they noticed Eykar come in, they gave no sign.

He paused to rest at the mixing room. His leg throbbed from shuffling around on stone, where once he had paced evenly as master of this dark domain. But he'd been young then, whole, keen-sighted.

He wondered what Daya had come here for. He did not believe for a moment that Galligan had forced her to accompany him. She had said not one word to Eykar since his arrival. Now she worked in a shallow alcove never meant for cooking but for preparation of the death drink.

She stirred the pot with the handle of the small tool Eykar has used to dig weeds in the terrace garden. The blade, a sharp strip of metal, now lay on the work counter, transformed into a knife to cut ingredients for the pot.

The pet fem ducked her head submissively when she saw him watching. Leeja, her assistant, covered her face and trembled.

He remembered Leeja at the Watchtower that night, with blood on her blade. Retribution had laid a hard hand on her. He could not find it in himself to feel sorry.

He was more affected by the spectacle of Daya, once the proud priestess of the moon, reduced in a few days of Servan's treatment to a cringing shadow padding barefoot over the cold stone floors. Whatever had brought her here—was she spying for Alldera, perhaps?—he was sure she regretted it now.

Servan must have bullied Galligan into sharing her in the old style. They had not shared gently. Daya moved slowly, favoring her right side. Her entire face seemed swollen, a grotesque distortion of her already marred beauty.

Maybe Galligan had beaten her himself, to prove his distance from her. The price of joining the winning team could be very high: a lesson for young Shareem, poor kitling, in the rites of Holdfast manhood.

Eykar did not want the Old days back. The present was hard and often unfair, but the past had been a nightmare of institutionalized cruelty. He had always hated the rule of the Seniors, and if he thought for one moment that Servan had a chance in hell of restoring some form of it—

Looking at these people, gathered in this place, he felt a sense of doomed futility. He had an impulse to step forward and empty the poison bottle into the kettle steaming over the coals. That was what people had always come here for; and he had been appointed to give it to them. If these few just lay down and died now, much suffering would surely be averted!

Except that he was not Endtendant any more; he was not the Oracle, who in a drugged dream might foresee all these deaths and so consider it his duty to make them happen. Besides, the dose in the flask wasn't enough.

He took up one of the mended cups (his hand remembered the rough feel of its grip) and held it out. "Just give me some of the gravy," he said.

Daya pressed her dipper down to fill its well with bubbling pot liquor for his cup. She whispered some placating formula from the Old days when a splash stung the back of his hand—a deliberate mistake? He knew a lot more now than he had before about the furtive gestures of resistance of those owned by others.

"Careful," he said softly, and he thought he saw the shadow of her twisted smile.

He entered the first of the private niches into which the more prominent men of those days had carried their lethal portions. No point trying to pull the rotting curtain, which hung half torn from its hooks; no one was watching him.

Turning his back on the larger room, he fumbled open the flask and poured the dose into his cup. It had a sickly scent that made his gorge rise; *still strong.* He set the cup quietly in a niche once used for a dreaming lamp and left it there.

He could not fall alive into Alldera's hands now, not after giving her daughter to Servan.

The men sat in a streaming cone of daylight from above, on benches they had dragged onto the round, raised dais in the center of the hall. Their table was a wooden gangway that he remembered had once crossed one of the sea drains. Now it was set on tall barrels from the storerooms.

He joined them. They were talking about the Conquest war, which Galligan was describing in gory detail for the wanderers who had missed it. Eykar's mind drifted.

On this dais he had prayed aloud to the forefathers before donning the mask and gown of his office. Then he had stepped onto the chamber floor to move among the doomed pilgrims, handing out the deadly drink. A callow stripling in such a place, with such a duty—he looked back at himself, appalled and unexpectedly tender. How on earth had he done it and not gone mad? Maybe he *had* gone mad.

Hot, full bowls were served to them now by Daya. The food was a salty stew with seedcake chunks lying sodden in it.

Jonko took his, gulped it down, and got up. Servan looked at him. "Going somewhere?"

"We should have a man on watch," Jonko said. "Hak would."

"Oh, sit down, man," Servan said with the easy expansiveness of a wealthy host. "Endpath was built to be held by one man, remember? It pretty well holds itself. The next move is ours, and I don't feel like making it yet." Over his shoulder he called, "Bread, bitch, where's the bread? And I hope you haven't cooked the fruit in seawater as you did this stew; it's salty enough to choke on!"

Galligan lowered his bowl, staring into it. "If we eat everything now—"

"We'll be full," Servan said, "and strong, and brave. Eat, man. This isn't a siege. We can't win a siege, so we're not staying. I know I said we would, but Eykar changed my mind. What's the good of having an Oracle around if you don't use it? We're going to bargain for supplies for a journey north. Won't old Blix be surprise to see us!"

"We can't!" Galligan said. "You don't know the fems any more if you think you can just stroll back the way you came! But they might give you Endpath to live in, close by where they can keep an eye on you."

"You think I don't know them?" Servan said, leaning his elbows on the table. He began to expound about fems, very entertainingly.

Eykar made himself eat. He studied Servan. The DarkDreamer certainly was not going to do and be whatever it was that Galligan's cult friends wanted their Sunbear to do and be. His youthful glow had been scoured off by hunger and hardship. His high spirits covered frustration and cynical bitterness now.

He had always been a clever man. He ate and smiled and joked in the face of defeat, and knew it, even reveled defiantly in that knowledge. Eykar recognized the reckless gleam in his eyes, and was carried back for a moment to his behavior when Bajerman had caught them and had tormented Servan for the fun of it, two decades ago and more. People changed so little!

He could see that Servan knew what Jonko refused to know, what the cultists denied: that a few worn-out adventurers and a rough half-hundred slave-men could not subdue the armed and victorious Free with knives, slingstones, and a few bullets. No, not even led and inspired by d Layo's daring and experience. Alldera's riders could put six arrows into a slingsman's heart before he could couch a stone, and she had allies over the mountains.

Servan said something that made Jonko bray with laughter, dropping food down the front of his shirt. In the light streaming down on them Eykar watched the thickset Ferryman lift his bowl in a tribute to the joke.

Galligan did not laugh; his gaze kept darting furtively, anxiously, toward Daya.

A faint vibration moved the air: death's laughter joining in. *If the Oracle spoke now it would say, If you love your life go now, this minute, while you still can.*

"Go along now, boys," Servan said grandly, "bring that little bitch up here for her meal. And don't maul her about, mind. She's to look pretty for me."

Jonko and Galligan, relieved to have something to do, went out laughing and swearing like old friends.

Daya silently collected the dishes and refilled their cups and beakers with water.

"Do you really want me to go away again, heart-man of mine?" Servan said, ignoring her and leaning toward Eykar. "I have to confess, I'm a little bit offended. You can't possibly come north with us, of course, lame as you are. They'll take our escape out on you, my lad, if you stay. But then again, you have protection from very high up, I hear."

Eykar looked at Servan's hands, that were square-palmed and strong, deeply sunbrowned now, the veins standing high and the nails crudely trimmed and none too clean. He wanted powerfully to kiss those hands. He was suddenly very, very frightened of what was going to happen here. This was his own house they took their ease in, and in his house Death was master.

Eykar looked at this handsome, confident man who commanded other men easily yet did not give a damn for command. It was this that men fell in love with—this aura of power without effort, power without respect for power. They were awed by a man for whom power was only a tool, to be cast aside on a whim as if he were invulnerable with power or without it.

I would go with you if I could, he thought with a deep stab of longing; *even though I see through your glamour and I know its cost.*

He had to answer, and he could not say that. He said instead, "It will mean something to the stickmen here, if you can force concessions from the Free."

"Oh yes, I'll be away north and they'll think kindly of me as they die of old age," Servan said sardonically, "because there'll be nobody left here but fem-shaped boys raised to lick the bitches' feet. So this is it, this is the blow you're willing to strike against your oppressors—handing over Alldera's kit and helping me sneak away? Pretty tame stuff from the man who killed his father with one righteous blow."

"You were always the wild one, not I."

"I have an amusing little story for you, later: something poor old One-Eyed Hak told me before he died." Servan reached out suddenly and touched Eykar's cheek with the crook of his warm, rough forefinger.

"You had a great smile when you were young. If you had smiled more, your life might have been different. Mine, too. I should have made you smile more."

"Here she is," Jonko boomed, "the 'Conqueror's' child!"

Fathers

I could walk pretty well. I had been walking in the fems' room, pacing and pacing to keep from thinking, and scraping my wrists along the wall to try to wear through the leather cord that bound them.

They kicked open the door, grabbed me, and marched very fast with me so that once I stumbled I couldn't catch up. That way they were able to drag me into the big room as if my legs were too weakened by fear to support me.

In the long fall of light from the ceiling I saw two men at a thick-planked table. They sat facing me with their backs to the table, which had plates and a pitcher and some cups on it.

I couldn't make out Eykar's face. The light dazzled me.

The man beside him lounged back on his elbows, both legs stretched out in front of him. He wore outlandish clothes, odd patches of this and that tied on with knotted laces, and big, clumsy sandals. His fair hair was tied back from his face with a bit of dirty braid.

Bending forward, one hand on his knee now and the other cupping his chin, he said in a smooth and pleasant voice, "Ever had a man, little bitch? Or did they put a horse to you already, as I hear those wild cunts do over the mountains?"

I thought Eykar winced, and I was glad. He was not a crude person, and crudeness in someone he loved must embarrass him. The man gripping my right arm sniggered.

I squinted, trying to see the DarkDreamer better.

"What's wrong with her? Is she mute?" he said.

I swallowed and said, "Untie me if you want to have a human conversation."

"Shut up," he replied pleasantly. "Now, listen to my question again, and think before you speak. Have you ever been fucked by a man?"

Galligan's fingers tightened spasmodically on my shoulder. He cleared his throat. "You said you would trade her back. They'll never let us go if we prong her first; not Alldera's own daughter! Other men will pay, too. You don't know how vengeful these people can be."

My other escort spat on the floor. "Shit, if I'd known we were going that way I'd have had her myself last night."

D Layo drawled, "Oh, she's not for you, Jonko; not Alldera's kit. She's for me. Maybe I can send her back carrying a little present for her mother; let them know how generous I am."

Eykar Bek said nothing.

D Layo stood up from the bench in a surprisingly quick movement. I got a sense of his being a graceful man, not tall—Galligan topped him by a head—but strong. He had raped my mother, but he was not my father. In no way could this smooth, blond bully be my father. In his balanced, compact muscularity I read a taste for swift, brutal action, and I thought he would swoop down on me then and there.

But he advanced no closer; he was thinking instead, and enjoying his thoughts.

Eykar Bek had never struck me as the sort of person who would love someone stupid (even Setteo was smart enough to survive despite being crazy). D Layo, I saw now, fairly glittered with intelligence. The focus was himself, of course, and the impression he was making. If he had a weakness (and he must, I told myself, he must), it was this showiness, this desire to parade his beauty, his cleverness, his effortless authority, for the admiration of those around him.

"I guess I came home for something special after all," he drawled. "Alldera can wait. We have food enough to hold out here while I teach this child a few things."

He smiled at Eykar now, smiled with tender malice at the lowered head of the man who had betrayed me to him.

My heart thundered. As if he heard, he turned back

toward me and his mouth, which was beautiful and shapely in repose, curled into a smirk.

I thought, *He's like a shorter, meaner version of the Jargasonna Line, back home. That's all he is, he's like those nasty women, and that's just exactly as scared as I have to be—as if I'd been caught lifting Jargasonna horses.*

But I thought of Leeja-Beda, and of how my hands were tied and how no one here but Eykar knew me, and the coppery taste of terror filled my mouth.

The DarkDreamer made a pass over his crotch with one hand, very casual, giving himself a little pat of approval. "These Free people love children, as I hear it. We'll do our best to please, won't we, little bitch?"

Eykar said suddenly in an acid tone, "You've already given Alldera that gift. The girl is your daughter."

"What?" d Layo looked startled. "They told me she was yours. Isn't that right, Ganni?"

Uncertainly, Galligan said, "Well, that's what they say."

Could they be wrong; had Eykar only played the concerned sire for reasons of his own? I could hardly breathe, I was suffocating in betrayal.

"Look under her hair," Eykar said impatiently, "at the back of the neck. She has a red birthmark, just as you do yourself. She's your child, Servan."

Rough fingers pushed my head forward and scraped aside the hair at my nape, where I did have, I'd been told as a child, a mark. If I was this strutting brute's child, this ragged devil's child, and if he forced another of his get onto me—

I almost laughed. I wanted to say, "What good Grassland studs couldn't do you certainly can't, little man."

I wanted to say it, and I couldn't, and I hated myself most bitterly for my cowardice.

Rage darkened my sight and drove it wide: I saw the whole room, every stone and seam of it, every mote dancing in the light from the domed roof. Off to my left was a shallow alcove adrift with the smoke of a cooking fire. Two figures stood against the glow. One, a long, ragged shape, made me think of Setteo by its crazy twitchings—Leeja-Beda.

With her was the smaller form of the pet fem, somehow

transported back in time to the days when she had been punished by assignment to her master's kitchens. She held a dripping ladle in her hand.

These two are my witnesses, I noted somewhere in my whirling mind, and each of them must see this bastard's body when I've gotten loose and killed him.

"She'll come crawling to me before a week is out," I heard the DarkDreamer say to Eykar. "All I need is a little time with her, and maybe a little manna to soften her brains as my fists soften her bones. What do you think, Eykar? You have to help with my little project."

That was when I realized that he had no real interest in me at all—not me, not Alldera, no one except Eykar. The rest of us were nothing but counters to him in the game he played of seeing how much he could torment his lover and still remain beloved. Why else would these threats against me be spoken to Eykar, and with such sensual pleasure?

Eykar's shoulders seemed to draw tighter together; his head drooped. Even I could read that shamed, defensive posture.

Was he sorry? Good! I was here because of him. Now he could not help me if he wanted to. Let him suffer. I hated him almost as much as I hated this lover of his, who drank others' pain with such relish, draught after burning draught.

"Come over here, come here to me," d Layo called. "Do what I tell you, girl. Your father wants you."

Jonko started to shove me forward, but d Layo, working at the knotted laces that held his ragged trousers closed, waved him and Galligan aside. They moved away.

"Come along, girl," he crooned, as if he were coaxing a recalcitrant horse, "don't make me come to you. I'm the master here; you do as I say. That's the first lesson."

Eykar looked up then, with an expression of utter despair. Plainly, he believed that d Layo could and would reduce me to a cringing slave like Daya or Leeja. When I saw that, my nerve broke; because now I believed it, too.

Panicked, I did the thing I had determined not to do: I spun on my heel and bolted for the doorway before Jonko and Galligan could stop me. Only Shareem blocked my way.

Behind me I heard panicky yells, and glancing back I

saw that Jonko and Galligan, instead of pursuing me, were crashing into each other in their haste to get clear: the DarkDreamer had something in his hand, lifting, pointing at me.

His face was flushed, his neck bulged like an excited stallion's, magnificent and ridiculous all at once. He shouted, "I said come here, you little bitch-spawn!"

The gun clicked, and I thought that was a shot and breathed deep in thanks that he had somehow missed me. Shareem squawked and leaped back from the doorway.

"No, Servan!" That was Eykar's voice, harsh and high. I stopped. Escape lay through the doorway, but I didn't go. I turned to see Eykar lunge up from the bench, snatching at the gun.

D Layo, swearing, swung his elbow into Eykar's midriff. Eykar whoofed air and folded, dropping to one knee with his lame leg splayed out. I winced for him, even while I thought, *Good, god damn you, you deserve it!*

The gun bucked in d Layo's grip and a huge sound filled the room. My hands jerked in their bonds, trying to fly up and cover my ears. Out of this thunderclap came a cracking echo and then a brief, high, zinging sound off to the left.

D Layo, peering down at the weapon and fiddling with something on it, swore. I heard the click again—the sound of preparation, I realized now, for another explosion. Eykar, still without breath, was gaping up at him like a worshipper kneeling in ecstasy at a moon cairn.

Then someone darted between me and d Layo. It was Daya, her hair flying wild and dirty like a clump of weeds. Something small and bright winked in her raised right hand.

Over her shoulder I saw d Layo's surprised expression as she threw herself on him, wrapping him in a tight embrace, her encircling grip cinching his upper arms to his sides, her left leg hiked up to crook around his thigh. Clinging, she screamed out something but her words were obliterated by another bellow of the gun.

Bright red bloomed on her back, low over one hip. While the echoes still skipped from the walls, she began to slide limply down his body onto the floor.

Part of the sound battering me was the cry from my own throat. Then came a howl of inchoate pain from Galligan, who hurled himself at d Layo with clawing hands and bared teeth.

The gun boomed again as they strugged together, reeling; something slapped hard off the opposite wall. Jonko, starting toward the fighting men, yipped and fell, clutching his elbow. He lay rocking from side to side, hugging his arm to his chest. Cries came from him in the rhythm of his breathing: in, scream, in, scream.

Galligan and d Layo rolled, flailing, on the table in a clatter of smashed crockery. They fell heavily off the other side onto the floor, still locked together. The gun, jarred from d Layo's hand by the impact, clattered across the paving and stopped, spinning slowly on its side.

I ran back, thinking to get hold of it myself. I couldn't have done much with it, tied as I was and knowing nothing of the weapon. I wasn't really thinking, just rushing where my fear drove me.

Eykar had pulled himself upright beside the table, and he swung toward me. His wide, pale stare told me clearly: I was not to step between him and his embattled lover. His will, like a hand planted on my chest, halted me. Then, still cramped over the blow he had taken, he returned his attention to the grunting, thrashing fighters.

Shaken and confused, I knelt beside Daya thinking to at least try to drag her out of danger. She lay with her hands pressed to her side, from which blood seeped in a slow stain on the floor beneath her. Her eyes were closed. I was afraid to make things worse by pulling at her with my clumsy, pinioned hands.

Kneeling there, I glanced under the table at Galligan and d Layo rolling and heaving against each other on the floor. I saw something glinting on the dull stone flagging. It was a metal blade, curved and sharpened, the thing I had seen in Daya's hand. It was something to cut my bonds.

But Galligan saw it, too. He snatched it up.

I scrambled to my feet to see better.

He straddled his supine enemy, pressing the sharp edge downward as d Layo, red-faced with the effort of holding off Galligan's purposeful weight and strength, bucked and twisted to dislodge the larger man.

The concentrated violence of their bowed torsos and thrashing limbs, the cords standing in Galligan's neck, d Layo's bared and bloody teeth, made me shrink back. Horses fight with similar muscular explosiveness, but with them it's blindingly quick. The loser runs away, and it's over.

This was about obliteration.

D Layo must have caught sight of the gun nearby, for he rolled suddenly toward it, letting go of Galligan's knife hand for an instant and blocking the blade with his other arm. His outstretched fingers clawed at the barrel of the gun.

I saw my future. With Galligan shot, d Layo would spring to his feet smiling, dust himself off, and get on with punishing me, my mothers, and as many of the Free as he could reach for everything that had gone wrong with his plans.

Eykar still stood between me and the gun I might have used to save myself. The pair of them, my two fathers, were about to destroy me.

I lunged for the gun again, hopeless as that was.

Eykar was quicker. I don't think he even saw my approach. He simply stepped across my path, planted his sound leg, and with a kick sent the gun skimming off the dais into the shadowed reaches of the chamber beyond.

I heard hardly a sound then but my own astonished breathing. Like me, the fighters froze, their eyes straining after the vanished weapon. Eykar stood canted over his lame leg, biting his lips white.

Blood smeared the floor beneath d Layo's cheek. I heard him gasp out, "The Oracle speaks at last!"

Then with a great, guttural roar he arched his back, lifting Galligan's knees clear of the floor and nearly toppling him. Galligan shouted. His arm swept powerfully down and across, and a scarlet fountain leaped between them.

I've slaughtered horses. I knew that I was saved, and I thought, *Good, that's done.*

The sounds were bad, though. A horse is easier, it accepts sooner. Mingled with Galligan's sobs of triumph and exhaustion came a thick, choking gurgle that went on and on, accompanied by the desperate thudding of d Layo's struggling limbs and the scraping of his heels on the stone flags.

I sprinted for the kitchen, afraid of what Galligan might do next. Leeja must cut my hands free so that I could defend myself. But the alcove was empty except for acrid smoke pouring from the abandoned cooking pot.

I grabbed the wooden stirrer and whacked the pot, which split and dumped its blackened contents on the hissing coals, and the smoke began to disperse. Eyes smarting, I turned with the stick wedged between my palms to see what threatened now.

Eykar was retreating, limping quickly out through the doorway (but why? I wondered, as no one was pursuing him). Jonko had crawled off somewhere—I could no longer hear his cries. Galligan knelt beside Daya, trying to stanch her bleeding with strips of cloth torn from his clothes. I saw no sign of Shareem, and no one was paying the slightest attention to me.

I padded cautiously over to look at d Layo. He had burned so bright with vitality and selfish will that I imagined him still holding his life inside his body somehow.

But his sprawled limbs had that unstrung look of death and the pool of blood around him no longer spread. His eyes alone held a semblance of life, as if watching his soul escape up the falling light to the skies outside. It was his beauty, which I could not deny now that his face was smoothed and refined by the pallor of death, that provoked this strange, sad notion.

I knelt gingerly to pick up the blade that Galligan had thrown aside. The edge was dull with clots of blood.

There was no way for me to hold the metal strip with my numb fingers so as to cut my own bonds. When I tried to wedge it into a split in the table's end and saw myself free against the sharpened edge, I dropped the thing and had to retrieve it again. I grew frightened that my hands were dying, as the skin was now swollen and discolored around the leather cords that bound me.

The floor shuddered slightly, and I heard a metallic, grinding shriek, muffled by distance. It dragged on, a stuttering cry that set my teeth on edge.

The gates. Someone had opened Endpath's rusty gates. If there were Free people keeping watch on this awful place, they would soon arrive.

I could not bear the thought that they would find me standing in the midst of all this gory mayhem still tied up, a helpless prisoner. I ran from alcove to alcove, searching for some fixed, sharp edge on which to cut my bonds, half-blinded by tears of frustration. I remember stumbling in one of the drains that indented the floor—they were big on cleaning up after death, those Old Holdfast men. I never saw so many drains and chutes for dumping offal in any building anywhere as in that great, black pile.

Then I heard someone speaking. I stopped to listen.

It was Eykar's voice, very reedy and bleak, chanting words I couldn't catch because of the odd echoes in that place. At first I looked up, but of course there was no way he could have mounted the rusting iron stair toward the domed ceiling, not with that leg of his.

Then I saw a bloody footprint pointing away from d Layo's body. While I was crashing about the place, Eykar must have returned, gone to his dead lover, and retreated again with the DarkDreamer's blood on his shoe.

I found him in the first little sidechamber off the cooking alcove. He stood with his back against the outer wall, holding a chipped clay cup and singing with his eyes closed:

—the memory of men of valor,
the memory of the tall men striding before us,
the memory of the sons of our brotherhood
fought free of their dams' black evil
by our bright and manly will—

Here he faltered, groaned, "Christ-God-son," in a tone of exhausted loathing, cleared his throat, and continued:

To this roll of names
inscribed on the endless wall of the daylight sky

I the Endtendant add the name of our dearest brother
the DarkDreamer Servan d Layo."

A deep breath.

And the name of one who loved him
And brought his destruction,
Great Father Death's servant, bearer and keeper,
Eykar Bek.

So then I knew what was in the cup. I went for it with all my might, using my tied hands like a club. The cup popped out of his grasp and shattered on the floor.

Eykar cried, "Oh no, no, no!"

I threw myself against him and held him pinned to the wall while the stinky stuff from the cup ran away over the floor. I was afraid he would throw himself down and try to lick it up.

He didn't struggle hard—for one thing, I put my weight where d Layo had gut-punched him. And he was at the end of his energy, while I was still running high. When I let him go, he crumpled like an empty shirt.

All very well, but I needed his help. I crouched down and retrieved the little blade from where I'd dropped it in my charge.

I only hesitated for a moment; what if he stabbed himself, or me? But his will had drained away with the poisoned drink. I could read in his face that a balance had shifted between us, and he had run out of resolve.

"Cut me loose," I commanded.

He stared at the bloody steel, then took it from me and began sawing mechanically at first one place and then another, till he found a bit of the cord exposed enough so that he could cut it without slicing into my swollen flesh.

I nearly bawled when the blood pushed back into my hands. I tried crashing my palms together to make it happen faster and to drown the agony in friction.

He said, "Don't do that," and began massaging my hands, first one and then the other, back and forth. I confess that for all my newfound authority over him, I was glad that he had to set the little blade down to do it.

"How did you open the gates?" I said between gritted teeth.

He said that as Endpath could be closed and held by just one person, so it could also be opened by just one. There was a standing lever by the main doors that could be thrown with relatively small effort, either to shut them or to open them. It still worked.

The only other question I could think to ask was, "Was he really my father? What you said, about the birthmark—"

"I have it, too; see?" He lowered his head and showed me. "Half the Holdfast population has that mark. We're a very inbred people."

"Then why did you tell him he was my father?"

"Because I thought he might be . . . less savage with you," he said, "if you were his. He was sometimes careful with things he thought of as belonging to him."

"If you cared about that," I snarled, "you shouldn't have handed me over to him in the first place."

"It was because of Setteo," he said.

"Oh," I said. *Well, of course,* I thought, feeling very tired and dispirited. "I'm sorry. Sheel shouldn't have killed him. What can I say? She's a Riding Woman. She carries a bow. Men are vermin where she comes from, so when she saw him on the Pilgrim Way she just let fly."

He went very still. I heard Galligan crooning reassurances to Daya out in the big room, that she wasn't going to die, he wouldn't let her.

Eykar said, "They told me *you* killed Setteo."

"Who told you that?" I said, astonished.

"Arjvall." His voice cracked. "My enemy. An enemy told me, and I believed him."

"By your Christ, Eykar," I exploded, "if I'd been there, I'd have stopped it! I'd have tried, anyway! I promised you I wouldn't hurt him, remember?"

He looked in my eyes, his cool hands motionless on my burning ones. He started to say, "I remember," but the words died away. He bent and pressed my hands against his face while he rocked and sighed and sobbed, as if he would bring his heart up from his chest and weep it out of his eyes in red, heavy drops.

A Story Ends

Daya took ten days to die.

At first they told Alldera that the pet would recover. The bullet seemed to have passed through her side without doing serious damage. Sheel observed, unsympathetically, that she had seen people recover after being chewed up much worse than that by sharu, and the Rois cousins vied with each other in offering stories of survival despite loss of blood and bone, the goriest of them probably made up for the occasion.

The Rois Motherline, Alldera remembered, was noted for its dramatic flair.

It shortly became apparent that an infection had set in. Lora-Lan said she thought the pet fem had developed the sort of fever caused by a burst appendix. People did not survive that, even if dosed on the bread mold that Fedeka had begun prescribing thanks to comments on the curative powers of this mold in an Ancient book.

Alldera, remaining in Lammintown, spent her time in an ongoing Whole Land Council session. At the moment they were arguing the fate of the Ferryman Jonko, who had been caught stealing meat from a smokehouse on the beach. He was staggering with pain and fever, but his shattered elbow already showed signs of healing.

His name was put down, along with Daya's, for trial in connection with actions taken during the period of the Ferrymen's Return. The list was being amended with charges made by the North Townwomen against their captors.

Alldera kept reminding the councilors, and observers from Midfast, New Forge, and the Bayo-born, that the last thing anyone needed right now was a rash of trials. There was still hay to be stacked for winter, grain to be threshed, seed to be selected for next spring. Summer harvests needed preparation for storage, the fences of winter pastures needed mending, there were roofs to be repaired before the storm season, and the second hemp cutting of the summer was still in progress at Oldtown.

She pointed out that she could go on at some length and still not account for it all. "And you can be certain," she told them, "that if we fall short of provisions this winter, we'll be at each other's throats by spring. In the absence of food, hunger eats up fellowship."

Kobba continued to press for the immediate punishment of Galligan, at least. She blamed him entirely for Daya's ruin, even while she excoriated Daya herself for treachery. Alldera suspected that Kobba blamed herself most of all for not having killed Galligan on the Steps when she'd had the chance.

Weary with hours of debate, Alldera excused herself and went to the sickroom, where Lora-Lan was mixing up a dose of something with a heavy, sweet smell. She had drawn up her table to the largest window for the light and for the air freshened by last night's early storm.

People with the usual run of colds and work injuries lay on pallets or sat up playing tile games on the deep windowsills. They nudged each other when Alldera entered, but did not approach her. They all knew why she had come.

Alldera had not seen Daya since the day of d Layo's death at Endpath. Now, with trepidation, she went over to the raised pallet indicated by Lora.

Daya's face was lumpy and mottled-looking, between the bruising from the men's hard usage and the hectic flare of fever. Sweat sheened her skin and glistened in the hollow between her collarbones. The hand lying outside the blanket looked like a tined claw for raking roasted taydo out of the ashes. Under the blanket her body stirred and twitched ceaselessly.

"Not you," Daya said, when she saw who had come. Her face seemed suddenly full of animation and passion, but her voice was barely audible. "*Beyarra.*"

"Beyarra's in Council," Alldera said. She could not bring herself to sit down—Lady, how desperately she longed to get away again!—although a stool was set beside the pallet for the use of nurses. "I can take a message back to her."

"No," Daya gasped. "Tell her myself. I must see her."

Her eyelids drifted shut and a low, whining sound came

from her open mouth. The restless stirring under the blanket became more pronounced.

Shaken, Alldera returned to Lora at her sunwashed work table. "She's in pain, Lor. Can't you give her something?"

Lora looked out at the sun. "It's too soon for more," she said unhappily. "I don't want to kill her—" Her eyes met Alldera's with a kind of shamed defiance. "Not till she asks me to. Can't you send Beyarra to her? I've asked, but Beyarra is always too busy. She's avoiding us."

"I'll go get her," Alldera said, glad of a good reason to escape.

She stepped out on a narrow balcony at a landing in the cliff stairs. For a few moments she stood and let the sea wind lift and cleanse her hair and clothing of the sickroom smells. The anxiety and pain remained, of course.

Beyarra, she found, had also left the meeting hall below and was pacing under the portico.

Through the open doorway Kobba's voice rang: "I don't care how men really *are* or how women really *are*, or why. 'How' and 'why' never brought anyone back to life or restored a crushed spirit. Whatever men are by nature, they can be taught to show us respect or they can deal with me."

A surf of applause, talk, and shouting greeted this.

Someone answered, words partly obscured by the noise: "—same for those among the Free who fail in their respect toward others of their own sex?"

"Who's that?" Alldera said, startled. "That's a man's voice."

"Payder. His sponsors brought him as an example"—

Alldera hushed her, leaning to listen.

"—higher standards of conduct for men than for women, Kobba?" That sounded like Ila-Illea, whose robust sympathy for sponsored men was well known.

"Of course!" Kobba shouted. "How else can you get men to behave like human beings?"

Someone else, it sounded like Kastia-Kai, added ironically, "They haven't required human behavior from each other for many generations. They must work harder at it than we do, just to catch up."

There was some knowing laughter at this, out of which Ila's voice came: "—always been exceptions—"

"And you know what the common run of men think of *those*," Kobba hooted. "Just listen to what they say about Eykar Bek!"

Kastia said, "If that's how they feel, they can stay on the stick. It's their choice whether to be people or not, which is more choice than they ever gave us."

"Please, go talk to them, Alldera," Beyarra begged. "Kobba wants not just trials, she wants all the men under yoke and stick for good because of what's happened. But there have to be rewards too, don't there? You can't teach anyone to act better by just hammering and hammering on them no matter what they do!"

"I agree," Alldera said, "but the behavior of Galligan and Setteo hasn't helped."

"Galligan would have followed Daya into fire if she'd said to, and Setteo was trying to save Veree, in his own weird way. Even Salalli thinks that he meant well. If a mad cutboy can care for a child, why shouldn't any sane man learn to do so too? And wash clothes and cook food and all the rest; there's plenty of work to go around! But stick and yoke are poor workers, and sticked men keep us busy supervising them, when we have our own work to do too! It's so obvious—"

"Bee," Alldera said. "This isn't going to get settled one way or another today. Daya needs to talk to you, now."

Beyarra stood swaying unhappily from one foot to the other, looking at the ground. "You finally went," she said softly. "To shame me."

Alldera reached out to hug her, but the younger fem turned away. "I don't know how to face her. Should I yell, spit on her, kiss her poor face, beg her pardon?"

"You can listen to her," Alldera said. "Take paper and pens with you, Bee. If I know Daya, she has a story to tell."

Four days later, Beyarra related that story. Daya said she had gone to d Layo determined to kill him, for Alldera and for all of them; that she had used Galligan to present herself to the DarkDreamer and get close to him; that she had endured the men's abuse, protecting Sorrel as best she could, until an opportunity had come to attack.

"She says she went for d Layo with a weapon in her hand," Beyarra said. "The blade Galligan killed him with." She shuddered. "I made that tool for Eykar's gardening, when we were at Endpath waiting for you to heal up."

Alldera shrugged. "Sorrel says Daya never used it; she dropped it or threw it down. She may have meant to strike at d Layo, Bee, but she didn't."

Beyarra riffled the thick buff pages on which she had inscribed Daya's story and said with shy insistence, "In a way she did. She got herself shot, and Galligan reacted as she knew he would: he killed d Layo. He *became* her weapon, you see?"

They sat in the courtyard of the old Hemaway Hall, now a drinking garden for people's leisure hours. They were quiet for a little, listening to the murmur of conversation around them.

"I think she was just acting out some sick, pet-minded fantasy that nearly got my daughter killed," Alldera said at length. "You have a generous nature, Bee, to see her as a hero. Is all this what she told you, or what you think happened?"

"Both," Beyarra said, flushing.

Alldera took her hand and kissed her ink-stained knuckles. "I wish I could be that faithful to the loves of my past," she said. She stood up. "Is she willing to see me now?"

"She's asked for you." Beyarra covered her eyes with that inky hand.

People would weep for Daya, Alldera thought, *despite it all.* The First Free who had come home from exile to triumph in the Holdfast had never been so many that they could lightly lose even one more of their number. And Daya had told great stories, once; still did, it seemed.

Beyarra shook her head. "I was so sure that Roona would be next."

Daya neither spoke to Alldera nor asked for the merciful draught that Lora had prepared. She accepted Alldera's presence, her ministrations and her watchfulness, without words. Alldera found this unnerving at first, then provoking, and at last perfectly fitting.

They had moved the pet fem into a smaller room used for contagious illness, so that she could speak with Beyarra in privacy. Alldera couldn't help wondering whether Daya missed having witnesses to her martyrdom.

Sorrel brought a dinner tray to the sickroom the next evening. It was for Alldera; Daya was beyond eating.

"I didn't expect to see you here," Alldera said.

The younger woman said uncomfortably. "They told me you were here. With her."

"I thought you were looking after Veree."

Sorrel's eyes were red-rimmed. "He's better now. He asks for his friends in the Children's House. He gets up to mischief. He's bored. And he keeps asking about Setteo. I don't know what to tell him."

"Sounds as if he needs company his own age," Alldera said. The meat pie on the tray was cold. It tasted good anyway.

"That's what people say." Sorrel gulped. "Send him down to the Midfast, to the Children's House. But I just got him back!"

Alldera made no comment. She hardly felt in a position to lecture her daughter on good mothering.

With a big breath Sorrel continued, "I can't take him home to the Grasslands. What happened to Setteo made that pretty clear. Sheel didn't dislike Setteo, she just reacted as any Riding Woman would. And there is no place else for Veree, except here. Fedeka says she'll look after him at the Children's House, specially closely, I mean." She made a wry face. "We both agree, she owes me that much."

Alldera said around a mouthful of pie, "Good idea."

"It's the only idea anybody's had," Sorrel said. "At least people are talking seriously now about how to raise the boy-kits to be more than pets or draught animals. Veree will find sponsors when the time comes. He's a good boy."

Alldera refrained from describing all the discussion, the passion, the hope and fear and idealism, that had been expended on the upbringing of the boys since the first of them had been born. Sorrel didn't stay long.

The next time she came to the sickroom, she was even less forthcoming at first. After pacing restlessly for a while, ignoring Daya entirely, she finally demanded, "Do I look like that man d Layo?"

Ah, here it came; now they must speak of the Dark-Dreamer. Alldera had persuaded herself that they might not need to, not for a long time still.

"Why?" she said.

"If people here are reminded of that man every time they look at me, then I should ride away home."

"People ought to be reminded."

"That's what Kobba says." Sorrel got a stool and brought it over to sit on. She watched Alldera sponge Daya's drawn, gleaming face and brush the hair back from her temples. Daya's closed eyelids did not flicker.

"Kobba says," Sorrel said, lowering her voice, "that you were prepared to let me die rather than negotiate with d Layo." Before Alldera could speak, she hurried on: "I hope that's true, blood-ma. It would have been a shame to me forever—and to you—if my life had been valued higher than other people's lives."

Alldera dipped a rag in a bowl of water and wrung a few drops into Daya's open mouth.

"I think Beyarra hasn't forgiven me for it, though," Alldera said.

Sorrel snorted. "Well, *I* haven't forgiven *her* for helping Daya sneak out of Midfast. Of all the stupid—"

Alldera said, "Much needs to be forgiven all around."

Sorrel inspected Alldera's tray and began wiping up the last of the cooling gravy with a scrap of bread. She chewed thoughtfully. "For a smart person, Beyarra can sure be a fool, like some lovestruck Caranaw back home. Some people say she's to blame for Daya's death, so I guess it's no wonder if she thinks so too." She stared at Daya's still features. "Can she hear me?"

"I don't know, but remember that she's not dead yet."

"Well," Sorrel said in a whisper, "who do you think is responsible for . . . this?"

Alldera said quietly, "Nobody but Daya is responsible for Daya's dying. It's what she set out to accomplish. It's how she's decided to end her own story."

Sorrel gazed at the pet fem's moist, scarred face with fascination now. "Has she said that?"

"To Beyarra. She hasn't said a word to me. I don't think she will. I think she's done with words."

She wanted suddenly to cry and wished Sorrel would leave her alone to do so privately.

"Beyarra worked all night in here again, writing," Sorrel said, looking curiously about. "Roona goes around complaining that she's using up all the paper on Daya and her—stories."

She set the empty tray back on the floor and hunched forward, her elbows on her knees. "Blood-ma, Beyarra wants Eykar Bek to tell his part of what happened, for her history. He won't. You could order him to speak."

A pungent odor of urine spread in the air. Alldera picked up a dented metal bell in the shape of a Ferryman's cap, a bit of salvage from Lammintown, and rang it a couple of times for assistance.

Then she said with forced patience, "Haven't I made myself clear about this? No one is to give that man any orders of any kind ever again. Do you understand why? You should."

Sorrel emitted a smothered giggle. "You can't give the Free orders not to give orders to a slave, blood-ma!" She sobered. "It's all too complicated for that anyway. He did hand me over to the DarkDreamer."

"Yes. And then he thought better of it and kicked that damned gun away, thereby saving your life and my sanity."

"I don't see how undoing his own bad actions makes him some kind of hero," Sorrel persisted, frowning.

"He's paid the price," Alldera said sharply. Sometimes she lost patience with Sorrel's youthful obduracy and her way of seeing everything as black or white. "Eykar was as close to the DarkDreamer as I am to—to Nenisi. They had a life bond, the kind nothing can erase.

"He'll never say it but I assure you, Eykar dreams every night of how he himself broke that bond, and he doesn't have Setteo to turn to now for comfort. But he'll manage. He's a very strong spirit struggling along in a frail and much-abused body. That's how he's been as long as I've known him."

"We don't know that he's my father, though," Sorrel said stubbornly. "It could have been the other one."

"Mothers protect children," Alldera said. She had thought about this a lot since riding into Endpath and finding Sorrel and Eykar in that sidechamber, huddled together. "The good mothers do, anyway; and that man did a better job of protecting you than your blood-ma did, didn't he?

"If he were a woman, we'd make him one of your sharemas for that. So a father must be a sort of male sharemother. You will kindly treat him with the same respect that you show to any of your other parents."

Sorrel scowled. "I do. But I can ask questions, can't I?"

Emla came in then, answering the bell at last. Sorrel retreated to a corner of the room while Alldera and the masseur lifted Daya and cleaned her and changed the bedding. When they were done, Daya lay breathing through her nose with a soft keening sound. Alldera had heard hours of it already that day and found it very hard to bear. She stayed in order to bear it, while Daya bore so much more.

Emla said, "Lora says she can take over here for a while."

"Let her stay where she can do some good."

"Why are you doing this?" Sorrel said in an angry whisper. "Let somebody else tend to the pet fem! She doesn't deserve your attention."

"Kobba told you that," Alldera said, and Sorrel's quick blush confirmed it. "Kobba doesn't know everything, she only thinks she does. When it came down to it Daya did what she could, and it turned out to be enough."

"For that you can thank the Lady," Emla said tartly, swinging the basket of bedclothes up onto her hip, "not Daya."

Sorrel drifted unwillingly to Daya's bedside again, gazing darkly down at the unconscious pet fem. "I shouldn't have needed any of this helping and saving, by her or anybody else. *I* should have killed that damned DarkDreamer for you."

Such a passionate regret, and so unnecessary! Alldera tried to explain: "That was Eykar's task, his and Galligan's. Men generally want someone to do it for them—us, of course—but in the end it's their own job."

"What is?" Sorrel said, looking confused.

"Drawing the line," Alldera said, "between what a man

may do and what he may not do and still have other men call him a man."

Sorrel considered, scowled, and shook her head. "I should have helped, at least, instead of running around waving my tied-up hands, like a—like a hobbled horse!"

Alldera arched her back, stretching. She crossed to the window. "Well," she said, leaning her elbows on the sunny sill, "I've needed saving a number of times. Does that make me a worthless person?"

Sorrel laughed angrily. "Of course not!"

A sea breeze suddenly spread into the room, invigorating the thick, dull air. Alldera took a slow, luscious breath and changed the subject. "Still planning to leave, now that the excitement's over?"

Sorrel fiddled with the frayed seam of one sleeve. "I can't think here. Things happen all the time, people pull in different directions. How can I figure things out?"

"Don't try," Alldera said. She turned to let the sun warm her back. "If you ever do, you're sure to be wrong."

"Why?" Sorrel countered. "I'm not stupid."

"Beyarra can explain it better. Everybody's got only part of the truth. And people do tell lies, or they are mistaken or forgetful, no matter how much time they spend *figuring*."

"Well, what do you think I should do?"

Alldera had never thought to hear that question from her daughter. She answered cautiously, "Stay on a while, help out. Get into our arguments, our plans, our work. There's so much to be done. What's happening with those goats, by the way? We're a long way from managing them well. I think the North Town folk aren't telling us everything."

"Oh, Shareem is working with us on that now. His mother had a huge fight with him when she got him back, and that put him off at first. The Rois cousins found him with his arm stuck down a drain up there at Endpath, scrabbling after that gun that got wedged down there. He's still trying to work things out, too, I guess.

"He's a natural teacher, Eykar says, about animals, anyway, and he likes the way we treat the horses." Sorrel came to the window and leaned beside her. "You want me to stay because you're going to leave, aren't you?"

The sun falling on the wing of her deep red hair was beautiful. Alldera wanted to touch that glossy shine, but she was afraid Sorrel would pull away. She was feeling so tired, and so untethered in her thoughts, that she couldn't trust her judgment of such things.

"Who says I'm leaving?" she said, stalling.

"Sheel. Those Roises are going back. You could travel with them."

"Sheel's not going herself? I haven't had a chance to really talk with her."

"No, she's planning a trip south, with Shanuay," Sorrel said. "To help those Breakaway people follow their horses like true Riding Women, she says; more likely just to criticize everything they do and drive them crazy.

"She's amazing, you know? She convinced those Roises not to just murder all the men at Midfast, because of Leeja and Tamansa and everything. I wish I'd been there to see Sheel face them down, and Kobba with them!"

Playing my part, Alldera thought, *as other people are doing too while I'm in here watching part of my old life dying.*

"So it is true?" Sorrel pressed on. "You are going back to the Grasslands after—after this?"

Alldera said, "I need to see Nenisi again. I want some space and some quiet around me. Don't you think I deserve that, daughter? I know I haven't been what you wanted me to be—"

Sorrel averted her face. "I just don't want to think," she said indistinctly, "that you're going because of me. I've come here and made such big mistakes—"

Alldera caught the surprised young woman in her arms. Gusts of laughter shook her like grass in a wind, and her tears darkened Sorrel's burnished hair where it pressed her cheek.

"And I've been worrying," she managed to gasp out, "that you would think I was abandoning you again!"

"Oh, blood-ma, we're way past that point, don't you think?"

She felt Sorrel's hands giving awkward little pats on her back, and heard her saying something more in a soothing tone with hiccups and sniffling sounds in it. The essence was that Sorrel was used to being separated from her, expected it even, and was a grown-up now.

What a relief to hear that; and what a sharp bite of guilt and regret!

After a while they were just standing there with sun on their shoulders, holding on to each other without speaking or moving. *I'm leaning on her,* Alldera thought, *like a weak old woman; if I don't break this up she won't either, for fear of offending me; or she will, and that will feel worse.*

She drew back just a little and they released each other, laughing with mutual embarrassment.

"I have to go," Alldera said, blotting her eyes with the corner of the headcloth she had draped around her neck. She glanced over Sorrel's shoulder at the cot against the far wall and added huskily, "I'll take Daya's body with me to the Grasslands. That was the one place where I ever saw her happy. Don't you think that would be a good thing?"

Sorrel shook her head. "I guess I've never known her, not really."

"Who has?"

"Galligan thinks he has," Sorrel said. "He won't like your taking her so far away. He's half crazy as it is, being kept away from her now, while she's—here." She absently shoved her hair back with both hands and shook it out on her shoulders. She was growing it out longer. A little vanity there, Alldera thought. It was nice to see her take pleasure in her own good looks. "If he loves her so much, how could he let d Layo abuse her like that?"

"Don't ask me," Alldera said. "I think it's something about how men always have to put themselves on a ladder, one above another, so they won't just kill each other, all grabbing for everything at once. d Layo was very, very high on that ladder, being the famous Sunbear. So what he wanted he could take, and Galligan had to let him."

"Eykar says Galligan could die of quarry cough."

"He could," Alldera said briskly, "but he'll have to do it in the men's sickroom. I'm not having him in here, giving his damn cough to me. We've got as much illness as we can handle. More in fact, thanks to what those north people brought with them."

She thought Sorrel understood: she wasn't going to

share Daya with Galligan, not here at the end. *I knew her first. I loved her first.*

"They made all the men come and see d Layo's body in Midfast," Sorrel was saying—Alldera had lost track for a minute—"so they would know he was really dead. It was grisly. I was down there settling Veree at the Children's House." She bit her lip and blinked hard. "I went to watch.

"Eykar stood on the Steps with the body on a plank and told what had happened. He held up this big black bowl and invited the men to come and drink the last of the Endpath poison if they wanted to follow the Sunbear, because there was no place for them in the Holdfast. Nobody moved, so he just poured it down the Steps. I wonder if it really was poison."

"Who thought this little ritual up?" Alldera asked with a grimace.

"Beyarra and Eykar together, I think. Kobba was the one who announced that if any men went after Eykar or Galligan, all the remaining men would be killed outright, *whack, whack, whack,* no trials or anything, and the Free would bet their posterity on the boys already born."

"Well, that's one way to handle it," Alldera said. It could also be read as the issuance of a challenge; but she did not think the men were up to much in the way of challenges now. "Did they believe that, do you think?"

"Well," Sorrel said judiciously, "you know Kobba. She was pretty convincing. A lot of sticks have asked for sponsors since then, and the spies told Beyarra that hardly anybody turned up at the last Bear dance.

"Beyarra wants to take off all the yokes and the sticks and just tell the men to make themselves useful if they want to eat. She proposed that in the Council yesterday. Kobba said she'd sooner cut off her own nose, right after cutting off Beyarra's."

Alldera laughed, picturing this brief but pungent debate. Then she said seriously, "If the men's place really does change, it's not going to happen for a while."

"I understand that a lot better than I did, but it has to happen sometime!" Sorrel said, warmly. "You think so too, don't you?"

"I do," Alldera said after a little. "When they learn to

carry their honor for themselves. That's the most heroic task there is, if they could only see it. Then Eykar and Setteo and a few others, not to mention us women, wouldn't have to break our backs trying to carry it for them.

"If you care about the little boys growing up to be people and not just the vengeful ghosts of their fathers, you should stay here and help raise them in better ways."

"How would *I* know better ways?" Sorrel objected. "There aren't any boys where I come from!"

"Nobody knows," Alldera said, "that's what I'm telling you. It's going to take everybody to come up with some answers, and to convince us all to try. And then spot what's not working and figure out how to fix it."

She could feel Sorrel's resistance, but all the younger woman said was, "They'll listen to you more than to me."

"No, love, they won't," Alldera said. She patted Sorrel's hand tentatively. The hand was not withdrawn. "Not the kits coming up, certainly. They're much more likely to listen to you. I'm used up, Sorrel. I just want to get myself out of the way."

She did not add that she had nearly as much blood on her hands, she sometimes felt, as Eykar had on his. She needed to go scrub away that blood with handfuls of long, clean prairie grass. She needed Nenisi to give her back the plains as if she were newly emerged from the childpack, dirty, wild, and naked.

There were things she could not even begin to explain to this insistent young woman.

She said lightly, "My stars, girl, do you want me doing everything around here forever? Don't you want anything left for anybody else?"

Daya uttered a series of gasps and a low cry, and Alldera hurried back to sit with her and stroke the backs of her hot, dry hands to keep her from tearing at her dressings.

"Just rest," she murmured in the pet fem's ear. "Get a leg over the pain and ride it quiet. You must be strong and rested for our journey. We'll go to the plains and ride all day, the way we used to do. I have a black mare picked out for you, the fastest, the prettiest ever. But first you have to rest."

When Daya quieted again, Sorrel had gone.

The pet fem died in the pit of night. When it was over, Alldera went to the window and said a prayer to Moonwoman although the moon was obscured by fresh banks of storm cloud and only in its first quarter. She prayed anyway, dipping in a bowl of clean water the white stones that had hung at Daya's belt, just in case it might do some good.

Sheel helped pack her saddlebags, nattering about how pleased Nenisi would be to see her, warning her not to let the Rois cousins eat more than their share on the way home because they were greedy creatures, though you'd never guess it by their leanness.

They were looking over a string of horses at the beach pens—Sheel was pumping her for information about the Islands in preparation for her own journey south—when Salalli marched determinedly toward them over the sand.

"She wants to go with you," Sheel said. "Some of these Townsfolk are unhappy here. People get too fussed about liking one place better than another."

She jumped on a young roan mare she had hopes for as a racer and trotted off to meet Shanuay.

Salalli hung back until Sheel was well out of earshot. She had her younger daughter with her. The dark woman wore a long tunic, boots, and a wide-brimmed hat woven out of beach grass. Luma had somebody's cut-down riding leathers on and fidgeted constantly at her mother's side.

"I want to ask something of you," Salalli began, and paused. At Alldera's nod she went on, "If some Town people ask to go with you to the Grasslands, please say no."

"Why is that?" Alldera leaned on the top rail of the pen.

"They think we can't live here with Holdfast people," Salalli said. "But I think we can, even if you are so crooked in your loves. It's not as if that has never happened among us, too. Then, sometimes these pale people of yours stare at us, but what is a look?

"Billyan says we should go south to the Swamp Islands, but I hear that they castrate boys there. I won't have my Shareem treated so. Now those Roises tell me that he would be unwelcome in their people's tents, although he is as dark as they are.

"But if the Townswomen all go with you and I stay here because of Shareem, it would not be good for any of my children. You have a child who grew up among strangers. Do you think it was good for her?"

Alldera said cautiously, "Not so good in some ways, excellent in others. Are most of your people determined to leave, then? I hadn't heard about it."

Salalli said, "We have not spoken of it to Free folk yet, but we talk among ourselves. I know you want us to stay, but now they say that you yourself are leaving."

"Yes," Alldera admitted, feeling guiltier about this now than when Sorrel had challenged her. She was moved by Salalli's dignity as an exile in a foreign land. She wanted to take her hard, dark hands and hold them and tell her how well she knew that feeling of being unalterably set apart, an alien shocked by the outlandish ways of her hosts.

"I have friends in the Grasslands," she explained, "people I haven't seen for years. I have a duty to my old companion Daya, who died. I'll go soon."

"I and my children," Salalli said, giving Luma's restless arm a little shake, "do not want to be left here feeling angry with Shareem because, out of worry about him, we let our people go off with you and leave us behind."

Alldera said, "The voices of you and your people should be heard in our Council. We need you all here, Salalli."

Salalli narrowed her eyes. "Very good, but do we need you? We did not, before your bloody-handed men came. Do we now?"

"I can only tell you what I think," Alldera replied, picking her way slowly among the possibilities, "but I certainly wouldn't encourage your friends to cross the mountains with me. We all need time to get used to each other. I will talk in our Council about this. Perhaps you would come and talk there yourself."

"Perhaps," Salalli said. "Luma, stand still! And will it be understood if I go and talk also sometimes with your Book Man, and bring my children? Shareem seems to respect him, and he, the Book Man, says he has things to teach and things he wishes to learn. And I want Luma to know the stories of the place she lives now, not only the place that we left behind."

Alldera blinked. "Well, you understand that relations between women and men are very—difficult here. You could find some objections raised—" She shuddered to think what people would say about Eykar Bek teaching Shareem to read.

"I do understand," Salalli said pointedly, "and I have more reason than most to know why. But that Book Man has had the devils of pride knocked out of him and maybe a few angels of wisdom knocked in, like yourself, Alldera Holdfaster. You both remind me of my own elder kindred, who lived hard and learned from their lives. There is nothing to object to in anyone studying what he has to teach."

"He's right, I think, that you are a good teacher yourself, Salalli of the Towns."

For a long moment the northwoman looked at her in silence, and then she decided to speak. "We Town people know of a cruel history between dark people and white ones which I doubt is written in your 'books'; we have been reminded of it pretty strongly just lately. Shall I teach that?"

"I hope so," Alldera said. "Perhaps someday you and Shareem and others will write it down for all of us to read."

"Perhaps," Salalli said, and they nodded to each other and left it, for now, at that.

The time came to say good-bye to Eykar. He was on the beach, limping along the margin of the waves. She walked alongside him and told him what Salalli had said.

He said, "Other people can teach reading to Salalli and her children. I'm not concentrating very well these days."

Beyarra had told her that he had not opened a book since d Layo's death, which was another reason she judged he should have the responsibility of pupils again.

"It's not just reading Salalli wants Shareem to learn from you," she said. "She thinks you have wisdom of your own to share with all her children. I think so, too."

"There, you see?" he exclaimed. "You treat one youngster decently, and suddenly everybody wants you for their children's father! You people will work me to death without ever raising a callus on my palm."

"Yes," she said. "It's unfair all around, isn't it?"

The sand hissed under her boot soles. Sunset had begun to flame without their noticing. She would be gone before the beach settled into winter this year.

"I'm sorry," she said. "Have I said so? About Setteo, not about the other."

He said, "Thank you. I wish I'd done better by Setteo." His breathing heaved for a moment, then steadied. "What does Beyarra say about your going back to the Grasslands?"

Alldera sighed unhappily. "She's upset about it. But we are not—she's very young, Eykar, more of an age to be bedding with my daughter than with me. Her impetuosity—I never would have guessed she would get herself involved in Daya's schemes. She's so ashamed that she's very uneasy with me now."

"She couldn't know what she was getting into," he said.

"That's what I mean." Something was bent, if not broken, between her and the young NewFree, but talking about it didn't help or clarify it in the least. He seemed to understand that, for he didn't prod her to continue or try to reassure her about repairing the relationship.

Two riders cantered by, yelling, and yanking at a sack they held between them: practicing for a game of pillo, by the look of things. They whooped in salute as they passed.

Turning to look after them, he stumbled. She took his arm to steady him.

He snickered, a coltish sound. "Someday they'll decide we were gods. Well, their descendants will, somewhere down the line. I, the Oracle, predict it."

"Everyone knows the Oracle is a fraud," Alldera said, tucking her arm through his.

"We'll both be long dead," he went on. "We won't care. Not even if they decide we were lovers, a divine pair coupling to bring forth the moon and the sun and all good things."

"Emla's right," she said. "You read too much."

He smelled of soap, she noticed; a great improvement over the first few days after the death of d Layo, when Eykar had sat in a heap, crying and brooding and rank. It surprised her sometimes to think that he and she were nearly of an age; you wouldn't think so to look at them now, even though she had taken her own share of hard knocks.

Maybe men would age less quickly in a world they did not run.

"Hard on Sorrel," he mused, "being a child of gods."

"She can handle it," Alldera said firmly. *She'd better.*

He poked with his toe at a wreath of deep green tide wrack lying on the crusted sand. "I think she has what's best of Servan. I know she has what's best in you. I wish I could be as certain that she has anything of mine."

"She has. She's yours, as much as anybody is ever anybody's, by your own choice, Eykar. I told her so, and I'm telling you." She pressed his elbow closer to her side. "And I'm also telling you that our daughter should know how to read. She can read to you when your own eyes are too tired."

"If she'll study, I'll teach her," he said shortly. "I've said so, haven't I? What about the other children? The boys as well as the girls?"

They turned and walked slowly up the beach again, toward the distant shape of Endpath as it melted into the dusk. The limping pace made her hip begin to ache. They talked around and around and over and under matters of literacy, history, and myth, enclosed together in the hush and hiss of the waves.

We'll never talk like this again, she thought. *I need to go away.*

Sand inside her right boot was making her heel sore. She ignored it, walking, talking the Holdfast's future further and further away from herself, while light silvered and died up the cliff on one hand and dimmed off the shifting surface of the sea on the other.

Epilog: The Wind

After a truly terrible winter, during which the passes through the mountains were blocked for months on end, I rode west to visit the tents of my home camp and to see my bloodmother again, and my sharemothers Nenisi Conor and Shayeen Bawn. Nothing had been heard from that quarter since the autumn before. I had been having uneasy dreams. So had some others, but we all put it down to the effects of the prolonged, severe weather.

For several years, Alldera had been living in Stone Dancing Camp. On visits during that time I had found her sunbrown, relaxed, and welcoming, carrying less—I thought—of that cloud of melancholy that Daya's death had drawn down upon her.

She was pleased, I think, by the things she had been hearing about me from traders who took pack trains of goods between the two peoples. She always sent greetings back with such venturers in return for mine, and sometimes a gift for me and whoever my current love might be. I think she wanted me to remember Grassland ways of sharing, even if I did eventually settle down for good in some Holdfast hearth.

I found this charming. She and Nenisi were tight as a rawhide braid, while I was too restless and impatient to stay in any stable household for long. I was earning a roving reputation, and enjoying it, too.

But Alldera's absence had begun to nag at me. Once the river swelled with snowmelt, I began making my preparations.

That spring showed promise of excellent, full crops due to all the moisture and the moderate temperatures that had come with the snows. I finished my work at Raysa's hearth, helping to dig cattail roots around the margins of the laver ponds, and attached myself to a small goods train carrying clay and metalware, salt, and bolts of cloth for trade among the Riding Women.

It was Cool Season west of the mountains. That was when the Free Fems' wagon had used to go out trading too, following the camps which followed the grazing.

The Tea Camp was now just a clearing with a few disintegrating timbers lying where the wagons had once stood. Charred sites of old fires showed where the Riding Women had come to do their own tea harvest, since the Free Fems weren't there any longer to do it for them.

We would have missed the place altogether if Lora-Lan had not been with us. She knew the way in her bones. She had brought some iron and steel items from New Forge to trade, but that was just an excuse, I think, to see the plains again.

Beyarra had a map Roona had drawn of the rounds of the Motherline camps. We unrolled it on a flat place on the ground and crouched around it, pointing and discussing the most likely place to find the Stone Dancing tents this time of year.

I had already given my opinion many times on the way, so I left them to it and walked around inhaling the scents of the place and squinting at the distant horizon that had been haunting my dreams.

Payder, our only male traveler, brought a leather bottle and offered me a drink. He drove our goods wagon for us, but he was also there as Eykar's eyes. My father was effectively blind by then, and Payder had gradually taken on some of the roles Setteo had once played in the Book Room. His sponsors had assigned him there, as a favor to me; he seldom danced for the entertainment of others any more because of a knee injury.

He also had bed space, as they said, in a half a dozen hearths, to which certain men, and women too, would happily repair with him when he came visiting on Book Room business.

He and I had stirred the broth together a couple of times, before I went to doing my baby-hunting using a syringe instead of a man. By then he had become Eykar's bedmate.

I had gone through a stage of curiosity about man-fucking which I deliberately pursued in defiance of Servan d Layo and his sort. I wanted a child of my own—Veree was growing up very attached to his Childhouse cohorts, like all the kits his age.

Anyway, Payder and I hadn't fucked together for years now, and we were easy together again. When my father was in an irascible mood—he had grown sharper, not mellower, with time and increasing physical debility—I often communicated with him through Payder.

Maybe "irascible" is too strong. Men were these days more prone than women to bouts of gloom about both the past and the future, and no wonder, people said, considering. Eykar was particularly inclined that way, not surprisingly. Men with less extreme histories of loss and pain had killed themselves around the time of d Layo's death, or not long after. I think sometimes his past nearly overwhelmed him, too.

One of my two daughters might have been Payder's, but the younger one, Allda-Tamann, was starting to look much more like a rather homely but fertile Ferryman named Laxen. She has his ears and his funny, wrinkle-faced frown.

"I can see why you miss this place," Payder said, stopping the bottle again and slinging its strap over his shoulder. "Thoughts fly out in all directions along with sight; there's nothing to contain them."

I knew he would convey the sense of the country to Eykar more effectively than I ever could. At that moment I resented him being there, taking possession in his own way of a land that had been, after all, my home; and I didn't answer.

Lora walked slowly toward us, head down, hands buried in her cloak. A rough, billowing breeze blew, but I thought I saw more in her posture than resistance to the wind.

"All the ashes are old," she said worriedly. "No one's built a fire here since before the winter."

"Well, who would?" I said. "There's been no traffic with the passes closed, and the tea bushes are still dormant."

"People used to come looking for our old treasure caches," Lora said. "Mares, I mean, hunting for something unusual to give to a friend or a lover. But nobody's been."

"Found it all, maybe," I said.

She said, "The wind smells different."

"How?" Payder said.

"Don't listen to her, she's daft," I said. "It smells the same as it ever did."

But I sensed it, too: a flatness to the air, a lack of something. An emptier emptiness.

"Let's get moving," I said.

I was nervous now, as well as excited. It was almost a full year since I had last ridden the plains. I should have gone the summer before, when the Rois cousins had left the Holdfast for the naming of a young kinswoman in Steep

Cloud Camp. The early snows must have kept them from returning east, for I knew how close they had grown to some of the Townswomen and their hearth friends.

Now I had news, gossip, things to tell everyone from Eelayenn to Cadermain Hayscall, whose famous horse I had lifted in my maiden raid, to my mothers themselves. I wished I had come sooner, snow in the mountains or no snow.

I'd been preoccupied. There was a great deal of outwash from the Ferrymen's return. Endpath had the word "end" in it, but I have learned how rare true endings are. Or perhaps we just don't recognize them, since new things come bursting out of them almost at once. d Layo's death proved not to be an ending at all.

Some people worried that if his gravesite were known, men would find ways to rifle it for bits of his corpse to keep as relics. This was a notion so repulsive that I could hardly believe anyone could do such a thing. It proved the desperation of the Bear devotees, if they would consider stooping to such behavior. And what did it say of the Free, that they could imagine it too?

On the other hand—and as Alldera told me many times, "There is always another hand"—if the DarkDreamer's body just vanished, that would give credence to his supposed identity as the magical "Sunbear" of the Cold Country, an immortal being. We had gone through too much over that man to allow this.

In the end, we opened a pit that had been dug after a battle of the Conquest. We buried the DarkDreamer there with neither fanfare nor insult and told the men that his body lay with other male casualties of that war, his bones mingled with theirs. We would not say where, exactly, which made some sticks very upset.

There was talk among them, which they even brought to the Whole Land Council through a chosen spokesman—dull Relki, of all people—of digging up d Layo's bones and sealing them in Endpath. This proposal, not surprisingly, came to nothing, although discussion of the idea continues, on and off. That's how it is in the New Holdfast; many matters are dealt with, but few resolved.

Well, they are not usually simple matters.

Arjvall began preaching that d Layo had become "part of the earth" of the Holdfast, not confined to any one spot. He and his cronies started building a religion on this. Almost at once the "Sunbear's Men" split into factions, which any observer of the Lady's rites could have predicted. Arjvall, the leader of the original movement, was found murdered—perhaps sacrificed—a year after d Layo died.

The cult withered thereafter. Arvjall had had a very strong and bitter spirit which they had needed, no longer having Setteo to give them Bear visions.

Recognized belatedly as the only authentic link with the Cold Country, Setteo became a mythic figure to the men before he was dead six months. They needed him on the other side of death to help them, with all the deaths they had among their own numbers that first winter after the Ferrymen's Return.

Eykar said it was despair that killed them.

Kobba, and not Kobba alone, said good riddance whatever the cause; the fewer men living who remember having been masters of fems, the better she feels about the future of our young boys. She argues always against allowing the men any contact with our children, who are also, of course, theirs.

I myself prefer to see the remaining men, sponsored and supervised, help with the young. How else are these boys and girls to see how a man may fit himself to the role of a human being, like the women whose hearth he shares? And I would not like to see men kept distant and mysterious, while it is the women that the children come to know.

Besides, raising children is hard work, and not all the Free make good mothers. This comes as no surprise. If the men of the Old days were taught to punish and abuse children, what can we expect the maltreated slaves of such men to have learned?

At least three bad-tempered women, two Free and one NewFree, have been sent south to live with the Breakaways, who keep no men or children. One came back changed for the better, and the other two have stayed there.

Otherwise, Raysa's stubborn friends remain a troublesome splinter off our society, a headstrong, selfish crew with a fierce yearning for their version of Grassland freedom. Having known it themselves, or dreamed of it in the case of most NewFree, they at first continued to aggressively expand their territory despite the objections of the Bayo-born.

A natural boundary appeared when these herders reached a southern forest infested by insects that made horses sicken and die. They turned back in disappointment, falling to some bitter feuding among themselves. I was asked to go down there with Sheel, and we persuaded them to sort themselves into two smaller camps with distinct grazing grounds. This seems to have settled them down considerably.

Lissie came along on that trip, and, falling in love with a woman of the Breakaways, stayed with their camp. This did not endear me to Salalli, who blamed me for leading her elder girl into corruption. The majority of the Townswomen remain staunch against our love customs and are champions of Ancient ways.

In fact Salalli eventually set up a hearth with Galligan, of all people, whom she joined two NewFree in sponsoring. He had been on the stick since Daya's death, an event for which many still hold him, fairly or unfairly, responsible. If he resents being blamed, he never shows it; but he has always blamed himself, I think, for having failed to protect her.

I've grown to like him myself. I believe he did love Daya and misses her still.

Salalli's hearth specializes very successfully in timber and other forest harvests, and, of course, the taming and raising of goats. Different people have moved through that household, as people tend to do everywhere in the New Holdfast. We are as restless a breed as the Riding Women, in our own way.

I lived at Salalli's hearth myself for a year and a half. Raysa joined me there. So did Veree. Raysa formally asked to sharemother him with me at the end of that time. So far this has worked out well, although Raysa and I are not currently hearth-sharing.

There is a song going around that began among the men, an acidly humorous plaint about the trials of being required to become the best woman that you can when you have been born a man. Raysa agrees with me that Veree will make a pretty fair woman.

She was the one who pointed out in Council that the sponsorship of men and boys is a way of providing them with what amounts to a family of sharemothers, who show them how decent people behave and require that they themselves do so. She felt that this was a great step toward humanizing those men capable of such a change, after the brutalizing lives they had all led from birth onward.

Better still, as an alternative to killing the men or keeping them permanently on the stick, sponsoring prevents the problem of having to explain to our sons and our daughters how we destroyed their fathers because we were afraid of them. As it is our past is hard enough to comprehend, for young people growing up in a world as different from the Old Holdfast as the moon must be from the earth.

Still, some people so distrusted the idea of sponsorship that they went to join the Breakaways' tents down south, where no males are tolerated on any terms.

Agreement is hard to come by and hard to maintain when it comes to assuring our daughters' freedom from the heavy hands of men.

I have heard that Relki argued one day that it is unfair that men must measure up to standards women set in order to attain the rights of merely subordinate persons. Kastia-Kai replied that in the Old Holdfast no matter what standards a fem managed to meet, she was never recognized as a human being of any degree, with any rights; and so the men have small grounds for complaint.

A satirical verse on this point was shortly afterward added to the men's song of protest. But when the boys and girls sing that song—and they do, as it has a lively rhythm—the satire is gone. They understand the new verse as a serious rebuttal of "Relki's Lament."

We sing many mourning songs, humorous and sad. Eykar and his students have gleaned from their reading the depressing fact that Ancient men—and women too—lived much longer than any of us can expect to live now. Many people have died younger than they should have, hardship, war, and anguish having crippled their bodies and their spirits. Liberty doesn't heal every wound.

No unsponsored men are left, resistance having finally collapsed after the murder of Arjvall. Chokky Vargindo held out a while, staying on the stick to show how tough men could be, but even he caved in at last. What is the point of a painful and futile gesture that nobody cares about?

As for what standards should be set and by whom, any fool can see what makes a reasonable society by looking at who rules a band of horses or a flock of goats. Despite noisy male pantomime of mastery, the chief invariably turns out to be the queen doe or the lead mare, not the randy, hysterical buck or the stallion with the arched neck and rolling eyes.

Roona said this explained why the Ancients' histories of the deeds of men were a record of foolishness, and no great loss.

I told this to Eykar, and he laughed and said she was by no means the first to think so. He talked often with Roona after that, until pneumonia ended her life during SevenStorm Winter. I heard him tell Veree once that he had come to think of bald old Roona as a sort of mother to him (his real dam was burned for witchery long ago).

The Townswomen departed northward the following spring, having found the Holdfast too uneasy a fit. Some were by then saying openly that light-skinned people were not fully human, something of the spirit having been left out of them along with coloration of the skin, and that this was why Holdfasters were quarrelsome, unfaithful, and sexually perverse.

They came back again before the winter was out, saying only that the ruins of their old homes were too sad and too haunted for them to stay there.

Luma, Salalli's younger daughter, told me that they had attempted to consult their sea deity, Sallah, by means of rituals local to the place which she could not describe to me, these things being secret and holy. No answer had come. Sadly concluding that Sallah too had abandoned their empty homeland, they turned south again.

Luma said she thought they had forgotten how many

graves of childen and adults they had left behind at the townsites. Winters are longer and harder up there.

She is a fine girl, and it pleases me that Veree looks up to her and shows every evidence of being fond of her, as she is of him. With little Biri, they make an inseparable threesome these days and may well home at the same hearth soon.

Upon returning Salalli's people at first chose to live apart, settling under the mountains by 'Troi ruins, where they could hunt freely. Wild goats, bred by escaped tame ones, had multiplied with startling speed in that upland country. The Council is continually mediating disputes between farmers and gardeners on the one hand, and hunters and herders of goats on the other, over the damage these incredibly persistent, agile, and voracious creatures do when they find a way to get into a cultivated field or orchard.

Trust the great find of d Layo's expedition to turn out to be not only a boon but also a nuisance and a cause of conflict! But roast kid and goat cheese are fine foods. The sweet-sap those men brought back from the north has also become much prized. Beyarra says that if we had tasted those delicious, sticky sheets sooner, we would have bargained away half our country for a map to the maple groves.

When the Bayo-born traded us two seagoing boats for some guns made in New Forge on the model of d Layo's gun, the Townswomen colony split in two. Some of those people came to the Lammintown to involve themselves in the crafts and wisdom of seagoing, of which they already had some knowledge from their lives on the north coast. They built the Sallah shrine at the foot of the Devil's Stair, and from their ranks have come two hardy coastal explorers who have made names for themselves.

Lammintown itself is becoming a boat-building harbor city, now that fish have begun to appear in the sea. The Townswomen say this is because they have brought us the worship of Sallah. Some of them press for converts among the Free.

Friction flares occasionally between the followers of Sallah and those of the Lady. Kastia in particular has taken a great dislike to Luma, who has become a very attractive proponent of the Townswomen's creed. Anyone can see that she is jealous of Luma's youth and beauty, just as Luma is impatient with Kastia's stubbornness and contemptuous of her increasing frailty. But none of this alters the fact that each has followers, and clashes occur.

I am working with Eykar on a study of the connections between the moon, symbol of the Lady, and the sea, the Encompassing Heart of Sallah, in hope of helping the steadier members of both groups to find common ground.

Eykar says religion seems to be necessary to the majority of any population (history again), but that it has been a major point of trouble for many people before us.

Payder, a quick student of anything in print, finds all this fascinating; but then, almost everything fascinates him. He says he can't understand why Chokky Vargindo still mourns the passing of the Old ways and decries the dullness of life empty of the free exercise of masculine passions and ambitions. I can. But it is nonsensical nostalgia all the same.

Nothing and no one ranged free in the Old Holdfast except the richest of Senior men. Even they were full of fears and hedged themselves about with protections of their vaunted power and privilege, however vainly in the end.

Payder finds his excitement in our own busy days and his many busy nights and in the piecing together of history's truths in the Book Room. I hope his enthusiasm will spread to Veree and the other young boys, whom he is helping to learn to read.

Kobba grimly warns that nothing could be more foolish and risky than educating the boys; but Beyarra maintains that ignorance is more dangerous than malice, because the ignorant can easily be used by the few who are truly malicious to mulitiply the effects of malice far beyond its natural scope.

Beyarra has become a redoubtable speaker, but refuses to serve on the Council in any formal capacity. She will remind you on any occasion of her past misjudgments, which she insists led to the deaths of Daya, Tamansa-Nan, and Leeja-Beda.

Of all the people who did not need to be chastened by events, Beyarra has suffered the most miserably, I think.

She and Eykar have worked with me on writing my own account of coming to the New Holdfast and what I found and did there. She said, "How are we to unlearn the crippling self-contempt our masters taught us? If you go around writing down songs full of the boasts, lies, and errors of a bunch of aging warriors but you don't bother to set down your own story, what can be learned?"

But I have outrun myself. I was writing here about my return to the Grasslands after Acorn Winter, and what I found west of the mountains.

What we did not find, rather.

We rode for weeks, up and down, consuming our trade goods and killing wild horses for meat. We searched at the wells, at the granaries that now held only a few dusty swags of desiccated grain, and at the great, wide grounds of the Gather. Payder found a drum frame there, with the head rotted out.

After the first few times we thought we had sighted a tent, or a wisp of smoke, or a herd being moved, we stopped shouting and pointing and slapping hands with each other in joy and relief.

The tent was just a crooked pole with a scorched hide hanging from it, the smoke rose from a small grass fire coming from nowhere and going nowhere, and the horses were wild ones, not being herded but moving where their bossmare took them.

Kenoma, who was breathing freely for the first time in years because she was away from whatever in the Holdfast makes her sneeze and cough, stood in her stirrups and stared after those horses. She reminded us—although we did not want to be reminded—that the last Holdfast visitors to the Grasslands, at the end of the previous summer, had in fact not met up with the camps they had meant to visit. They had only seen some riders in the distance, who had waved to them but had ridden away without pausing to gossip over the tea-fire.

A raiding party, those Free folk had concluded, Women preoccupied with serious business of their own.

Now I felt, and I knew the others with me did too, that those riders had been stragglers behind others gone ahead, or a few sent back to do some last task before final departure.

Silent, tired, with tears in our eyes that no one spoke of, we rode to the western edge of the Grasslands, where earth turns to mud. This was the miles-long shore of the Great Salty River, a gently rippling sheet of water reaching farther than the eye could see.

"Sheel was raised along here somewhere," I said. I silently thanked the Lady that Sheel Torrinor had not come with us, being away again in the Islands where she and Shanuay often traveled.

The water was printed with wind scrawls out beyond the cattails. Payder walked up beside me, frowning under his raised hand. He said, "We've missed them. Maybe they've gone north."

"No," I said.

I knew. I had known for days, maybe even from the time Lora found cold ashes at the Tea Camp. We all knew, but dared not say out loud what we knew: the grass was too high everywhere except where we saw wild horses grazing, the sharu burrows too many and undisturbed. Even the old squat grounds outside the traditional campsites were stale and scentless.

We had not missed the Riding Women. They were not there to be found.

That day by the wide river, Lora turned her horse and rode north along the bank at a steady, determined walk. She didn't come back for two days. We made a small, quiet camp and waited.

When she returned, she said nothing. Her face was drawn and still. She had aged. Huddled around our fire that night, we could scarcely look at one another.

"But why would they leave their homeland?" Payder burst out at last. "They've lived here for so long and so proudly; and where can they have gone?"

He had met some of the Grassland traders who had crossed the mountains to visit us from time to time. They had regarded him as a curiosity, a conjuring trick—one of these new young males who knew how to behave. He had regarded them with awe.

Now we were too shaken and in too much pain to be careful or tactful, and I was sorry when Kobba growled, "They smelled you coming, boy. They wouldn't want their country any more if they knew men would set foot on it."

"If they really are gone," Payder said with dignity, "I am sorry for your loss, Hera. But the wind blows from the west here. They could not have caught my scent."

The Rois cousins had gone home the previous summer carrying word that I was planning to visit my bloodmother and that I would bring Eykar with me, although as it turned out Payder had come in his place. So in a way, Kobba could be right.

Later I found Payder sitting off by himself, his head in his hands, the picture of desolation.

He said to me, "I wanted to see them, too. I wanted to see the warriors galloping over the plain, the speakers crowded into the Chief Tent. We hear wonderful stories—why have they gone?"

"Maybe they'll come back," I said.

But I did not believe it; and they have not.

They wouldn't have gone into the southern forests or the cold, dense northern woods, not with their horse herds. On our way across the mountains we had seen none but Holdfastish signs of habitation.

"They've left us," Lora said. "What will we do?"

"Follow," said Kobba, rubbing her crooked fist with her other hand. She stood canted forward into the breeze, as if she could fly over the Great Salty River by sheer will.

I said, "They don't want us to follow, or they'd have left us a guide. We don't own them. No one owns them, and they would sooner die than own us, or anyone. Let them go."

"Your blood-ma is with them," Lora said, her voice full of tears and pleading. "Your share-mas would be glad to see you come to them again."

I said, "They are Free people, they go where they wish. I won't have them tracked down like runaway slaves."

We headed home by way of Fedeka's valley, the place where Alldera had camped with the one-armed dyer before walking out on the plains to capture wild horses. The spring still flowed, and some of the poles Fedeka had used to use to build drying frames were stacked under a bent tree.

Here riders had camped fairly recently, and they had left something else behind.

On the bare ground where Fedeka had once spread plants to dry, someone had driven tall stakes into the earth and placed objects in a pattern. It made no sense to me at first. Then Lora-Lan walked to the center and said, "This cluster marks the wells of Steep Cloud Camp, and those are the wells of Wind Grass. There is Royo, down there is Leaf Shadow—"

I saw the way sand had blown against the bases of these stakes, fine sand that had once been spread smoothly out among them. I saw that she was right.

There was a glittering stone representing the site of a famous fight to the death between women of the Caranaws and a faction of the Bawns, locked in feud. The rusted bit-shank half-buried just west of it reminded me of a story about a horse race won by an ancient mare without a rider which had joined the race on her own. A lump of sand-blasted glass represented the Phantom Well on Red Sand territory, the scent of whose waters had lured three tired and thirsty horse raiders to their deaths in a sandslide.

There were many such markers, more than I knew the significances of. But I knew what their presence meant.

"It's a map," I said, "of the Grasslands."

The last time I had seen this was when a sharechild of my heartfriend Eelayenn had come out of the childpack for naming. A map was made in a sweat-tent and her family danced there with her, marking out the whole history of the Riding Women for her to learn and know and have. It was how mothers gave the plains to their children.

The Riding Women had not only relinquished the plains but had given them to us, with all of their own history in that place.

We rode east with sore eyes and weeping hearts, too. All the way I thought and thought, searching my memory for what I had said or done the last time I had visited Alldera at Holdfaster Tent that could have sent her away with the Riding Women.

There were many possibilities. By then, I was grown-up enough not to believe any of them. The Women had decided to go, and she had gone with them; that was all. Their reasons for leaving were their own, and did not belong to us.

Some weeks after our return, Eykar came with Payder to where I was twisting straw rope with someone—Janna, I think—in the Children's House. Eykar limped in without ceremony and lowered himself to sit under the lattice with us. He had Payder read to me, and the listening children, from books about the Ancients. These were tales of heroes who did great works for their people and then went away westward, to legendary lands of peace and healing.

I thought it was all horseshit or else a fancy way of saying they did their work and died; but I didn't interrupt. The names of the imaginary haven sounded like the feeling in my heart: Westernesse, the Isles of the Blest, Avalon. They do not need to be real, and I doubt Eykar meant me to take them as such.

What I do think is that there are sandbars close to the surface of the Great Salty River, at least in some seasons. I think the Riding Women drove their herds out over those, going west and west until they reached dry plains rising from the far side. I think they have settled there, to live with wide water between them and the people of the coast, we women and men who live so riskily side by side.

Many other stories are told now about the passing of the horse herders of the plains. Some of the Breakaways have gone to live there, but few can bear the vastness of the place and its winds that echo the voices of vanished warriors.

I never go there now. The Grasslands that I knew, the earth that hummed softly with the drumming of the hooves of hard-ridden horses, is gone for good. I subscribe to none of the wishful tales people tell of how those Women will come back someday, shouting their self-songs and jeering at us for our soft, silly, Holdfast ways.

One, of course, still lived among us at the time that I returned from that journey into the void. When Sheel got word she came to 'Troi, where I was staying at Lora's hearth, and she and I spent a short time together.

She listened to everything I had to tell her about what we had found in the Grasslands, and for the first time ever

I saw despair settle on her keen, pale face and dim the ironical fire in her eyes.

"I will stay here, of course," she said at last, angrily. "How are you to get along without a single one of your sharemothers near you to tell you right from wrong?"

I knew what it cost her to say this, and I could not accept such a sacrifice. I kept insisting that she must do her heart's will and rejoin her own people until she bowed her head and was silent. That was a good thing, since it gave me a chance to wipe my tears without her seeing them.

She spent some time with Shanuay and other friends while she gathered good horses and some stores for travel. On a summer morning she kissed me good-bye and rode away toward the lowest pass, singing her self-song. She was rehearsing all the new verses she had added while living in the Holdfast.

Nothing has been seen of her since by any of us.

Shibann and a few others went looking for Leeja a few years ago and came home reporting that they had seen someone they were sure was Sheel, a rider with long white hair on a ridge some distance off. She held a strung bow high, like a sign, they said, before turning and galloping off on her big-headed plains pony, and they couldn't find her again.

I should say that poor Leeja-Beda was never found after she vanished from that terrible scene in Endpath. People sometimes ride out to be alone with their anger or their grief over one thing or another. If they wish to show deep disagreement with some decision or policy about how our sons are raised and how they live among us, such riders say they are going "looking for Leeja," meaning they want to remind everyone of what can come of relaxing our vigilance over the men of our hearths and houses.

At any rate, I feel sure that Shibann and her friends did not see Sheel Torrinor. For many obvious reasons it is not possible that they did, although I am moved by the tribute paid in their strong wish to have seen her.

I have often dreamed of her in the years since those great events, more often than I dream of Alldera herself.

In my dream, my slim, light-haired plains mother, with

her eyes narrowed against the brightness of the enormous sky, gallops her horses west over the surface of the Great Salty River. Sitting straight as a lance in her saddle, she rides into a setting sun and a firm west wind, and in the dusk far ahead the lights of tent fires gleam, to guide and welcome her.

But here in the lands she left behind, if there are to be women like those Women—riders and fighters and lovers and true-speakers, making their lives from day to day with all their powers—it seems they will be ourselves and our daughters, or no one.